World Classic Reading Book

20 GREAT SHORT STORIES Vol. 01

[English Version]

by Various Writers

20 Great Short Stories Vol. 01
[English Version]

발 행 | 2021년 03월 10일
저 자 | Various Writers
펴낸이 | 한건희
펴낸곳 | 주식회사 부크크
출판사등록 | 2014.07.15.(제2014—16호)
주 소 | 서울 금천구 가산디지털1로 119 SK트윈테크타워 A동 305-7호
전 화 | 1670—8316
이메일 | info@bookk.co.kr

ISBN | 979-11-372-3899-2

www.bookk.co.kr

이 책은 'English Version' 영어 원서와 국가별(예, 러시아 / 프랑스 등) 작품을 영어 번역한 도서로 이름, 지명 등 일부 단어는 그 나라의 언어로 표기로 되어 있습니다.

World Classic Reading Book

20 Great Short Stories Vol. 01

[English Version]

by Various Writers

CONTENTS

20 Great Short Stories Vol. 01

20 GREAT SHORT STORIES Vol. 01

by Various Writers

The Gift of the Magi

O. Henry

ONE dollar and eighty-seven cents. That was all. And sixty cents of it was in pennies. Pennies saved one and two at a time by bulldozing the grocer and the vegetable man and the butcher until one's cheeks burned with the silent imputation of parsimony that such close dealing implied. Three times Della counted it. One dollar and eighty-seven cents. And the next day would be Christmas.

There was clearly nothing to do but flop down on the shabby little couch and howl. So Della did it. Which instigates the moral reflection that life is made up of sobs, sniffles, and smiles, with sniffles predominating.

While the mistress of the home is gradually subsiding from the first stage to the second, take a look at the home. A furnished flat at $8 per week. It did not exactly beggar description, but it certainly had that word on the lookout for the mendicancy squad.

In the vestibule below was a letter-box into which no letter would go, and an electric button from which no mortal finger could coax a ring. Also appertaining thereunto was a card bearing the name "Mr. James Dillingham Young." The "Dillingham" had been flung to the breeze during a former period of prosperity when its possessor was being paid $30 per week. Now, when the income was shrunk to $20, though, they were thinking seriously of contracting to a modest and unassuming D. But whenever Mr. James Dillingham Young came home and reached his flat above he was called "Jim" and greatly hugged by Mrs. James Dillingham Young, already introduced to you as Della. Which is all very good.

Della finished her cry and attended to her cheeks with

the powder rag. She stood by the window and looked out dully at a gray cat walking a gray fence in a gray backyard. Tomorrow would be Christmas Day, and she had only $1.87 with which to buy Jim a present. She had been saving every penny she could for months, with this result. Twenty dollars a week doesn't go far. Expenses had been greater than she had calculated. They always are. Only $1.87 to buy a present for Jim. Her Jim. Many a happy hour she had spent planning for something nice for him. Something fine and rare and sterling—something just a little bit near to being worthy of the honor of being owned by Jim.

There was a pier glass between the windows of the room. Perhaps you have seen a pier glass in an $8 flat. A very thin and very agile person may, by observing his reflection in a rapid sequence of longitudinal strips, obtain a fairly accurate conception of his looks. Della, being slender, had mastered the art.

Suddenly she whirled from the window and stood before the glass. Her eyes were shining brilliantly, but her face had lost its color within twenty seconds. Rapidly she pulled down her hair and let it fall to its full length.

Now, there were two possessions of the James Dillingham Youngs in which they both took a mighty pride. One was Jim's gold watch that had been his father's and his grandfather's. The other was Della's hair. Had the queen of Sheba lived in the flat across the airshaft, Della would have let her hair hang out the window some day to dry just to depreciate Her Majesty's jewels and gifts. Had King Solomon been the janitor, with all his treasures piled up in the basement, Jim would have pulled out his watch every time he passed, just to see him pluck at his beard from envy.

So now Della's beautiful hair fell about her rippling and shining like a cascade of brown waters. It reached below her knee and made itself almost a garment for her. And then she did it up again nervously and quickly. Once she faltered for a minute and stood still while a tear or two splashed on the worn red carpet.

On went her old brown jacket; on went her old brown hat. With a whirl of skirts and with the brilliant sparkle still in her eyes, she fluttered out the door and down the stairs to the street.

Where she stopped the sign read: "Mme. Sofronie. Hair Goods of All Kinds." One flight up Della ran, and collected herself, panting. Madame, large, too white, chilly, hardly looked the "Sofronie."

"Will you buy my hair?" asked Della.

"I buy hair," said Madame. "Take yer hat off and let's have a sight at the looks of it."

Down rippled the brown cascade.

"Twenty dollars," said Madame, lifting the mass with a practised hand.

"Give it to me quick," said Della.

Oh, and the next two hours tripped by on rosy wings. Forget the hashed metaphor. She was ransacking the stores for Jim's present.

She found it at last. It surely had been made for Jim and no one else. There was no other like it in any of the stores, and she had turned all of them inside out. It was a platinum fob chain simple and chaste in design, properly proclaiming its value by substance alone and not by meretricious ornamentation—as all good things should do. It was even worthy of The Watch. As soon as she saw it she knew that it must be Jim's. It was like him. Quietness and value—the description applied to both. Twenty-one dollars they took from her for it, and she hurried home with the 87 cents. With that chain on his watch Jim might be properly anxious about the time in any company. Grand as the watch was, he sometimes looked at it on the sly on account of the old leather strap that he used in place of a chain.

When Della reached home her intoxication gave way a little to prudence and reason. She got out her curling irons and lighted the gas and went to work repairing the ravages made by generosity added to love. Which is always a tremendous task, dear friends—a mammoth task.

Within forty minutes her head was covered with tiny, close-lying curls that made her look wonderfully like a truant schoolboy. She looked at her reflection in the mirror long, carefully, and critically.

"If Jim doesn't kill me," she said to herself, "before he takes a second look at me, he'll say I look like a Coney Island chorus girl. But what could I do—oh! what could I do with a dollar and eighty-seven cents?" At 7 o'clock the coffee was made and the frying-pan was on the back of the stove hot and ready to cook the chops.

Jim was never late. Della doubled the fob chain in her hand and sat on the corner of the table near the door that he always entered. Then she heard his step on the stair away down on the first flight, and she turned white for just a moment. She had a habit of saying a little silent prayer about the simplest everyday things, and now she whispered: "Please God, make him think I am still pretty." The door opened and Jim stepped in and closed it. He looked thin and very serious. Poor fellow, he was only twenty-two—and to be burdened with a family! He needed a new overcoat and he was without gloves.

Jim stopped inside the door, as immovable as a setter at the scent of quail. His eyes were fixed upon Della, and there was an expression in them that she could not read, and it terrified her. It was not anger, nor surprise, nor disapproval, nor horror, nor any of the sentiments that she had been prepared for. He simply stared at her fixedly with that peculiar expression on his face.

Della wriggled off the table and went for him.

"Jim, darling," she cried, "don't look at me that way. I had my hair cut off and sold because I couldn't have lived through Christmas without giving you a present. It'll grow out again—you won't mind, will you? I just had to do it. My hair grows awfully fast. Say 'Merry Christmas!' Jim, and let's be happy. You don't know what a nice—what a beautiful, nice gift I've got for you." "You've cut off your hair?" asked Jim, laboriously, as if he had not arrived at that patent fact yet even after the hardest mental labor.

"Cut it off and sold it," said Della. "Don't you like me just as well, anyhow? I'm me without my hair, ain't I?"

Jim looked about the room curiously.

"You say your hair is gone?" he said, with an air almost of idiocy.

"You needn't look for it," said Della. "It's sold, I tell you—sold and gone, too. It's Christmas Eve, boy. Be good to me, for it went for you. Maybe the hairs of my head were numbered," she went on with sudden serious sweetness, "but nobody could ever count my love for you. Shall I put the chops on, Jim?" Out of his trance Jim seemed quickly to wake. He enfolded his Della. For ten seconds let us regard with discreet scrutiny some inconsequential object in the other direction. Eight dollars a week or a million a year—what is the difference? A mathematician or a wit would give you the wrong answer. The magi brought valuable gifts, but that was not among them. This dark assertion will be illuminated later on.

Jim drew a package from his overcoat pocket and threw it upon the table.

"Don't make any mistake, Dell," he said, "about me. I don't think there's anything in the way of a haircut or a shave or a shampoo that could make me like my girl any less. But if you'll unwrap that package you may see why you had me going a while at first." White fingers and nimble tore at the string and paper. And then an ecstatic scream of joy; and then, alas! a quick feminine change to hysterical tears and wails, necessitating the immediate employment of all the comforting powers of the lord of the flat.

For there lay The Combs—the set of combs, side and back, that Della had worshipped long in a Broadway window. Beautiful combs, pure tortoise shell, with jewelled rims—just the shade to wear in the beautiful vanished hair. They were expensive combs, she knew, and her heart had simply craved and yearned over them without the least hope of possession. And now, they were hers, but the tresses that should have adorned the coveted adornments were gone.

But she hugged them to her bosom, and at length she was able to look up with dim eyes and a smile and say: "My hair grows so fast, Jim!"

And then Della leaped up like a little singed cat and cried, "Oh, oh!"

Jim had not yet seen his beautiful present. She held it out to him eagerly upon her open palm. The dull precious metal seemed to flash with a reflection of her bright and ardent spirit.

"Isn't it a dandy, Jim? I hunted all over town to find it. You'll have to look at the time a hundred times a day now. Give me your watch. I want to see how it looks on it."

Instead of obeying, Jim tumbled down on the couch and put his hands under the back of his head and smiled.

"Dell," said he, "let's put our Christmas presents away and keep 'em a while. They're too nice to use just at present. I sold the watch to get the money to buy your combs. And now suppose you put the chops on."

The magi, as you know, were wise men—wonderfully wise men—who brought gifts to the Babe in the manger. They invented the art of giving Christmas presents. Being wise, their gifts were no doubt wise ones, possibly bearing the privilege of exchange in case of duplication. And here I have lamely related to you the uneventful chronicle of two foolish children in a flat who most unwisely sacrificed for each other the greatest treasures of their house. But in a last word to the wise of these days let it be said that of all who give gifts these two were the wisest. Of all who give and receive gifts, such as they are wisest. Everywhere they are wisest. They are the magi.

Ball of Fat (Boule de suif)

Guy de Maupassant

For several days in succession fragments of a defeated army had passed through the town. They were mere disorganized bands, not disciplined forces. The men wore long, dirty beards and tattered uniforms; they advanced in listless fashion, without a flag, without a leader. All seemed exhausted, worn out, incapable of thought or resolve, marching onward merely by force of habit, and dropping to the ground with fatigue the moment they halted. One saw, in particular, many enlisted men, peaceful citizens, men who lived quietly on their income, bending beneath the weight of their rifles; and little active volunteers, easily frightened but full of enthusiasm, as eager to attack as they were ready to take to flight; and amid these, a sprinkling of red-breeched soldiers, the pitiful remnant of a division cut down in a great battle; somber artillerymen, side by side with nondescript foot-soldiers; and, here and there, the gleaming helmet of a heavy-footed dragoon who had difficulty in keeping up with the quicker pace of the soldiers of the line. Legions of irregulars with high-sounding names "Avengers of Defeat," "Citizens of the Tomb," "Brethren in Death"—passed in their turn, looking like banditti. Their leaders, former drapers or grain merchants, or tallow or soap chandlers—warriors by force of circumstances, officers by reason of their mustachios or their money—covered with weapons, flannel and gold lace, spoke in an impressive manner, discussed plans of campaign, and behaved as though they alone bore the fortunes of dying France on their braggart shoulders; though, in truth, they frequently were afraid of their own men—scoundrels often brave beyond measure, but pillagers and debauchees.

Rumor had it that the Prussians were about to enter Rouen.

The members of the National Guard, who for the past two months had been reconnoitering with the utmost caution in the neighboring woods, occasionally shooting their own sentinels, and making ready for fight whenever a rabbit rustled in the undergrowth, had now returned to their homes. Their arms, their uniforms, all the death-dealing paraphernalia with which they had terrified all the milestones along the highroad for eight miles round, had suddenly and marvellously disappeared.

The last of the French soldiers had just crossed the Seine on their way to Pont-Audemer, through Saint-Sever and Bourg-Achard, and in their rear the vanquished general, powerless to do aught with the forlorn remnants of his army, himself dismayed at the final overthrow of a nation accustomed to victory and disastrously beaten despite its legendary bravery, walked between two orderlies.

Then a profound calm, a shuddering, silent dread, settled on the city. Many a round-paunched citizen, emasculated by years devoted to business, anxiously awaited the conquerors, trembling lest his roasting-jacks or kitchen knives should be looked upon as weapons.

Life seemed to have stopped short; the shops were shut, the streets deserted. Now and then an inhabitant, awed by the silence, glided swiftly by in the shadow of the walls. The anguish of suspense made men even desire the arrival of the enemy.

In the afternoon of the day following the departure of the French troops, a number of uhlans, coming no one knew whence, passed rapidly through the town. A little later on, a black mass descended St. Catherine's Hill, while two other invading bodies appeared respectively on the Darnetal and the Boisguillaume roads. The advance guards of the three corps arrived at precisely the same moment at the Square of the Hotel de Ville, and the German army poured through all the adjacent streets, its battalions making the pavement ring with their firm, measured tread.

Orders shouted in an unknown, guttural tongue rose to the windows of the seemingly dead, deserted houses; while behind the fast-closed shutters eager eyes peered forth at the victors-masters now of the city, its fortunes, and its lives, by "right of war." The inhabitants, in their darkened rooms, were possessed by that terror which follows in the wake of cataclysms, of deadly upheavals of the earth, against which all human skill and strength are vain. For the same thing happens whenever the established order of things is upset, when security no longer exists, when all those rights usually protected by the law of man or of Nature are at the mercy of unreasoning, savage force. The earthquake crushing a whole nation under falling roofs; the flood let loose, and engulfing in its swirling depths the corpses of drowned peasants, along with dead oxen and beams torn from shattered houses; or the army, covered with glory, murdering those who defend themselves, making prisoners of the rest, pillaging in the name of the Sword, and giving thanks to God to the thunder of cannon—all these are appalling scourges, which destroy all belief in eternal justice, all that confidence we have been taught to feel in the protection of Heaven and the reason of man.

Small detachments of soldiers knocked at each door, and then disappeared within the houses; for the vanquished saw they would have to be civil to their conquerors.

At the end of a short time, once the first terror had

subsided, calm was again restored. In many houses the Prussian officer ate at the same table with the family. He was often well-bred, and, out of politeness, expressed sympathy with France and repugnance at being compelled to take part in the war. This sentiment was received with gratitude; besides, his protection might be needful some day or other. By the exercise of tact the number of men quartered in one's house might be reduced; and why should one provoke the hostility of a person on whom one's whole welfare depended? Such conduct would savor less of bravery than of fool-hardiness. And foolhardiness is no longer a failing of the citizens of Rouen as it was in the days when their city earned renown by its heroic defenses. Last of all-final argument based on the national politeness—the folk of Rouen said to one another that it was only right to be civil in one's own house, provided there was no public exhibition of familiarity with the foreigner. Out of doors, therefore, citizen and soldier did not know each other; but in the house both chatted freely, and each evening the German remained a little longer warming himself at the hospitable hearth.

Even the town itself resumed by degrees its ordinary aspect. The French seldom walked abroad, but the streets swarmed with Prussian soldiers. Moreover, the officers of the Blue Hussars, who arrogantly dragged their instruments of death along the pavements, seemed to hold the simple townsmen in but little more contempt than did the French cavalry officers who had drunk at the same cafes the year before.

But there was something in the air, a something strange and subtle, an intolerable foreign atmosphere like a penetrating odor—the odor of invasion. It permeated dwellings and places of public resort, changed the taste of food, made one imagine one's self in far-distant lands, amid dangerous, barbaric tribes.

The conquerors exacted money, much money. The inhabitants paid what was asked; they were rich. But, the wealthier a Norman tradesman becomes, the more he suffers at having to part with anything that belongs to him, at having to see any portion of his substance pass into the hands of another.

Nevertheless, within six or seven miles of the town, along the course of the river as it flows onward to Croisset, Dieppedalle and Biessart, boat-men and fishermen often hauled to the surface of the water the body of a German, bloated in his uniform, killed by a blow from knife or club, his head crushed by a stone, or perchance pushed from some bridge into the stream below. The mud of the river-bed swallowed up these obscure acts of vengeance—savage, yet legitimate; these unrecorded deeds of bravery; these silent attacks fraught with greater danger than battles fought in broad day, and surrounded, moreover, with no halo of romance. For hatred of the foreigner ever arms a few intrepid souls, ready to die for an idea.

At last, as the invaders, though subjecting the town to the strictest discipline, had not committed any of the deeds of horror with which they had been credited while on their triumphal march, the people grew bolder, and the necessities of business again animated the breasts of the local merchants. Some of these had important commercial interests at Havre —occupied at present by the French army—and wished to attempt to reach that port by overland route to Dieppe, taking the boat from there.

Through the influence of the German officers whose acquaintance they had made, they obtained a permit to leave town from the general in command.

A large four-horse coach having, therefore, been

engaged for the journey, and ten passengers having given in their names to the proprietor, they decided to start on a certain Tuesday morning before daybreak, to avoid attracting a crowd.

The ground had been frozen hard for some time-past, and about three o'clock on Monday afternoon—large black clouds from the north shed their burden of snow uninterruptedly all through that evening and night.

At half-past four in the morning the travellers met in the courtyard of the Hotel de Normandie, where they were to take their seats in the coach.

They were still half asleep, and shivering with cold under their wraps. They could see one another but indistinctly in the darkness, and the mountain of heavy winter wraps in which each was swathed made them look like a gathering of obese priests in their long cassocks. But two men recognized each other, a third accosted them, and the three began to talk. "I am bringing my wife," said one. "So am I." "And I, too." The first speaker added: "We shall not return to Rouen, and if the Prussians approach Havre we will cross to England." All three, it turned out, had made the same plans, being of similar disposition and temperament.

Still the horses were not harnessed. A small lantern carried by a stable-boy emerged now and then from one dark doorway to disappear immediately in another. The stamping of horses' hoofs, deadened by the dung and straw of the stable, was heard from time to time, and from inside the building issued a man's voice, talking to the animals and swearing at them. A faint tinkle of bells showed that the harness was being got ready; this tinkle soon developed into a continuous jingling, louder or softer according to the movements of the horse, sometimes stopping altogether, then breaking out in a sudden peal accompanied by a pawing of the ground by an iron-shod hoof.

The door suddenly closed. All noise ceased.

The frozen townsmen were silent; they remained motionless, stiff with cold.

A thick curtain of glistening white flakes fell ceaselessly to the ground; it obliterated all outlines, enveloped all objects in an icy mantle of foam; nothing was to be heard throughout the length and breadth of the silent, winter-bound city save the vague, nameless rustle of falling snow—a sensation rather than a sound—the gentle mingling of light atoms which seemed to fill all space, to cover the whole world.

The man reappeared with his lantern, leading by a rope a melancholy-looking horse, evidently being led out against his inclination. The hostler placed him beside the pole, fastened the traces, and spent some time in walking round him to make sure that the harness was all right; for he could use only one hand, the other being engaged in holding the lantern. As he was about to fetch the second horse he noticed the motionless group of travellers, already white with snow, and said to them: "Why don't you get inside the coach? You'd be under shelter, at least." This did not seem to have occurred to them, and they at once took his advice. The three men seated their wives at the far end of the coach, then got in themselves; lastly the other vague, snow-shrouded forms clambered to the remaining places without a word.

The floor was covered with straw, into which the feet sank. The ladies at the far end, having brought with them little copper foot-warmers heated by means of a kind of chemical fuel, proceeded to light these, and spent some time in expatiating in low tones on their advantages, saying over and over again things which they had all known for a long time.

At last, six horses instead of four having been harnessed

to the diligence, on account of the heavy roads, a voice outside asked: "Is every one there?" To which a voice from the interior replied: "Yes," and they set out.

The vehicle moved slowly, slowly, at a snail's pace; the wheels sank into the snow; the entire body of the coach creaked and groaned; the horses slipped, puffed, steamed, and the coachman's long whip cracked incessantly, flying hither and thither, coiling up, then flinging out its length like a slender serpent, as it lashed some rounded flank, which instantly grew tense as it strained in further effort.

But the day grew apace. Those light flakes which one traveller, a native of Rouen, had compared to a rain of cotton fell no longer. A murky light filtered through dark, heavy clouds, which made the country more dazzlingly white by contrast, a whiteness broken sometimes by a row of tall trees spangled with hoarfrost, or by a cottage roof hooded in snow.

Within the coach the passengers eyed one another curiously in the dim light of dawn.

Right at the back, in the best seats of all, Monsieur and Madame Loiseau, wholesale wine merchants of the Rue Grand-Pont, slumbered opposite each other. Formerly clerk to a merchant who had failed in business, Loiseau had bought his master's interest, and made a fortune for himself. He sold very bad wine at a very low price to the retail-dealers in the country, and had the reputation, among his friends and acquaintances, of being a shrewd rascal a true Norman, full of quips and wiles. So well established was his character as a cheat that, in the mouths of the citizens of Rouen, the very name of Loiseau became a byword for sharp practice.

Above and beyond this, Loiseau was noted for his practical jokes of every description—his tricks, good or ill-natured; and no one could mention his name without adding at once: "He's an extraordinary man—Loiseau." He was undersized and potbellied, had a florid face with grayish whiskers.

His wife-tall, strong, determined, with a loud voice and decided manner —represented the spirit of order and arithmetic in the business house which Loiseau enlivened by his jovial activity.

Beside them, dignified in bearing, belonging to a superior caste, sat Monsieur Carre-Lamadon, a man of considerable importance, a king in the cotton trade, proprietor of three spinning-mills, officer of the Legion of Honor, and member of the General Council. During the whole time the Empire was in the ascendancy he remained the chief of the well-disposed Opposition, merely in order to command a higher value for his devotion when he should rally to the cause which he meanwhile opposed with "courteous weapons," to use his own expression.

Madame Carre-Lamadon, much younger than her husband, was the consolation of all the officers of good family quartered at Rouen. Pretty, slender, graceful, she sat opposite her husband, curled up in her furs, and gazing mournfully at the sorry interior of the coach.

Her neighbors, the Comte and Comtesse Hubert de Breville, bore one of the noblest and most ancient names in Normandy. The count, a nobleman advanced in years and of aristocratic bearing, strove to enhance by every artifice of the toilet, his natural resemblance to King Henry IV, who, according to a legend of which the family were inordinately proud, had been the favored lover of a De Breville lady, and father of her child —the frail one's husband having, in recognition of this fact, been made a count and governor of a province.

A colleague of Monsieur Carre-Lamadon in the General Council, Count Hubert represented the Orleanist party in his department. The story of his marriage with the daughter of a small shipowner at Nantes had always remained more or less of a mystery. But as the countess had an air of unmistakable breeding, entertained faultlessly, and was even supposed to have been loved by a son of Louis-Philippe, the nobility vied with one another in doing her honor, and her drawing-room remained the most select in the whole countryside—the only one which retained the old spirit of gallantry, and to which access was not easy.

The fortune of the Brevilles, all in real estate, amounted, it was said, to five hundred thousand francs a year.

These six people occupied the farther end of the coach, and represented Society—with an income—the strong, established society of good people with religion and principle.

It happened by chance that all the women were seated on the same side; and the countess had, moreover, as neighbors two nuns, who spent the time in fingering their long rosaries and murmuring paternosters and aves. One of them was old, and so deeply pitted with smallpox that she looked for all the world as if she had received a charge of shot full in the face. The other, of sickly appearance, had a pretty but wasted countenance, and a narrow, consumptive chest, sapped by that devouring faith which is the making of martyrs and visionaries.

A man and woman, sitting opposite the two nuns, attracted all eyes.

The man—a well-known character—was Cornudet, the democrat, the terror of all respectable people. For the past twenty years his big red beard had been on terms of intimate acquaintance with the tankards of all the republican cafes. With the help of his comrades and brethren he had dissipated a respectable fortune left him by his father, an old-established confectioner, and he now impatiently awaited the Republic, that he might at last be rewarded with the post he had earned by his revolutionary orgies. On the fourth of September—possibly as the result of a practical joke—he was led to believe that he had been appointed prefect; but when he attempted to take up the duties of the position the clerks in charge of the office refused to recognize his authority, and he was compelled in consequence to retire. A good sort of fellow in other respects, inoffensive and obliging, he had thrown himself zealously into the work of making an organized defence of the town. He had had pits dug in the level country, young forest trees felled, and traps set on all the roads; then at the approach of the enemy, thoroughly satisfied with his preparations, he had hastily returned to the town. He thought he might now do more good at Havre, where new intrenchments would soon be necessary.

The woman, who belonged to the courtesan class, was celebrated for an embonpoint unusual for her age, which had earned for her the sobriquet of "Boule de Suif" (Tallow Ball). Short and round, fat as a pig, with puffy fingers constricted at the joints, looking like rows of short sausages; with a shiny, tightly-stretched skin and an enormous bust filling out the bodice of her dress, she was yet attractive and much sought after, owing to her fresh and pleasing appearance. Her face was like a crimson apple, a peony-bud just bursting into bloom; she had two magnificent dark eyes, fringed with thick, heavy lashes, which cast a shadow into their depths; her mouth was small, ripe, kissable, and was furnished with the tiniest of white teeth.

As soon as she was recognized the respectable matrons of the party began to whisper among themselves, and the words "hussy" and "public scandal" were uttered so loudly that Boule de Suif raised her head. She forthwith cast such a challenging, bold look at her neighbors that a sudden silence fell on the company, and all lowered their eyes, with the exception of Loiseau, who watched her with evident interest.

But conversation was soon resumed among the three ladies, whom the presence of this girl had suddenly drawn together in the bonds of friendship—one might almost say in those of intimacy. They decided that they ought to combine, as it were, in their dignity as wives in face of this shameless hussy; for legitimized love always despises its easygoing brother.

The three men, also, brought together by a certain conservative instinct awakened by the presence of Cornudet, spoke of money matters in a tone expressive of contempt for the poor. Count Hubert related the losses he had sustained at the hands of the Prussians, spoke of the cattle which had been stolen from him, the crops which had been ruined, with the easy manner of a nobleman who was also a tenfold millionaire, and whom such reverses would scarcely inconvenience for a single year. Monsieur Carre-Lamadon, a man of wide experience in the cotton industry, had taken care to send six hundred thousand francs to England as provision against the rainy day he was always anticipating. As for Loiseau, he had managed to sell to the French commissariat department all the wines he had in stock, so that the state now owed him a considerable sum, which he hoped to receive at Havre.

And all three eyed one another in friendly, well-disposed fashion. Although of varying social status, they were united in the brotherhood of money—in that vast freemasonry made up of those who possess, who can jingle gold wherever they choose to put their hands into their breeches' pockets.

The coach went along so slowly that at ten o'clock in the morning it had not covered twelve miles. Three times the men of the party got out and climbed the hills on foot. The passengers were becoming uneasy, for they had counted on lunching at Totes, and it seemed now as if they would hardly arrive there before nightfall. Every one was eagerly looking out for an inn by the roadside, when, suddenly, the coach foundered in a snowdrift, and it took two hours to extricate it.

As appetites increased, their spirits fell; no inn, no wine shop could be discovered, the approach of the Prussians and the transit of the starving French troops having frightened away all business.

The men sought food in the farmhouses beside the road, but could not find so much as a crust of bread; for the suspicious peasant invariably hid his stores for fear of being pillaged by the soldiers, who, being entirely without food, would take violent possession of everything they found.

About one o'clock Loiseau announced that he positively had a big hollow in his stomach. They had all been suffering in the same way for some time, and the increasing gnawings of hunger had put an end to all conversation.

Now and then some one yawned, another followed his example, and each in turn, according to his character, breeding and social position, yawned either quietly or noisily, placing his hand before the gaping void whence issued breath condensed into vapor.

Several times Boule de Suif stooped, as if searching for something under her petticoats. She would hesitate a moment, look at her neighbors, and then quietly sit upright again. All faces were pale and drawn. Loiseau declared he would give a thousand francs for a knuckle of ham. His wife made an involuntary and quickly checked gesture of protest. It always hurt her to hear of money being squandered, and she could not even understand jokes on such a subject.

"As a matter of fact, I don't feel well," said the count. "Why did I not think of bringing provisions?" Each one reproached himself in similar fashion.

Cornudet, however, had a bottle of rum, which he offered to his neighbors. They all coldly refused except Loiseau, who took a sip, and returned the bottle with thanks, saying: "That's good stuff; it warms one up, and cheats the appetite." The alcohol put him in good humor, and he proposed they should do as the sailors did in the song: eat the fattest of the passengers. This indirect allusion to Boule de Suif shocked the respectable members of the party. No one replied; only Cornudet smiled. The two good sisters had ceased to mumble their rosary, and, with hands enfolded in their wide sleeves, sat motionless, their eyes steadfastly cast down, doubtless offering up as a sacrifice to Heaven the suffering it had sent them.

At last, at three o'clock, as they were in the midst of an apparently limitless plain, with not a single village in sight, Boule de Suif stooped quickly, and drew from underneath the seat a large basket covered with a white napkin.

From this she extracted first of all a small earthenware plate and a silver drinking cup, then an enormous dish containing two whole chickens cut into joints and imbedded in jelly. The basket was seen to contain other good things: pies, fruit, dainties of all sorts-provisions, in fine, for a three days' journey, rendering their owner independent of wayside inns. The necks of four bottles protruded from among the food. She took a chicken wing, and began to eat it daintily, together with one of those rolls called in Normandy "Regence." All looks were directed toward her. An odor of food filled the air, causing nostrils to dilate, mouths to water, and jaws to contract painfully. The scorn of the ladies for this disreputable female grew positively ferocious; they would have liked to kill her, or throw, her and her drinking cup, her basket, and her provisions, out of the coach into the snow of the road below.

But Loiseau's gaze was fixed greedily on the dish of chicken. He said:

"Well, well, this lady had more forethought than the rest of us. Some people think of everything."

She looked up at him.

"Would you like some, sir? It is hard to go on fasting all day."

He bowed.

"Upon my soul, I can't refuse; I cannot hold out another minute. All is fair in war time, is it not, madame?" And, casting a glance on those around, he added:

"At times like this it is very pleasant to meet with obliging people."

He spread a newspaper over his knees to avoid soiling his trousers, and, with a pocketknife he always carried, helped himself to a chicken leg coated with jelly, which he thereupon proceeded to devour.

Then Boule le Suif, in low, humble tones, invited the nuns to partake of her repast. They both accepted the offer unhesitatingly, and after a few stammered words of thanks began to eat quickly, without raising their eyes. Neither did Cornudet refuse his neighbor's offer, and, in combination with the nuns, a sort of table was formed by opening out the newspaper over the four pairs of knees.

Mouths kept opening and shutting, ferociously masticating and devouring the food. Loiseau, in his corner, was hard at work, and in low tones urged his wife to follow his example. She held out for a long time, but overstrained Nature gave way at last. Her husband, assuming his politest manner, asked their "charming companion" if he might be allowed to offer Madame Loiseau a small helping.

"Why, certainly, sir," she replied, with an amiable smile, holding out the dish.

When the first bottle of claret was opened some embarrassment was caused by the fact that there was only one drinking cup, but this was passed from one to another, after being wiped. Cornudet alone, doubtless in a spirit of gallantry, raised to his own lips that part of the rim which was still moist from those of his fair neighbor.

Then, surrounded by people who were eating, and well-nigh suffocated by the odor of food, the Comte and Comtesse de Breville and Monsieur and Madame Carre-Lamadon endured that hateful form of torture which has perpetuated the name of Tantalus. All at once the manufacturer's young wife heaved a sigh which made every one turn and look at her; she was white as the snow without; her eyes closed, her head fell forward; she had fainted. Her husband, beside himself, implored the help of his neighbors. No one seemed to know what to do until the elder of the two nuns, raising the patient's head, placed Boule de Suif's drinking cup to her lips, and made her swallow a few drops of wine. The pretty invalid moved, opened her eyes, smiled, and declared in a feeble voice that she was all right again. But, to prevent a recurrence of the catastrophe, the nun made her drink a cupful of claret, adding: "It's just hunger — that's what is wrong with you." Then Boule de Suif, blushing and embarrassed, stammered, looking at the four passengers who were still fasting:

"'Mon Dieu', if I might offer these ladies and gentlemen

——"

She stopped short, fearing a snub. But Loiseau continued:

"Hang it all, in such a case as this we are all brothers and sisters and ought to assist each other. Come, come, ladies, don't stand on ceremony, for goodness' sake! Do we even know whether we shall find a house in which to pass the night? At our present rate of going we sha'n't be at Totes till midday to-morrow." They hesitated, no one daring to be the first to accept. But the count settled the question. He turned toward the abashed girl, and in his most distinguished manner said:

"We accept gratefully, madame."

As usual, it was only the first step that cost. This Rubicon once crossed, they set to work with a will. The basket was emptied. It still contained a pate de foie gras, a lark pie, a piece of smoked tongue, Crassane pears, Pont-Leveque gingerbread, fancy cakes, and a cup full of pickled gherkins and onions—Boule de Suif, like all women, being very fond of indigestible things.

They could not eat this girl's provisions without speaking to her. So they began to talk, stiffly at first; then, as she seemed by no means forward, with greater freedom. Mesdames de Breville and Carre-Lamadon, who were accomplished women of the world, were gracious and tactful. The countess especially displayed that amiable condescension characteristic of great ladies whom no contact with baser mortals can sully, and was absolutely charming. But the sturdy Madame Loiseau, who had the soul of a gendarme, continued morose, speaking little and eating much.

Conversation naturally turned on the war. Terrible stories were told about the Prussians, deeds of bravery were recounted of the French; and all these people who were fleeing themselves were ready to pay homage to the courage of their compatriots. Personal experiences soon followed, and Boule le Suif related with genuine emotion, and with that warmth of language not uncommon in women of her class and temperament, how it came about that she had left Rouen.

"I thought at first that I should be able to stay," she said. "My house was well stocked with provisions, and it seemed better to put up with feeding a few soldiers than to banish myself goodness knows where. But when I saw these Prussians it was too much for me! My blood boiled with rage; I wept the whole day for very shame. Oh, if only I had been a man! I looked at them from my window—the fat swine, with their pointed helmets!—and my maid held my hands to keep me from throwing my furniture down on them. Then some of them were quartered on me; I flew at the throat of the first one who entered. They are just as easy to strangle as other men! And I'd have been the death of that one if I hadn't been dragged away from him by my hair. I had to hide after that. And as soon as I could get an opportunity I left the place, and here I am." She was warmly congratulated. She rose in the estimation of her companions, who had not been so brave; and Cornudet listened to her with the approving and benevolent smile of an apostle, the smile a priest might wear in listening to a devotee praising God; for long-bearded democrats of his type have a monopoly of patriotism, just as priests have a monopoly of religion. He held forth in turn, with dogmatic self-assurance, in the style of the proclamations daily pasted on the walls of the town, winding up with a specimen of stump oratory in which he reviled "that besotted fool of a Louis-Napoleon." But Boule de Suif was indignant, for she was an ardent Bonapartist. She turned as red as a cherry, and stammered in her wrath: "I'd just like to have seen you in his place—you and your sort! There would have been a nice mix-up. Oh, yes! It was you who betrayed that man. It would be impossible to live in France if we were governed by such rascals as you!" Cornudet, unmoved by this tirade, still smiled a superior, contemptuous smile; and one felt that high words were impending, when the count interposed, and, not without difficulty, succeeded in calming the exasperated woman, saying that all sincere opinions ought to be respected. But the countess and the manufacturer's wife, imbued with the unreasoning hatred of the upper classes for the Republic, and instinct, moreover, with the affection felt by all women for the pomp and circumstance of despotic government, were drawn, in spite of themselves, toward this dignified young woman, whose opinions coincided so closely with their own.

The basket was empty. The ten people had finished its contents without difficulty amid general regret that it did not hold more. Conversation went on a little longer, though it flagged somewhat after the passengers had finished eating.

Night fell, the darkness grew deeper and deeper, and the cold made Boule de Suif shiver, in spite of her plumpness. So Madame de Breville offered her her foot-warmer, the fuel of which had been several times renewed since the morning, and she accepted the offer at once, for her feet were icy cold. Mesdames Carre-Lamadon and Loiseau gave theirs to the nuns.

The driver lighted his lanterns. They cast a bright gleam on a cloud of vapor which hovered over the sweating flanks of the horses, and on the roadside snow, which seemed to unroll as they went along in the changing light of the lamps.

All was now indistinguishable in the coach; but suddenly a movement occurred in the corner occupied by Boule de Suif and Cornudet; and Loiseau, peering into the gloom, fancied he saw the big, bearded democrat move hastily to one side, as if he had received a well-directed, though noiseless, blow in the dark.

Tiny lights glimmered ahead. It was Totes. The coach had been on the road eleven hours, which, with the three hours allotted the horses in four periods for feeding and breathing, made fourteen. It entered the town, and stopped before the Hotel du Commerce.

The coach door opened; a well-known noise made all the travellers start; it was the clanging of a scabbard, on the pavement; then a voice called out something in German.

Although the coach had come to a standstill, no one got out; it looked as if they were afraid of being murdered the moment they left their seats. Thereupon the driver appeared, holding in his hand one of his lanterns, which cast a sudden glow on the interior of the coach, lighting up the double row of startled faces, mouths agape, and eyes wide open in surprise and terror.

Beside the driver stood in the full light a German officer, a tall young man, fair and slender, tightly encased in his uniform like a woman in her corset, his flat shiny cap, tilted to one side of his head, making him look like an English hotel runner. His exaggerated mustache, long and straight and tapering to a point at either end in a single blond hair that could hardly be seen, seemed to weigh down the corners of his mouth and give a droop to his lips.

In Alsatian French he requested the travellers to alight, saying stiffly:

"Kindly get down, ladies and gentlemen."

The two nuns were the first to obey, manifesting the docility of holy women accustomed to submission on every occasion. Next appeared the count and countess, followed by the manufacturer and his wife, after whom came Loiseau, pushing his larger and better half before him.

"Good-day, sir," he said to the officer as he put his foot to the ground, acting on an impulse born of prudence rather than of politeness. The other, insolent like all in authority, merely stared without replying.

Boule de Suif and Cornudet, though near the door, were the last to alight, grave and dignified before the enemy. The stout girl tried to control herself and appear calm; the democrat stroked his long russet beard with a somewhat trembling hand. Both strove to maintain their dignity, knowing well that at such a time each individual is always looked upon as more or less typical of his nation; and, also, resenting the complaisant attitude of their companions, Boule de Suif tried to wear a bolder front than her neighbors, the virtuous women, while he, feeling that it was incumbent on him to set a good example, kept up the attitude of resistance which he had first assumed when he undertook to mine the high roads round Rouen.

They entered the spacious kitchen of the inn, and the German, having demanded the passports signed by the general in command, in which were mentioned the name, description and profession of each traveller, inspected them all minutely, comparing their appearance with the written particulars.

Then he said brusquely: "All right," and turned on his heel.

They breathed freely, All were still hungry; so supper was ordered. Half an hour was required for its preparation, and while two servants were apparently engaged in getting it ready the travellers went to look at their rooms. These all opened off a long corridor, at the end of which was a glazed door with a number on it.

They were just about to take their seats at table when the innkeeper appeared in person. He was a former horse dealer—a large, asthmatic individual, always wheezing, coughing, and clearing his throat. Follenvie was his patronymic.

He called:

"Mademoiselle Elisabeth Rousset?"

Boule de Suif started, and turned round.

"That is my name."

"Mademoiselle, the Prussian officer wishes to speak to you immediately."

"To me?"

"Yes; if you are Mademoiselle Elisabeth Rousset."

She hesitated, reflected a moment, and then declared roundly:

"That may be; but I'm not going."

They moved restlessly around her; every one wondered and speculated as to the cause of this order. The count approached:

"You are wrong, madame, for your refusal may bring trouble not only on yourself but also on all your companions. It never pays to resist those in authority. Your compliance with this request cannot possibly be fraught with any danger; it has probably been made because some formality or other was forgotten." All added their voices to that of the count; Boule de Suif was begged, urged, lectured, and at last convinced; every one was afraid of the complications which might result from headstrong action on her part. She said finally:

"I am doing it for your sakes, remember that!"

The countess took her hand.

"And we are grateful to you."

She left the room. All waited for her return before commencing the meal. Each was distressed that he or she had not been sent for rather than this impulsive, quick-tempered girl, and each mentally rehearsed platitudes in case of being summoned also.

But at the end of ten minutes she reappeared breathing hard, crimson with indignation.

"Oh! the scoundrel! the scoundrel!" she stammered.

All were anxious to know what had happened; but she declined to enlighten them, and when the count pressed the point, she silenced him with much dignity, saying:

"No; the matter has nothing to do with you, and I cannot speak of it."

Then they took their places round a high soup tureen, from which issued an odor of cabbage. In spite of this coincidence, the supper was cheerful. The cider was good; the Loiseaus and the nuns drank it from motives of economy. The others ordered wine; Cornudet demanded beer. He had his own fashion of uncorking the bottle and making the beer foam, gazing at it as he inclined his glass and then raised it to a position between the lamp and his eye that he might judge of its color. When he drank, his great beard, which matched the color of his favorite beverage, seemed to tremble with affection; his eyes positively squinted in the endeavor not to lose sight of the beloved glass, and he looked for all the world as if he were fulfilling the only function for which he was born. He seemed to have established in his mind an affinity between the two great passions of his life—pale ale and revolution—and assuredly he could not taste the one without dreaming of the other.

Monsieur and Madame Follenvie dined at the end of the table. The man, wheezing like a broken-down locomotive, was too short-winded to talk when he was eating. But the wife was not silent a moment; she told how the Prussians had impressed her on their arrival, what they did, what they said; execrating them in the first place because they cost her money, and in the second because she had two sons in the army. She addressed herself principally to the countess, flattered at the opportunity of talking to a lady of quality.

Then she lowered her voice, and began to broach delicate subjects. Her husband interrupted her from time to time, saying:

"You would do well to hold your tongue, Madame Follenvie."

But she took no notice of him, and went on:

"Yes, madame, these Germans do nothing but eat potatoes and pork, and then pork and potatoes. And don't imagine for a moment that they are clean! No, indeed! And if only you saw them drilling for hours, indeed for days, together; they all collect in a field, then they do nothing but march backward and forward, and wheel this way and that. If only they would cultivate the land, or remain at home and work on their high roads! Really, madame, these soldiers are of no earthly use! Poor people have to feed and keep them, only in order that they may learn how to kill! True, I am only an old woman with no education, but when I see them wearing themselves out marching about from morning till night, I say to myself: When there are people who make discoveries that are of use to people, why should others take so much trouble to do harm? Really, now, isn't it a terrible thing to kill people, whether they are Prussians, or English, or Poles, or French? If we revenge ourselves on any one who injures us we do wrong, and are punished for it; but when our sons are shot down like partridges, that is all right, and decorations are given to the man who kills the most. No, indeed, I shall never be able to understand it." Cornudet raised his voice:

"War is a barbarous proceeding when we attack a peaceful neighbor, but it is a sacred duty when undertaken in defence of one's country."

The old woman looked down:

"Yes; it's another matter when one acts in self-defence; but would it not be better to kill all the kings, seeing that they make war just to amuse themselves?"

Cornudet's eyes kindled.

"Bravo, citizens!" he said.

Monsieur Carre-Lamadon was reflecting profoundly. Although an ardent admirer of great generals, the peasant woman's sturdy common sense made him reflect on the wealth which might accrue to a country by the employment of so many idle hands now maintained at a great expense, of so much unproductive force, if they were employed in those great industrial enterprises which it will take centuries to complete.

But Loiseau, leaving his seat, went over to the innkeeper and began chatting in a low voice. The big man chuckled, coughed, sputtered; his enormous carcass shook with merriment at the pleasantries of the other; and he ended by buying six casks of claret from Loiseau to be delivered in spring, after the departure of the Prussians.

The moment supper was over every one went to bed, worn out with fatigue.

But Loiseau, who had been making his observations on the sly, sent his wife to bed, and amused himself by placing first his ear, and then his eye, to the bedroom keyhole, in order to discover what he called "the mysteries of the corridor." At the end of about an hour he heard a rustling, peeped out quickly, and caught sight of Boule de Suif, looking more rotund than ever in a dressing-gown of blue cashmere trimmed with white lace. She held a candle in her hand, and directed her steps to the numbered door at the end of the corridor. But one of the side doors was partly opened, and when, at the end of a few minutes, she returned, Cornudet, in his shirt-sleeves, followed her. They spoke in low tones, then stopped short. Boule de Suif seemed to be stoutly denying him admission to her room. Unfortunately, Loiseau could not at first hear what they said; but toward the end of the conversation they raised their voices, and he caught a few words. Cornudet was loudly insistent.

"How silly you are! What does it matter to you?" he said.

She seemed indignant, and replied:

"No, my good man, there are times when one does not do that sort of thing; besides, in this place it would be shameful."

Apparently he did not understand, and asked the reason. Then she lost her temper and her caution, and, raising her voice still higher, said:

"Why? Can't you understand why? When there are Prussians in the house! Perhaps even in the very next room!"

He was silent. The patriotic shame of this wanton, who would not suffer herself to be caressed in the neighborhood of the enemy, must have roused his dormant dignity, for after bestowing on her a simple kiss he crept softly back to his room. Loiseau, much edified, capered round the bedroom before taking his place beside his slumbering spouse.

Then silence reigned throughout the house. But soon there arose from some remote part—it might easily have been either cellar or attic—a stertorous, monotonous, regular snoring, a dull, prolonged rumbling, varied by tremors like those of a boiler under pressure of steam. Monsieur Follenvie had gone to sleep.

As they had decided on starting at eight o'clock the next morning, every one was in the kitchen at that hour; but the coach, its roof covered with snow, stood by itself in the middle of the yard, without either horses or driver. They sought the latter in the stables, coach-houses and barns —but in vain. So the men of the party resolved to scour the country for him, and sallied forth. They found themselves in the square, with the church at the farther side, and to right and left low-roofed houses where there were some Prussian soldiers. The first soldier they saw was peeling potatoes. The second, farther on, was washing out a barber's shop. Another, bearded to the eyes, was fondling a crying infant, and dandling it on his knees to quiet it; and the stout peasant women, whose men-folk were for the most part at the war, were, by means of signs, telling their obedient conquerors what work they were to do: chop wood, prepare soup, grind coffee; one of them even was doing the washing for his hostess, an infirm old grandmother.

The count, astonished at what he saw, questioned the beadle who was coming out of the presbytery. The old man answered:

"Oh, those men are not at all a bad sort; they are not Prussians, I am told; they come from somewhere farther off, I don't exactly know where. And they have all left wives and children behind them; they are not fond of war either, you may be sure! I am sure they are mourning for the men where they come from, just as we do here; and the war causes them just as much unhappiness as it does us. As a matter of fact, things are not so very bad here just now, because the soldiers do no harm, and work just as if they were in their own homes. You see, sir, poor folk always help one another; it is the great ones of this world who make war." Cornudet indignant at the friendly understanding established between conquerors and conquered, withdrew, preferring to shut himself up in the inn.

"They are repeopling the country," jested Loiseau.

"They are undoing the harm they have done," said Monsieur Carre-Lamadon gravely.

But they could not find the coach driver. At last he was discovered in the village cafe, fraternizing cordially with the officer's orderly.

"Were you not told to harness the horses at eight o'clock?" demanded the count.

"Oh, yes; but I've had different orders since."

"What orders?"

"Not to harness at all."

"Who gave you such orders?"

"Why, the Prussian officer."

"But why?"

"I don't know. Go and ask him. I am forbidden to harness the horses, so I don't harness them—that's all."

"Did he tell you so himself?"

"No, sir; the innkeeper gave me the order from him."

"When?"

"Last evening, just as I was going to bed."

The three men returned in a very uneasy frame of mind.

They asked for Monsieur Follenvie, but the servant replied that on account of his asthma he never got up before ten o'clock. They were strictly forbidden to rouse him earlier, except in case of fire.

They wished to see the officer, but that also was impossible, although he lodged in the inn. Monsieur Follenvie alone was authorized to interview him on civil matters. So they waited. The women returned to their rooms, and occupied themselves with trivial matters.

Cornudet settled down beside the tall kitchen fireplace, before a blazing fire. He had a small table and a jug of beer placed beside him, and he smoked his pipe—a pipe which enjoyed among democrats a consideration almost equal to his own, as though it had served its country in serving Cornudet. It was a fine meerschaum, admirably colored to a black the shade of its owner's teeth, but sweet-smelling, gracefully curved, at home in its master's hand, and completing his physiognomy. And Cornudet sat motionless, his eyes fixed now on the dancing flames, now on the froth which crowned his beer; and after each draught he passed his long, thin fingers with an air of satisfaction through his long, greasy hair, as he sucked the foam from his mustache.

Loiseau, under pretence of stretching his legs, went out to see if he could sell wine to the country dealers. The count and the manufacturer began to talk politics. They forecast the future of France. One believed in the Orleans dynasty, the other in an unknown savior—a hero who should rise up in the last extremity: a Du Guesclin, perhaps a Joan of Arc? or another Napoleon the First? Ah! if only the Prince Imperial were not so young! Cornudet, listening to them, smiled like a man who holds the keys of destiny in his hands. His pipe perfumed the whole kitchen.

As the clock struck ten, Monsieur Follenvie appeared. He was immediately surrounded and questioned, but could only repeat, three or four times in succession, and without variation, the words:

"The officer said to me, just like this: 'Monsieur Follenvie, you will forbid them to harness up the coach for those travellers to-morrow. They are not to start without an order from me. You hear? That is sufficient.'"

Then they asked to see the officer. The count sent him his card, on which Monsieur Carre-Lamadon also inscribed his name and titles. The Prussian sent word that the two men would be admitted to see him after his luncheon—that is to say, about one o'clock.

The ladies reappeared, and they all ate a little, in spite

of their anxiety. Boule de Suif appeared ill and very much worried.

They were finishing their coffee when the orderly came to fetch the gentlemen.

Loiseau joined the other two; but when they tried to get Cornudet to accompany them, by way of adding greater solemnity to the occasion, he declared proudly that he would never have anything to do with the Germans, and, resuming his seat in the chimney corner, he called for another jug of beer.

The three men went upstairs, and were ushered into the best room in the inn, where the officer received them lolling at his ease in an armchair, his feet on the mantelpiece, smoking a long porcelain pipe, and enveloped in a gorgeous dressing-gown, doubtless stolen from the deserted dwelling of some citizen destitute of taste in dress. He neither rose, greeted them, nor even glanced in their direction. He afforded a fine example of that insolence of bearing which seems natural to the victorious soldier.

After the lapse of a few moments he said in his halting French:

"What do you want?"

"We wish to start on our journey," said the count.

"No."

"May I ask the reason of your refusal?"

"Because I don't choose."

"I would respectfully call your attention, monsieur, to the fact that your general in command gave us a permit to proceed to Dieppe; and I do not think we have done anything to deserve this harshness at your hands."

"I don't choose—that's all. You may go."

They bowed, and retired.

The afternoon was wretched. They could not understand the caprice of this German, and the strangest ideas came into their heads. They all congregated in the kitchen, and talked the subject to death, imagining all kinds of unlikely things. Perhaps they were to be kept as hostages—but for what reason? or to be extradited as prisoners of war? or possibly they were to be held for ransom? They were panic-stricken at this last supposition. The richest among them were the most alarmed, seeing themselves forced to empty bags of gold into the insolent soldier's hands in order to buy back their lives. They racked their brains for plausible lies whereby they might conceal the fact that they were rich, and pass themselves off as poor—very poor. Loiseau took off his watch chain, and put it in his pocket. The approach of night increased their apprehension. The lamp was lighted, and as it wanted yet two hours to dinner Madame Loiseau proposed a game of trente et un. It would distract their thoughts. The rest agreed, and Cornudet himself joined the party, first putting out his pipe for politeness' sake.

The count shuffled the cards—dealt—and Boule de Suif had thirty-one to start with; soon the interest of the game assuaged the anxiety of the players. But Cornudet noticed that Loiseau and his wife were in league to cheat.

They were about to sit down to dinner when Monsieur Follenvie appeared, and in his grating voice announced:

"The Prussian officer sends to ask Mademoiselle Elisabeth Rousset if she has changed her mind yet."

Boule de Suif stood still, pale as death. Then, suddenly turning crimson with anger, she gasped out:

"Kindly tell that scoundrel, that cur, that carrion of a Prussian, that I will never consent—you understand?—never, never, never!"

The fat innkeeper left the room. Then Boule de Suif was surrounded, questioned, entreated on all sides to reveal the mystery of her visit to the officer. She refused at first; but her wrath soon got the better of her.

"What does he want? He wants to make me his mistress!" she cried.

No one was shocked at the word, so great was the general indignation. Cornudet broke his jug as he banged it down on the table. A loud outcry arose against this base soldier. All were furious. They drew together in common resistance against the foe, as if some part of the sacrifice exacted of Boule de Suif had been demanded of each. The count declared, with supreme disgust, that those people behaved like ancient barbarians. The women, above all, manifested a lively and tender sympathy for Boule de Suif. The nuns, who appeared only at meals, cast down their eyes, and said nothing.

They dined, however, as soon as the first indignant outburst had subsided; but they spoke little and thought much.

The ladies went to bed early; and the men, having lighted their pipes, proposed a game of ecarte, in which Monsieur Follenvie was invited to join, the travellers hoping to question him skillfully as to the best means of vanquishing the officer's obduracy. But he thought of nothing but his cards, would listen to nothing, reply to nothing, and repeated, time after time: "Attend to the game, gentlemen! attend to the game!" So absorbed was his attention that he even forgot to expectorate. The consequence was that his chest gave forth rumbling sounds like those of an organ. His wheezing lungs struck every note of the asthmatic scale, from deep, hollow tones to a shrill, hoarse piping resembling that of a young cock trying to crow.

He refused to go to bed when his wife, overcome with sleep, came to fetch him. So she went off alone, for she was an early bird, always up with the sun; while he was addicted to late hours, ever ready to spend the night with friends. He merely said: "Put my egg-nogg by the fire," and went on with the game. When the other men saw that nothing was to be got out of him they declared it was time to retire, and each sought his bed.

They rose fairly early the next morning, with a vague hope of being allowed to start, a greater desire than ever to do so, and a terror at having to spend another day in this wretched little inn.

Alas! the horses remained in the stable, the driver was invisible. They spent their time, for want of something better to do, in wandering round the coach.

Luncheon was a gloomy affair; and there was a general coolness toward Boule de Suif, for night, which brings counsel, had somewhat modified the judgment of her companions. In the cold light of the morning they almost bore a grudge against the girl for not having secretly sought out the Prussian, that the rest of the party might receive a joyful surprise when they awoke. What more simple?

Besides, who would have been the wiser? She might have saved appearances by telling the officer that she had taken pity on their distress. Such a step would be of so little consequence to her.

But no one as yet confessed to such thoughts.

In the afternoon, seeing that they were all bored to death, the count proposed a walk in the neighborhood of the village. Each one wrapped himself up well, and the little party set out, leaving behind only Cornudet, who preferred to sit over the fire, and the two nuns, who were in the habit of spending their day in the church or at the presbytery.

The cold, which grew more intense each day, almost froze the noses and ears of the pedestrians, their feet began to pain them so that each step was a penance, and when they reached the open country it looked so mournful and depressing in its limitless mantle of white that they all hastily retraced their steps, with bodies benumbed and hearts heavy.

The four women walked in front, and the three men followed a little in their rear.

Loiseau, who saw perfectly well how matters stood, asked suddenly "if that trollop were going to keep them waiting much longer in this Godforsaken spot." The count, always courteous, replied that they could not exact so painful a sacrifice from any woman, and that the first move must come from herself. Monsieur Carre-Lamadon remarked that if the French, as they talked of doing, made a counter attack by way of Dieppe, their encounter with the enemy must inevitably take place at Totes. This reflection made the other two anxious.

"Supposing we escape on foot?" said Loiseau.

The count shrugged his shoulders.

"How can you think of such a thing, in this snow? And with our wives? Besides, we should be pursued at once, overtaken in ten minutes, and brought back as prisoners at the mercy of the soldiery."

This was true enough; they were silent.

The ladies talked of dress, but a certain constraint seemed to prevail among them.

Suddenly, at the end of the street, the officer appeared. His tall, wasp-like, uniformed figure was outlined against the snow which bounded the horizon, and he walked, knees apart, with that motion peculiar to soldiers, who are always anxious not to soil their carefully polished boots.

He bowed as he passed the ladies, then glanced scornfully at the men, who had sufficient dignity not to raise their hats, though Loiseau made a movement to do so.

Boule de Suif flushed crimson to the ears, and the three married women felt unutterably humiliated at being met thus by the soldier in company with the girl whom he had treated with such scant ceremony.

Then they began to talk about him, his figure, and his face. Madame Carre-Lamadon, who had known many officers and judged them as a connoisseur, thought him not at all bad-looking; she even regretted that he was not a Frenchman, because in that case he would have made a very handsome hussar, with whom all the women would assuredly have fallen in love.

When they were once more within doors they did not know what to do with themselves. Sharp words even were exchanged apropos of the merest trifles. The silent dinner was quickly over, and each one went to bed early in the hope of sleeping, and thus killing time.

They came down next morning with tired faces and irritable tempers; the women scarcely spoke to Boule de Suif.

A church bell summoned the faithful to a baptism. Boule de Suif had a child being brought up by peasants at Yvetot. She did not see him once a year, and never thought of him; but the idea of the child who was about to be baptized induced a sudden wave of tenderness for her own, and she insisted on being present at the ceremony.

As soon as she had gone out, the rest of the company looked at one another and then drew their chairs together; for they realized that they must decide on some course of action. Loiseau had an inspiration: he proposed that they should ask the officer to detain Boule de Suif only, and to let the rest depart on their way.

Monsieur Follenvie was intrusted with this commission, but he returned to them almost immediately. The

German, who knew human nature, had shown him the door. He intended to keep all the travellers until his condition had been complied with.

Whereupon Madame Loiseau's vulgar temperament broke bounds.

"We're not going to die of old age here!" she cried. "Since it's that vixen's trade to behave so with men I don't see that she has any right to refuse one more than another. I may as well tell you she took any lovers she could get at Rouen—even coachmen! Yes, indeed, madame—the coachman at the prefecture! I know it for a fact, for he buys his wine of us. And now that it is a question of getting us out of a difficulty she puts on virtuous airs, the drab! For my part, I think this officer has behaved very well. Why, there were three others of us, any one of whom he would undoubtedly have preferred. But no, he contents himself with the girl who is common property. He respects married women. Just think. He is master here. He had only to say: 'I wish it!' and he might have taken us by force, with the help of his soldiers." The two other women shuddered; the eyes of pretty Madame Carre-Lamadon glistened, and she grew pale, as if the officer were indeed in the act of laying violent hands on her.

The men, who had been discussing the subject among themselves, drew near. Loiseau, in a state of furious resentment, was for delivering up "that miserable woman," bound hand and foot, into the enemy's power. But the count, descended from three generations of ambassadors, and endowed, moreover, with the lineaments of a diplomat, was in favor of more tactful measures.

"We must persuade her," he said.

Then they laid their plans.

The women drew together; they lowered their voices,

and the discussion became general, each giving his or her opinion. But the conversation was not in the least coarse. The ladies, in particular, were adepts at delicate phrases and charming subtleties of expression to describe the most improper things. A stranger would have understood none of their allusions, so guarded was the language they employed. But, seeing that the thin veneer of modesty with which every woman of the world is furnished goes but a very little way below the surface, they began rather to enjoy this unedifying episode, and at bottom were hugely delighted —feeling themselves in their element, furthering the schemes of lawless love with the gusto of a gourmand cook who prepares supper for another.

Their gaiety returned of itself, so amusing at last did the whole business seem to them. The count uttered several rather risky witticisms, but so tactfully were they said that his audience could not help smiling. Loiseau in turn made some considerably broader jokes, but no one took offence; and the thought expressed with such brutal directness by his wife was uppermost in the minds of all: "Since it's the girl's trade, why should she refuse this man more than another?" Dainty Madame Carre-Lamadon seemed to think even that in Boule de Suif's place she would be less inclined to refuse him than another.

The blockade was as carefully arranged as if they were investing a fortress. Each agreed on the role which he or she was to play, the arguments to be used, the maneuvers to be executed. They decided on the plan of campaign, the stratagems they were to employ, and the surprise attacks which were to reduce this human citadel and force it to receive the enemy within its walls.

But Cornudet remained apart from the rest, taking no share in the plot.

So absorbed was the attention of all that Boule de Suif's

entrance was almost unnoticed. But the count whispered a gentle "Hush!" which made the others look up. She was there. They suddenly stopped talking, and a vague embarrassment prevented them for a few moments from addressing her. But the countess, more practiced than the others in the wiles of the drawing-room, asked her: "Was the baptism interesting?"

The girl, still under the stress of emotion, told what she had seen and heard, described the faces, the attitudes of those present, and even the appearance of the church. She concluded with the words:

"It does one good to pray sometimes."

Until lunch time the ladies contented themselves with being pleasant to her, so as to increase her confidence and make her amenable to their advice.

As soon as they took their seats at table the attack began. First they opened a vague conversation on the subject of self-sacrifice. Ancient examples were quoted: Judith and Holofernes; then, irrationally enough, Lucrece and Sextus; Cleopatra and the hostile generals whom she reduced to abject slavery by a surrender of her charms. Next was recounted an extraordinary story, born of the imagination of these ignorant millionaires, which told how the matrons of Rome seduced Hannibal, his lieutenants, and all his mercenaries at Capua. They held up to admiration all those women who from time to time have arrested the victorious progress of conquerors, made of their bodies a field of battle, a means of ruling, a weapon; who have vanquished by their heroic caresses hideous or detested beings, and sacrificed their chastity to vengeance and devotion.

All was said with due restraint and regard for propriety, the effect heightened now and then by an outburst of forced enthusiasm calculated to excite emulation.

A listener would have thought at last that the one role

of woman on earth was a perpetual sacrifice of her person, a continual abandonment of herself to the caprices of a hostile soldiery.

The two nuns seemed to hear nothing, and to be lost in thought. Boule de Suif also was silent.

During the whole afternoon she was left to her reflections. But instead of calling her "madame" as they had done hitherto, her companions addressed her simply as "mademoiselle," without exactly knowing why, but as if desirous of making her descend a step in the esteem she had won, and forcing her to realize her degraded position.

Just as soup was served, Monsieur Follenvie reappeared, repeating his phrase of the evening before:

"The Prussian officer sends to ask if Mademoiselle Elisabeth Rousset has changed her mind."

Boule de Suif answered briefly:

"No, monsieur."

But at dinner the coalition weakened. Loiseau made three unfortunate remarks. Each was cudgeling his brains for further examples of self-sacrifice, and could find none, when the countess, possibly without ulterior motive, and moved simply by a vague desire to do homage to religion, began to question the elder of the two nuns on the most striking facts in the lives of the saints. Now, it fell out that many of these had committed acts which would be crimes in our eyes, but the Church readily pardons such deeds when they are accomplished for the glory of God or the good of mankind. This was a powerful argument, and the countess made the most of it. Then, whether by reason of a tacit understanding, a thinly veiled act of complaisance such as those who wear the ecclesiastical habit excel in, or whether merely as the result of sheer stupidity—a stupidity admirably adapted to further their designs—the old nun rendered formidable aid to the conspirator. They had thought her timid; she proved herself bold, talkative, bigoted. She was not troubled by the ins and outs of casuistry; her doctrines were as iron bars; her faith knew no doubt; her conscience no scruples. She looked on Abraham's sacrifice as natural enough, for she herself would not have hesitated to kill both father and mother if she had received a divine order to that effect; and nothing, in her opinion, could displease our Lord, provided the motive were praiseworthy. The countess, putting to good use the consecrated authority of her unexpected ally, led her on to make a lengthy and edifying paraphrase of that axiom enunciated by a certain school of moralists: "The end justifies the means." "Then, sister," she asked, "you think God accepts all methods, and pardons the act when the motive is pure?"

"Undoubtedly, madame. An action reprehensible in itself often derives merit from the thought which inspires it."

And in this wise they talked on, fathoming the wishes of God, predicting His judgments, describing Him as interested in matters which assuredly concern Him but little.

All was said with the utmost care and discretion, but every word uttered by the holy woman in her nun's garb weakened the indignant resistance of the courtesan. Then the conversation drifted somewhat, and the nun began to talk of the convents of her order, of her Superior, of herself, and of her fragile little neighbor, Sister St. Nicephore. They had been sent for from Havre to nurse the hundreds of soldiers who were in hospitals, stricken with smallpox. She described these wretched invalids and their malady. And, while they themselves were detained on their way by the caprices of the Prussian officer, scores of Frenchmen might be dying, whom they would otherwise have saved! For the nursing of soldiers was the old nun's specialty; she had been in the Crimea, in Italy, in Austria; and as she told the story of her campaigns she revealed herself as one of those holy sisters of the fife and drum who seem designed by nature to follow camps, to snatch the wounded from amid the strife of battle, and to quell with a word, more effectually than any general, the rough and insubordinate troopers—a masterful woman, her seamed and pitted face itself an image of the devastations of war.

No one spoke when she had finished for fear of spoiling the excellent effect of her words.

As soon as the meal was over the travellers retired to their rooms, whence they emerged the following day at a late hour of the morning.

Luncheon passed off quietly. The seed sown the preceding evening was being given time to germinate and bring forth fruit.

In the afternoon the countess proposed a walk; then the count, as had been arranged beforehand, took Boule de Suif's arm, and walked with her at some distance behind the rest.

He began talking to her in that familiar, paternal, slightly contemptuous tone which men of his class adopt in speaking to women like her, calling her "my dear child," and talking down to her from the height of his exalted social position and stainless reputation. He came straight to the point.

"So you prefer to leave us here, exposed like yourself to all the violence which would follow on a repulse of the Prussian troops, rather than consent to surrender yourself, as you have done so many times in your life?"

The girl did not reply.

He tried kindness, argument, sentiment. He still bore himself as count, even while adopting, when desirable, an attitude of gallantry, and making pretty—nay, even tender

—speeches. He exalted the service she would render them, spoke of their gratitude; then, suddenly, using the familiar "thou": "And you know, my dear, he could boast then of having made a conquest of a pretty girl such as he won't often find in his own country."

Boule de Suif did not answer, and joined the rest of the party.

As soon as they returned she went to her room, and was seen no more. The general anxiety was at its height. What would she do? If she still resisted, how awkward for them all!

The dinner hour struck; they waited for her in vain. At last Monsieur Follenvie entered, announcing that Mademoiselle Rousset was not well, and that they might sit down to table. They all pricked up their ears. The count drew near the innkeeper, and whispered: "Is it all right?"

"Yes."

Out of regard for propriety he said nothing to his companions, but merely nodded slightly toward them. A great sigh of relief went up from all breasts; every face was lighted up with joy.

"By Gad!" shouted Loiseau, "I'll stand champagne all round if there's any to be found in this place." And great was Madame Loiseau's dismay when the proprietor came back with four bottles in his hands. They had all suddenly become talkative and merry; a lively joy filled all hearts. The count seemed to perceive for the first time that Madame Carre-Lamadon was charming; the manufacturer paid compliments to the countess. The conversation was animated, sprightly, witty, and, although many of the jokes were in the worst possible taste, all the company were amused by them, and none offended—indignation being dependent, like other emotions, on surroundings. And the mental atmosphere had gradually become filled with gross imaginings and unclean thoughts.

At dessert even the women indulged in discreetly worded allusions. Their glances were full of meaning; they had drunk much. The count, who even in his moments of relaxation preserved a dignified demeanor, hit on a much-appreciated comparison of the condition of things with the termination of a winter spent in the icy solitude of the North Pole and the joy of shipwrecked mariners who at last perceive a southward track opening out before their eyes.

Loiseau, fairly in his element, rose to his feet, holding aloft a glass of champagne.

"I drink to our deliverance!" he shouted.

All stood up, and greeted the toast with acclamation. Even the two good sisters yielded to the solicitations of the ladies, and consented to moisten their lips with the foaming wine, which they had never before tasted. They declared it was like effervescent lemonade, but with a pleasanter flavor.

"It is a pity," said Loiseau, "that we have no piano; we might have had a quadrille."

Cornudet had not spoken a word or made a movement; he seemed plunged in serious thought, and now and then tugged furiously at his great beard, as if trying to add still further to its length. At last, toward midnight, when they were about to separate, Loiseau, whose gait was far from steady, suddenly slapped him on the back, saying thickly: "You're not jolly to-night; why are you so silent, old man?"

Cornudet threw back his head, cast one swift and scornful glance over the assemblage, and answered:

"I tell you all, you have done an infamous thing!"

He rose, reached the door, and repeating: "Infamous!" disappeared.

A chill fell on all. Loiseau himself looked foolish and disconcerted for a moment, but soon recovered his aplomb, and, writhing with laughter, exclaimed:

"Really, you are all too green for anything!"

Pressed for an explanation, he related the "mysteries of the corridor," whereat his listeners were hugely amused. The ladies could hardly contain their delight. The count and Monsieur Carre-Lamadon laughed till they cried. They could scarcely believe their ears.

"What! you are sure? He wanted—"

"I tell you I saw it with my own eyes."

"And she refused?"

"Because the Prussian was in the next room!"

"Surely you are mistaken?"

"I swear I'm telling you the truth."

The count was choking with laughter. The manufacturer held his sides. Loiseau continued:

"So you may well imagine he doesn't think this evening's business at all amusing."

And all three began to laugh again, choking, coughing, almost ill with merriment.

Then they separated. But Madame Loiseau, who was nothing if not spiteful, remarked to her husband as they were on the way to bed that "that stuck-up little minx of a Carre-Lamadon had laughed on the wrong side of her mouth all the evening." "You know," she said, "when women run after uniforms it's all the same to them whether the men who wear them are French or Prussian. It's perfectly sickening!"

The next morning the snow showed dazzling white tinder a clear winter sun. The coach, ready at last, waited before the door; while a flock of white pigeons, with pink eyes spotted in the centres with black, puffed out their white feathers and walked sedately between the legs of the six horses, picking at the steaming manure.

The driver, wrapped in his sheepskin coat, was smoking a pipe on the box, and all the passengers, radiant with delight at their approaching departure, were putting up provisions for the remainder of the journey.

They were waiting only for Boule de Suif. At last she appeared.

She seemed rather shamefaced and embarrassed, and advanced with timid step toward her companions, who with one accord turned aside as if they had not seen her. The count, with much dignity, took his wife by the arm, and removed her from the unclean contact.

The girl stood still, stupefied with astonishment; then, plucking up courage, accosted the manufacturer's wife with a humble "Good-morning, madame," to which the other replied merely with a slight and insolent nod, accompanied by a look of outraged virtue. Every one suddenly appeared extremely busy, and kept as far from Boule de Suif as if her skirts had been infected with some deadly disease. Then they hurried to the coach, followed by the despised courtesan, who, arriving last of all, silently took the place she had occupied during the first part of the journey.

The rest seemed neither to see nor to know her—all save Madame Loiseau, who, glancing contemptuously in her direction, remarked, half aloud, to her husband:

"What a mercy I am not sitting beside that creature!"

The lumbering vehicle started on its way, and the journey began afresh.

At first no one spoke. Boule de Suif dared not even raise her eyes. She felt at once indignant with her neighbors, and humiliated at having yielded to the Prussian into whose arms they had so hypocritically cast her.

But the countess, turning toward Madame Carre-Lamadon, soon broke the painful silence:

"I think you know Madame d'Etrelles?"
"Yes; she is a friend of mine."
"Such a charming woman!"
"Delightful! Exceptionally talented, and an artist to the finger tips. She sings marvellously and draws to perfection."
The manufacturer was chatting with the count, and amid the clatter of the window-panes a word of their conversation was now and then distinguishable: "Shares—maturity—premium—time-limit."
Loiseau, who had abstracted from the inn the timeworn pack of cards, thick with the grease of five years' contact with half-wiped-off tables, started a game of bezique with his wife.
The good sisters, taking up simultaneously the long rosaries hanging from their waists, made the sign of the cross, and began to mutter in unison interminable prayers, their lips moving ever more and more swiftly, as if they sought which should outdistance the other in the race of orisons; from time to time they kissed a medal, and crossed themselves anew, then resumed their rapid and unintelligible murmur.
Cornudet sat still, lost in thought.
Ah the end of three hours Loiseau gathered up the cards, and remarked that he was hungry.
His wife thereupon produced a parcel tied with string, from which she extracted a piece of cold veal. This she cut into neat, thin slices, and both began to eat.
"We may as well do the same," said the countess. The rest agreed, and she unpacked the provisions which had been prepared for herself, the count, and the Carre-Lamadons. In one of those oval dishes, the lids of which are decorated with an earthenware hare, by way of showing that a game pie lies within, was a succulent delicacy consisting of the brown flesh of the game larded

with streaks of bacon and flavored with other meats chopped fine. A solid wedge of Gruyere cheese, which had been wrapped in a newspaper, bore the imprint: "Items of News," on its rich, oily surface.

The two good sisters brought to light a hunk of sausage smelling strongly of garlic; and Cornudet, plunging both hands at once into the capacious pockets of his loose overcoat, produced from one four hard-boiled eggs and from the other a crust of bread. He removed the shells, threw them into the straw beneath his feet, and began to devour the eggs, letting morsels of the bright yellow yolk fall in his mighty beard, where they looked like stars.

Boule de Suif, in the haste and confusion of her departure, had not thought of anything, and, stifling with rage, she watched all these people placidly eating. At first, ill-suppressed wrath shook her whole person, and she opened her lips to shriek the truth at them, to overwhelm them with a volley of insults; but she could not utter a word, so choked was she with indignation.

No one looked at her, no one thought of her. She felt herself swallowed up in the scorn of these virtuous creatures, who had first sacrificed, then rejected her as a thing useless and unclean. Then she remembered her big basket full of the good things they had so greedily devoured: the two chickens coated in jelly, the pies, the pears, the four bottles of claret; and her fury broke forth like a cord that is overstrained, and she was on the verge of tears. She made terrible efforts at self-control, drew herself up, swallowed the sobs which choked her; but the tears rose nevertheless, shone at the brink of her eyelids, and soon two heavy drops coursed slowly down her cheeks. Others followed more quickly, like water filtering from a rock, and fell, one after another, on her rounded bosom. She sat upright, with a fixed expression, her face pale and rigid, hoping desperately that no one saw her give way.

But the countess noticed that she was weeping, and with a sign drew her husband's attention to the fact. He shrugged his shoulders, as if to say: "Well, what of it? It's not my fault." Madame Loiseau chuckled triumphantly, and murmured: "She's weeping for shame."

The two nuns had betaken themselves once more to their prayers, first wrapping the remainder of their sausage in paper:

Then Cornudet, who was digesting his eggs, stretched his long legs under the opposite seat, threw himself back, folded his arms, smiled like a man who had just thought of a good joke, and began to whistle the Marseillaise.

The faces of his neighbors clouded; the popular air evidently did not find favor with them; they grew nervous and irritable, and seemed ready to howl as a dog does at the sound of a barrel-organ. Cornudet saw the discomfort he was creating, and whistled the louder; sometimes he even hummed the words: Amour sacre de la patrie,

Conduis, soutiens, nos bras vengeurs,
Liberte, liberte cherie,
Combats avec tes defenseurs!

The coach progressed more swiftly, the snow being harder now; and all the way to Dieppe, during the long, dreary hours of the journey, first in the gathering dusk, then in the thick darkness, raising his voice above the rumbling of the vehicle, Cornudet continued with fierce obstinacy his vengeful and monotonous whistling, forcing his weary and exasperated-hearers to follow the song from end to end, to recall every word of every line, as each was repeated over and over again with untiring persistency.

And Boule de Suif still wept, and sometimes a sob she could not restrain was heard in the darkness between two verses of the song.

The Lady With the Dog

Anton Pavlovich Chekhov

I

IT was said that a new person had appeared on the sea-front: a lady with a little dog. Dmitri Dmitritch Gurov, who had by then been a fortnight at Yalta, and so was fairly at home there, had begun to take an interest in new arrivals. Sitting in Verney's pavilion, he saw, walking on the sea-front, a fair-haired young lady of medium height, wearing a béret; a white Pomeranian dog was running behind her.

And afterwards he met her in the public gardens and in the square several times a day. She was walking alone, always wearing the same béret, and always with the same white dog; no one knew who she was, and every one called her simply "the lady with the dog."

"If she is here alone without a husband or friends, it wouldn't be amiss to make her acquaintance," Gurov reflected.

He was under forty, but he had a daughter already twelve years old, and two sons at school. He had been married young, when he was a student in his second year, and by now his wife seemed half as old again as he. She was a tall, erect woman with dark eyebrows, staid and dignified, and, as she said of herself, intellectual. She read a great deal, used phonetic spelling, called her husband, not Dmitri, but Dimitri, and he secretly considered her unintelligent, narrow, inelegant, was afraid of her, and did not like to be at home. He had begun being unfaithful to her long ago—had been unfaithful to her often, and, probably on that account, almost always spoke ill of women, and when they were talked about in his presence, used to call them "the lower race."

It seemed to him that he had been so schooled by bitter experience that he might call them what he liked, and yet he could not get on for two days together without "the lower race." In the society of men he was bored and not himself, with them he was cold and uncommunicative; but when he was in the company of women he felt free, and knew what to say to them and how to behave; and he was at ease with them even when he was silent. In his appearance, in his character, in his whole nature, there was something attractive and elusive which allured women and disposed them in his favour; he knew that, and some force seemed to draw him, too, to them.

Experience often repeated, truly bitter experience, had taught him long ago that with decent people, especially Moscow people—always slow to move and irresolute—every intimacy, which at first so agreeably diversifies life and appears a light and charming adventure, inevitably grows into a regular problem of extreme intricacy, and in the long run the situation becomes unbearable. But at every fresh meeting with an interesting woman this experience seemed to slip out of his memory, and he was eager for life, and everything seemed simple and amusing.

One evening he was dining in the gardens, and the lady in the béret came up slowly to take the next table. Her expression, her gait, her dress, and the way she did her hair told him that she was a lady, that she was married, that she was in Yalta for the first time and alone, and that she was dull there.... The stories told of the immorality in such places as Yalta are to a great extent untrue; he despised them, and knew that such stories were for the most part made up by persons who would themselves have been glad to sin if they had been able; but when the lady sat down at the next table three paces from him, he remembered these tales of easy conquests, of trips to the mountains, and the tempting thought of a swift, fleeting love affair, a romance with an unknown woman, whose name he did not know, suddenly took possession of him.

He beckoned coaxingly to the Pomeranian, and when the dog came up to him he shook his finger at it. The Pomeranian growled: Gurov shook his finger at it again.

The lady looked at him and at once dropped her eyes.

"He doesn't bite," she said, and blushed.

"May I give him a bone?" he asked; and when she nodded he asked courteously, "Have you been long in Yalta?"

"Five days."

"And I have already dragged out a fortnight here."

There was a brief silence.

"Time goes fast, and yet it is so dull here!" she said, not looking at him.

"That's only the fashion to say it is dull here. A provincial will live in Belyov or Zhidra and not be dull, and when he comes here it's 'Oh, the dulness! Oh, the dust!' One would think he came from Grenada."

She laughed. Then both continued eating in silence, like strangers, but after dinner they walked side by side; and there sprang up between them the light jesting conversation of people who are free and satisfied, to whom it does not matter where they go or what they talk about. They walked and talked of the strange light on the sea: the water was of a soft warm lilac hue, and there was a golden streak from the moon upon it. They talked of how sultry it was after a hot day. Gurov told her that he came from Moscow, that he had taken his degree in Arts, but had a post in a bank; that he had trained as an opera-singer, but had given it up, that he owned two houses in Moscow.... And from her he learnt that she had grown up in Petersburg, but had lived in S —— since her marriage two years before, that she was staying another month in Yalta, and that her husband, who needed a holiday too, might perhaps come and fetch her. She was not sure whether her husband had a post in a Crown Department or under the Provincial Council—and was amused by her own ignorance. And Gurov learnt, too, that she was called Anna Sergeyevna.

Afterwards he thought about her in his room at the hotel—thought she would certainly meet him next day; it would be sure to happen. As he got into bed he thought how lately she had been a girl at school, doing lessons like his own daughter; he recalled the diffidence, the angularity, that was still manifest in her laugh and her manner of talking with a stranger. This must have been the first time in her life she had been alone in surroundings in which she was followed, looked at, and spoken to merely from a secret motive which she could hardly fail to guess. He recalled her slender, delicate neck, her lovely grey eyes.

"There's something pathetic about her, anyway," he thought, and fell asleep.

II

A week had passed since they had made acquaintance. It was a holiday. It was sultry indoors, while in the street the wind whirled the dust round and round, and blew people's hats off. It was a thirsty day, and Gurov often went into the pavilion, and pressed Anna Sergeyevna to have syrup and water or an ice. One did not know what to do with oneself.

In the evening when the wind had dropped a little, they went out on the groyne to see the steamer come in.

There were a great many people walking about the harbour; they had gathered to welcome some one, bringing bouquets. And two peculiarities of a well-dressed Yalta crowd were very conspicuous: the elderly ladies were dressed like young ones, and there were great numbers of generals.

Owing to the roughness of the sea, the steamer arrived late, after the sun had set, and it was a long time turning about before it reached the groyne. Anna Sergeyevna looked through her lorgnette at the steamer and the passengers as though looking for acquaintances, and when she turned to Gurov her eyes were shining. She talked a great deal and asked disconnected questions, forgetting next moment what she had asked; then she dropped her lorgnette in the crush.

The festive crowd began to disperse; it was too dark to see people's faces. The wind had completely dropped, but Gurov and Anna Sergeyevna still stood as though waiting to see some one else come from the steamer. Anna Sergeyevna was silent now, and sniffed the flowers without looking at Gurov.

"The weather is better this evening," he said. "Where shall we go now? Shall we drive somewhere?"

She made no answer.

Then he looked at her intently, and all at once put his arm round her and kissed her on the lips, and breathed in the moisture and the fragrance of the flowers; and he immediately looked round him, anxiously wondering whether any one had seen them.

"Let us go to your hotel," he said softly. And both walked quickly.

The room was close and smelt of the scent she had bought at the Japanese shop. Gurov looked at her and thought: "What different people one meets in the world!" From the past he preserved memories of careless, good-natured women, who loved cheerfully and were grateful to him for the happiness he gave them, however brief it might be; and of women like his wife who loved without any genuine feeling, with superfluous phrases, affectedly, hysterically, with an expression that suggested that it was not love nor passion, but something more significant; and of two or three others, very beautiful, cold women, on whose faces he had caught a glimpse of a rapacious expression—an obstinate desire to snatch from life more than it could give, and these were capricious, unreflecting, domineering, unintelligent women not in their first youth, and when Gurov grew cold to them their beauty excited his hatred, and the lace on their linen seemed to him like scales.

But in this case there was still the diffidence, the angularity of inexperienced youth, an awkward feeling; and there was a sense of consternation as though some one had suddenly knocked at the door. The attitude of Anna Sergeyevna—"the lady with the dog"—to what had happened was somehow peculiar, very grave, as though it were her fall—so it seemed, and it was strange and inappropriate. Her face dropped and faded, and on both sides of it her long hair hung down mournfully; she mused in a dejected attitude like "the woman who was a sinner" in an old-fashioned picture.

"It's wrong," she said. "You will be the first to despise me now."

There was a water-melon on the table. Gurov cut himself a slice and began eating it without haste. There followed at least half an hour of silence.

Anna Sergeyevna was touching; there was about her the purity of a good, simple woman who had seen little of life. The solitary candle burning on the table threw a faint light on her face, yet it was clear that she was very unhappy.

"How could I despise you?" asked Gurov. "You don't know what you are saying."

"God forgive me," she said, and her eyes filled with tears. "It's awful."

"You seem to feel you need to be forgiven."

"Forgiven? No. I am a bad, low woman; I despise myself and don't attempt to justify myself. It's not my husband but myself I have deceived. And not only just now; I have been deceiving myself for a long time. My husband may be a good, honest man, but he is a flunkey! I don't know what he does there, what his work is, but I know he is a flunkey! I was twenty when I was married to him. I have been tormented by curiosity; I wanted something better. 'There must be a different sort of life,' I said to myself. I wanted to live! To live, to live!... I was fired by curiosity ... you don't understand it, but, I swear to God, I could not control myself; something happened to me: I could not be restrained. I told my husband I was ill, and came here.... And here I have been walking about as though I were dazed, like a mad creature; ... and now I have become a vulgar, contemptible woman whom any one may despise."

Gurov felt bored already, listening to her. He was irritated by the naïve tone, by this remorse, so unexpected and inopportune; but for the tears in her eyes, he might have thought she was jesting or playing a part.

"I don't understand," he said softly. "What is it you want?"

She hid her face on his breast and pressed close to him.

"Believe me, believe me, I beseech you ..." she said. "I love a pure, honest life, and sin is loathsome to me. I don't know what I am doing. Simple people say: 'The Evil One has beguiled me.' And I may say of myself now that the Evil One has beguiled me."

"Hush, hush!..." he muttered.

He looked at her fixed, scared eyes, kissed her, talked softly and affectionately, and by degrees she was comforted, and her gaiety returned; they both began laughing.

Afterwards when they went out there was not a soul on the sea-front. The town with its cypresses had quite a deathlike air, but the sea still broke noisily on the shore; a single barge was rocking on the waves, and a lantern was blinking sleepily on it.

They found a cab and drove to Oreanda.

"I found out your surname in the hall just now: it was written on the board—Von Diderits," said Gurov. "Is your husband a German?"

"No; I believe his grandfather was a German, but he is an Orthodox Russian himself."

At Oreanda they sat on a seat not far from the church, looked down at the sea, and were silent. Yalta was hardly visible through the morning mist; white clouds stood motionless on the mountain-tops. The leaves did not stir on the trees, grasshoppers chirruped, and the monotonous hollow sound of the sea rising up from below, spoke of the peace, of the eternal sleep awaiting us. So it must have sounded when there was no Yalta, no Oreanda here; so it sounds now, and it will sound as indifferently and monotonously when we are all no more. And in this constancy, in this complete indifference to the life and death of each of us, there lies hid, perhaps, a pledge of our eternal salvation, of the unceasing movement of life upon earth, of unceasing progress towards perfection. Sitting beside a young woman who in the dawn seemed so lovely, soothed and spellbound in these magical surroundings—the sea, mountains, clouds, the open sky—Gurov thought how in reality everything is beautiful in this world when one reflects: everything except what we think or do ourselves when we forget our human dignity and the higher aims of our existence.

A man walked up to them—probably a keeper—looked at them and walked away. And this detail seemed mysterious and beautiful, too. They saw a steamer come from Theodosia, with its lights out in the glow of dawn.

"There is dew on the grass," said Anna Sergeyevna, after a silence.

"Yes. It's time to go home."

They went back to the town.

Then they met every day at twelve o'clock on the sea-front, lunched and dined together, went for walks, admired the sea. She complained that she slept badly, that her heart throbbed violently; asked the same questions, troubled now by jealousy and now by the fear that he did not respect her sufficiently. And often in the square or gardens, when there was no one near them, he suddenly drew her to him and kissed her passionately. Complete idleness, these kisses in broad daylight while he looked round in dread of some one's seeing them, the heat, the smell of the sea, and the continual passing to and fro before him of idle, well-dressed, well-fed people, made a new man of him; he told Anna Sergeyevna how beautiful she was, how fascinating. He was impatiently passionate, he would not move a step away from her, while she was often pensive and continually urged him to confess that he did not respect her, did not love her in the least, and thought of her as nothing but a common woman. Rather late almost every evening they drove somewhere out of town, to Oreanda or to the waterfall; and the expedition was always a success, the scenery invariably impressed them as grand and beautiful.

They were expecting her husband to come, but a letter came from him, saying that there was something wrong with his eyes, and he entreated his wife to come home as quickly as possible. Anna Sergeyevna made haste to go.

"It's a good thing I am going away," she said to Gurov. "It's the finger of destiny!"

She went by coach and he went with her. They were driving the whole day. When she had got into a compartment of the express, and when the second bell had rung, she said:

"Let me look at you once more ... look at you once again. That's right."

She did not shed tears, but was so sad that she seemed ill, and her face was quivering.

"I shall remember you ... think of you," she said. "God be with you; be happy. Don't remember evil against me. We are parting forever—it must be so, for we ought never to have met. Well, God be with you."

The train moved off rapidly, its lights soon vanished from sight, and a minute later there was no sound of it, as though everything had conspired together to end as quickly as possible that sweet delirium, that madness. Left alone on the platform, and gazing into the dark distance, Gurov listened to the chirrup of the grasshoppers and the hum of the telegraph wires, feeling as though he had only just waked up. And he thought, musing, that there had been another episode or adventure in his life, and it, too, was at an end, and nothing was left of it but a memory.... He was moved, sad, and conscious of a slight remorse. This young woman whom he would never meet again had not been happy with him; he was genuinely warm and affectionate with her, but yet in his manner, his tone, and his caresses there had been a shade of light irony, the coarse condescension of a happy man who was, besides, almost twice her age. All the time she had called him kind, exceptional, lofty; obviously he had seemed to her different from what he really was, so he had unintentionally deceived her....

Here at the station was already a scent of autumn; it was a cold evening.

"It's time for me to go north," thought Gurov as he left the platform. "High time!"

III

At home in Moscow everything was in its winter routine; the stoves were heated, and in the morning it was still dark when the children were having breakfast and getting ready for school, and the nurse would light the lamp for a short time. The frosts had begun already. When the first snow has fallen, on the first day of sledge-driving it is pleasant to see the white earth, the white roofs, to draw soft, delicious breath, and the season brings back the days of one's youth. The old limes and birches, white with hoar-frost, have a good-natured expression; they are nearer to one's heart than cypresses and palms, and near them one doesn't want to be thinking of the sea and the mountains.

Gurov was Moscow born; he arrived in Moscow on a fine frosty day, and when he put on his fur coat and warm gloves, and walked along Petrovka, and when on Saturday evening he heard the ringing of the bells, his recent trip and the places he had seen lost all charm for him. Little by little he became absorbed in Moscow life, greedily read three newspapers a day, and declared he did not read the Moscow papers on principle! He already felt a longing to go to restaurants, clubs, dinner-parties, anniversary celebrations, and he felt flattered at entertaining distinguished lawyers and artists, and at playing cards with a professor at the doctors' club. He could already eat a whole plateful of salt fish and cabbage.

In another month, he fancied, the image of Anna Sergeyevna would be shrouded in a mist in his memory, and only from time to time would visit him in his dreams with a touching smile as others did. But more than a month passed, real winter had come, and everything was still clear in his memory as though he had parted with Anna Sergeyevna only the day before. And his memories glowed more and more vividly. When in the evening stillness he heard from his study the voices of his children, preparing their lessons, or when he listened to a song or the organ at the restaurant, or the storm howled in the chimney, suddenly everything would rise up in his memory: what had happened on the groyne, and the early morning with the mist on the mountains, and the steamer coming from Theodosia, and the kisses. He would pace a long time about his room, remembering it all and smiling; then his memories passed into dreams, and in his fancy the past was mingled with what was to come. Anna Sergeyevna did not visit him in dreams, but followed him about everywhere like a shadow and haunted him. When he shut his eyes he saw her as though she were living before him, and she seemed to him lovelier, younger, tenderer than she was; and he imagined himself finer than he had been in Yalta. In the evenings she peeped out at him from the bookcase, from the fireplace, from the corner—he heard her breathing, the caressing rustle of her dress. In the street he watched the women, looking for some one like her.

He was tormented by an intense desire to confide his memories to some one. But in his home it was impossible to talk of his love, and he had no one outside; he could not talk to his tenants nor to any one at the bank. And what had he to talk of? Had he been in love, then? Had there been anything beautiful, poetical, or edifying or simply interesting in his relations with Anna Sergeyevna? And there was nothing for him but to talk vaguely of love, of woman, and no one guessed what it meant; only his wife twitched her black eyebrows, and said: "The part of a lady-killer does not suit you at all, Dimitri."

One evening, coming out of the doctors' club with an official with whom he had been playing cards, he could not resist saying:

"If only you knew what a fascinating woman I made the acquaintance of in Yalta!"

The official got into his sledge and was driving away, but turned suddenly and shouted:

"Dmitri Dmitritch!"

"What?"

"You were right this evening: the sturgeon was a bit too strong!"

These words, so ordinary, for some reason moved Gurov to indignation, and struck him as degrading and unclean. What savage manners, what people! What senseless nights, what uninteresting, uneventful days! The rage for card-playing, the gluttony, the drunkenness, the continual talk always about the same thing. Useless pursuits and conversations always about the same things absorb the better part of one's time, the better part of one's strength, and in the end there is left a life grovelling and curtailed, worthless and trivial, and there is no escaping or getting away from it—just as though one were in a madhouse or a prison.

Gurov did not sleep all night, and was filled with indignation. And he had a headache all next day. And the next night he slept badly; he sat up in bed, thinking, or paced up and down his room. He was sick of his children, sick of the bank; he had no desire to go anywhere or to talk of anything.

In the holidays in December he prepared for a journey, and told his wife he was going to Petersburg to do something in the interests of a young friend—and he set off for S——. What for? He did not very well know himself. He wanted to see Anna Sergeyevna and to talk with her—to arrange a meeting, if possible.

He reached S—— in the morning, and took the best room at the hotel, in which the floor was covered with grey army cloth, and on the table was an inkstand, grey with dust and adorned with a figure on horseback, with its hat in its hand and its head broken off. The hotel porter gave him the necessary information; Von Diderits lived in a house of his own in Old Gontcharny Street—it was not far from the hotel: he was rich and lived in good style, and had his own horses; every one in the town knew him. The porter pronounced the name "Dridirits."

Gurov went without haste to Old Gontcharny Street and found the house. Just opposite the house stretched a long grey fence adorned with nails.

"One would run away from a fence like that," thought Gurov, looking from the fence to the windows of the house and back again.

He considered: to-day was a holiday, and the husband would probably be at home. And in any case it would be tactless to go into the house and upset her. If he were to send her a note it might fall into her husband's hands, and then it might ruin everything. The best thing was to trust to chance. And he kept walking up and down the street by the fence, waiting for the chance. He saw a beggar go in at the gate and dogs fly at him; then an hour later he heard a piano, and the sounds were faint and indistinct. Probably it was Anna Sergeyevna playing. The front door suddenly opened, and an old woman came out, followed by the familiar white Pomeranian. Gurov was on the point of calling to the dog, but his heart began beating violently, and in his excitement he could not remember the dog's name.

He walked up and down, and loathed the grey fence more and more, and by now he thought irritably that Anna Sergeyevna had forgotten him, and was perhaps already amusing herself with some one else, and that that was very natural in a young woman who had nothing to look at from morning till night but that confounded fence. He went back to his hotel room and sat for a long while on the sofa, not knowing what to do, then he had dinner and a long nap.

"How stupid and worrying it is!" he thought when he woke and looked at the dark windows: it was already evening. "Here I've had a good sleep for some reason. What shall I do in the night?"

He sat on the bed, which was covered by a cheap grey blanket, such as one sees in hospitals, and he taunted himself in his vexation:

"So much for the lady with the dog ... so much for the adventure.... You're in a nice fix...."

That morning at the station a poster in large letters had caught his eye. "The Geisha" was to be performed for the first time. He thought of this and went to the theatre.

"It's quite possible she may go to the first performance," he thought.

The theatre was full. As in all provincial theatres, there was a fog above the chandelier, the gallery was noisy and restless; in the front row the local dandies were standing up before the beginning of the performance, with their hands behind them; in the Governor's box the Governor's daughter, wearing a boa, was sitting in the front seat, while the Governor himself lurked modestly behind the curtain with only his hands visible; the orchestra was a long time tuning up; the stage curtain swayed. All the time the audience were coming in and taking their seats Gurov looked at them eagerly.

Anna Sergeyevna, too, came in. She sat down in the third row, and when Gurov looked at her his heart contracted, and he understood clearly that for him there was in the whole world no creature so near, so precious, and so important to him; she, this little woman, in no way remarkable, lost in a provincial crowd, with a vulgar lorgnette in her hand, filled his whole life now, was his sorrow and his joy, the one happiness that he now desired for himself, and to the sounds of the inferior orchestra, of the wretched provincial violins, he thought how lovely she was. He thought and dreamed.

A young man with small side-whiskers, tall and stooping, came in with Anna Sergeyevna and sat down beside her; he bent his head at every step and seemed to be continually bowing. Most likely this was the husband whom at Yalta, in a rush of bitter feeling, she had called a flunkey. And there really was in his long figure, his side-whiskers, and the small bald patch on his head, something of the flunkey's obsequiousness; his smile was sugary, and in his buttonhole there was some badge of distinction like the number on a waiter.

During the first interval the husband went away to smoke; she remained alone in her stall. Gurov, who was sitting in the stalls, too, went up to her and said in a trembling voice, with a forced smile:

"Good-evening."

She glanced at him and turned pale, then glanced again with horror, unable to believe her eyes, and tightly gripped the fan and the lorgnette in her hands, evidently struggling with herself not to faint. Both were silent. She was sitting, he was standing, frightened by her confusion and not venturing to sit down beside her. The violins and the flute began tuning up. He felt suddenly frightened; it seemed as though all the people in the boxes were looking at them. She got up and went quickly to the door; he followed her, and both walked senselessly along passages, and up and down stairs, and figures in legal, scholastic, and civil service uniforms, all wearing badges, flitted before their eyes. They caught glimpses of ladies, of fur coats hanging on pegs; the draughts blew on them, bringing a smell of stale tobacco. And Gurov, whose heart was beating violently, thought: "Oh, heavens! Why are these people here and this orchestra!..."

And at that instant he recalled how when he had seen Anna Sergeyevna off at the station he had thought that everything was over and they would never meet again. But how far they were still from the end!

On the narrow, gloomy staircase over which was written "To the Amphitheatre," she stopped.

"How you have frightened me!" she said, breathing hard, still pale and overwhelmed. "Oh, how you have frightened me! I am half dead. Why have you come? Why?"

"But do understand, Anna, do understand ..." he said hastily in a low voice. "I entreat you to understand...."

She looked at him with dread, with entreaty, with love; she looked at him intently, to keep his features more distinctly in her memory.

"I am so unhappy," she went on, not heeding him. "I have thought of nothing but you all the time; I live only in the thought of you. And I wanted to forget, to forget you; but why, oh, why, have you come?"

On the landing above them two schoolboys were smoking and looking down, but that was nothing to Gurov; he drew Anna Sergeyevna to him, and began kissing her face, her cheeks, and her hands.

"What are you doing, what are you doing!" she cried in horror, pushing him away. "We are mad. Go away to-day;

go away at once.... I beseech you by all that is sacred, I implore you.... There are people coming this way!"

Some one was coming up the stairs.

"You must go away," Anna Sergeyevna went on in a whisper. "Do you hear, Dmitri Dmitritch? I will come and see you in Moscow. I have never been happy; I am miserable now, and I never, never shall be happy, never! Don't make me suffer still more! I swear I'll come to Moscow. But now let us part. My precious, good, dear one, we must part!"

She pressed his hand and began rapidly going downstairs, looking round at him, and from her eyes he could see that she really was unhappy. Gurov stood for a little while, listened, then, when all sound had died away, he found his coat and left the theatre.

IV

And Anna Sergeyevna began coming to see him in Moscow. Once in two or three months she left S——, telling her husband that she was going to consult a doctor about an internal complaint—and her husband believed her, and did not believe her. In Moscow she stayed at the Slaviansky Bazaar hotel, and at once sent a man in a red cap to Gurov. Gurov went to see her, and no one in Moscow knew of it.

Once he was going to see her in this way on a winter morning (the messenger had come the evening before when he was out). With him walked his daughter, whom he wanted to take to school: it was on the way. Snow was falling in big wet flakes.

"It's three degrees above freezing-point, and yet it is snowing," said Gurov to his daughter. "The thaw is only on the surface of the earth; there is quite a different temperature at a greater height in the atmosphere."

"And why are there no thunderstorms in the winter,

father?"

He explained that, too. He talked, thinking all the while that he was going to see her, and no living soul knew of it, and probably never would know. He had two lives: one, open, seen and known by all who cared to know, full of relative truth and of relative falsehood, exactly like the lives of his friends and acquaintances; and another life running its course in secret. And through some strange, perhaps accidental, conjunction of circumstances, everything that was essential, of interest and of value to him, everything in which he was sincere and did not deceive himself, everything that made the kernel of his life, was hidden from other people; and all that was false in him, the sheath in which he hid himself to conceal the truth—such, for instance, as his work in the bank, his discussions at the club, his "lower race," his presence with his wife at anniversary festivities—all that was open. And he judged of others by himself, not believing in what he saw, and always believing that every man had his real, most interesting life under the cover of secrecy and under the cover of night. All personal life rested on secrecy, and possibly it was partly on that account that civilised man was so nervously anxious that personal privacy should be respected.

After leaving his daughter at school, Gurov went on to the Slaviansky Bazaar. He took off his fur coat below, went upstairs, and softly knocked at the door. Anna Sergeyevna, wearing his favourite grey dress, exhausted by the journey and the suspense, had been expecting him since the evening before. She was pale; she looked at him, and did not smile, and he had hardly come in when she fell on his breast. Their kiss was slow and prolonged, as though they had not met for two years.

"Well, how are you getting on there?" he asked. "What news?"

"Wait; I'll tell you directly.... I can't talk."
She could not speak; she was crying. She turned away from him, and pressed her handkerchief to her eyes.
"Let her have her cry out. I'll sit down and wait," he thought, and he sat down in an arm-chair.
Then he rang and asked for tea to be brought him, and while he drank his tea she remained standing at the window with her back to him. She was crying from emotion, from the miserable consciousness that their life was so hard for them; they could only meet in secret, hiding themselves from people, like thieves! Was not their life shattered?
"Come, do stop!" he said.
It was evident to him that this love of theirs would not soon be over, that he could not see the end of it. Anna Sergeyevna grew more and more attached to him. She adored him, and it was unthinkable to say to her that it was bound to have an end some day; besides, she would not have believed it!
He went up to her and took her by the shoulders to say something affectionate and cheering, and at that moment he saw himself in the looking-glass.
His hair was already beginning to turn grey. And it seemed strange to him that he had grown so much older, so much plainer during the last few years. The shoulders on which his hands rested were warm and quivering. He felt compassion for this life, still so warm and lovely, but probably already not far from beginning to fade and wither like his own. Why did she love him so much? He always seemed to women different from what he was, and they loved in him not himself, but the man created by their imagination, whom they had been eagerly seeking all their lives; and afterwards, when they noticed their mistake, they loved him all the same. And not one of them had been happy with him. Time passed, he had

made their acquaintance, got on with them, parted, but he had never once loved; it was anything you like, but not love.

And only now when his head was grey he had fallen properly, really in love—for the first time in his life.

Anna Sergeyevna and he loved each other like people very close and akin, like husband and wife, like tender friends; it seemed to them that fate itself had meant them for one another, and they could not understand why he had a wife and she a husband; and it was as though they were a pair of birds of passage, caught and forced to live in different cages. They forgave each other for what they were ashamed of in their past, they forgave everything in the present, and felt that this love of theirs had changed them both.

In moments of depression in the past he had comforted himself with any arguments that came into his mind, but now he no longer cared for arguments; he felt profound compassion, he wanted to be sincere and tender....

"Don't cry, my darling," he said. "You've had your cry; that's enough.... Let us talk now, let us think of some plan."

Then they spent a long while taking counsel together, talked of how to avoid the necessity for secrecy, for deception, for living in different towns and not seeing each other for long at a time. How could they be free from this intolerable bondage?

"How? How?" he asked, clutching his head. "How?"

And it seemed as though in a little while the solution would be found, and then a new and splendid life would begin; and it was clear to both of them that they had still a long, long road before them, and that the most complicated and difficult part of it was only just beginning.

The Stars

A tale from a Provencal shepherd.
Alphonse Daudet

When I used to be in charge of the animals on the Luberon, I was in the pasture for many weeks with my dog Labri and the flock without seeing another living soul. Occasionally the hermit from Mont-de-l'Ure would pass by looking for medicinal herbs, or I might see the blackened face of a chimney sweep from Piémont. But these were simple folk, silenced by the solitude, having lost the taste for chit-chat, and knowing nothing of what was going on down in the villages and towns. So, I was truly happy, when every fortnight I heard the bells on our farm's mule which brought my provisions, and I saw the bright little face of the farm boy, or the red hat of old aunty Norade appear over the hill. I asked them for news from the village, the baptisms, marriages, and so on. But what particularly interested me, was to know what was happening to my master's daughter, Mademoiselle Stephanette, the loveliest thing for fifty kilometres around. Without wishing to seem over-curious, I managed to find out if she was going to village fetes and evening farm gatherings, and if she still turned up with a new admirer every time. If someone asked me how that concerned a poor mountain shepherd, I would say that I was twenty years old and that Stephanette was the loveliest thing I had seen in my whole life.

One Sunday, however, the fortnight's supplies were very late arriving. In the morning, I had thought, "It's because of High Mass." Then about midday, a big storm got up, which made me think that bad road conditions had kept the mule from setting out. Then, just after three o'clock, as the sky cleared and the wet mountain glistened in the sunshine, I could hear the mule's bells above the sound of the dripping leaves and the raging streams. To me they were as welcome, happy, and lively as a peal of bells on Easter Day. But there was no little farm boy or old aunty Norade at the head. It was … you'll never guess … my heart's very own desire, friends! Stephanette in person, sitting comfortably between the wicker baskets, her lovely face flushed by the mountain air and the bracing storm.

Apparently, the young lad was ill and aunty Norade was on holiday at her childrens' place. Stephanette told me all this as she got off the mule, and explained that she was late because she had lost her way. But to see her there in her Sunday best, with her ribbon of flowers, her silk skirt and lace bodice; it looked more like she had just come from a dance, rather than trying to find her way through the bushes. Oh, the little darling! My eyes never tired of looking at her. I had never seen her so close before. Sometimes in winter, after the flocks had returned to the plain, and I was in the farm for supper in the evening, she would come into the dining room, always overdressed and rather proud, and rush across the room, virtually ignoring us…. But now, there she was, right in front of me, all to myself. Now wasn't that something to lose your head over?

Once she had taken the provisions out of the pannier, Stephanette began to take an interest in everything. Hitching up her lovely Sunday skirt, which otherwise might have got marked, she went into the compound, to look at the place where I slept. The straw crib with its lambskin cover, my long cape hanging on the wall, my shepherd's crook, and my catapult; all these things fascinated her.

—So, this is where you live, my little shepherd? How

tedious it must be to be alone all the time. What do you do with yourself? What do you think about?

I wanted to say, "About you, my lady," and I wouldn't have been lying, but I was so greatly nonplussed that I couldn't find a single word by way of a reply. Obviously, she picked this up, and certainly she would now take some gentle malicious pleasure in turning the screw:

—What about your girlfriend, shepherd, doesn't she come up to see you sometimes? Of course, it would have to be the fairy Esterelle, who only runs at the top of the mountain, or the fabled, golden she-goat….

As she talked on, she seemed to me like the real fairy Esterelle. She threw her head back with a cheeky laugh and hurried away, which made her visit seem like a dream.

—Goodbye, shepherd.

—Bye, Bye, lady.

And there she was—gone—taking the empty baskets with her.

As she disappeared along the steep path, stones disturbed by the mule's hooves, seemed to take my heart with them as they rolled away. I could hear them for a very long time. For the rest of the day, I stood there daydreaming, hardly daring to move, fearing to break the spell. Towards the evening, as the base of the valleys became a deeper blue, and the bleating animals flocked together for their return to the compound, I heard someone calling to me on the way down, and there she was; mademoiselle herself. But she wasn't laughing any more; she was trembling, and wet, and fearful, and cold. She would have me believe that at the bottom of the hill, she had found the River Sorgue was swollen by the rain storm and, wanting to cross at all costs, had risked getting drowned. The worse thing, was that at that time of night, there was no chance of her getting back to the farm. She would never be able to find the way to the crossing place alone, and I couldn't leave the flock. The thought of staying the night on the mountain troubled her a great deal, particularly as her family would worry about her. I reassured her as best I could: —The nights are short in July, my Lady. It's only going to seem like a passing, unpleasant moment.

I quickly lit a good fire to dry her feet and her dress soaked by the river. I then placed some milk and cheese in front of her, but the poor little thing couldn't turn her thoughts to either warming herself or eating. Seeing the huge tears welling up in her eyes, made me want to cry myself.

Meanwhile night had almost fallen. There was just the faintest trace of the sunset left on the mountains' crests. I wanted mademoiselle to go on into in the compound to rest and recover. I covered the fresh straw with a beautiful brand new skin, and I bid her good night. I was going to sit outside the door. As God is my witness, I never had an unclean thought, despite my burning desire for her. I had nothing but a great feeling of pride in considering that, there, in a corner of the compound, close up to the flock watching curiously over her sleeping form, my masters' daughter rested,—just like a sheep, though one whiter and much more precious than all the others,—trusting me to guard her. To me, never had the sky seemed darker, nor the stars brighter…. Suddenly, the wicker fence opened and the beautiful Stephanette appeared. She couldn't sleep; the animals were scrunching the hay as they moved, or bleating in their dreams. For now, she just wanted to come close to the fire. I threw my goat-skin over her shoulders, tickled the fire, and we sat there together not saying anything. If you know what's it's like to sleep under the stars at night, you'll know that, when we are normally asleep, a mysterious world awakens in the solitude and silence. It's the time the springs babble more clearly, and the ponds light up their will o' the wisps. All mountain spirits roam freely about, and there are rustlings in the air, imperceptible sounds, that might be branches thickening or grass growing. Day-time is for everyday living things; night-time is for strange, unknown things. If you're not used to it, it can terrify you···. So it was with mademoiselle, who was all of a shiver, and clung to me very tightly at the slightest noise. Once, a long gloomy cry, from the darkest of the ponds, rose and fell in intensity as it came towards us. At the same time, a shooting star flashed above our heads going in the same direction, as if the moan we had just heard was carrying a light.

—What's that? Stephanette asked me in a whisper.

—A soul entering heaven, my Lady; and I crossed myself.

She did the same, but stayed looking at the heavens in rapt awe. Then she said to me:

—Is it true then, that you shepherds are magicians?

—No, no, mademoiselle, but here we live closer to the stars, and we know more about what happens up there than people who live in the plains.

She kept looking at the stars, her head on her hands, wrapped in the sheepskin like a small heavenly shepherd:

—How many there are! How beautiful! I have never seen so many. Do you know their names, shepherd?

—Of course, lady. There you are! Just above our heads, that's the Milky Way. Further on you have the Great Bear. And so, he described to her in great detail, some of the magic of the star-filled panoply···.

—One of the stars, which the shepherds name, Maguelonne, I said, chases Saturn and marries him every seven years.

—What, shepherd! Are there star marriages, then?

—Oh yes, my Lady.

I was trying to explain to her what these marriages were about, when I felt something cool and fine on my shoulder. It was her head, heavy with sleep, placed on me with just a delightful brush of her ribbons, lace, and dark tresses. She stayed just like that, unmoving, right until the stars faded in the coming daylight. As for me, I watched her sleeping, being somewhat troubled in my soul, but that clear night, which had only ever given me beautiful thoughts, had kept me in an innocent frame of mind. The stars all around us continued their stately, silent journey like a great docile flock in the sky. At times, I imagined that one of these stars, the finest one, the most brilliant, having lost its way, had come to settle, gently, on my shoulder, to sleep….

The Black Cat

Edgar Allan Po

For the most wild, yet most homely narrative which I am about to pen, I neither expect nor solicit belief. Mad indeed would I be to expect it in a case where my very senses reject their own evidence. Yet mad am I not—and very surely do I not dream. But to-morrow I die, and to-day I would unburthen my soul. My immediate purpose is to place before the world plainly, succinctly, and without comment, a series of mere household events. In their consequences these events have terrified—have tortured—have destroyed me. Yet I will not attempt to expound them. To me they presented little but horror—to many they will seem less terrible than baroques. Hereafter, perhaps, some intellect may be found which will reduce my phantasm to the commonplace—some intellect more calm, more logical, and far less excitable than my own, which will perceive, in the circumstances I detail with awe, nothing more than an ordinary succession of very natural causes and effects.

From my infancy I was noted for the docility and humanity of my disposition. My tenderness of heart was even so conspicuous as to make me the jest of my companions. I was especially fond of animals, and was indulged by my parents with a great variety of pets. With these I spent most of my time, and never was so happy as when feeding and caressing them. This peculiarity of character grew with my growth, and in my manhood I derived from it one of my principal sources of pleasure. To those who have cherished an affection for a faithful and sagacious dog, I need hardly be at the trouble of explaining the nature or the intensity of the gratification thus derivable. There is something in the unselfish and self-sacrificing love of a brute which goes directly to the heart of him who has had frequent occasion to test the paltry friendship and gossamer fidelity of mere Man.

I married early, and was happy to find in my wife a disposition not uncongenial with my own. Observing my partiality for domestic pets, she lost no opportunity of procuring those of the most agreeable kind. We had birds, gold-fish, a fine dog, rabbits, a small monkey, and a cat.

This latter was a remarkably large and beautiful animal, entirely black, and sagacious to an astonishing degree. In speaking of his intelligence, my wife, who at heart was not a little tinctured with superstition, made frequent allusion to the ancient popular notion which regarded all black cats as witches in disguise. Not that she was ever serious upon this point, and I mention the matter at all for no better reason than that it happens just now to be remembered.

Pluto—this was the cat's name—was my favorite pet and playmate. I alone fed him, and he attended me wherever I went about the house. It was even with difficulty that I could prevent him from following me through the streets.

Our friendship lasted in this manner for several years, during which my general temperament and character—through the instrumentality of the Fiend Intemperance—had (I blush to confess it) experienced a radical alteration for the worse. I grew, day by day, more moody, more irritable, more regardless of the feelings of others. I suffered myself to use intemperate language to my wife. At length, I even offered her personal violence. My pets of course were made to feel the change in my disposition. I not only neglected but ill-used them. For Pluto, however, I still retained sufficient regard to restrain me from maltreating him, as I made no scruple of maltreating the rabbits, the monkey, or even the dog, when by accident, or through affection, they came in my way. But my disease grew upon me—for what disease is like Alcohol!—and at length even Pluto, who was now becoming old, and consequently somewhat peevish—even Pluto began to experience the effects of my ill-temper.

One night, returning home much intoxicated from one of my haunts about town, I fancied that the cat avoided my presence. I seized him, when, in his fright at my violence, he inflicted a slight wound upon my hand with his teeth. The fury of a demon instantly possessed me. I knew myself no longer. My original soul seemed at once to take its flight from my body, and a more than fiendish malevolence, gin-nurtured, thrilled every fiber of my frame. I took from my waistcoat-pocket a pen-knife, opened it, grasped the poor beast by the throat, and deliberately cut one of its eyes from the socket! I blush, I burn, I shudder, while I pen the damnable atrocity.

When reason returned with the morning—when I had slept off the fumes of the night's debauch—I experienced a sentiment half of horror, half of remorse, for the crime of which I had been guilty, but it was at best a feeble and equivocal feeling, and the soul remained untouched. I again plunged into excess, and soon drowned in wine all memory of the deed.

In the meantime the cat slowly recovered. The socket of the lost eye presented, it is true, a frightful appearance, but he no longer appeared to suffer any pain. He went about the house as usual, but, as might be expected, fled in extreme terror at my approach. I had so much of my old heart left as to be at first grieved by this evident dislike on the part of a creature which had once so loved me. But this feeling soon gave place to irritation. And then came, as if to my final and irrevocable overthrow, the spirit of Perverseness. Of this spirit philosophy takes no account. Yet I am not more sure that my soul lives than I am that perverseness is one of the primitive impulses of the human heart—one of the indivisible primary faculties or sentiments which give direction to the character of Man. Who has not, a hundred times, found himself committing a vile or a silly action for no other reason than because he knows he should not? Have we not a perpetual inclination, in the teeth of our best judgment, to violate that which is Law, merely because we understand it to be such? This spirit of perverseness, I say, came to my final overthrow. It was this unfathomable longing of the soul to vex itself—to offer violence to its own nature—to do wrong for the wrong's sake only—that urged me to continue and finally to consummate the injury I had inflicted upon the unoffending brute. One morning, in cool blood, I slipped a noose about its neck and hung it to the limb of a tree; hung it with the tears streaming from my eyes, and with the bitterest remorse at my heart; hung it because I knew that it had loved me, and because I felt it had given me no reason of offense; hung it because I knew that in so doing I was committing a sin—a deadly sin that would so jeopardize my immortal soul as to place it, if such a thing were possible, even beyond the reach of the infinite mercy of the Most Merciful and Most Terrible God.

On the night of the day on which this cruel deed was done, I was aroused from sleep by the cry of fire. The curtains of my bed were in flames. The whole house was blazing. It was with great difficulty that my wife, a servant, and myself, made our escape from the conflagration. The destruction was complete. My entire worldly wealth was swallowed up, and I resigned myself thenceforward to despair.

I am above the weakness of seeking to establish a

sequence of cause and effect between the disaster and the atrocity. But I am detailing a chain of facts, and wish not to leave even a possible link imperfect. On the day succeeding the fire, I visited the ruins. The walls with one exception had fallen in. This exception was found in a compartment wall, not very thick, which stood about the middle of the house, and against which had rested the head of my bed. The plastering had here in great measure resisted the action of the fire, a fact which I attributed to its having been recently spread. About this wall a dense crowd were collected, and many persons seemed to be examining a particular portion of it with very minute and eager attention. The words "Strange!" "Singular!" and other similar expressions, excited my curiosity. I approached and saw, as if graven in bas relief upon the white surface the figure of a gigantic cat. The impression was given with an accuracy truly marvelous. There as a rope about the animal's neck.

When I first beheld this apparition—for I could scarcely regard it as less—my wonder and my terror were extreme. But at length reflection came to my aid. The cat, I remembered, had been hung in a garden adjacent to the house. Upon the alarm of fire this garden had been immediately filled by the crowd, by some one of whom the animal must have been cut from the tree and thrown through an open window into my chamber. This had probably been done with the view of arousing me from sleep. The falling of other walls had compressed the victim of my cruelty into the substance of the freshly spread plaster; the lime of which, with the flames and the ammonia from the carcass, had then accomplished the portraiture as I saw it.

Although I thus readily accounted to my reason, if not altogether to my conscience, for the startling fact just detailed, it did not the less fail to make a deep impression upon my fancy. For months I could not rid myself of the phantasm of the cat, and during this period there came back into my spirit a half-sentiment that seemed, but was not, remorse. I went so far as to regret the loss of the animal, and to look about me among the vile haunts which I now habitually frequented for another pet of the same species, and of somewhat similar appearance, with which to supply its place.

One night, as I sat half-stupefied in a den of more than infamy, my attention was suddenly drawn to some black object, reposing upon the head of one of the immense hogsheads of gin or of rum, which constituted the chief furniture of the apartment. I had been looking steadily at the top of this hogshead for some minutes, and what now caused me surprise was the fact that I had not sooner perceived the object thereupon. I approached it, and touched it with my hand. It was a black cat—a very large one—fully as large as Pluto, and closely resembling him in every respect but one. Pluto had not a white hair upon any portion of his body; but this cat had a large, although indefinite splotch of white, covering nearly the whole region of the breast.

Upon my touching him he immediately arose, purred loudly, rubbed against my hand, and appeared delighted with my notice. This, then, was the very creature of which I was in search. I at once offered to purchase it of the landlord; but this person made no claim to it—knew nothing of it—had never seen it before.

I continued my caresses, and when I prepared to go home the animal evinced a disposition to accompany me. I permitted it to do so, occasionally stooping and patting it as I proceeded. "When it reached the house it domesticated itself at once, and became immediately a great favorite with my wife.

For my own part, I soon found a dislike to it arising within me. This was just the reverse of what I had anticipated, but—I know not how or why it was—its evident fondness for myself rather disgusted and annoyed. By slow degrees these feelings of disgust and annoyance rose into the bitterness of hatred. I avoided the creature; a certain sense of shame, and the remembrance of my former deed of cruelty, preventing me from physically abusing it. I did not, for some weeks, strike or otherwise violently ill-use it, but gradually—very gradually—I came to look upon it with unutterable loathing, and to flee silently from its odious presence as from the breath of a pestilence.

What added, no doubt, to my hatred of the beast was the discovery, on the morning after I brought it home, that, like Pluto, it also had been deprived of one of its eyes. This circumstance, however, only endeared it to my wife, who, as I have already said, possessed in a high degree that humanity of feeling which had once been my distinguishing trait, and the source of many of my simplest and purest pleasures.

With my aversion to this cat, however, its partiality for myself seemed to increase. It followed my footsteps with a pertinacity which it would be difficult to make tho reader comprehend. Whenever I sat, it would crouch beneath my chair or spring upon my knees, covering me with its loathsome caresses. If I arose to walk it would get between my feet and thus nearly throw me down, or, fastening its long and sharp claws in my dress, clamber in this manner to my breast. At such times, although I longed to destroy it with a blow, I was yet withheld from so doing, partly by a memory of my former crime, but chiefly—let me confess it at once—by absolute dread of the beast.

This dread was not exactly a dread of physical evil—and

yet I should be at a loss how otherwise to define it. I am almost ashamed to own—yes, even in this felon's cell, I am almost ashamed to own—that the terror and horror with which the animal inspired me had been heightened by one of the merest chimeras it would be possible to conceive. My wife had called my attention more than once to the character of the mark of white hair, of which I have spoken, and which constituted the sole visible difference between the strange beast and the one I had destroyed. The reader will remember that this mark, although large, had been originally very indefinite, but by slow degrees—degrees nearly imperceptible, and which for a long time my reason struggled to reject as fanciful—it had at length assumed a rigorous distinctness of outline. It was now the representation of an object that I shudder to name—and for this above all I loathed and dreaded, and would have rid myself of the monster had I dared—it was now, I say, the image of a hideous—of a ghastly thing—of the Gallows!—O, mournful and terrible engine of horror and of crime—of agony and of death!

And now was I indeed wretched beyond the wretchedness of mere humanity. And a brute beast—whose fellow I had contemptuously destroyed—a brute beast to work out for me—for me a man, fashioned in the image of the High God—so much of insufferable woe! Alas! neither by day nor by night knew I the blessing of rest any more! During the former the creature left me no moment alone; and in the latter I started hourly from dreams of unutterable fear, to find the hot breath of the thing upon my face, and its vast weight—an incarnate nightmare that I had no power to shake off—incumbent eternally upon my heart!

Beneath the pressure of torments such as these, the feeble remnant of the good within me succumbed. Evil thoughts became my sole intimates—the darkest and most evil of thoughts. The moodiness of my usual temper increased to hatred of all things and of all mankind; while from the sudden frequent and ungovernable outbursts of a fury to which I now blindly abandoned myself, my uncomplaining wife, alas! was the most usual and the most patient of sufferers.

One day she accompanied me upon some household errand into the cellar of the old building which our poverty compelled us to inhabit. The cat followed me down the steep stairs, and nearly throwing me headlong, exasperated me to madness. Uplifting an ax, and forgetting in my wrath the childish dread which had hitherto stayed my hand, I aimed a blow at the animal, which of course would have proved instantly fatal had it descended as I wished. But this blow was arrested by the hand of my wife. Goaded by the interference into a rage more than demoniacal, I withdrew my arm from her grasp and buried the ax in her brain. She fell dead upon the spot without a groan.

This hideous murder accomplished, I set myself forthwith and with entire deliberation to the task of concealing the body. I knew that I could not remove it from the house, either by day or by night, without the risk of being observed by the neighbors. Many projects entered my mind. At one period I thought of cutting the corpse into minute fragments and destroying them by fire. At another I resolved to dig a grave for it in the floor of the cellar. Again, I deliberated about casting it in the well in the yard—about packing it in a box, as if merchandise, with the usual arrangements, and so getting a porter to take it from the house. Finally I hit upon what I considered a far better expedient than either of these. I determined to wall it up in the cellar—as the monks of the middle ages are recorded to have walled up their victims.

For a purpose such as this the cellar was well adapted. Its walls were loosely constructed and had lately been plastered throughout with a rough plaster, which the dampness of the atmosphere had prevented from hardening. Moreover, in one of the walls was a projection caused by a false chimney or fireplace, that had been filled up and made to resemble the rest of the cellar. I made no doubt that I could readily displace the bricks at this point, insert the corpse, and wall the whole up as before, so that no eye could detect anything suspicious.

And in this calculation I was not deceived. By means of a crowbar I easily dislodged the bricks, and having carefully deposited the body against the inner wall, I propped it in that position, while with little trouble I relaid the whole structure as it originally stood. Having procured mortar, sand, and hair with every possible precaution, I prepared a plaster which could not be distinguished from the old, and with this I very carefully went over the new brick-work. When I had finished I felt satisfied that all was right. The wall did not present the slightest appearance of having been disturbed. The rubbish on the floor was picked up with the minutest care. I looked around triumphantly, and said to myself—"Here at last, then, my labor has not been in vain."

My next step was to look for the beast which had been the cause of so much wretchedness, for I had at length firmly resolved to put it to death. Had I been able to meet with it at the moment there could have been been no doubt of its fate, but it appeared that the crafty animal had been alarmed at the violence of my previous anger, and forbore to present itself in my present mood. It is impossible to describe or to imagine the deep, the blissful sense of relief which the absence of the detested creature occasioned in my bosom. It did not make its appearance during the night—and thus for one night at least since its introduction into the house I soundly and tranquilly slept, aye, slept even with the burden of murder upon my soul!

The second and the third day passed, and still my tormentor came not. Once again I breathed as a freeman. The monster, in terror, had fled the premises forever! I should behold it no more! My happiness was supreme! The guilt of my dark deed disturbed me but little. Some few inquiries had been made, but these had been readily answered. Even a search had been instituted—but of course nothing was to be discovered. I looked upon my future felicity as secured.

Upon the fourth day of the assassination, a party of the police came very unexpectedly into the house, and proceeded again to make rigorous investigation of the premises. Secure, however, in the inscrutability of my place of concealment, I felt no embarrassment whatever. The officers bade me accompany them in their search. They left no nook or corner unexplored. At length, for the third or fourth time, they descended into the cellar. I quivered not in a muscle. My heart beat calmly as that of one who slumbers in innocence. I walked the cellar from end to end. I folded my arms upon my bosom, and roamed easily to and fro. The police were thoroughly satisfied, and prepared to depart. The glee at my heart was too strong to be restrained. I burned to say if but one word by way of triumph, and to render doubly sure their assurance of my guiltlessness.

"Gentlemen," I said at last, as the party ascended the steps, "I delight to have allayed your suspicions. I wish you all health, and a little more courtesy. By the by, gentlemen, this—this is a very well-constructed house." [In the rabid desire to say something easily, I scarcely knew what I uttered at all.] "I may say an excellently well-constructed house. These walls—are you going, gentlemen?—these walls are solidly put together;" and here, through the mere frenzy of bravado, I rapped heavily with a cane which I held in my hand upon that very portion of the brick-work behind which stood the corpse of the wife of my bosom.

But may God shield and deliver me from the fangs of the arch-fiend! No sooner had the reverberation of my blows sunk into silence than I was answered by a voice from within the tomb!—by a cry, at first muffled and broken, like the sobbing of a child, and then quickly swelling into one long, loud, and continuous scream, utterly anomalous and inhuman—a howl—a wailing shriek, half of horror and half of triumph, such as might have arisen only out of hell, conjointly from the throats of the damned in their agony and of the demons that exult in the damnation.

Of my own thoughts it is folly to speak. Swooning, I staggered to the opposite wall. For one instant the party upon the stairs remained motionless, through extremity of terror and of awe. In the next a dozen stout arms were toiling at the wall. It fell bodily. The corpse, already greatly decayed and clotted with gore, stood erect before the eyes of the spectators. Upon its head, with red extended mouth and solitary eye of fire, sat the hideous beast whose craft had seduced me into murder, and whose informing voice had consigned me to the hangman. I had walled the monster up within the tomb!

What Men Live By

Leo Tolstoy

A shoemaker named Simon, who had neither house nor land of his own, lived with his wife and children in a peasant's hut, and earned his living by his work. Work was cheap, but bread was dear, and what he earned he spent for food. The man and his wife had but one sheepskin coat between them for winter wear, and even that was torn to tatters, and this was the second year he had been wanting to buy sheep-skins for a new coat. Before winter Simon saved up a little money: a three-rouble note lay hidden in his wife's box, and five roubles and twenty kopeks were owed him by customers in the village.

So one morning he prepared to go to the village to buy the sheep-skins. He put on over his shirt his wife's wadded nankeen jacket, and over that he put his own cloth coat. He took the three-rouble note in his pocket, cut himself a stick to serve as a staff, and started off after breakfast. "I'll collect the five roubles that are due to me," thought he, "add the three I have got, and that will be enough to buy sheep-skins for the winter coat." He came to the village and called at a peasant's hut, but the man was not at home. The peasant's wife promised that the money should be paid next week, but she would not pay it herself. Then Simon called on another peasant, but this one swore he had no money, and would only pay twenty kopeks which he owed for a pair of boots Simon had mended. Simon then tried to buy the sheep-skins on credit, but the dealer would not trust him.

"Bring your money," said he, "then you may have your

pick of the skins. We know what debt-collecting is like." So all the business the shoemaker did was to get the twenty kopeks for boots he had mended, and to take a pair of felt boots a peasant gave him to sole with leather.

Simon felt downhearted. He spent the twenty kopeks on vodka, and started homewards without having bought any skins. In the morning he had felt the frost; but now, after drinking the vodka, he felt warm, even without a sheep-skin coat. He trudged along, striking his stick on the frozen earth with one hand, swinging the felt boots with the other, and talking to himself.

I

"I'm quite warm," said he, "though I have no sheep-skin coat. I've had a drop, and it runs through all my veins. I need no sheep-skins. I go along and don't worry about anything. That's the sort of man I am! What do I care? I can live without sheep-skins. I don't need them. My wife will fret, to be sure. And, true enough, it is a shame; one works all day long, and then does not get paid. Stop a bit! If you don't bring that money along, sure enough I'll skin you, blessed if I don't. How's that? He pays twenty kopeks at a time! What can I do with twenty kopeks? Drink it-that's all one can do! Hard up, he says he is! So he may be—but what about me? You have a house, and cattle, and everything; I've only what I stand up in! You have corn of your own growing; I have to buy every grain. Do what I will, I must spend three roubles every week for bread alone. I come home and find the bread all used up, and I have to fork out another rouble and a half. So just pay up what you owe, and no nonsense about it!" By this time he had nearly reached the shrine at the bend of the road. Looking up, he saw something whitish behind the shrine. The daylight was fading, and the shoemaker peered at the thing without being able to make out what it was. "There was no white stone here before. Can it be an ox? It's not like an ox. It has a head like a man, but it's too white; and what could a man be doing there?" He came closer, so that it was clearly visible. To his surprise it really was a man, alive or dead, sitting naked, leaning motionless against the shrine. Terror seized the shoemaker, and he thought, "Some one has killed him, stripped him, and left him there. If I meddle I shall surely get into trouble." So the shoemaker went on. He passed in front of the shrine so that he could not see the man. When he had gone some way, he looked back, and saw that the man was no longer leaning against the shrine, but was moving as if looking towards him. The shoemaker felt more frightened than before, and thought, "Shall I go back to him, or shall I go on? If I go near him something dreadful may happen. Who knows who the fellow is? He has not come here for any good. If I go near him he may jump up and throttle me, and there will be no getting away. Or if not, he'd still be a burden on one's hands. What could I do with a naked man? I couldn't give him my last clothes. Heaven only help me to get away!" So the shoemaker hurried on, leaving the shrine behind him-when suddenly his conscience smote him, and he stopped in the road.

"What are you doing, Simon?" said he to himself. "The man may be dying of want, and you slip past afraid. Have you grown so rich as to be afraid of robbers? Ah, Simon, shame on you!" So he turned back and went up to the man.

II

Simon approached the stranger, looked at him, and saw that he was a young man, fit, with no bruises on his body, only evidently freezing and frightened, and he sat there leaning back without looking up at Simon, as if too faint to lift his eyes. Simon went close to him, and then the man seemed to wake up. Turning his head, he opened his eyes and looked into Simon's face. That one look was enough to make Simon fond of the man. He threw the felt boots on the ground, undid his sash, laid it on the boots, and took off his cloth coat.

"It's not a time for talking," said he. "Come, put this coat on at once!" And Simon took the man by the elbows and helped him to rise. As he stood there, Simon saw that his body was clean and in good condition, his hands and feet shapely, and his face good and kind. He threw his coat over the man's shoulders, but the latter could not find the sleeves. Simon guided his arms into them, and drawing the coat well on, wrapped it closely about him, tying the sash round the man's waist.

Simon even took off his torn cap to put it on the man's head, but then his own head felt cold, and he thought: "I'm quite bald, while he has long curly hair." So he put his cap on his own head again. "It will be better to give him something for his feet," thought he; and he made the man sit down, and helped him to put on the felt boots, saying, "There, friend, now move about and warm yourself. Other matters can be settled later on. Can you walk?" The man stood up and looked kindly at Simon, but could not say a word.

"Why don't you speak?" said Simon. "It's too cold to stay here, we must be getting home. There now, take my stick, and if you're feeling weak, lean on that. Now step out!" The man started walking, and moved easily, not lagging behind.

As they went along, Simon asked him, "And where do you belong to?" "I'm not from these parts."

"I thought as much. I know the folks hereabouts. But, how did you come to be there by the shrine?"

"I cannot tell."

"Has some one been ill-treating you?"

"No one has ill-treated me. God has punished me."

"Of course God rules all. Still, you'll have to find food and shelter somewhere. Where do you want to go to?"

"It is all the same to me."

Simon was amazed. The man did not look like a rogue, and he spoke gently, but yet he gave no account of himself. Still Simon thought, "Who knows what may have happened?" And he said to the stranger: "Well then, come home with me, and at least warm yourself awhile."

So Simon walked towards his home, and the stranger kept up with him, walking at his side. The wind had risen and Simon felt it cold under his shirt. He was getting over his tipsiness by now, and began to feel the frost. He went along sniffling and wrapping his wife's coat round him, and he thought to himself: "There now—talk about sheep-skins! I went out for sheep-skins and come home without even a coat to my back, and what is more, I'm bringing a naked man along with me. Matryona won't be pleased!" And when he thought of his wife he felt sad; but when he looked at the stranger and remembered how he had looked up at him at the shrine, his heart was glad.

III

Simon's wife had everything ready early that day. She had cut wood, brought water, fed the children, eaten her own meal, and now she sat thinking. She wondered when she ought to make bread: now or tomorrow? There was still a large piece left.

"If Simon has had some dinner in town," thought she, "and does not eat much for supper, the bread will last out another day."

She weighed the piece of bread in her hand again and

again, and thought: "I won't make any more today. We have only enough flour left to bake one batch; We can manage to make this last out till Friday." So Matryona put away the bread, and sat down at the table to patch her husband's shirt. While she worked she thought how her husband was buying skins for a winter coat.

"If only the dealer does not cheat him. My good man is much too simple; he cheats nobody, but any child can take him in. Eight roubles is a lot of money—he should get a good coat at that price. Not tanned skins, but still a proper winter coat. How difficult it was last winter to get on without a warm coat. I could neither get down to the river, nor go out anywhere. When he went out he put on all we had, and there was nothing left for me. He did not start very early today, but still it's time he was back. I only hope he has not gone on the spree!" Hardly had Matryona thought this, when steps were heard on the threshold, and some one entered. Matryona stuck her needle into her work and went out into the passage. There she saw two men: Simon, and with him a man without a hat, and wearing felt boots.

Matryona noticed at once that her husband smelt of spirits. "There now, he has been drinking," thought she. And when she saw that he was coatless, had only her jacket on, brought no parcel, stood there silent, and seemed ashamed, her heart was ready to break with disappointment. "He has drunk the money," thought she, "and has been on the spree with some good-for-nothing fellow whom he has brought home with him." Matryona let them pass into the hut, followed them in, and saw that the stranger was a young, slight man, wearing her husband's coat. There was no shirt to be seen under it, and he had no hat. Having entered, he stood, neither moving, nor raising his eyes, and Matryona thought: "He must be a bad man—he's afraid." Matryona frowned, and stood beside the oven looking to see what they would do.

Simon took off his cap and sat down on the bench as if things were all right.

"Come, Matryona; if supper is ready, let us have some."

Matryona muttered something to herself and did not move, but stayed where she was, by the oven. She looked first at the one and then at the other of them, and only shook her head. Simon saw that his wife was annoyed, but tried to pass it off. Pretending not to notice anything, he took the stranger by the arm.

"Sit down, friend," said he, "and let us have some supper."

The stranger sat down on the bench.

"Haven't you cooked anything for us?" said Simon.

Matryona's anger boiled over. "I've cooked, but not for you. It seems to me you have drunk your wits away. You went to buy a sheep-skin coat, but come home without so much as the coat you had on, and bring a naked vagabond home with you. I have no supper for drunkards like you." "That's enough, Matryona. Don't wag your tongue without reason. You had better ask what sort of man—"

"And you tell me what you've done with the money?"

Simon found the pocket of the jacket, drew out the three-rouble note, and unfolded it.

"Here is the money. Trifonof did not pay, but promises to pay soon."

Matryona got still more angry; he had bought no sheep-skins, but had put his only coat on some naked fellow and had even brought him to their house.

She snatched up the note from the table, took it to put away in safety, and said: "I have no supper for you. We can't feed all the naked drunkards in the world."

"There now, Matryona, hold your tongue a bit. First

hear what a man has to say-"

"Much wisdom I shall hear from a drunken fool. I was right in not wanting to marry you-a drunkard. The linen my mother gave me you drank; and now you've been to buy a coat-and have drunk it, too!" Simon tried to explain to his wife that he had only spent twenty kopeks; tried to tell how he had found the man—but Matryona would not let him get a word in. She talked nineteen to the dozen, and dragged in things that had happened ten years before.

Matryona talked and talked, and at last she flew at Simon and seized him by the sleeve.

"Give me my jacket. It is the only one I have, and you must needs take it from me and wear it yourself. Give it here, you mangy dog, and may the devil take you."

Simon began to pull off the jacket, and turned a sleeve of it inside out; Matryona seized the jacket and it burst its seams, She snatched it up, threw it over her head and went to the door. She meant to go out, but stopped undecided—she wanted to work off her anger, but she also wanted to learn what sort of a man the stranger was.

IV

Matryona stopped and said: "If he were a good man he would not be naked. Why, he hasn't even a shirt on him. If he were all right, you would say where you came across the fellow." "That's just what I am trying to tell you," said Simon. "As I came to the shrine I saw him sitting all naked and frozen. It isn't quite the weather to sit about naked! God sent me to him, or he would have perished. What was I to do? How do we know what may have happened to him? So I took him, clothed him, and brought him along. Don't be so angry, Matryona. It is a sin. Remember, we all must die one day." Angry words rose to Matryona's lips, but she looked at the stranger and was silent. He sat on the edge of the bench, motionless, his hands folded on his knees, his head drooping on his breast, his eyes closed, and his brows knit as if in pain. Matryona was silent: and Simon said: "Matryona, have you no love of God?" Matryona heard these words, and as she looked at the stranger, suddenly her heart softened towards him. She came back from the door, and going to the oven she got out the supper. Setting a cup on the table, she poured out some kvas. Then she brought out the last piece of bread, and set out a knife and spoons.

"Eat, if you want to," said she.

Simon drew the stranger to the table.

"Take your place, young man," said he.

Simon cut the bread, crumbled it into the broth, and they began to eat. Matryona sat at the corner of the table resting her head on her hand and looking at the stranger.

And Matryona was touched with pity for the stranger, and began to feel fond of him. And at once the stranger's face lit up; his brows were no longer bent, he raised his eyes and smiled at Matryona.

When they had finished supper, the woman cleared away the things and began questioning the stranger. "Where are you from?" said she.

"I am not from these parts."

"But how did you come to be on the road?"

"I may not tell."

"Did some one rob you?"

"God punished me."

"And you were lying there naked?"

"Yes, naked and freezing. Simon saw me and had pity on me. He took off his coat, put it on me and brought me here. And you have fed me, given me drink, and shown pity on me. God will reward you!" Matryona rose, took from the window Simon's old shirt she had been patching, and gave it to the stranger. She also brought out a pair of trousers for him.

"There," said she, "I see you have no shirt. Put this on, and lie down where you please, in the loft or on the oven."

The stranger took off the coat, put on the shirt, and lay down in the loft. Matryona put out the candle, took the coat, and climbed to where her husband lay.

Matryona drew the skirts of the coat over her and lay down, but could not sleep; she could not get the stranger out of her mind.

When she remembered that he had eaten their last piece of bread and that there was none for tomorrow, and thought of the shirt and trousers she had given away, she felt grieved; but when she remembered how he had smiled, her heart was glad.

Long did Matryona lie awake, and she noticed that Simon also was awake—he drew the coat towards him.

"Simon!"

"Well?"

"You have had the last of the bread, and I have not put any to rise. I don't know what we shall do tomorrow. Perhaps I can borrow some of neighbor Martha."

"If we're alive we shall find something to eat."

The woman lay still awhile, and then said, "He seems a good man, but why does he not tell us who he is?"

"I suppose he has his reasons."

"Simon!"

"Well?"

"We give; but why does nobody give us anything?"

Simon did not know what to say; so he only said, "Let us stop talking," and turned over and went to sleep.

V

In the morning Simon awoke. The children were still asleep; his wife had gone to the neighbor's to borrow some bread. The stranger alone was sitting on the bench, dressed in the old shirt and trousers, and looking upwards. His face was brighter than it had been the day before.

Simon said to him, "Well, friend; the belly wants bread, and the naked body clothes. One has to work for a living What work do you know?"

"I do not know any."

This surprised Simon, but he said, "Men who want to learn can learn anything."

"Men work, and I will work also."

"What is your name?"

"Michael."

"Well, Michael, if you don't wish to talk about yourself, that is your own affair; but you'll have to earn a living for yourself. If you will work as I tell you, I will give you food and shelter." "May God reward you! I will learn. Show me what to do."

Simon took yarn, put it round his thumb and began to twist it.

"It is easy enough—see!"

Michael watched him, put some yarn round his own thumb in the same way, caught the knack, and twisted the yarn also.

Then Simon showed him how to wax the thread. This also Michael mastered. Next Simon showed him how to twist the bristle in, and how to sew, and this, too, Michael learned at once.

Whatever Simon showed him he understood at once, and after three days he worked as if he had sewn boots all his life. He worked without stopping, and ate little. When work was over he sat silently, looking upwards. He hardly went into the street, spoke only when necessary, and neither joked nor laughed. They never saw him smile, except that first evening when Matryona gave them supper.

VI

Day by day and week by week the year went round. Michael lived and worked with Simon. His fame spread till people said that no one sewed boots so neatly and strongly as Simon's workman, Michael; and from all the district round people came to Simon for their boots, and he began to be well off.

One winter day, as Simon and Michael sat working, a carriage on sledge-runners, with three horses and with bells, drove up to the hut. They looked out of the window; the carriage stopped at their door, a fine servant jumped down from the box and opened the door. A gentleman in a fur coat got out and walked up to Simon's hut. Up jumped Matryona and opened the door wide. The gentleman stooped to enter the hut, and when he drew himself up again his head nearly reached the ceiling, and he seemed quite to fill his end of the room.

Simon rose, bowed, and looked at the gentleman with astonishment. He had never seen any one like him. Simon himself was lean, Michael was thin, and Matryona was dry as a bone, but this man was like some one from another world: red-faced, burly, with a neck like a bull's, and looking altogether as if he were cast in iron.

The gentleman puffed, threw off his fur coat, sat down on the bench, and said, "Which of you is the master bootmaker?"

"I am, your Excellency," said Simon, coming forward.

Then the gentleman shouted to his lad, "Hey, Fedka, bring the leather!"

The servant ran in, bringing a parcel. The gentleman

took the parcel and put it on the table.

"Untie it," said he. The lad untied it.

The gentleman pointed to the leather.

"Look here, shoemaker," said he, "do you see this leather?"

"Yes, your honor."

"But do you know what sort of leather it is?"

Simon felt the leather and said, "It is good leather."

"Good, indeed! Why, you fool, you never saw such leather before in your life. It's German, and cost twenty roubles."

Simon was frightened, and said, "Where should I ever see leather like that?"

"Just so! Now, can you make it into boots for me?"

"Yes, your Excellency, I can."

Then the gentleman shouted at him: "You can, can you? Well, remember whom you are to make them for, and what the leather is. You must make me boots that will wear for a year, neither losing shape nor coming unsown. If you can do it, take the leather and cut it up; but if you can't, say so. I warn you now if your boots become unsewn or lose shape within a year, I will have you put in prison. If they don't burst or lose shape for a year I will pay you ten roubles for your work." Simon was frightened, and did not know what to say. He glanced at Michael and nudging him with his elbow, whispered: "Shall I take the work?"

Michael nodded his head as if to say, "Yes, take it."

Simon did as Michael advised, and undertook to make boots that would not lose shape or split for a whole year.

Calling his servant, the gentleman told him to pull the boot off his left leg, which he stretched out.

"Take my measure!" said he.

Simon stitched a paper measure seventeen inches long,

smoothed it out, knelt down, wiped his hand well on his apron so as not to soil the gentleman's sock, and began to measure. He measured the sole, and round the instep, and began to measure the calf of the leg, but the paper was too short. The calf of the leg was as thick as a beam.

"Mind you don't make it too tight in the leg."

Simon stitched on another strip of paper. The gentleman twitched his toes about in his sock, looking round at those in the hut, and as he did so he noticed Michael.

"Whom have you there?" asked he.

"That is my workman. He will sew the boots."

"Mind," said the gentleman to Michael, "remember to make them so that they will last me a year."

Simon also looked at Michael, and saw that Michael was not looking at the gentleman, but was gazing into the corner behind the gentleman, as if he saw some one there. Michael looked and looked, and suddenly he smiled, and his face became brighter.

"What are you grinning at, you fool?" thundered the gentleman. "You had better look to it that the boots are ready in time."

"They shall be ready in good time," said Michael.

"Mind it is so," said the gentleman, and he put on his boots and his fur coat, wrapped the latter round him, and went to the door. But he forgot to stoop, and struck his head against the lintel.

He swore and rubbed his head. Then he took his seat in the carriage and drove away.

When he had gone, Simon said: "There's a figure of a man for you! You could not kill him with a mallet. He almost knocked out the lintel, but little harm it did him."

And Matryona said: "Living as he does, how should he

not grow strong? Death itself can't touch such a rock as that."

VII

Then Simon said to Michael: "Well, we have taken the work, but we must see we don't get into trouble over it. The leather is dear, and the gentleman hot-tempered. We must make no mistakes. Come, your eye is truer and your hands have become nimbler than mine, so you take this measure and cut out the boots. I will finish off the sewing of the vamps." Michael did as he was told. He took the leather, spread it out on the table, folded it in two, took a knife and began to cut out.

Matryona came and watched him cutting, and was surprised to see how he was doing it. Matryona was accustomed to seeing boots made, and she looked and saw that Michael was not cutting the leather for boots, but was cutting it round.

She wished to say something, but she thought to herself: "Perhaps I do not understand how gentleman's boots should be made. I suppose Michael knows more about it—and I won't interfere." When Michael had cut up the leather, he took a thread and began to sew not with two ends, as boots are sewn, but with a single end, as for soft slippers.

Again Matryona wondered, but again she did not interfere. Michael sewed on steadily till noon. Then Simon rose for dinner, looked around, and saw that Michael had made slippers out of the gentleman's leather.

"Ah," groaned Simon, and he thought, "How is it that Michael, who has been with me a whole year and never made a mistake before, should do such a dreadful thing? The gentleman ordered high boots, welted, with whole fronts, and Michael has made soft slippers with single soles, and has wasted the leather. What am I to say to the gentleman? I can never replace leather such as this." And he said to Michael, "What are you doing, friend? You have ruined me! You know the gentleman ordered high boots, but see what you have made!"

Hardly had he begun to rebuke Michael, when "rat-tat" went the iron ring that hung at the door. Some one was knocking. They looked out of the window; a man had come on horseback, and was fastening his horse. They opened the door, and the servant who had been with the gentleman came in.

"Good day," said he.

"Good day," replied Simon. "What can we do for you?"

"My mistress has sent me about the boots."

"What about the boots?"

"Why, my master no longer needs them. He is dead."

"Is it possible?"

"He did not live to get home after leaving you, but died in the carriage. When we reached home and the servants came to help him alight, he rolled over like a sack. He was dead already, and so stiff that he could hardly be got out of the carriage. My mistress sent me here, saying: 'Tell the bootmaker that the gentleman who ordered boots of him and left the leather for them no longer needs the boots, but that he must quickly make soft slippers for the corpse. Wait till they are ready, and bring them back with you.' That is why I have come."

Michael gathered up the remnants of the leather; rolled them up, took the soft slippers he had made, slapped them together, wiped them down with his apron, and handed them and the roll of leather to the servant, who took them and said: "Good-bye, masters, and good day to you!"

VIII

Another year passed, and another, and Michael was now living his sixth year with Simon. He lived as before. He went nowhere, only spoke when necessary, and had only smiled twice in all those years—once when Matryona gave him food, and a second time when the gentleman was in their hut. Simon was more than pleased with his workman. He never now asked him where he came from, and only feared lest Michael should go away.

They were all at home one day. Matryona was putting iron pots in the oven; the children were running along the benches and looking out of the window; Simon was sewing at one window, and Michael was fastening on a heel at the other.

One of the boys ran along the bench to Michael, leant on his shoulder, and looked out of the window.

"Look, Uncle Michael! There is a lady with little girls! She seems to be coming here. And one of the girls is lame."

When the boy said that, Michael dropped his work, turned to the window, and looked out into the street.

Simon was surprised. Michael never used to look out into the street, but now he pressed against the window, staring at something. Simon also looked out, and saw that a well-dressed woman was really coming to his hut, leading by the hand two little girls in fur coats and woolen shawls. The girls could hardly be told one from the other, except that one of them was crippled in her left leg and walked with a limp.

The woman stepped into the porch and entered the passage. Feeling about for the entrance she found the latch, which she lifted, and opened the door. She let the two girls go in first, and followed them into the hut.

"Good day, good folk!"

"Pray come in," said Simon. "What can we do for you?"

The woman sat down by the table. The two little girls pressed close to her knees, afraid of the people in the hut.

"I want leather shoes made for these two little girls for spring."

"We can do that. We never have made such small shoes, but we can make them; either welted or turnover shoes, linen lined. My man, Michael, is a master at the work."

Simon glanced at Michael and saw that he had left his work and was sitting with his eyes fixed on the little girls. Simon was surprised. It was true the girls were pretty, with black eyes, plump, and rosy-cheeked, and they wore nice kerchiefs and fur coats, but still Simon could not understand why Michael should look at them like that—just as if he had known them before. He was puzzled, but went on talking with the woman, and arranging the price. Having fixed it, he prepared the measure. The woman lifted the lame girl on to her lap and said: "Take two measures from this little girl. Make one shoe for the lame foot and three for the sound one. They both have the same size feet. They are twins." Simon took the measure and, speaking of the lame girl, said: "How did it happen to her? She is such a pretty girl. Was she born so?"

"No, her mother crushed her leg."

Then Matryona joined in. She wondered who this woman was, and whose the children were, so she said: "Are not you their mother then?"

"No, my good woman; I am neither their mother nor any relation to them. They were quite strangers to me, but I adopted them."

"They are not your children and yet you are so fond of them?"

"How can I help being fond of them? I fed them both at my own breasts. I had a child of my own, but God took him. I was not so fond of him as I now am of them."

"Then whose children are they?"

IX

The woman, having begun talking, told them the whole story.

"It is about six years since their parents died, both in one week: their father was buried on the Tuesday, and their mother died on the Friday. These orphans were born three days after their father's death, and their mother did not live another day. My husband and I were then living as peasants in the village. We were neighbors of theirs, our yard being next to theirs. Their father was a lonely man; a wood-cutter in the forest. When felling trees one day, they let one fall on him. It fell across his body and crushed his bowels out. They hardly got him home before his soul went to God; and that same week his wife gave birth to twins—these little girls. She was poor and alone; she had no one, young or old, with her. Alone she gave them birth, and alone she met her death." "The next morning I went to see her, but when I entered the hut, she, poor thing, was already stark and cold. In dying she had rolled on to this child and crushed her leg. The village folk came to the hut, washed the body, laid her out, made a coffin, and buried her. They were good folk. The babies were left alone. What was to be done with them? I was the only woman there who had a baby at the time. I was nursing my first-born—eight weeks old. So I took them for a time. The peasants came together, and thought and thought what to do with them; and at last they said to me: 'For the present, Mary, you had better keep the girls, and later on we will arrange what to do for them.' So I nursed the sound one at my breast, but at first I did not feed this crippled one. I did not suppose she would live. But then I thought to myself, why should the poor innocent suffer? I pitied her, and began to feed her. And so I fed my own boy and these two—the three of them—at my own breast. I was young and strong, and had good food, and God gave me so much milk that at times it even overflowed. I used sometimes to feed two at a time, while the third was waiting. When one had enough I nursed the third. And God so ordered it that these grew up, while my own was buried before he was two years old. And I had no more children, though we prospered. Now my husband is working for the corn merchant at the mill. The pay is good, and we are well off. But I have no children of my own, and how lonely I should be without these little girls! How can I help loving them! They are the joy of my life!" She pressed the lame little girl to her with one hand, while with the other she wiped the tears from her cheeks.

And Matryona sighed, and said: "The proverb is true that says, 'One may live without father or mother, but one cannot live without God.'"

So they talked together, when suddenly the whole hut was lighted up as though by summer lightning from the corner where Michael sat. They all looked towards him and saw him sitting, his hands folded on his knees, gazing upwards and smiling.

X

The woman went away with the girls. Michael rose from the bench, put down his work, and took off his apron. Then, bowing low to Simon and his wife, he said: "Farewell, masters. God has forgiven me. I ask your forgiveness, too, for anything done amiss." And they saw that a light shone from Michael. And Simon rose, bowed down to Michael, and said: "I see, Michael, that you are no common man, and I can neither keep you nor question you. Only tell me this: how is it that when I found you and brought you home, you were gloomy, and when my wife gave you food you smiled at her and became brighter? Then when the gentleman came to order the boots, you smiled again and became brighter still? And now, when this woman brought the little girls, you smiled a third time, and have become as bright as day? Tell me, Michael, why does your face shine so, and why did you smile those three times?" And Michael answered: "Light shines from me because I have been punished, but now God has pardoned me. And I smiled three times, because God sent me to learn three truths, and I have learnt them. One I learnt when your wife pitied me, and that is why I smiled the first time. The second I learnt when the rich man ordered the boots, and then I smiled again. And now, when I saw those little girls, I learn the third and last truth, and I smiled the third time." And Simon said, "Tell me, Michael, what did God punish you for? and what were the three truths? that I, too, may know them."

And Michael answered: "God punished me for disobeying Him. I was an angel in heaven and disobeyed God. God sent me to fetch a woman's soul. I flew to earth, and saw a sick woman lying alone, who had just given birth to twin girls. They moved feebly at their mother's side, but she could not lift them to her breast. When she saw me, she understood that God had sent me for her soul, and she wept and said: 'Angel of God! My husband has just been buried, killed by a falling tree. I have neither sister, nor aunt, nor mother: no one to care for my orphans. Do not take my soul! Let me nurse my babes, feed them, and set them on their feet before I die. Children cannot live without father or mother.' And I hearkened to her. I placed one child at her breast and gave the other into her arms, and returned to the Lord in heaven. I flew to the Lord, and said: 'I could not take the soul of the mother. Her husband was killed by a tree; the woman has twins, and prays that her soul may not be taken. She says: "Let me nurse and feed my children, and set them on their feet. Children cannot live without father or mother." I have not taken her soul.' And God said: 'Go-take the mother's soul, and learn three truths: Learn What dwells in man, What is not given to man, and What men live by. When thou has learnt these things, thou shalt return to heaven.' So I flew again to earth and took the mother's soul. The babes dropped from her breasts. Her body rolled over on the bed and crushed one babe, twisting its leg. I rose above the village, wishing to take her soul to God; but a wind seized me, and my wings drooped and dropped off. Her soul rose alone to God, while I fell to earth by the roadside."

XI

And Simon and Matryona understood who it was that had lived with them, and whom they had clothed and fed. And they wept with awe and with joy. And the angel said: "I was alone in the field, naked. I had never known human needs, cold and hunger, till I became a man. I was famished, frozen, and did not know what to do. I saw, near the field I was in, a shrine built for God, and I went to it hoping to find shelter. But the shrine was locked, and I could not enter. So I sat down behind the shrine to shelter myself at least from the wind. Evening drew on. I was hungry, frozen, and in pain. Suddenly I heard a man coming along the road. He carried a pair of boots, and was talking to himself. For the first time since I became a man I saw the mortal face of a man, and his face seemed terrible to me and I turned from it.

And I heard the man talking to himself of how to cover his body from the cold in winter, and how to feed wife and children. And I thought: 'I am perishing of cold and hunger, and here is a man thinking only of how to clothe himself and his wife, and how to get bread for themselves. He cannot help me.' When the man saw me he frowned and became still more terrible, and passed me by on the other side. I despaired; but suddenly I heard him coming back. I looked up, and did not recognize the same man; before, I had seen death in his face; but now he was alive, and I recognized in him the presence of God. He came up to me, clothed me, took me with him, and brought me to his home. I entered the house; a woman came to meet us and began to speak. The woman was still more terrible than the man had been; the spirit of death came from her mouth; I could not breathe for the stench of death that spread around her. She wished to drive me out into the cold, and I knew that if she did so she would die. Suddenly her husband spoke to her of God, and the woman changed at once. And when she brought me food and looked at me, I glanced at her and saw that death no longer dwelt in her; she had become alive, and in her, too, I saw God.

"Then I remembered the first lesson God had set me: 'Learn what dwells in man.' And I understood that in man dwells Love! I was glad that God had already begun to show me what He had promised, and I smiled for the first time. But I had not yet learnt all. I did not yet know What is not given to man, and What men live by.

"I lived with you, and a year passed. A man came to order boots that should wear for a year without losing shape or cracking. I looked at him, and suddenly, behind his shoulder, I saw my comrade—the angel of death. None but me saw that angel; but I knew him, and knew that before the sun set he would take that rich man's soul. And I thought to myself, 'The man is making preparations for a year, and does not know that he will die before evening.' And I remembered God's second saying, 'Learn what is not given to man.' "What dwells in man I already knew. Now I learnt what is not given him. It is not given to man to know his own needs. And I smiled for the second time. I was glad to have seen my comrade angel—glad also that God had revealed to me the second saying.

"But I still did not know all. I did not know What men live by. And I lived on, waiting till God should reveal to me the last lesson. In the sixth year came the girl-twins with the woman; and I recognized the girls, and heard how they had been kept alive. Having heard the story, I thought, 'Their mother besought me for the children's sake, and I believed her when she said that children cannot live without father or mother; but a stranger has nursed them, and has brought them up.' And when the woman showed her love for the children that were not her own, and wept over them, I saw in her the living God and understood What men live by. And I knew that God had revealed to me the last lesson, and had forgiven my sin. And then I smiled for the third time."

XII

And the angel's body was bared, and he was clothed in light so that eye could not look on him; and his voice grew louder, as though it came not from him but from heaven above. And the angel said: "I have learnt that all men live not by care for themselves but by love.

"It was not given to the mother to know what her children needed for their life. Nor was it given to the rich man to know what he himself needed. Nor is it given to any man to know whether, when evening comes, he will need boots for his body or slippers for his corpse.

"I remained alive when I was a man, not by care of myself, but because love was present in a passer-by, and because he and his wife pitied and loved me. The orphans remained alive not because of their mother's care, but because there was love in the heart of a woman, a stranger to them, who pitied and loved them. And all men live not by the thought they spend on their own welfare, but because love exists in man.

"I knew before that God gave life to men and desires that they should live; now I understood more than that.

"I understood that God does not wish men to live apart, and therefore he does not reveal to them what each one needs for himself; but he wishes them to live united, and therefore reveals to each of them what is necessary for all.

"I have now understood that though it seems to men that they live by care for themselves, in truth it is love alone by which they live. He who has love, is in God, and God is in him, for God is love." And the angel sang praise to God, so that the hut trembled at his voice. The roof opened, and a column of fire rose from earth to heaven. Simon and his wife and children fell to the ground. Wings appeared upon the angel's shoulders, and he rose into the heavens.

And when Simon came to himself the hut stood as before, and there was no one in it but his own family.

The Offshore Pirate

Francis Scott Key Fitzgerald

I

This unlikely story begins on a sea that was a blue dream, as colorful as blue-silk stockings, and beneath a sky as blue as the irises of children's eyes. From the western half of the sky the sun was shying little golden disks at the sea—if you gazed intently enough you could see them skip from wave tip to wave tip until they joined a broad collar of golden coin that was collecting half a mile out and would eventually be a dazzling sunset. About half-way between the Florida shore and the golden collar a white steam-yacht, very young and graceful, was riding at anchor and under a blue-and-white awning aft a yellow-haired girl reclined in a wicker settee reading The Revolt of the Angels, by Anatole France.

She was about nineteen, slender and supple, with a spoiled alluring mouth and quick gray eyes full of a radiant curiosity. Her feet, stockingless, and adorned rather than clad in blue-satin slippers which swung nonchalantly from her toes, were perched on the arm of a settee adjoining the one she occupied. And as she read she intermittently regaled herself by a faint application to her tongue of a half-lemon that she held in her hand. The other half, sucked dry, lay on the deck at her feet and rocked very gently to and fro at the almost imperceptible motion of the tide.

The second half-lemon was well-nigh pulpless and the golden collar had grown astonishing in width, when suddenly the drowsy silence which enveloped the yacht was broken by the sound of heavy footsteps and an elderly man topped with orderly gray hair and clad in a white-flannel suit appeared at the head of the companionway. There he paused for a moment until his eyes became accustomed to the sun, and then seeing the girl under the awning he uttered a long even grunt of disapproval.

If he had intended thereby to obtain a rise of any sort he was doomed to disappointment. The girl calmly turned over two pages, turned back one, raised the lemon mechanically to tasting distance, and then very faintly but quite unmistakably yawned.

"Ardita!" said the gray-haired man sternly.

Ardita uttered a small sound indicating nothing.

"Ardita!" he repeated. "Ardita!"

Ardita raised the lemon languidly, allowing three words to slip out before it reached her tongue.

"Oh, shut up."

"Ardita!"

"What?"

"Will you listen to me—or will I have to get a servant to hold you while I talk to you?"

The lemon descended very slowly and scornfully.

"Put it in writing."

"Will you have the decency to close that abominable book and discard that damn lemon for two minutes?"

"Oh, can't you lemme alone for a second?"

"Ardita, I have just received a telephone message from the shore——"

"Telephone?" She showed for the first time a faint interest.

"Yes, it was——"

"Do you mean to say," she interrupted wonderingly, "'at they let you run a wire out here?"

"Yes, and just now——"

"Won't other boats bump into it?"

"No. It's run along the bottom. Five min——"

"Well, I'll be darned! Gosh! Science is golden or something—isn't it?"

"Will you let me say what I started to?"

"Shoot!"

"Well it seems—well, I am up here—" He paused and swallowed several times distractedly. "Oh, yes. Young woman, Colonel Moreland has called up again to ask me to be sure to bring you in to dinner. His son Toby has come all the way from New York to meet you and he's invited several other young people. For the last time, will you——"

"No," said Ardita shortly, "I won't. I came along on this darn cruise with the one idea of going to Palm Beach, and you knew it, and I absolutely refuse to meet any darn old colonel or any darn young Toby or any darn old young people or to set foot in any other darn old town in this crazy state. So you either take me to Palm Beach or else shut up and go away."

"Very well. This is the last straw. In your infatuation for this man.—a man who is notorious for his excesses—a man your father would not have allowed to so much as mention your name—you have rejected the demi-monde rather than the circles in which you have presumably grown up. From now on——"

"I know," interrupted Ardita ironically, "from now on you go your way and I go mine. I've heard that story before. You know I'd like nothing better."

"From now on," he announced grandiloquently, "you are no niece of mine. I——"

"O-o-o-oh!" The cry was wrung from Ardita with the agony of a lost soul. "Will you stop boring me! Will you go 'way! Will you jump overboard and drown! Do you want me to throw this book at you!"

"If you dare do any——"

Smack! The Revolt of the Angels sailed through the air, missed its target by the length of a short nose, and bumped cheerfully down the companionway.

The gray-haired man made an instinctive step backward and then two cautious steps forward. Ardita jumped to her five feet four and stared at him defiantly, her gray eyes blazing.

"Keep off!"

"How dare you!" he cried.

"Because I darn please!"

"You've grown unbearable! Your disposition——"

"You've made me that way! No child ever has a bad disposition unless it's her fancy's fault! Whatever I am, you did it."

Muttering something under his breath her uncle turned and, walking forward called in a loud voice for the launch. Then he returned to the awning, where Ardita had again seated herself and resumed her attention to the lemon.

"I am going ashore," he said slowly. "I will be out again at nine o'clock to-night. When I return we start back to New York, wither I shall turn you over to your aunt for the rest of your natural, or rather unnatural, life." He paused and looked at her, and then all at once something in the utter childness of her beauty seemed to puncture his anger like an inflated tire, and render him helpless, uncertain, utterly fatuous.

"Ardita," he said not unkindly, "I'm no fool. I've been round. I know men. And, child, confirmed libertines don't reform until they're tired—and then they're not themselves—they're husks of themselves." He looked at her as if expecting agreement, but receiving no sight or sound of it he continued. "Perhaps the man loves you—that's possible. He's loved many women and he'll love many more. Less than a month ago, one month, Ardita, he was involved in a notorious affair with that red-haired woman, Mimi Merril; promised to give her the diamond bracelet that the Czar of Russia gave his mother. You know—you read the papers."

"Thrilling scandals by an anxious uncle," yawned Ardita. "Have it filmed. Wicked clubman making eyes at virtuous flapper. Virtuous flapper conclusively vamped by his lurid past. Plans to meet him at Palm Beach. Foiled by anxious uncle."

"Will you tell me why the devil you want to marry him?"

"I'm sure I couldn't say," said Audits shortly. "Maybe because he's the only man I know, good or bad, who has an imagination and the courage of his convictions. Maybe it's to get away from the young fools that spend their vacuous hours pursuing me around the country. But as for the famous Russian bracelet, you can set your mind at rest on that score. He's going to give it to me at Palm Beach—if you'll show a little intelligence."

"How about the—red-haired woman?"

"He hasn't seen her for six months," she said angrily. "Don't you suppose I have enough pride to see to that? Don't you know by this time that I can do any darn thing with any darn man I want to?"

She put her chin in the air like the statue of France Aroused, and then spoiled the pose somewhat by raising the lemon for action.

"Is it the Russian bracelet that fascinates you?"

"No, I'm merely trying to give you the sort of argument that would appeal to your intelligence. And I wish you'd go 'way," she said, her temper rising again. "You know I never change my mind. You've been boring me for three days until I'm about to go crazy. I won't go ashore! Won't! Do you hear? Won't!"

"Very well," he said, "and you won't go to Palm Beach either. Of all the selfish, spoiled, uncontrolled disagreeable, impossible girl I have——"

Splush! The half-lemon caught him in the neck. Simultaneously came a hail from over the side.

"The launch is ready, Mr. Farnam."

Too full of words and rage to speak, Mr. Farnam cast one utterly condemning glance at his niece and, turning, ran swiftly down the ladder.

II

Five o'clock robed down from the sun and plumped soundlessly into the sea. The golden collar widened into a glittering island; and a faint breeze that had been playing with the edges of the awning and swaying one of the dangling blue slippers became suddenly freighted with song. It was a chorus of men in close harmony and in perfect rhythm to an accompanying sound of oars dealing the blue writers. Ardita lifted her head and listened.

"Carrots and Peas,
Beans on their knees,
Pigs in the seas,
Lucky fellows!
Blow us a breeze,
Blow us a breeze,
Blow us a breeze,
With your bellows."

Ardita's brow wrinkled in astonishment. Sitting very still she listened eagerly as the chorus took up a second verse.

"Onions and beans,
Marshalls and Deans,
Goldbergs and Greens
And Costellos.
Blow us a breeze,
Blow us a breeze,

Blow us a breeze,
With your bellows."

With an exclamation she tossed her book to the desk, where it sprawled at a straddle, and hurried to the rail. Fifty feet away a large rowboat was approaching containing seven men, six of them rowing and one standing up in the stern keeping time to their song with an orchestra leader's baton.

"Oysters and Rocks,
Sawdust and socks,
Who could make clocks
Out of cellos?——"

The leader's eyes suddenly rested on Ardita, who was leaning over the rail spellbound with curiosity. He made a quick movement with his baton and the singing instantly ceased. She saw that he was the only white man in the boat—the six rowers were negroes.

"Narcissus ahoy!" he called politely.

"What's the idea of all the discord?" demanded Ardita cheerfully. "Is this the varsity crew from the county nut farm?"

By this time the boat was scraping the side of the yacht and a great bulking negro in the bow turned round and grasped the ladder. Thereupon the leader left his position in the stern and before Ardita had realized his intention he ran up the ladder and stood breathless before her on the deck.

"The women and children will be spared!" he said briskly. "All crying babies will be immediately drowned and all males put in double irons!" Digging her hands excitedly down into the pockets of her dress Ardita stared at him, speechless with astonishment. He was a young man with a scornful mouth and the bright blue eyes of a healthy baby set in a dark sensitive face. His hair was pitch black, damp and curly—the hair of a

Grecian statue gone brunette. He was trimly built, trimly dressed, and graceful as an agile quarter-back.

"Well, I'll be a son of a gun!" she said dazedly.

They eyed each other coolly.

"Do you surrender the ship?"

"Is this an outburst of wit?" demanded Ardita. "Are you an idiot—or just being initiated to some fraternity?"

"I asked you if you surrendered the ship."

"I thought the country was dry," said Ardita disdainfully. "Have you been drinking finger-nail enamel? You better get off this yacht!"

"What?" the young man's voice expressed incredulity.

"Get off the yacht! You heard me!"

He looked at her for a moment as if considering what she had said.

"No," said his scornful mouth slowly; "No, I won't get off the yacht. You can get off if you wish."

Going to the rail be gave a curt command and immediately the crew of the rowboat scrambled up the ladder and ranged themselves in line before him, a coal-black and burly darky at one end and a miniature mulatto of four feet nine at to other. They seemed to be uniformly dressed in some sort of blue costume ornamented with dust, mud, and tatters; over the shoulder of each was slung a small, heavy-looking white sack, and under their arms they carried large black cases apparently containing musical instruments.

"'Ten-shun!" commanded the young man, snapping his own heels together crisply. "Right driss! Front! Step out here, Babe!"

The smallest Negro took a quick step forward and saluted.

"Take command, go down below, catch the crew and tie 'em up—all except the engineer. Bring him up to me. Oh, and pile those bags by the rail there."

"Yas-suh!"

Babe saluted again and wheeling about motioned for the five others to gather about him. Then after a short whispered consultation they all filed noiselessly down the companionway.

"Now," said the young man cheerfully to Ardita, who had witnessed this last scene in withering silence, "if you will swear on your honor as a flapper—which probably isn't worth much—that you'll keep that spoiled little mouth of yours tight shut for forty-eight hours, you can row yourself ashore in our rowboat."

"Otherwise what?"

"Otherwise you're going to sea in a ship."

With a little sigh as for a crisis well passed, the young man sank into the settee Ardita had lately vacated and stretched his arms lazily. The corners of his mouth relaxed appreciatively as he looked round at the rich striped awning, the polished brass, and the luxurious fittings of the deck. His eye felt on the book, and then on the exhausted lemon.

"Hm," he said, "Stonewall Jackson claimed that lemon-juice cleared his head. Your head feel pretty clear?"

Ardita disdained to answer.

"Because inside of five minutes you'll have to make a clear decision whether it's go or stay."

He picked up the book and opened it curiously.

"The Revolt of the Angels. Sounds pretty good. French, eh?" He stared at her with new interest "You French?"

"No."

"What's your name?"

"Farnam."

"Farnam what?"

"Ardita Farnam."

"Well Ardita, no use standing up there and chewing out

the insides of your mouth. You ought to break those nervous habits while you're young. Come over here and sit down."

Ardita took a carved jade case from her pocket, extracted a cigarette and lit it with a conscious coolness, though she knew her hand was trembling a little; then she crossed over with her supple, swinging walk, and sitting down in the other settee blew a mouthful of smoke at the awning.

"You can't get me off this yacht," she raid steadily; "and you haven't got very much sense if you think you'll get far with it. My uncle'll have wirelesses zigzagging all over this ocean by half past six."

"Hm."

She looked quickly at his face, caught anxiety stamped there plainly in the faintest depression of the mouth's corners.

"It's all the same to me," she said, shrugging her shoulders. "'Tisn't my yacht. I don't mind going for a coupla hours' cruise. I'll even lend you that book so you'll have something to read on the revenue boat that takes you up to Sing-Sing."

He laughed scornfully.

"If that's advice you needn't bother. This is part of a plan arranged before I ever knew this yacht existed. If it hadn't been this one it'd have been the next one we passed anchored along the coast."

"Who are you?" demanded Ardita suddenly. "And what are you?"

"You've decided not to go ashore?"

"I never even faintly considered it."

"We're generally known," he said "all seven of us, as Curtis Carlyle and his Six Black Buddies late of the Winter Garden and the Midnight Frolic."

"You're singers?"

"We were until to-day. At present, due to those white bags you see there we're fugitives from justice and if the reward offered for our capture hasn't by this time reached twenty thousand dollars I miss my guess."
"What's in the bags?" asked Ardita curiously.
"Well," he said "for the present we'll call it—mud—Florida mud."

III

Within ten minutes after Curtis Carlyle's interview with a very frightened engineer the yacht Narcissus was under way, steaming south through a balmy tropical twilight. The little mulatto, Babe, who seems to have Carlyle's implicit confidence, took full command of the situation. Mr. Farnam's valet and the chef, the only members of the crew on board except the engineer, having shown fight, were now reconsidering, strapped securely to their bunks below. Trombone Mose, the biggest negro, was set busy with a can of paint obliterating the name Narcissus from the bow, and substituting the name Hula Hula, and the others congregated aft and became intently involved in a game of craps.

Having given order for a meal to be prepared and served on deck at seven-thirty, Carlyle rejoined Ardita, and, sinking back into his settee, half closed his eyes and fell into a state of profound abstraction.

Ardita scrutinized him carefully—and classed him immediately as a romantic figure. He gave the effect of towering self-confidence erected on a slight foundation—just under the surface of each of his decisions she discerned a hesitancy that was in decided contrast to the arrogant curl of his lips.

"He's not like me," she thought "There's a difference somewhere." Being a supreme egotist Ardita frequently thought about herself; never having had her egotism disputed she did it entirely naturally and with no detraction from her unquestioned charm. Though she was nineteen she gave the effect of a high-spirited precocious child, and in the present glow of her youth and beauty all the men and women she had known were but driftwood on the ripples of her temperament. She had met other egotists—in fact she found that selfish people bored her rather less than unselfish people—but as yet there had not been one she had not eventually defeated and brought to her feet.

But though she recognized an egotist in the settee, she felt none of that usual shutting of doors in her mind which meant clearing ship for action; on the contrary her instinct told her that this man was somehow completely pregnable and quite defenseless. When Ardita defied convention—and of late it had been her chief amusement—it was from an intense desire to be herself, and she felt that this man, on the contrary, was preoccupied with his own defiance.

She was much more interested in him than she was in her own situation, which affected her as the prospect of a matineé might affect a ten-year-old child. She had implicit confidence in her ability to take care of herself under any and all circumstances.

The night deepened. A pale new moon smiled misty-eyed upon the sea, and as the shore faded dimly out and dark clouds were blown like leaves along the far horizon a great haze of moonshine suddenly bathed the yacht and spread an avenue of glittering mail in her swift path. From time to time there was the bright flare of a match as one of them lighted a cigarette, but except for the low under-tone of the throbbing engines and the even wash of the waves about the stern the yacht was quiet as a dream boat star-bound through the heavens. Round them bowed the smell of the night sea, bringing with it an infinite languor.

Carlyle broke the silence at last.

"Lucky girl," he sighed "I've always wanted to be rich—and buy all this beauty."

Ardita yawned.

"I'd rather be you," she said frankly.

"You would—for about a day. But you do seem to possess a lot of nerve for a flapper."

"I wish you wouldn't call me that."

"Beg your pardon."

"As to nerve," she continued slowly, "it's my one redeemiug feature. I'm not afraid of anything in heaven or earth."

"Hm, I am."

"To be afraid," said Ardita, "a person has either to be very great and strong—or else a coward. I'm neither." She paused for a moment, and eagerness crept into her tone. "But I want to talk about you. What on earth have you done—and how did you do it?"

"Why?" he demanded cynically. "Going to write a movie, about me?"

"Go on," she urged. "Lie to me by the moonlight. Do a fabulous story."

A negro appeared, switched on a string of small lights under the awning, and began setting the wicker table for supper. And while they ate cold sliced chicken, salad, artichokes and strawberry jam from the plentiful larder below, Carlyle began to talk, hesitatingly at first, but eagerly as he saw she was interested. Ardita scarcely touched her food as she watched his dark young face—handsome, ironic faintly ineffectual.

He began life as a poor kid in a Tennessee town, he said, so poor that his people were the only white family in their street. He never remembered any white children —but there were inevitably a dozen pickaninnies streaming in his trail, passionate admirers whom he kept in tow by the vividness of his imagination and the amount of trouble he was always getting them in and out of. And it seemed that this association diverted a rather unusual musical gift into a strange channel.

There had been a colored woman named Belle Pope Calhoun who played the piano at parties given for white children—nice white children that would have passed Curtis Carlyle with a sniff. But the ragged little "poh white" used to sit beside her piano by the hour and try to get in an alto with one of those kazoos that boys hum through. Before he was thirteen he was picking up a living teasing ragtime out of a battered violin in little cafés round Nashville. Eight years later the ragtime craze hit the country, and he took six darkies on the Orpheum circuit. Five of them were boys he had grown up with; the other was the little mulatto, Babe Divine, who was a wharf nigger round New York, and long before that a plantation hand in Bermuda, until he stuck an eight-inch stiletto in his master's back. Almost before Carlyle realized his good fortune he was on Broadway, with offers of engagements on all sides, and more money than he had ever dreamed of.

It was about then that a change began in his whole attitude, a rather curious, embittering change. It was when he realized that he was spending the golden years of his life gibbering round a stage with a lot of black men. His act was good of its kind—three trombones, three saxaphones, and Carlyle's flute—and it was his own peculiar sense of rhythm that made all the difference; but he began to grow strangely sensitive about it, began to hate the thought of appearing, dreaded it from day to day.

They were making money—each contract he signed called for more—but when he went to managers and told them that he wanted to separate from his sextet and go on as a regular pianist, they laughed at him and told him he was crazy—it would be an artistic suicide. He used to laugh afterward at the phrase "artistic suicide." They all used it.

Half a dozen times they played at private dances at three thousand dollars a night, and it seemed as if these crystallized all his distaste for his mode of livlihood. They took place in clubs and houses that he couldn't have gone into in the daytime. After all, he was merely playing to rôle of the eternal monkey, a sort of sublimated chorus man. He was sick of the very smell of the theatre, of powder and rouge and the chatter of the greenroom, and the patronizing approval of the boxes. He couldn't put his heart into it any more. The idea of a slow approach to the luxury of leisure drove him wild. He was, of course, progressing toward it, but, like a child, eating his ice-cream so slowly that he couldn't taste it at all.

He wanted to have a lot of money and time and opportunity to read and play, and the sort of men and women round him that he could never have—the kind who, if they thought of him at all, would have considered him rather contemptible; in short he wanted all those things which he was beginning to lump under the general head of aristocracy, an aristocracy which it seemed almost any money could buy except money made as he was making it. He was twenty-five then, without family or education or any promise that he would succeed in a business career. He began speculating wildly, and within three weeks he had lost every cent he had saved.

Then the war came. He went to Plattsburg, and even there his profession followed him. A brigadier-general called him up to headquarters and told him he could serve his country better as a band leader—so he spent the war entertaining celebrities behind the line with a headquarters band. It was not so bad—except that when the infantry came limping back from the trenches he wanted to be one of them. The sweat and mud they wore seemed only one of those ineffable symbols of aristocracy that were forever eluding him.

"It was the private dances that did it. After I came back from the war the old routine started. We had an offer from a syndicate of Florida hotels. It was only a question of time then."

He broke off and Ardita looked at him expectantly, but he shook his head.

"No," he said, "I'm going to tell you about it. I'm enjoying it too much, and I'm afraid I'd lose a little of that enjoyment if I shared it with anyone else. I want to hang on to those few breathless, heroic moments when I stood out before them all and let them know I was more than a damn bobbing, squawking clown."

From up forward came suddenly the low sound of singing. The negroes had gathered together on the deck and their voices rose together in a haunting melody that soared in poignant harmonics toward the moon. And Ardita listens in enchantment.

"Oh down——
oh down,
Mammy wanna take me down milky way,
Oh down,
oh down,
Pappy say to-morra-a-a-ah
But mammy say to-day,
Yes—mammy say to-day!"

Carlyle sighed and was silent for a moment looking up at the gathered host of stars blinking like arc-lights in the warm sky. The negroes' song had died away to a plaintive humming and it seemed as if minute by minute the brightness and the great silence were increasing until he could almost hear the midnight toilet of the mermaids as they combed their silver dripping curls under the moon and gossiped to each other of the fine wrecks they lived on the green opalescent avenues below.

"You see," said Carlyle softly, "this is the beauty I want. Beauty has got to be astonishing, astounding—it's got to burst in on you like a dream, like the exquisite eyes of a girl."

He turned to her, but she was silent.

"You see, don't you, Anita—I mean, Ardita?"

Again she made no answer. She had been sound asleep for some time.

IV

In the dense sun-flooded noon of next day a spot in the sea before them resolved casually into a green-and-gray islet, apparently composed of a great granite cliff at its northern end which slanted south through a mile of vivid coppice and grass to a sandy beach melting lazily into the surf. When Ardita, reading in her favorite seat, came to the last page of The Revolt of the Angels, and slamming the book shut looked up and saw it, she gave a little cry of delight, and called to Carlyle, who was standing moodily by the rail.

"Is this it? Is this where you're going?"

Carlyle shrugged his shoulders carelessly.

"You've got me." He raised his voice and called up to the acting skipper: "Oh, Babe, is this your island?"

The mulatto's miniature head appeared from round the corner of the deck-house.

"Yas-suh! This yeah's it."

Carlyle joined Ardita.

"Looks sort of sporting, doesn't it?"

"Yes," she agreed; "but it doesn't look big enough to be much of a hiding-place."

"You still putting your faith in those wirelesses your uncle was going to have zigzagging round?"

"No," said Ardita frankly. "I'm all for you. I'd really like to see you make a get-away."

He laughed.

"You're our Lady Luck. Guess we'll have to keep you with us as a mascot—for the present anyway."

"You couldn't very well ask me to swim back," she said coolly. "If you do I'm going to start writing dime novels founded on that interminable history of your life you gave me last night."

He flushed and stiffened slightly.

"I'm very sorry I bored you."

"Oh, you didn't—until just at the end with some story about how furious you were because you couldn't dance with the ladies you played music for."

He rose angrily.

"You have got a darn mean little tongue."

"Excuse me," she said melting into laughter, "but I'm not used to having men regale me with the story of their life ambitions—especially if they've lived such deathly platonic lives."

"Why? What do men usually regale you with?"

"Oh, they talk about me," she yawned. "They tell me I'm the spirit of youth and beauty."

"What do you tell them?"

"Oh, I agree quietly."

"Does every man you meet tell you he loves you?"

Ardita nodded.

"Why shouldn't he? All life is just a progression toward, and then a recession from, one phrase—'I love you.'"

Carlyle laughed and sat down.

"That's very true. That's—that's not bad. Did you make

that up?"

"Yes—or rather I found it out. It doesn't mean anything especially. It's just clever."

"It's the sort of remark," he said gravely, "that's typical of your class."

"Oh," she interrupted impatiently, "don't start that lecture on aristocracy again! I distrust people who can be intense at this hour in the morning. It's a mild form of insanity—a sort of breakfast-food jag. Morning's the time to sleep, swim, and be careless."

Ten minutes later they had swung round in a wide circle as if to approach the island from the north.

"There's a trick somewhere," commented Ardita thoughtfully. "He can't mean just to anchor up against this cliff."

They were heading straight in now toward the solid rock, which must have been well over a hundred feet tall, and not until they were within fifty yards of it did Ardita see their objective. Then she clapped her hands in delight. There was a break in the cliff entirely hidden by a curious overlapping of rock, and through this break the yacht entered and very slowly traversed a narrow channel of crystal-clear water between high gray walls. Then they were riding at anchor in a miniature world of green and gold, a gilded bay smooth as glass and set round with tiny palms, the whole resembling the mirror lakes and twig trees that children set up in sand piles.

"Not so darned bad!" cried Carlyle excitedly.

"I guess that little coon knows his way round this corner of the Atlantic."

His exuberance was contagious, and Ardita became quite jubilant.

"It's an absolutely sure-fire hiding-place!"

"Lordy, yes! It's the sort of island you read about."

The rowboat was lowered into the golden lake and they

pulled to shore.

"Come on," said Carlyle as they landed in the slushy sand, "we'll go exploring."

The fringe of palms was in turn ringed in by a round mile of flat, sandy country. They followed it south and brushing through a farther rim of tropical vegetation came out on a pearl-gray virgin beach where Ardita kicked of her brown golf shoes—she seemed to have permanently abandoned stockings—and went wading. Then they sauntered back to the yacht, where the indefatigable Babe had luncheon ready for them. He had posted a lookout on the high cliff to the north to watch the sea on both sides, though he doubted if the entrance to the cliff was generally known—he had never even seen a map on which the island was marked.

"What's its name," asked Ardita—"the island, I mean?"

"No name 'tall," chuckled Babe. "Reckin she jus' island, 'at's all."

In the late afternoon they sat with their backs against great boulders on the highest part of the cliff and Carlyle sketched for her his vague plans. He was sure they were hot after him by this time. The total proceeds of the coup he had pulled off and concerning which he still refused to enlighten her, he estimated as just under a million dollars. He counted on lying up here several weeks and then setting off southward, keeping well outside the usual channels of travel rounding the Horn and heading for Callao, in Peru. The details of coaling and provisioning he was leaving entirely to Babe who, it seemed, had sailed these seas in every capacity from cabin-boy aboard a coffee trader to virtual first mate on a Brazillian pirate craft, whose skipper had long since been hung.

"If he'd been white he'd have been king of South America long ago," said Carlyle emphatically. "When it comes to intelligence he makes Booker T. Washington look like a moron. He's got the guile of every race and nationality whose blood is in his veins, and that's half a dozen or I'm a liar. He worships me because I'm the only man in the world who can play better ragtime than he can. We used to sit together on the wharfs down on the New York water-front, he with a bassoon and me with an oboe, and we'd blend minor keys in African harmonics a thousand years old until the rats would crawl up the posts and sit round groaning and squeaking like dogs will in front of a phonograph."

Ardita roared.

"How you can tell 'em!"

Carlyle grinned.

"I swear that's the gos——"

"What you going to do when you get to Callao?" she interrupted.

"Take ship for India. I want to be a rajah. I mean it. My idea is to go up into Afghanistan somewhere, buy up a palace and a reputation, and then after about five years appear in England with a foreign accent and a mysterious past. But India first. Do you know, they say that all the gold in the world drifts very gradually back to India. Something fascinating about that to me. And I want leisure to read—an immense amount."

"How about after that?"

"Then," he answered defiantly, "comes aristocracy. Laugh if you want to—but at least you'll have to admit that I know what I want—which I imagine is more than you do."

"On the contrary," contradicted Ardita, reaching in her pocket for her cigarette case, "when I met you I was in the midst of a great uproar of all my friends and relatives because I did know what I wanted."

"What was it?"

"A man."

He started.

"You mean you were engaged?"

"After a fashion. If you hadn't come aboard I had every intention of slipping ashore yesterday evening—how long ago it seems—and meeting him in Palm Beach. He's waiting there for me with a bracelet that once belonged to Catherine of Russia. Now don't mutter anything about aristocracy," she put in quickly. "I liked him simply because he had had an imagination and the utter courage of his convictions."

"But your family disapproved, eh?"

"What there is of it—only a silly uncle and a sillier aunt. It seems he got into some scandal with a red-haired woman name Mimi something—it was frightfully exaggerated, he said, and men don't lie to me—and anyway I didn't care what he'd done; it was the future that counted. And I'd see to that. When a man's in love with me he doesn't care for other amusements. I told him to drop her like a hot cake, and he did."

"I feel rather jealous," said Carlyle, frowning—and then he laughed. "I guess I'll just keep you along with us until we get to Callao. Then I'll lend you enough money to get back to the States. By that time you'll have had a chance to think that gentleman over a little more."

"Don't talk to me like that!" fired up Ardita. "I won't tolerate the parental attitude from anybody! Do you understand me?" He chuckled and then stopped, rather abashed, as her cold anger seemed to fold him about and chill him.

"I'm sorry," he offered uncertainly.

"Oh, don't apologize! I can't stand men who say 'I'm sorry' in that manly, reserved tone. Just shut up!"

A pause ensued, a pause which Carlyle found rather awkward, but which Ardita seemed not to notice at all as she sat contentedly enjoying her cigarette and gazing out at the shining sea. After a minute she crawled out on the rock and lay with her face over the edge looking down. Carlyle, watching her, reflected how it seemed impossible for her to assume an ungraceful attitude.

"Oh, look," she cried. "There's a lot of sort of ledges down there. Wide ones of all different heights."

"We'll go swimming to-night!" she said excitedly. "By moonlight."

"Wouldn't you rather go in at the beach on the other end?"

"Not a chance. I like to dive. You can use my uncle's bathing suit, only it'll fit you like a gunny sack, because he's a very flabby man. I've got a one-piece that's shocked the natives all along the Atlantic coast from Biddeford Pool to St. Augustine."

"I suppose you're a shark."

"Yes, I'm pretty good. And I look cute too. A sculptor up at Rye last summer told me my calves are worth five hundred dollars."

There didn't seem to be any answer to this, so Carlyle was silent, permitting himself only a discreet interior smile.

V

When the night crept down in shadowy blue and silver they threaded the shimmering channel in the rowboat and, tying it to a jutting rock, began climbing the cliff together. The first shelf was ten feet up, wide, and furnishing a natural diving platform. There they sat down in the bright moonlight and watched the faint incessant surge of the waters almost stilled now as the tide set seaward.

"Are you happy?" he asked suddenly.

She nodded.

"Always happy near the sea. You know," she went on, "I've been thinking all day that you and I are somewhat alike. We're both rebels—only for different reasons. Two years ago, when I was just eighteen and you were——"

"Twenty-five."

"——well, we were both conventional successes. I was an utterly devastating débutante and you were a prosperous musician just commissioned in the army——"

"Gentleman by act of Congress," he put in ironically.

"Well, at any rate, we both fitted. If our corners were not rubbed off they were at least pulled in. But deep in us both was something that made us require more for happiness. I didn't know what I wanted. I went from man to man, restless, impatient, month by month getting less acquiescent and more dissatisfied. I used to sit sometimes chewing at the insides of my mouth and thinking I was going crazy—I had a frightful sense of transiency. I wanted things now—now—now! Here I was—beautiful—I am, aren't I?"

"Yes," agreed Carlyle tentatively.

Ardita rose suddenly.

"Wait a second. I want to try this delightful-looking sea."

She walked to the end of the ledge and shot out over the sea, doubling up in mid-air and then straightening out and entering to water straight as a blade in a perfect jack-knife dive.

In a minute her voice floated up to him.

"You see, I used to read all day and most of the night. I began to resent society——"

"Come on up here," he interrupted. "What on earth are you doing?"

"Just floating round on my back. I'll be up in a minute. Let me tell you. The only thing I enjoyed was shocking people; wearing something quite impossible and quite charming to a fancy-dress party, going round with the fastest men in New York, and getting into some of the most hellish scrapes imaginable."

The sounds of splashing mingled with her words, and then he heard her hurried breathing as she began climbing up side to the ledge.

"Go on in!" she called

Obediently he rose and dived. When he emerged, dripping, and made the climb he found that she was no longer on the ledge, but after a second frightened he heard her light laughter from another shelf ten feet up. There he joined her and they both sat quietly for a moment, their arms clasped round their knees, panting a little from the climb.

"The family were wild," she said suddenly. "They tried to marry me off. And then when I'd begun to feel that after all life was scarcely worth living I found something"—her eyes went skyward exultantly——"I found something!"

Carlyle waited and her words came with a rush.

"Courage—just that; courage as a rule of life, and something to cling to always. I began to build up this enormous faith in myself. I began to see that in all my idols in the past some manifestation of courage had unconsciously been the thing that attracted me. I began separating courage from the other things of life. All sorts of courage—the beaten, bloody prize-fighter coming up for more—I used to make men take me to prize-fights; the déclassé woman sailing through a nest of cats and looking at them as if they were mud under her feet; the liking what you like always; the utter disregard for other people's opinions—just to live as I liked always and to die in my own way— Did you bring up the cigarettes?"

He handed one over and held a match for her gently.

"Still," Ardita continued, "the men kept gathering—old men and young men, my mental and physical inferiors, most of them, but all intensely desiring to have me—to own this rather magnificent proud tradition I'd built up round me. Do you see?"

"Sort of. You never were beaten and you never apologized."

"Never!"

She sprang to the edge, poised for a moment like a crucified figure against the sky; then describing a dark parabola plunked without a slash between two silver ripples twenty feet below.

Her voice floated up to him again.

"And courage to me meant ploughing through that dull gray mist that comes down on life—not only overriding people and circumstances but overriding the bleakness of living. A sort of insistence on the value of life and the worth of transient things."

She was climbing up now, and at her last words her head, with the damp yellow hair slicked symmetrically back appeared on his level.

"All very well," objected Carlyle. "You can call it courage, but your courage is really built, after all, on a pride of birth. You were bred to that defiant attitude. On my gray days even courage is one of the things that's gray and lifeless."

She was sitting near the edge, hugging her knees and gazing abstractedly at the white moon; he was farther back, crammed like a grotesque god into a niche in the rock.

"I don't want to sound like Pollyanna," she began, "but you haven't grasped me yet. My courage is faith—faith in the eternal resilience of me—that joy'll come back, and hope and spontaneity. And I feel that till it does I've got to keep my lips shut and my chin high, and my eyes wide—not necessarily any silly smiling. Oh, I've been through hell without a whine quite often—and the female hell is deadlier than the male."

"But supposing," suggested Carlyle, "that before joy and hope and all that came back the curtain was drawn on you for good?"

Ardita rose, and going to the wall climbed with some difficulty to the next ledge, another ten or fifteen feet above.

"Why," she called back "then I'd have won!"

He edged out till he could see her.

"Better not dive from there! You'll break your back," he said quickly.

She laughed.

"Not I!"

Slowly she spread her arms and stood there swan-like, radiating a pride in her young perfection that lit a warm glow in Carlyle's heart.

"We're going through the black air with our arms wide and our feet straight out behind like a dolphin's tail, and we're going to think we'll never hit the silver down there till suddenly it'll be all warm round us and full of little kissing, caressing waves."

Then she was in the air, and Carlyle involuntarily held his breath. He had not realized that the dive was nearly forty feet. It seemed an eternity before he heard the swift compact sound as she reached the sea.

And it was with his glad sigh of relief when her light watery laughter curled up the side of the cliff and into his anxious ears that he knew he loved her.

VI

Time, having no axe to grind, showered down upon them three days of afternoons. When the sun cleared the port-hole of Ardita's cabin an hour after dawn she rose cheerily, donned her bathing-suit, and went up on deck. The negroes would leave their work when they saw her, and crowd, chuckling and chattering, to the rail as she floated, an agile minnow, on and under the surface of the clear water. Again in the cool of the afternoon she would swim—and loll and smoke with Carlyle upon the cliff; or else they would lie on their sides in the sands of the southern beach, talking little, but watching the day fade colorfully and tragically into the infinite langour of a tropical evening.

And with the long, sunny hours Ardita's idea of the episode as incidental, madcap, a sprig of romance in a desert of reality, gradually left her. She dreaded the time when he would strike off southward; she dreaded all the eventualities that presented themselves to her; thoughts were suddenly troublesome and decisions odious. Had prayers found place in the pagan rituals of her soul she would have asked of life only to be unmolested for a while, lazily acquiescent to the ready, naïf flow of Carlyle's ideas, his vivid boyish imagination, and the vein of monomania that seemed to run crosswise through his temperament and colored his every action.

But this is not a story of two on an island, nor concerned primarily with love bred of isolation. It is merely the presentation of two personalities, and its idyllic setting among the palms of the Gulf Stream is quite incidental. Most of us are content to exist and breed and fight for the right to do both, and the dominant idea, the foredoomed attest to control one's destiny, is reserved for the fortunate or unfortunate few. To me the interesting thing about Ardita is the courage that will tarnish with her beauty and youth.

"Take me with you," she said late one night as they sat lazily in the grass under the shadowy spreading palms. The negroes had brought ashore their musical instruments, and the sound of weird ragtime was drifting softly over on the warm breath of the night. "I'd love to reappear in ten years, as a fabulously wealthy high-caste

Indian lady," she continued.
Carlyle looked at her quickly.
"You can, you know."
She laughed.
"Is it a proposal of marriage? Extra! Ardita Farnam becomes pirate's bride. Society girl kidnapped by ragtime bank robber."
"It wasn't a bank."
"What was it? Why won't you tell me?"
"I don't want to break down your illusions."
"My dear man, I have no illusions about you."
"I mean your illusions about yourself."
She looked up in surprise.
"About myself! What on earth have I got to do with whatever stray felonies you've committed?"
"That remains to be seen."
She reached over and patted his hand.
"Dear Mr. Curtis Carlyle," she said softly, "are you in love with me?"
"As if it mattered."
"But it does—because I think I'm in love with you."
He looked at her ironically.
"Thus swelling your January total to half a dozen," he suggested. "Suppose I call your bluff and ask you to come to India with me?"
"Shall I?"
He shrugged his shoulders.
"We can get married in Callao."
"What sort of life can you offer me? I don't mean that unkindly, but seriously; what would become of me if the people who want that twenty-thousand-dollar reward ever catch up with you?"
"I thought you weren't afraid."
"I never am—but I won't throw my life away just to show one man I'm not."

"I wish you'd been poor. Just a little poor girl dreaming over a fence in a warm cow country."

"Wouldn't it have been nice?"

"I'd have enjoyed astonishing you—watching your eyes open on things. If you only wanted things! Don't you see?"

"I know—like girls who stare into the windows of jewelry-stores."

"Yes—and want the big oblong watch that's platinum and has diamonds all round the edge. Only you'd decide it was too expensive and choose one of white gold for a hundred dollar. Then I'd say: 'Expensive? I should say not!' And we'd go into the store and pretty soon the platinum one would be gleaming on your wrist."

"That sounds so nice and vulgar—and fun, doesn't it?" murmured Ardita.

"Doesn't it? Can't you see us travelling round and spending money right and left, and being worshipped by bell-boys and waiters? Oh, blessed are the simple rich for they inherit the earth!"

"I honestly wish we were that way."

"I love you, Ardita," he said gently.

Her face lost its childish look for moment and became oddly grave.

"I love to be with you," she said, "more than with any man I've ever met. And I like your looks and your dark old hair, and the way you go over the side of the rail when we come ashore. In fact, Curtis Carlyle, I like all the things you do when you're perfectly natural. I think you've got nerve and you know how I feel about that. Sometimes when you're around I've been tempted to kiss you suddenly and tell you that you were just an idealistic boy with a lot of caste nonsense in his head. Perhaps if I were just a little bit older and a little more bored I'd go with you. As it is, I think I'll go back and marry—that other man."

Over across the silver lake the figures of the negroes writhed and squirmed in the moonlight like acrobats who, having been too long inactive, must go through their tacks from sheer surplus energy. In single file they marched, weaving in concentric circles, now with their heads thrown back, now bent over their instruments like piping fauns. And from trombone and saxaphone ceaselessly whined a blended melody, sometimes riotous and jubilant, sometimes haunting and plaintive as a death-dance from the Congo's heart.

"Let's dance," cried Ardita. "I can't sit still with that perfect jazz going on."

Taking her hand he led her out into a broad stretch of hard sandy soil that the moon flooded with great splendor. They floated out like drifting moths under the rich hazy light, and as the fantastic symphony wept and exulted and wavered and despaired Ardita's last sense of reality dropped away, and she abandoned her imagination to the dreamy summer scents of tropical flowers and the infinite starry spaces overhead, feeling that if she opened her eyes it would be to find herself dancing with a ghost in a land created by her own fancy.

"This is what I should call an exclusive private dance," he whispered.

"I feel quite mad—but delightfully mad!"

"We're enchanted. The shades of unnumbered generations of cannibals are watching us from high up on the side of the cliff there."

"And I'll bet the cannibal women are saying that we dance too close, and that it was immodest of me to come without my nose-ring."

They both laughed softly—and then their laughter died as over across the lake they heard the trombones stop in the middle of a bar, and the saxaphones give a startled moan and fade out.

"What's the matter?" called Carlyle.

After a moment's silence they made out the dark figure of a man rounding the silver lake at a run. As he came closer they saw it was Babe in a state of unusual excitement. He drew up before them and gasped out his news in a breath.

"Ship stan'in' off sho' 'bout half a mile suh. Mose, he uz on watch, he say look's if she's done ancho'd."

"A ship—what kind of a ship?" demanded Carlyle anxiously.

Dismay was in his voice, and Ardita's heart gave a sudden wrench as she saw his whole face suddenly droop.

"He say he don't know, suh."

"Are they landing a boat?"

"No, suh."

"We'll go up," said Carlyle.

They ascended the hill in silence, Ardita's hand still resting in Carlyle's as it had when they finished dancing. She felt it clinch nervously from time to time as though he were unaware of the contact, but though he hurt her she made no attempt to remove it. It seemed an hour's climb before they reached the top and crept cautiously across the silhouetted plateau to the edge of the cliff. After one short look Carlyle involuntarily gave a little cry. It was a revenue boat with six-inch guns mounted fore and aft.

"They know!" he said with a short intake of breath. "They know! They picked up the trail somewhere."

"Are you sure they know about the channel? They may be only standing by to take a look at the island in the morning. From where they are they couldn't see the opening in the cliff."

"They could with field-glasses," he said hopelessly. He

looked at his wrist-watch. "It's nearly two now. They won't do anything until dawn, that's certain. Of course there's always the faint possibility that they're waiting for some other ship to join; or for a coaler."

"I suppose we may as well stay right here."

The hour passed and they lay there side by side, very silently, their chins in their hands like dreaming children. In back of them squatted the negroes, patient, resigned, acquiescent, announcing now and then with sonorous snores that not even the presence of danger could subdue their unconquerable African craving for sleep.

Just before five o'clock Babe approached Carlyle. There were half a dozen rifles aboard the Narcissus he said. Had it been decided to offer no resistance?

A pretty good fight might be made, he thought, if they worked out some plan.

Carlyle laughed and shook his head.

"That isn't a Spic army out there, Babe. That's a revenue boat. It'd be like a bow and arrow trying to fight a machine-gun. If you want to bury those bags somewhere and take a chance on recovering them later, go on and do it. But it won't work—they'd dig this island over from one end to the other. It's a lost battle all round, Babe."

Babe inclined his head silently and turned away, and Carlyle's voice was husky as he turned to Ardita.

"There's the best friend I ever had. He'd die for me, and be proud to, if I'd let him."

"You've given up?"

"I've no choice. Of course there's always one way out—the sure way—but that can wait. I wouldn't miss my trial for anything—it'll be an interesting experiment in notoriety. 'Miss Farnam testifies that the pirate's attitude to her was at all times that of a gentleman.'"

"Don't!" she said. "I'm awfully sorry."

When the color faded from the sky and lustreless blue changed to leaden gray a commotion was visible on the ship's deck, and they made out a group of officers clad in white duck, gathered near the rail. They had field-glasses in their hands and were attentively examining the islet.

"It's all up," said Carlyle grimly.

"Damn," whispered Ardita. She felt tears gathering in her eyes "We'll go back to the yacht," he said. "I prefer that to being hunted out up here like a 'possum."

Leaving the plateau they descended the hill, and reaching the lake were rowed out to the yacht by the silent negroes. Then, pale and weary, they sank into the settees and waited.

Half an hour later in the dim gray light the nose of the revenue boat appeared in the channel and stopped, evidently fearing that the bay might be too shallow. From the peaceful look of the yacht, the man and the girl in the settees, and the negroes lounging curiously against the rail, they evidently judged that there would be no resistance, for two boats were lowered casually over the side, one containing an officer and six bluejackets, and the other, four rowers and in the stern two gray-haired men in yachting flannels. Ardita and Carlyle stood up, and half unconsciously started toward each other.

Then he paused and putting his hand suddenly into his pocket he pulled out a round, glittering object and held it out to her.

"What is it?" she asked wonderingly.

"I'm not positive, but I think from the Russian inscription inside that it's your promised bracelet."

"Where—where on earth——"

"It came out of one of those bags. You see, Curtis Carlyle and his Six Black Buddies, in the middle of their performance in the tea-room of the hotel at Palm Beach, suddenly changed their instruments for automatics and held up the crowd. I took this bracelet from a pretty, overrouged woman with red hair."

Ardita frowned and then smiled.

"So that's what you did! You have got nerve!"

He bowed.

"A well-known bourgeois quality," he said.

And then dawn slanted dynamically across the deck and flung the shadows reeling into gray corners. The dew rose and turned to golden mist, thin as a dream, enveloping them until they seemed gossamer relics of the late night, infinitely transient and already fading. For a moment sea and sky were breathless, and dawn held a pink hand over the young mouth of life—then from out in the lake came the complaint of a rowboat and the swish of oars.

Suddenly against the golden furnace low in the east their two graceful figures melted into one, and he was kissing her spoiled young mouth.

"It's a sort of glory," he murmured after a second.

She smiled up at him.

"Happy, are you?"

Her sigh was a benediction—an ecstatic surety that she was youth and beauty now as much as she would ever know. For another instant life was radiant and time a phantom and their strength eternal—then there was a bumping, scraping sound as the rowboat scraped alongside.

Up the ladder scrambled the two gray-haired men, the officer and two of the sailors with their hands on their revolvers. Mr. Farnam folded his arms and stood looking at his niece.

"So," he said nodding his head slowly.

With a sigh her arms unwound from Carlyle's neck, and her eyes, transfigured and far away, fell upon the boarding party. Her uncle saw her upper lip slowly swell into that arrogant pout he knew so well.

"So," he repeated savagely. "So this is your idea of—of romance. A runaway affair, with a high-seas pirate."

Ardita glanced at him carelessly.

"What an old fool you are!" she said quietly.

"Is that the best you can say for yourself?"

"No," she said as if considering. "No, there's something else. There's that well-known phrase with which I have ended most of our conversations for the past few years—'Shut up!'"

And with that she turned, included the two old men, the officer, and the two sailors in a curt glance of contempt, and walked proudly down the companionway.

But had she waited an instant longer she would have heard a sound from her uncle quite unfamiliar in most of their interviews. He gave vent to a whole-hearted amused chuckle, in which the second old man joined.

The latter turned briskly to Carlyle, who had been regarding this scene with an air of cryptic amusement.

"Well Toby," he said genially, "you incurable, hare-brained romantic chaser of rainbows, did you find that she was the person you wanted?"

Carlyle smiled confidently.

"Why—naturally," he said "I've been perfectly sure ever since I first heard tell of her wild career. That'd why I had Babe send up the rocket last night."

"I'm glad you did," said Colonel Moreland gravely. "We've been keeping pretty close to you in case you should have trouble with those six strange niggers. And we hoped we'd find you two in some such compromising position," he sighed. "Well, set a crank to catch a crank!"

"Your father and I sat up all night hoping for the best—or perhaps it's the worst. Lord knows you're welcome to her, my boy. She's run me crazy. Did you give her the

Russian bracelet my detective got from that Mimi woman?"

Carlyle nodded.

"Sh!" he said. "She's coming on deck."

Ardita appeared at the head of the companionway and gave a quick involuntary glance at Carlyle's wrists. A puzzled look passed across her face. Back aft the negroes had begun to sing, and the cool lake, fresh with dawn, echoed serenely to their low voices.

"Ardita," said Carlyle unsteadily.

She swayed a step toward him.

"Ardita," he repeated breathlessly, "I've got to tell you the—the truth. It was all a plant, Ardita. My name isn't Carlyle. It's Moreland, Toby Moreland. The story was invented, Ardita, invented out of thin Florida air."

She stared at him, bewildered, amazement, disbelief, and anger flowing in quick waves across her face. The three men held their breaths. Moreland, Senior, took a step toward her; Mr. Farnam's mouth dropped a little open as he waited, panic-stricken, for the expected crash.

But it did not come. Ardita's face became suddenly radiant, and with a little laugh she went swiftly to young Moreland and looked up at him without a trace of wrath in her gray eyes.

"Will you swear," she said quietly "That it was entirely a product of your own brain?"

"I swear," said young Moreland eagerly.

She drew his head down and kissed him gently.

"What an imagination!" she said softly and almost enviously. "I want you to lie to me just as sweetly as you know how for the rest of my life."

The negroes' voices floated drowsily back, mingled in an air that she had heard them singing before.

"Time is a thief;
Gladness and grief

Cling to the leaf
As it yellows——"

"What was in the bags?" she asked softly.

"Florida mud," he answered. "That was one of the two true things I told you."

"Perhaps I can guess the other one," she said; and reaching up on her tiptoes she kissed him softly in the illustration.

The Happy Prince

Oscar Wilde

High above the city, on a tall column, stood the statue of the Happy Prince. He was gilded all over with thin leaves of fine gold, for eyes he had two bright sapphires, and a large red ruby glowed on his sword-hilt.

He was very much admired indeed. "He is as beautiful as a weathercock," remarked one of the Town Councillors who wished to gain a reputation for having artistic tastes; "only not quite so useful," he added, fearing lest people should think him unpractical, which he really was not.

"Why can't you be like the Happy Prince?" asked a sensible mother of her little boy who was crying for the moon. "The Happy Prince never dreams of crying for anything."

"I am glad there is some one in the world who is quite happy," muttered a disappointed man as he gazed at the wonderful statue.

"He looks just like an angel," said the Charity Children as they came out of the cathedral in their bright scarlet cloaks and their clean white pinafores.

"How do you know?" said the Mathematical Master, "you have never seen one."

"Ah! but we have, in our dreams," answered the children; and the Mathematical Master frowned and looked very severe, for he did not approve of children dreaming.

One night there flew over the city a little Swallow. His friends had gone away to Egypt six weeks before, but he had stayed behind, for he was in love with the most beautiful Reed. He had met her early in the spring as he was flying down the river after a big yellow moth, and had been so attracted by her slender waist that he had stopped to talk to her.

"Shall I love you?" said the Swallow, who liked to come to the point at once, and the Reed made him a low bow. So he flew round and round her, touching the water with his wings, and making silver ripples. This was his courtship, and it lasted all through the summer.

"It is a ridiculous attachment," twittered the other Swallows; "she has no money, and far too many relations"; and indeed the river was quite full of Reeds. Then, when the autumn came they all flew away.

After they had gone he felt lonely, and began to tire of his lady-love. "She has no conversation," he said, "and I am afraid that she is a coquette, for she is always flirting with the wind." And certainly, whenever the wind blew, the Reed made the most graceful curtseys. "I admit that she is domestic," he continued, "but I love travelling, and my wife, consequently, should love travelling also." "Will you come away with me?" he said finally to her; but the Reed shook her head, she was so attached to her home.

"You have been trifling with me," he cried. "I am off to the Pyramids. Good-bye!" and he flew away.

All day long he flew, and at night-time he arrived at the city. "Where shall I put up?" he said; "I hope the town has made preparations."

Then he saw the statue on the tall column.

"I will put up there," he cried; "it is a fine position, with plenty of fresh air." So he alighted just between the feet of the Happy Prince.

"I have a golden bedroom," he said softly to himself as he looked round, and he prepared to go to sleep; but just as he was putting his head under his wing a large drop of water fell on him. "What a curious thing!" he cried; "there is not a single cloud in the sky, the stars are quite clear and bright, and yet it is raining. The climate in the north of Europe is really dreadful. The Reed used to like the rain, but that was merely her selfishness." Then another drop fell.

"What is the use of a statue if it cannot keep the rain off?" he said; "I must look for a good chimney-pot," and he determined to fly away.

But before he had opened his wings, a third drop fell, and he looked up, and saw—Ah! what did he see?

The eyes of the Happy Prince were filled with tears, and tears were running down his golden cheeks. His face was so beautiful in the moonlight that the little Swallow was filled with pity.

"Who are you?" he said.

"I am the Happy Prince."

"Why are you weeping then?" asked the Swallow; "you have quite drenched me."

"When I was alive and had a human heart," answered the statue, "I did not know what tears were, for I lived in the Palace of Sans-Souci, where sorrow is not allowed to enter. In the daytime I played with my companions in the garden, and in the evening I led the dance in the Great Hall. Round the garden ran a very lofty wall, but I never cared to ask what lay beyond it, everything about me was so beautiful. My courtiers called me the Happy Prince, and happy indeed I was, if pleasure be happiness. So I lived, and so I died. And now that I am dead they have set me up here so high that I can see all the ugliness and all the misery of my city, and though my heart is made of lead yet I cannot chose but weep." "What! is he not solid gold?" said the Swallow to himself. He was too polite to make any personal remarks out loud.

"Far away," continued the statue in a low musical voice, "far away in a little street there is a poor house. One of the windows is open, and through it I can see a woman seated at a table. Her face is thin and worn, and she has coarse, red hands, all pricked by the needle, for she is a seamstress. She is embroidering passion-flowers on a satin gown for the loveliest of the Queen's maids-of-honour to wear at the next Court-ball. In a bed in the corner of the room her little boy is lying ill. He has a fever, and is asking for oranges. His mother has nothing to give him but river water, so he is crying. Swallow, Swallow, little Swallow, will you not bring her the ruby out of my sword-hilt? My feet are fastened to this pedestal and I cannot move." "I am waited for in Egypt," said the Swallow. "My friends are flying up and down the Nile, and talking to the large lotus-flowers. Soon they will go to sleep in the tomb of the great King. The King is there himself in his painted coffin. He is wrapped in yellow linen, and embalmed with spices. Round his neck is a chain of pale green jade, and his hands are like withered leaves." "Swallow, Swallow, little Swallow," said the Prince, "will you not stay with me for one night, and be my messenger? The boy is so thirsty, and the mother so sad."

"I don't think I like boys," answered the Swallow. "Last summer, when I was staying on the river, there were two rude boys, the miller's sons, who were always throwing stones at me. They never hit me, of course; we swallows fly far too well for that, and besides, I come of a family famous for its agility; but still, it was a mark of disrespect." But the Happy Prince looked so sad that the little Swallow was sorry. "It is very cold here," he said; "but I will stay with you for one night, and be your messenger."

"Thank you, little Swallow," said the Prince.

So the Swallow picked out the great ruby from the Prince's sword, and flew away with it in his beak over the roofs of the town.

He passed by the cathedral tower, where the white marble angels were sculptured. He passed by the palace and heard the sound of dancing. A beautiful girl came out on the balcony with her lover. "How wonderful the stars are," he said to her, "and how wonderful is the power of love!" "I hope my dress will be ready in time for the State-ball," she answered; "I have ordered passion-flowers to be embroidered on it; but the seamstresses are so lazy."

He passed over the river, and saw the lanterns hanging to the masts of the ships. He passed over the Ghetto, and saw the old Jews bargaining with each other, and weighing out money in copper scales. At last he came to the poor house and looked in. The boy was tossing feverishly on his bed, and the mother had fallen asleep, she was so tired. In he hopped, and laid the great ruby on the table beside the woman's thimble. Then he flew gently round the bed, fanning the boy's forehead with his wings. "How cool I feel," said the boy, "I must be getting better"; and he sank into a delicious slumber.

Then the Swallow flew back to the Happy Prince, and told him what he had done. "It is curious," he remarked, "but I feel quite warm now, although it is so cold."

"That is because you have done a good action," said the Prince. And the little Swallow began to think, and then he fell asleep. Thinking always made him sleepy.

When day broke he flew down to the river and had a bath. "What a remarkable phenomenon," said the Professor of Ornithology as he was passing over the bridge. "A swallow in winter!" And he wrote a long letter about it to the local newspaper. Every one quoted it, it was full of so many words that they could not understand.

"To-night I go to Egypt," said the Swallow, and he was in high spirits at the prospect. He visited all the public monuments, and sat a long time on top of the church steeple. Wherever he went the Sparrows chirruped, and said to each other, "What a distinguished stranger!" so he enjoyed himself very much.

When the moon rose he flew back to the Happy Prince. "Have you any commissions for Egypt?" he cried; "I am just starting."

"Swallow, Swallow, little Swallow," said the Prince, "will you not stay with me one night longer?"

"I am waited for in Egypt," answered the Swallow. "To-morrow my friends will fly up to the Second Cataract. The river-horse couches there among the bulrushes, and on a great granite throne sits the God Memnon. All night long he watches the stars, and when the morning star shines he utters one cry of joy, and then he is silent. At noon the yellow lions come down to the water's edge to drink. They have eyes like green beryls, and their roar is louder than the roar of the cataract." "Swallow, Swallow, little Swallow," said the Prince, "far away across the city I see a young man in a garret. He is leaning over a desk covered with papers, and in a tumbler by his side there is a bunch of withered violets. His hair is brown and crisp, and his lips are red as a pomegranate, and he has large and dreamy eyes. He is trying to finish a play for the Director of the Theatre, but he is too cold to write any more. There is no fire in the grate, and hunger has made him faint." "I will wait with you one night longer," said the Swallow, who really had a good heart. "Shall I take him another ruby?"

"Alas! I have no ruby now," said the Prince; "my eyes are all that I have left. They are made of rare sapphires, which were brought out of India a thousand years ago. Pluck out one of them and take it to him. He will sell it to the jeweller, and buy food and firewood, and finish his play." "Dear Prince," said the Swallow, "I cannot do that"; and he began to weep.

"Swallow, Swallow, little Swallow," said the Prince, "do as I command you."

So the Swallow plucked out the Prince's eye, and flew away to the student's garret. It was easy enough to get in, as there was a hole in the roof. Through this he darted, and came into the room. The young man had his head buried in his hands, so he did not hear the flutter of the bird's wings, and when he looked up he found the beautiful sapphire lying on the withered violets.

"I am beginning to be appreciated," he cried; "this is from some great admirer. Now I can finish my play," and he looked quite happy.

The next day the Swallow flew down to the harbour. He sat on the mast of a large vessel and watched the sailors hauling big chests out of the hold with ropes. "Heave a-hoy!" they shouted as each chest came up. "I am going to Egypt"! cried the Swallow, but nobody minded, and when the moon rose he flew back to the Happy Prince.

"I am come to bid you good-bye," he cried.

"Swallow, Swallow, little Swallow," said the Prince, "will you not stay with me one night longer?"

"It is winter," answered the Swallow, "and the chill snow will soon be here. In Egypt the sun is warm on the green palm-trees, and the crocodiles lie in the mud and look lazily about them. My companions are building a nest in the Temple of Baalbec, and the pink and white doves are watching them, and cooing to each other. Dear Prince, I must leave you, but I will never forget you, and next spring I will bring you back two beautiful jewels in place of those you have given away. The ruby shall be redder than a red rose, and the sapphire shall be as blue as the great sea." "In the square below," said the Happy Prince, "there stands a little match-girl. She has let her matches fall in the gutter, and they are all spoiled. Her father will beat her if she does not bring home some money, and she is crying. She has no shoes or stockings, and her little head is bare. Pluck out my other eye, and give it to her, and her father will not beat her." "I will stay with you one night longer," said the Swallow, "but I cannot pluck out your eye. You would be quite blind then."

"Swallow, Swallow, little Swallow," said the Prince, "do as I command you."

So he plucked out the Prince's other eye, and darted down with it. He swooped past the match-girl, and slipped the jewel into the palm of her hand. "What a lovely bit of glass," cried the little girl; and she ran home, laughing.

Then the Swallow came back to the Prince. "You are blind now," he said, "so I will stay with you always."

"No, little Swallow," said the poor Prince, "you must go away to Egypt."

"I will stay with you always," said the Swallow, and he slept at the Prince's feet.

All the next day he sat on the Prince's shoulder, and told him stories of what he had seen in strange lands. He told him of the red ibises, who stand in long rows on the banks of the Nile, and catch gold-fish in their beaks; of the Sphinx, who is as old as the world itself, and lives in the desert, and knows everything; of the merchants, who walk slowly by the side of their camels, and carry amber beads in their hands; of the King of the Mountains of the Moon, who is as black as ebony, and worships a large crystal; of the great green snake that sleeps in a palm-tree, and has twenty priests to feed it with honey-cakes; and of the pygmies who sail over a big lake on large flat leaves, and are always at war with the butterflies.

"Dear little Swallow," said the Prince, "you tell me of marvellous things, but more marvellous than anything is the suffering of men and of women. There is no Mystery so great as Misery. Fly over my city, little Swallow, and tell me what you see there." So the Swallow flew over the great city, and saw the rich making merry in their beautiful houses, while the beggars were sitting at the gates. He flew into dark lanes, and saw the white faces of starving children looking out listlessly at the black streets. Under the archway of a bridge two little boys were lying in one another's arms to try and keep themselves warm. "How hungry we are!" they said. "You must not lie here," shouted the Watchman, and they wandered out into the rain.

Then he flew back and told the Prince what he had seen.

"I am covered with fine gold," said the Prince, "you must take it off, leaf by leaf, and give it to my poor; the living always think that gold can make them happy."

Leaf after leaf of the fine gold the Swallow picked off, till the Happy Prince looked quite dull and grey. Leaf after leaf of the fine gold he brought to the poor, and the children's faces grew rosier, and they laughed and played games in the street. "We have bread now!" they cried.

Then the snow came, and after the snow came the frost. The streets looked as if they were made of silver, they were so bright and glistening; long icicles like crystal daggers hung down from the eaves of the houses, everybody went about in furs, and the little boys wore scarlet caps and skated on the ice.

The poor little Swallow grew colder and colder, but he would not leave the Prince, he loved him too well. He picked up crumbs outside the baker's door when the baker was not looking and tried to keep himself warm by flapping his wings.

But at last he knew that he was going to die. He had just strength to fly up to the Prince's shoulder once more. "Good-bye, dear Prince!" he murmured, "will you let me kiss your hand?"

"I am glad that you are going to Egypt at last, little Swallow," said the Prince, "you have stayed too long here; but you must kiss me on the lips, for I love you."

"It is not to Egypt that I am going," said the Swallow. "I am going to the House of Death. Death is the brother of Sleep, is he not?"

And he kissed the Happy Prince on the lips, and fell down dead at his feet.

At that moment a curious crack sounded inside the statue, as if something had broken. The fact is that the leaden heart had snapped right in two. It certainly was a dreadfully hard frost.

Early the next morning the Mayor was walking in the square below in company with the Town Councillors. As they passed the column he looked up at the statue: "Dear me! how shabby the Happy Prince looks!" he said.

"How shabby indeed!" cried the Town Councillors, who always agreed with the Mayor; and they went up to look at it.

"The ruby has fallen out of his sword, his eyes are gone, and he is golden no longer," said the Mayor in fact, "he is litttle better than a beggar!"

"Little better than a beggar," said the Town Councillors.

"And here is actually a dead bird at his feet!" continued the Mayor. "We must really issue a proclamation that birds are not to be allowed to die here." And the Town

Clerk made a note of the suggestion.

So they pulled down the statue of the Happy Prince. "As he is no longer beautiful he is no longer useful," said the Art Professor at the University.

Then they melted the statue in a furnace, and the Mayor held a meeting of the Corporation to decide what was to be done with the metal. "We must have another statue, of course," he said, "and it shall be a statue of myself." "Of myself," said each of the Town Councillors, and they quarrelled. When I last heard of them they were quarrelling still.

"What a strange thing!" said the overseer of the workmen at the foundry. "This broken lead heart will not melt in the furnace. We must throw it away." So they threw it on a dust-heap where the dead Swallow was also lying.

"Bring me the two most precious things in the city," said God to one of His Angels; and the Angel brought Him the leaden heart and the dead bird.

"You have rightly chosen," said God, "for in my garden of Paradise this little bird shall sing for evermore, and in my city of gold the Happy Prince shall praise me."

King Lear

William Shakespeare

Lear, King of Britain, had three daughters: Goneril, wife to the Duke of Albany; Regan, wife to the Duke of Cornwall; and Cordelia, a young maid, for whose love the King of France and Duke of Burgundy were joint suitors, and were at this time making stay for that purpose in the court of Lear.

The old king, worn out with age and the fatigues of government, he being more than fourscore years old, determined to take no further part in state affairs, but to leave the management to younger strengths, that he might have time to prepare for death, which must at no long period ensue. With this intent he called his three daughters to him, to know from their own lips which of them loved him best, that he might part his kingdom among them in such proportions as their affection for him should seem to deserve.

Goneril, the eldest, declared that she loved her father more than words could give out, that he was dearer to her than the light of her own eyes, dearer than life and liberty, with a deal of such professing stuff, which is easy to counterfeit where there is no real love, only a few fine words delivered with confidence being wanted in that case. The king, delighted to hear from her own mouth this assurance of her love, and thinking truly that her heart went with it, in a fit of fatherly fondness bestowed upon her and her husband one-third of his ample kingdom.

Then calling to him his second daughter he demanded what she had to say. Regan, who was made of the same hollow metal as her sister, was not a whit behind in her professions, but rather declared that what her sister had spoken came short of the love which she professed to bear for his Highness; in so much that she found all other joys dead in comparison with the pleasure which she took in the love of her dear king and father.

Lear blessed himself in having such loving children, as he thought; and could do no less, after the handsome assurances which Regan had made, than bestow a third of his kingdom upon her and her husband, equal in size to that which he had already given away to Goneril.

Then turning to his youngest daughter, Cordelia, whom he called his joy, he asked what she had to say,thinking no doubt that she would glad his ears with the same loving speeches which her sisters had uttered, or rather that her expressions would be so much stronger than theirs, as she had always been his darling, and favored by him above either of them. But Cordelia, disgusted with the flattery of her sisters, whose hearts she knew were far from their lips, and seeing that all their coaxing speeches were only intended to wheedle the old king out of his dominions, that they and their husbands might reign in his lifetime, made no other reply but this—that she loved his Majesty according to her duty, neither more nor less.

The king, shocked with this appearance of ingratitude in his favorite child, desired her to consider her words and to mend her speech, lest it should mar her fortunes.

Cordelia then told her father that he was her father, that he had given her breeding, and loved her; that she returned those duties back as was most fit, and did obey him, love him, and most honor him. But that she could not frame her mouth to such large speeches as her sisters had done, or promise to love nothing else in the world. Why had her sisters husbands if (as they said) they had no love for anything but their father? If she should ever wed, she was sure the lord to whom she gave her husband would want half her love, half of her care and duty; she should never marry like her sisters, to love her father all.

Cordelia, who in earnest loved her old father even almost extravagantly as her sisters pretended to do, would have plainly told him so at any other time, in more daughter-like and loving terms, and without these qualifications, which did indeed sound a little ungracious; but after the crafty, flattering speeches of her sisters, which she had seen draw such extravagant rewards, she thought the handsomest thing she could do was to love and be silent. This put her affection out of suspicion of mercenary ends, and showed that she loved, but not for gain; and that her professions, the less ostentatious they were, had so much the more of truth and sincerity than her sisters'.

This plainness of speech, which Lear called pride, so enraged the old monarch—who in his best of times always showed much of spleen and rashness, and in whom the dotage incident to old age had so clouded over his reason that he could not discern truth from flattery, nor a gaypainted speech from words that came from the heart—that in a fury of resentment he retracted the third part of his kingdom which yet remained, and which he had reserved for Cordelia, and gave it away from her, sharing it equally between her two sisters and their husbands, the Dukes of Albany and Cornwall, whom he now called to him and in presence of all his courtiers, bestowing a coronet between them, invested them jointly with all the power, revenue, and execution of government, only retaining to himself the name of king; all the rest of royalty he resigned, with this reservation, that himself, with a hundred knights for his attendants, was to be maintained by monthly course in each of his daughters' palaces in turn.

So preposterous a disposal of his kingdom, so little guided by reason, and so much by passion, filled all his courtiers with astonishment and sorrow; but none of them had the courage to interpose between this incensed king and his wrath, except the Earl of Kent, who was beginning to speak a good word for Cordelia, when the passionate Lear on pain of death commanded him to desist; but the good Kent was not so to be repelled. He had been ever loyal to Lear, whom he had honored as a king, loved as a father, followed as a master; and he had never esteemed his life further than as a pawn to wage against his royal master's enemies, nor feared to lose it when Lear's safety was the motive; nor, now that Lear was most his own enemy, did this faithful servant of the king forget his old principles, but manfully opposed Lear to do Lear good; and was unmannerly only because Lear was mad. He had been a most faithful counselor in times past to the king, and he besought him now that he would see with his eyes (as he had done in many weighty matters) and go by his advice still, and in his best consideration recall this hideous rashness; for he would answer with his life his judgment that Lear's youngest daughter did not love him least, nor were those empty-hearted whose low sound gave no token of hollowness. When power bowed to flattery, honor was bound to plainness. For Lear's threats, what could he do to him whose life was already at his service? That should not hinder duty from speaking.

The honest freedom of this good Earl of Kent only stirred up the king's wrath the more, and, like a frantic patient who kills his physician and loves his mortal disease, he banished this true servant, and allotted him but five days to make his preparations for departure; but if on the sixth his hated person was found within the realm of Britain, that moment was to be his death. And Kent bade farewell to the king, and said that, since he chose to show himself in such fashion, it was but banishment to stay there; and before he went he recommended Cordelia to the protection of the gods, the maid who had so rightly thought and so discreetly spoken; and only wished that her sisters' large speeches might be answered with deeds of love; and then he went, as he said, to shape his old course to a new country.

The King of France and Duke of Burgundy were now called in to hear the determination of Lear about his youngest daughter, and to know whether they would persist in their courtship to Cordelia, now that she was under her father's displeasure and had no fortune but her own person to recommend her. And the Duke of Burgundy declined the match, and would not take her to wife upon such conditions. But the King of France, understanding what the nature of the fault had been which had lost her the love of her father—that it was only a tardiness of speech and the not being able to frame her tongue to flattery like her sisters—took this young maid by the hand and, saying that her virtues were a dowry above a kingdom, bade Cordelia to take farewell of her sisters and of her father, though he had been unkind, and she should go with him and be Queen of him and of fair France, and reign over fairer possessions than her sisters. And he called the Duke of Burgundy, in contempt, a waterish duke, because his love for this young maid had in a moment run all away like water.

Then Cordelia with weeping eyes took leave of her sisters, and besought them to love their father well and make good their professions; and they sullenly told her not to prescribe to them, for they knew their duty, but to strive to content her husband, who had taken her (as they tauntingly expressed it) as Fortune's alms. And Cordelia with a heavy heart departed, for she knew the cunning of her sisters and she wished her father in better hands than she was about to leave him in.

Cordelia was no sooner gone than the devilish dispositions of her sisters began to show themselves 'in their true colors. Even before the expiration of the first month, which Lear was to spend by agreement ,with his , daughter, Goneril, the old king began to find out the difference between promises and performances. This wretch, having got from her father all that he had to bestow, even to the giving away of the crown from off his head, began to grudge even those small remnants of royalty which the old man had reserved to himself, to please his fancy with the idea of being still a king. She could not bear to see him and his knights. Every time she met her father she put on a frowning countenance; and when the old man wanted to speak with her she would feign sickness or anything to get rid of the sight of him, for it was plain that she esteemed his old age a useless burden and his attendants an unnecessary expense; not only she herself slackened in her expressions of duty to the king, but by her example, and (it is to be feared) not without her private instructions, her very servants affected to treat him with neglect, and would either refuse to obey his orders or still more contemptuously pretend not to hear them. Lear could not but perceive this alteration in the behavior of his daughter, but he shut his eyes against it as long as he could, as people commonly are unwilling to believe the unpleasant consequences which their own mistakes and obstinacy have brought upon them.

True love and fidelity are no more to be estranged by ILL, than falsehood and hollow-heartedness can be conciliated by GOOD, USAGE. This eminently appears in the instance of the good Earl of Kent, who, though banished by Lear, and his life made forfeit if he were found in Britain, chose to stay and abide all consequences as long as there was a chance of his being useful to the king his master. See to what mean shifts and disguises poor loyalty is forced to submit sometimes; yet it counts nothing base or unworthy so as it can but do service where it owes an obligation! In the disguise of a serving-man, all his greatness and pomp laid aside, this good earl proffered his services to the king, who, not knowing him to be Kent in that disguise, but pleased with a certain plainness, or rather bluntness, in his answers, which the earl put on (so different from that smooth, oily flattery which he had so much reason to be sick of, having found the effects not answerable in his daughter), a bargain was quickly struck, and Lear took Kent into his service by the name of Caius, as he called himself, never suspecting him to be his once great favorite, the high and mighty Earl of Kent.

This Caius quickly found means to show his fidelity and love to his royal master, for, Goneril's steward that same day behaving in a disrespectful manner to Lear, and giving him saucy looks and language, as no doubt he was secretly encouraged to do by his mistress, Caius, not enduring to hear so open an affront put upon his Majesty, made no more ado, but presently tripped up his heels and laid the unmannerly slave in the kennel; for which friendly service Lear became more and more attached to him.

Nor was Kent the only friend Lear had. In his degree, and as far as so insignificant a personage could show his love, the poor fool, or jester, that had been of his palace while Lear had a palace, as it was the custom of kings and great personages at that time to keep a fool (as he was called) to make them sport after serious business—

this poor fool clung to Lear after he had given away his crown, and by his witty sayings would keep up his good-humor, though he could not refrain sometimes from jeering at his master for his imprudence in uncrowning himself and giving all away to his daughters; at which time, as he rhymingly expressed it, these daughters— "For sudden joy did weep,

And I for sorrow sung,
That such a king should play bo-peep
And go the fools among."

And in such wild sayings, and scraps of songs, of which he had plenty, this pleasant, honest fool poured out his heart even in the presence of Goneril herself, in many a bitter taunt and jest which cut to the quick, such as comparing the king to the hedgesparrow, who feeds the young of the cuckoo till they grow old enough, and then has its head bit off for its pains; and saying that an ass may know when the cart draws the horse (meaning that Lear's daughters, that ought to go behind, now ranked before their father); and that Lear was no longer Lear, but the shadow of Lear. For which free speeches he was once or twice threatened to be whipped.

The coolness and falling off of respect which Lear had begun to perceive were not all which this foolish fond father was to suffer from his unworthy daughter. She now plainly told him that his staying in her palace was inconvenient so long as he insisted upon keeping up an establishment of a hundred knights; that this establishment was useless and expensive and only served to fill her court with riot and feasting; and she prayed him that he would lessen their number and keep none but old men about him, such as himself, and fitting his age.

Lear at first could not believe his eyes or ears, nor that it was his daughter who spoke so unkindly. He could not believe that she who had received a crown from him could seek to cut off his train and grudge him the respect due to his old age. But she persisting in her undutiful demand, the old man's rage was so excited that he called her a detested kite and said that she spoke an untruth; and so indeed she did, for the hundred knights were all men of choice behavior and sobriety of manners, skilled in all particulars of duty, and not given to rioting or feasting, as she said. And he bid his horses to be prepared, for he would go to his other daughter, Regan, he and his hundred knights; and he spoke of ingratitude, and said it was a marble-hearted devil, and showed more hideous in a child than the sea-monster. And he cursed his eldest daughter, Goneril, so as was terrible to hear, praying that she might never have a child, or, if she had, that it might live to return that scorn and contempt upon her which she had shown to him; that she might feel how sharper than a serpent's tooth it was to have a thankless child. And Goneril's husband, the Duke of Albany, beginning to excuse himself for any share which Lear might suppose he had in the unkindness, Lear would not hear him out, but in a rage ordered his horses to be saddled and set out with his followers for the abode of Regan, his other daughter. And Lear thought to himself how small the fault of Cordelia (if it was a fault) now appeared in comparison with her sister's, and he wept; and then he was ashamed that such a creature as Goneril should have so much power over his manhood as to make him weep.

Regan and her husband were keeping their court in great pomp and state at their palace; and Lear despatched his servant Caius with letters to his daughter, that she might be prepared for his reception, while he and his train followed after. But it seems that Goneril had been beforehand with him, sending letters also to

Regan, accusing her father of waywardness and ill-humors, and advising her not to receive so great a train as he was bringing with him. This messenger arrived at the same time with Caius, and Caius and he met, and who should it be but Caius's old enemy the steward, whom he had formerly tripped up by the heels for his saucy behavior to Lear. Caius not liking the fellow's look, and, suspecting what he came for, began to revile him and challenged him to fight, which the fellow refusing, Caius, in a fit of honest passion, beat him soundly, as such a mischief-maker and carrier of wicked messages deserved; which coming to the ears of Regan and her husband, they ordered Caius to be put in the stocks, though he was a messenger from the king her father and in that character demanded the highest respect. So that the first thing the king saw when he entered the castle was his faithful servant Caius sitting in that disgraceful situation.

This was but a bad omen of the reception which he was to expect; but a worse followed when, upon inquiry for his daughter and her husband, he was told they were weary with traveling all night and could not see him; and when, lastly, upon his insisting in a positive and angry manner to see them, they came to greet him, whom should he see in their company but the hated Goneril, who had come to tell her own story and set her sister against the king her father!

This sight much moved the old man, and still more to see Regan take her by the hand; and he asked Goneril if she was not ashamed to look upon his old white beard. And Regan advised him to go home again with Goneril, and live with her peaceably, dismissing half of his attendants, and to ask her forgiveness; for he was old and wanted discretion, and must be ruled and led by persons that had more discretion than himself. And Lear showed how preposterous that would sound, if he were to go down on his knees and beg of his own daughter for food and raiment; and he argued against such an unnatural dependence, declaring his resolution never to return with her, but to stay where he was with Regan, he and his hundred knights; for he said that she had not forgot the half of the kingdom which he had endowed her with, and that her eyes were not fierce like Goneril's, but mild and kind. And he said that rather than return to Goneril, with half his train cut off, he would go over to France and beg a wretched pension of the king there, who had married his youngest daughter without a portion.

But he was mistaken in expecting kinder treatment of Regan than he had experienced from her sister Goneril. As if willing to outdo her sister in unfilial behavior, she declared that she thought fifty knights too many to wait upon him; that five-and-twenty were enough. Then Lear, nigh heartbroken, turned to Goneril and said that he would go back with her, for her fifty doubled five-and-twenty, and so her love was twice as much as Regan's. But Goneril excused herself, and said, what need of so many as five-and twenty? or even ten? or five? when he might be waited upon by her servants or her sister's servants? So these two wicked daughters, as if they strove to exceed each other in cruelty to their old father, who had been so good to them, by little and little would have abated him of all his train, all respect (little enough for him that once commanded a kingdom) which was left him to show that he had once been a king! Not that a splendid train is essential to happiness, but from a king to a beggar is a hard change, from commanding millions to be without one attendant; and it was the ingratitude in his daughters' denying more than what he would suffer by the want of it, which pierced this poor king to the heart; in so much that, with this double ill-usage, and vexation for having so foolishly given away a kingdom, his wits began to be unsettled, and while he said he knew not what, he vowed revenge against those unnatural hags and to make examples of them that should be a terror to the earth!

While he was thus idly threatening what his weak arm could never execute, night came on, and a loud storm of thunder and lightning with rain; and his daughters still persisting in their resolution not to admit his followers, he called for his horses, and chose rather to encounter the utmost fury of the storm abroad than stay under the same roof with these ungrateful daughters; and they, saying that the injuries which wilful men procure to themselves are their just punishment, suffered him to go in that condition and shut their doors upon him.

The winds were high, and the rain and storm increased, when the old man sallied forth to combat with the elements, less sharp than his daughters' unkindness. For many miles about there was scarce a bush; and there upon a heath, exposed to the fury of the storm in a dark night, did King Lear wander out, and defy the winds and the thunder; and he bid the winds to blow the earth into the sea, or swell the waves of the sea till they drowned the earth, that no token might remain of any such ungrateful animal as man. The old king was now left with no other companion than the poor fool, who still abided with him, with his merry conceits striving to outjest misfortune, saying it was but a naughty night to swim in, and truly the king had better go in and ask his daughter's blessing: But he that has a little tiny wit—

With heigh ho, the wind and the rain,—
Must make content with his fortunes fit
Though the rain it raineth every day,

and swearing it was a brave night to cool a lady's pride.

Thus poorly accompanied, this once great monarch was found by his ever-faithful servant the good Earl of Kent, now transformed to Caius, who ever followed close at his side, though the king did not know him to be the earl; and be said:

"Alas, sir, are you here? Creatures that love night love not such nights as these. This dreadful storm has driven the beasts to their hiding-places. Man's nature cannot endure the affliction or the fear."

And Lear rebuked him and said these lesser evils were not felt where a greater malady was fixed. When the mind is at ease the body has leisure to be delicate, but the tempest in his mind did take all feeling else from his senses but of that which beat at his heart. And he spoke of filial ingratitude, and said it was all one as if the mouth should tear the hand for lifting food to it; for parents were hands and food and everything to children.

But the good Caius still persisting in his entreaties that the king would not stay out in the open air, at last persuaded him to enter a little wretched hovel which stood upon the heath, where the fool first entering, suddenly ran back terrified, saying that he had seen a spirit. But upon examination this spirit proved to be nothing more than a poor Bedlam beggar who had crept into this deserted hovel for shelter, and with his talk about devils frighted the fool, one of those poor lunatics who are either mad, or feign to be so, the better to extort charity from the compassionate country people, who go about the country calling themselves poor Tom and poor Turlygood, saying, "Who gives anything to poor Tom?" sticking pins and nails and sprigs of rosemary into their arms to make them bleed; and with horrible actions, partly by prayers, and partly with lunatic curses, they move or terrify the ignorant country folk into giving them alms. This poor fellow was such a one; and the king, seeing him in so wretched a plight, with nothing but a blanket about his loins to cover his nakedness, could not be persuaded but that the fellow was some father who had given all away to his daughters and brought himself to that pass; for nothing, he thought, could bring a man to such wretchedness but the having unkind daughters.

And from this and many such wild speeches which he uttered the good Caius plainly perceived that he was not in his perfect mind, but that his daughters' ill-usage had really made him go mad. And now the loyalty of this worthy Earl of Kent showed itself in more essential services than he had hitherto found opportunity to perform. For with the assistance of some of the king's attendants who remained loyal he had the person of his royal master removed at daybreak to the castle of Dover, where his own friends and influence, as Earl of Kent, chiefly lay; and himself, embarking for France, hastened to the court of Cordelia, and did there in such moving terms represent the pitiful condition of her royal father, and set out in such lively colors the inhumanity of her sisters, that this good and loving child with many tears besought the king, her husband, that he would give her leave to embark for England, with a sufficient power to subdue these cruel daughters and their husbands and restore the old king, her father, to his throne; which being granted, she set forth, and with a royal army landed at Dover.

Lear, having by some chance escaped from the guardians which' the good Earl of Kent had put over him to take care of him in his lunacy, was found by some of Cordelia's train, wandering about the fields near Dover, in a pitiable condition, stark mad, and singing aloud to himself, with a crown upon his head which he had made of straw and nettles and other wild weeds that he had picked up in the corn-fields. By the advice of the physicians, Cordelia, though earnestly desirous of seeing her father, was prevailed upon to put off the meeting till, by sleep and the operation of herbs which they gave him, he should be restored to greater composure. By the aid of these skilful physicians, to whom Cordelia promised all her gold and jewels for the recovery of the old king, Lear was soon in a condition to see his daughter.

A tender sight it was to see the meeting between this father and daughter; to see the struggles between the joy of this poor old king at beholding again his once darling child, and the shame at receiving such filial kindness from her whom he had cast off for so small a fault in his displeasure; both these passions struggling with the remains of his malady, which in his half-crazed brain sometimes made him that he scarce remembered where he was or who it was tb at so kindly kissed him and spoke to him. And then he would beg the standers-by not to laugh at him if he were mistaken in thinking this lady to be his daughter Cordelia! And then to see him fall on his knees to beg pardon of his child; and she, good lady, kneeling all the while to ask a blessing of him, and telling him that it did not become him to kneel, but it was her duty, for she was his child, his true and very child Cordelia! And she kissed him (as she said) to kiss away all her sisters' unkindness, and said that they might be ashamed of themselves, to turn their old kind father with his white beard out into the cold air, when her enemy's dog, though it had bit her (as she prettily expressed it), should have stayed by her fire such a night as that, and warmed himself. And she told her father how she had come from France with purpose to bring him assistance; and he said that she must forget and forgive, for he was old and foolish and did not know what he did; but that to be sure she had great cause not to love him, but her sisters had none. And Cordelia said that she had no cause, no more than they had.

So we will leave this old king in the protection of his dutiful and loving child, where, by the help of sleep and medicine, she and her physicians at length succeeded in winding up the untuned and jarring senses which the cruelty of his other daughters had so violently shaken. Let us return to say a word or two about those cruel daughters.

These monsters of ingratitude, who had been so false to their old father, could not be expected to prove more faithful to their own husbands. They soon grew tired of paying even the appearance of duty and affection, and in an open way showed they had fixed their loves upon another. It happened that the object of their guilty loves was the same. It was Edmund, a natural son of the late Earl of Gloucester, who by his treacheries had succeeded in disinheriting his brother Edgar, the lawful heir, from his earldom, and by his wicked practices was now earl himself; a wicked man, and a fit object for the love of such wicked creatures as Goneril and Regan. It falling out about this time that the Duke of Cornwall, Regan's husband, died, Regan immediately declared her intention of wedding this Earl of Gloucester, which rousing the jealousy of her sister, to whom as well as to Regan this wicked earl had at sundry times professed love, Goneril found means to make away with her sister by poison; but being detected in her practices, and imprisoned by her husband, the Duke of Albany, for this deed, and for her guilty passion for the earl which had come to his ears, she, in a fit of disappointed love and rage, shortly put an end to her own life. Thus the justice of Heaven at last overtook these wicked daughters.

While the eyes of all men were upon this event,

admiring the justice displayed in their deserved deaths, the same eyes were suddenly taken off from this sight to admire at the mysterious ways of the same power in the melancholy fate of the young and virtuous daughter, the Lady Cordelia, whose good deeds did seem to deserve a more fortunate conclusion. But it is an awful truth that innocence and piety are not always successful in this world. The forces which Goneril and Regan had sent out under the command of the bad Earl of Gloucester were victorious, and Cordelia, by the practices of this wicked earl, who did not like that any should stand between him and the throne, ended her life in prison. Thus heaven took this innocent lady to itself in her young years, after showing her to the world an illustrious example of filial duty. Lear did not long survive this kind child.

Before he died, the good Earl of Kent, who had still attended his old master's steps from the first of his daughters' ill-usage to this sad period of his decay, tried to make him understand that it was he who had followed him under the name of Caius; but Lear's care-crazed brain at that time could not comprehend how that could be, or how Kent and Caius could be the same person, so Kent thought it needless to trouble him with explanations at such a time; and, Lear soon after expiring, this faithful servant to the king, between age and grief for his old master's vexations, soon followed him to the grave.

How the judgment of Heaven overtook the bad Earl of Gloucester, whose treasons were discovered, and himself slain in single combat with his brother, the lawful earl, and how Goneril's husband, the Duke of Albany, who was innocent of the death of Cordelia, and had never encouraged his lady in her wicked proceedings against her father, ascended the throne of Britain after the death of Lear, it is needless here to narrate, Lear and his three daughters being dead, whose adventures alone concern our story.

A Scandal in Bohemia

Arthur Conan Doyle

I.

To Sherlock Holmes she is always the woman. I have seldom heard him mention her under any other name. In his eyes she eclipses and predominates the whole of her sex. It was not that he felt any emotion akin to love for Irene Adler. All emotions, and that one particularly, were abhorrent to his cold, precise but admirably balanced mind. He was, I take it, the most perfect reasoning and observing machine that the world has seen, but as a lover he would have placed himself in a false position. He never spoke of the softer passions, save with a gibe and a sneer. They were admirable things for the observer—excellent for drawing the veil from men's motives and actions. But for the trained reasoner to admit such intrusions into his own delicate and finely adjusted temperament was to introduce a distracting factor which might throw a doubt upon all his mental results. Grit in a sensitive instrument, or a crack in one of his own high-power lenses, would not be more disturbing than a strong emotion in a nature such as his. And yet there was but one woman to him, and that woman was the late Irene Adler, of dubious and questionable memory.

I had seen little of Holmes lately. My marriage had drifted us away from each other. My own complete happiness, and the home-centred interests which rise up around the man who first finds himself master of his own establishment, were sufficient to absorb all my attention, while Holmes, who loathed every form of society with his whole Bohemian soul, remained in our lodgings in Baker Street, buried among his old books, and alternating from week to week between cocaine and ambition, the drowsiness of the drug, and the fierce energy of his own keen nature. He was still, as ever, deeply attracted by the study of crime, and occupied his immense faculties and extraordinary powers of observation in following out those clues, and clearing up those mysteries which had been abandoned as hopeless by the official police. From time to time I heard some vague account of his doings: of his summons to Odessa in the case of the Trepoff murder, of his clearing up of the singular tragedy of the Atkinson brothers at Trincomalee, and finally of the mission which he had accomplished so delicately and successfully for the reigning family of Holland. Beyond these signs of his activity, however, which I merely shared with all the readers of the daily press, I knew little of my former friend and companion.

One night—it was on the twentieth of March, 1888—I was returning from a journey to a patient (for I had now returned to civil practice), when my way led me through Baker Street. As I passed the well-remembered door, which must always be associated in my mind with my wooing, and with the dark incidents of the Study in Scarlet, I was seized with a keen desire to see Holmes again, and to know how he was employing his extraordinary powers. His rooms were brilliantly lit, and, even as I looked up, I saw his tall, spare figure pass twice in a dark silhouette against the blind. He was pacing the room swiftly, eagerly, with his head sunk upon his chest and his hands clasped behind him. To me, who knew his every mood and habit, his attitude and manner told their own story. He was at work again. He had risen out of his drug-created dreams and was hot upon the scent of some new problem. I rang the bell and was shown up to the chamber which had formerly been in part my own.

His manner was not effusive. It seldom was; but he was glad, I think, to see me. With hardly a word spoken, but with a kindly eye, he waved me to an armchair, threw across his case of cigars, and indicated a spirit case and a gasogene in the corner. Then he stood before the fire and looked me over in his singular introspective fashion.

"Wedlock suits you," he remarked. "I think, Watson, that you have put on seven and a half pounds since I saw you."

"Seven!" I answered.

"Indeed, I should have thought a little more. Just a trifle more, I fancy, Watson. And in practice again, I observe. You did not tell me that you intended to go into harness." "Then, how do you know?"

"I see it, I deduce it. How do I know that you have been getting yourself very wet lately, and that you have a most clumsy and careless servant girl?"

"My dear Holmes," said I, "this is too much. You would certainly have been burned, had you lived a few centuries ago. It is true that I had a country walk on Thursday and came home in a dreadful mess, but as I have changed my clothes I can't imagine how you deduce it. As to Mary Jane, she is incorrigible, and my wife has given her notice, but there, again, I fail to see how you work it out." He chuckled to himself and rubbed his long, nervous hands together.

"It is simplicity itself," said he; "my eyes tell me that on the inside of your left shoe, just where the firelight strikes it, the leather is scored by six almost parallel cuts. Obviously they have been caused by someone who has very carelessly scraped round the edges of the sole in order to remove crusted mud from it. Hence, you see, my double deduction that you had been out in vile weather, and that you had a particularly malignant boot-slitting specimen of the London slavey. As to your practice, if a gentleman walks into my rooms smelling of iodoform, with a black mark of nitrate of silver upon his right forefinger, and a bulge on the right side of his top-hat to show where he has secreted his stethoscope, I must be dull, indeed, if I do not pronounce him to be an active member of the medical profession." I could not help laughing at the ease with which he explained his process of deduction. "When I hear you give your reasons," I remarked, "the thing always appears to me to be so ridiculously simple that I could easily do it myself, though at each successive instance of your reasoning I am baffled until you explain your process. And yet I believe that my eyes are as good as yours." "Quite so," he answered, lighting a cigarette, and throwing himself down into an armchair. "You see, but you do not observe. The distinction is clear. For example, you have frequently seen the steps which lead up from the hall to this room." "Frequently."

"How often?"

"Well, some hundreds of times."

"Then how many are there?"

"How many? I don't know."

"Quite so! You have not observed. And yet you have seen. That is just my point. Now, I know that there are seventeen steps, because I have both seen and observed. By the way, since you are interested in these little problems, and since you are good enough to chronicle one or two of my trifling experiences, you may be interested in this." He threw over a sheet of thick, pink-tinted notepaper which had been lying open upon the table. "It came by the last post," said he. "Read it aloud." The note was undated, and without either signature or address.

"There will call upon you to-night, at a quarter to eight

o'clock," it said, "a gentleman who desires to consult you upon a matter of the very deepest moment. Your recent services to one of the royal houses of Europe have shown that you are one who may safely be trusted with matters which are of an importance which can hardly be exaggerated. This account of you we have from all quarters received. Be in your chamber then at that hour, and do not take it amiss if your visitor wear a mask." "This is indeed a mystery," I remarked. "What do you imagine that it means?"

"I have no data yet. It is a capital mistake to theorise before one has data. Insensibly one begins to twist facts to suit theories, instead of theories to suit facts. But the note itself. What do you deduce from it?" I carefully examined the writing, and the paper upon which it was written.

"The man who wrote it was presumably well to do," I remarked, endeavouring to imitate my companion's processes. "Such paper could not be bought under half a crown a packet. It is peculiarly strong and stiff." "Peculiar—that is the very word," said Holmes. "It is not an English paper at all. Hold it up to the light."

I did so, and saw a large "E" with a small "g," a "P," and a large "G" with a small "t" woven into the texture of the paper.

"What do you make of that?" asked Holmes.

"The name of the maker, no doubt; or his monogram, rather."

"Not at all. The 'G' with the small 't' stands for 'Gesellschaft,' which is the German for 'Company.' It is a customary contraction like our 'Co.' 'P,' of course, stands for 'Papier.' Now for the 'Eg.' Let us glance at our Continental Gazetteer." He took down a heavy brown volume from his shelves. "Eglow, Eglonitz—here we are, Egria. It is in a German-speaking country—in Bohemia, not far from Carlsbad. 'Remarkable as being the scene of the death of Wallenstein, and for its numerous glass-factories and paper-mills.' Ha, ha, my boy, what do you make of that?" His eyes sparkled, and he sent up a great blue triumphant cloud from his cigarette.

"The paper was made in Bohemia," I said.

"Precisely. And the man who wrote the note is a German. Do you note the peculiar construction of the sentence—'This account of you we have from all quarters received.' A Frenchman or Russian could not have written that. It is the German who is so uncourteous to his verbs. It only remains, therefore, to discover what is wanted by this German who writes upon Bohemian paper and prefers wearing a mask to showing his face. And here he comes, if I am not mistaken, to resolve all our doubts." As he spoke there was the sharp sound of horses' hoofs and grating wheels against the curb, followed by a sharp pull at the bell. Holmes whistled.

"A pair, by the sound," said he. "Yes," he continued, glancing out of the window. "A nice little brougham and a pair of beauties. A hundred and fifty guineas apiece. There's money in this case, Watson, if there is nothing else." "I think that I had better go, Holmes."

"Not a bit, Doctor. Stay where you are. I am lost without my Boswell. And this promises to be interesting. It would be a pity to miss it."

"But your client—"

"Never mind him. I may want your help, and so may he. Here he comes. Sit down in that armchair, Doctor, and give us your best attention."

A slow and heavy step, which had been heard upon the stairs and in the passage, paused immediately outside the door. Then there was a loud and authoritative tap.

"Come in!" said Holmes.

A man entered who could hardly have been less than

six feet six inches in height, with the chest and limbs of a Hercules. His dress was rich with a richness which would, in England, be looked upon as akin to bad taste. Heavy bands of astrakhan were slashed across the sleeves and fronts of his double-breasted coat, while the deep blue cloak which was thrown over his shoulders was lined with flame-coloured silk and secured at the neck with a brooch which consisted of a single flaming beryl. Boots which extended halfway up his calves, and which were trimmed at the tops with rich brown fur, completed the impression of barbaric opulence which was suggested by his whole appearance. He carried a broad-brimmed hat in his hand, while he wore across the upper part of his face, extending down past the cheekbones, a black vizard mask, which he had apparently adjusted that very moment, for his hand was still raised to it as he entered. From the lower part of the face he appeared to be a man of strong character, with a thick, hanging lip, and a long, straight chin suggestive of resolution pushed to the length of obstinacy.

"You had my note?" he asked with a deep harsh voice and a strongly marked German accent. "I told you that I would call." He looked from one to the other of us, as if uncertain which to address.

"Pray take a seat," said Holmes. "This is my friend and colleague, Dr. Watson, who is occasionally good enough to help me in my cases. Whom have I the honour to address?" "You may address me as the Count Von Kramm, a Bohemian nobleman. I understand that this gentleman, your friend, is a man of honour and discretion, whom I may trust with a matter of the most extreme importance. If not, I should much prefer to communicate with you alone." I rose to go, but Holmes caught me by the wrist and pushed me back into my chair. "It is both, or none," said he. "You may say before this gentleman anything which you may say to me." The Count shrugged his broad shoulders. "Then I must begin," said he, "by binding you both to absolute secrecy for two years; at the end of that time the matter will be of no importance. At present it is not too much to say that it is of such weight it may have an influence upon European history." "I promise," said Holmes.

"And I."

"You will excuse this mask," continued our strange visitor. "The august person who employs me wishes his agent to be unknown to you, and I may confess at once that the title by which I have just called myself is not exactly my own." "I was aware of it," said Holmes dryly.

"The circumstances are of great delicacy, and every precaution has to be taken to quench what might grow to be an immense scandal and seriously compromise one of the reigning families of Europe. To speak plainly, the matter implicates the great House of Ormstein, hereditary kings of Bohemia." "I was also aware of that," murmured Holmes, settling himself down in his armchair and closing his eyes.

Our visitor glanced with some apparent surprise at the languid, lounging figure of the man who had been no doubt depicted to him as the most incisive reasoner and most energetic agent in Europe. Holmes slowly reopened his eyes and looked impatiently at his gigantic client.

"If your Majesty would condescend to state your case," he remarked, "I should be better able to advise you."

The man sprang from his chair and paced up and down the room in uncontrollable agitation. Then, with a gesture of desperation, he tore the mask from his face and hurled it upon the ground. "You are right," he cried; "I am the King. Why should I attempt to conceal it?" "Why, indeed?" murmured Holmes. "Your Majesty had not spoken before I was aware that I was addressing Wilhelm

Gottsreich Sigismond von Ormstein, Grand Duke of Cassel-Felstein, and hereditary King of Bohemia." "But you can understand," said our strange visitor, sitting down once more and passing his hand over his high white forehead, "you can understand that I am not accustomed to doing such business in my own person. Yet the matter was so delicate that I could not confide it to an agent without putting myself in his power. I have come incognito from Prague for the purpose of consulting you." "Then, pray consult," said Holmes, shutting his eyes once more.

"The facts are briefly these: Some five years ago, during a lengthy visit to Warsaw, I made the acquaintance of the well-known adventuress, Irene Adler. The name is no doubt familiar to you." "Kindly look her up in my index, Doctor," murmured Holmes without opening his eyes. For many years he had adopted a system of docketing all paragraphs concerning men and things, so that it was difficult to name a subject or a person on which he could not at once furnish information. In this case I found her biography sandwiched in between that of a Hebrew rabbi and that of a staff-commander who had written a monograph upon the deep-sea fishes.

"Let me see!" said Holmes. "Hum! Born in New Jersey in the year 1858. Contralto—hum! La Scala, hum! Prima donna Imperial Opera of Warsaw—yes! Retired from operatic stage—ha! Living in London—quite so! Your Majesty, as I understand, became entangled with this young person, wrote her some compromising letters, and is now desirous of getting those letters back." "Precisely so. But how—"

"Was there a secret marriage?"

"None."

"No legal papers or certificates?"

"None."

"Then I fail to follow your Majesty. If this young person should produce her letters for blackmailing or other purposes, how is she to prove their authenticity?" "There is the writing."

"Pooh, pooh! Forgery."

"My private note-paper."

"Stolen."

"My own seal."

"Imitated."

"My photograph."

"Bought."

"We were both in the photograph."

"Oh, dear! That is very bad! Your Majesty has indeed committed an indiscretion."

"I was mad—insane."

"You have compromised yourself seriously."

"I was only Crown Prince then. I was young. I am but thirty now."

"It must be recovered."

"We have tried and failed."

"Your Majesty must pay. It must be bought."

"She will not sell."

"Stolen, then."

"Five attempts have been made. Twice burglars in my pay ransacked her house. Once we diverted her luggage when she travelled. Twice she has been waylaid. There has been no result." "No sign of it?"

"Absolutely none."

Holmes laughed. "It is quite a pretty little problem," said he.

"But a very serious one to me," returned the King reproachfully.

"Very, indeed. And what does she propose to do with the photograph?"

"To ruin me."

"But how?"
"I am about to be married."
"So I have heard."
"To Clotilde Lothman von Saxe-Meningen, second daughter of the King of Scandinavia. You may know the strict principles of her family. She is herself the very soul of delicacy. A shadow of a doubt as to my conduct would bring the matter to an end." "And Irene Adler?"
"Threatens to send them the photograph. And she will do it. I know that she will do it. You do not know her, but she has a soul of steel. She has the face of the most beautiful of women, and the mind of the most resolute of men. Rather than I should marry another woman, there are no lengths to which she would not go—none."
"You are sure that she has not sent it yet?"
"I am sure."
"And why?"
"Because she has said that she would send it on the day when the betrothal was publicly proclaimed. That will be next Monday."
"Oh, then we have three days yet," said Holmes with a yawn. "That is very fortunate, as I have one or two matters of importance to look into just at present. Your Majesty will, of course, stay in London for the present?"
"Certainly. You will find me at the Langham under the name of the Count Von Kramm."
"Then I shall drop you a line to let you know how we progress."
"Pray do so. I shall be all anxiety."
"Then, as to money?"
"You have carte blanche."
"Absolutely?"
"I tell you that I would give one of the provinces of my kingdom to have that photograph."
"And for present expenses?"

The King took a heavy chamois leather bag from under his cloak and laid it on the table.

"There are three hundred pounds in gold and seven hundred in notes," he said.

Holmes scribbled a receipt upon a sheet of his note-book and handed it to him.

"And Mademoiselle's address?" he asked.

"Is Briony Lodge, Serpentine Avenue, St. John's Wood."

Holmes took a note of it. "One other question," said he. "Was the photograph a cabinet?"

"It was."

"Then, good-night, your Majesty, and I trust that we shall soon have some good news for you. And good-night, Watson," he added, as the wheels of the royal brougham rolled down the street. "If you will be good enough to call to-morrow afternoon at three o'clock I should like to chat this little matter over with you."

II.

At three o'clock precisely I was at Baker Street, but Holmes had not yet returned. The landlady informed me that he had left the house shortly after eight o'clock in the morning. I sat down beside the fire, however, with the intention of awaiting him, however long he might be. I was already deeply interested in his inquiry, for, though it was surrounded by none of the grim and strange features which were associated with the two crimes which I have already recorded, still, the nature of the case and the exalted station of his client gave it a character of its own. Indeed, apart from the nature of the investigation which my friend had on hand, there was something in his masterly grasp of a situation, and his keen, incisive reasoning, which made it a pleasure to me to study his system of work, and to follow the quick, subtle methods by which he disentangled the most inextricable mysteries. So accustomed was I to his invariable success that the very possibility of his failing had ceased to enter into my head.

It was close upon four before the door opened, and a drunken-looking groom, ill-kempt and side-whiskered, with an inflamed face and disreputable clothes, walked into the room. Accustomed as I was to my friend's amazing powers in the use of disguises, I had to look three times before I was certain that it was indeed he. With a nod he vanished into the bedroom, whence he emerged in five minutes tweed-suited and respectable, as of old. Putting his hands into his pockets, he stretched out his legs in front of the fire and laughed heartily for some minutes.

"Well, really!" he cried, and then he choked and laughed again until he was obliged to lie back, limp and helpless, in the chair.

"What is it?"

"It's quite too funny. I am sure you could never guess how I employed my morning, or what I ended by doing."

"I can't imagine. I suppose that you have been watching the habits, and perhaps the house, of Miss Irene Adler."

"Quite so; but the sequel was rather unusual. I will tell you, however. I left the house a little after eight o'clock this morning in the character of a groom out of work. There is a wonderful sympathy and freemasonry among horsey men. Be one of them, and you will know all that there is to know. I soon found Briony Lodge. It is a bijou villa, with a garden at the back, but built out in front right up to the road, two stories. Chubb lock to the door. Large sitting-room on the right side, well furnished, with long windows almost to the floor, and those preposterous English window fasteners which a child could open. Behind there was nothing remarkable, save that the passage window could be reached from the top of the coach-house. I walked round it and examined it closely from every point of view, but without noting anything else of interest.

"I then lounged down the street and found, as I expected, that there was a mews in a lane which runs down by one wall of the garden. I lent the ostlers a hand in rubbing down their horses, and received in exchange twopence, a glass of half-and-half, two fills of shag tobacco, and as much information as I could desire about Miss Adler, to say nothing of half a dozen other people in the neighbourhood in whom I was not in the least interested, but whose biographies I was compelled to listen to." "And what of Irene Adler?" I asked.

"Oh, she has turned all the men's heads down in that part. She is the daintiest thing under a bonnet on this planet. So say the Serpentine-mews, to a man. She lives quietly, sings at concerts, drives out at five every day, and returns at seven sharp for dinner. Seldom goes out at other times, except when she sings. Has only one male visitor, but a good deal of him. He is dark, handsome, and dashing, never calls less than once a day, and often twice. He is a Mr. Godfrey Norton, of the Inner Temple. See the advantages of a cabman as a confidant. They had driven him home a dozen times from Serpentine-mews, and knew all about him. When I had listened to all they had to tell, I began to walk up and down near Briony Lodge once more, and to think over my plan of campaign.

"This Godfrey Norton was evidently an important factor in the matter. He was a lawyer. That sounded ominous. What was the relation between them, and what the object of his repeated visits? Was she his client, his friend, or his mistress? If the former, she had probably transferred the photograph to his keeping. If the latter, it was less likely. On the issue of this question depended whether I should continue my work at Briony Lodge, or turn my attention to the gentleman's chambers in the Temple. It was a delicate point, and it widened the field of my inquiry. I fear that I bore you with these details, but I have to let you see my little difficulties, if you are to understand the situation." "I am following you closely," I answered.

"I was still balancing the matter in my mind when a hansom cab drove up to Briony Lodge, and a gentleman sprang out. He was a remarkably handsome man, dark, aquiline, and moustached—evidently the man of whom I had heard. He appeared to be in a great hurry, shouted to the cabman to wait, and brushed past the maid who opened the door with the air of a man who was thoroughly at home.

"He was in the house about half an hour, and I could catch glimpses of him in the windows of the sitting-room, pacing up and down, talking excitedly, and waving his arms. Of her I could see nothing. Presently he emerged, looking even more flurried than before. As he stepped up to the cab, he pulled a gold watch from his pocket and looked at it earnestly, 'Drive like the devil,' he shouted, 'first to Gross & Hankey's in Regent Street, and then to the Church of St. Monica in the Edgeware Road. Half a guinea if you do it in twenty minutes!'

"Away they went, and I was just wondering whether I should not do well to follow them when up the lane came a neat little landau, the coachman with his coat only half-buttoned, and his tie under his ear, while all the tags of his harness were sticking out of the buckles. It hadn't pulled up before she shot out of the hall door and into it. I only caught a glimpse of her at the moment, but she was a lovely woman, with a face that a man might die for.

"'The Church of St. Monica, John,' she cried, 'and half a sovereign if you reach it in twenty minutes.'

"This was quite too good to lose, Watson. I was just balancing whether I should run for it, or whether I should perch behind her landau when a cab came through the street. The driver looked twice at such a shabby fare, but I jumped in before he could object. 'The Church of St. Monica,' said I, 'and half a sovereign if you reach it in twenty minutes.' It was twenty-five minutes to twelve, and of course it was clear enough what was in the wind.

"My cabby drove fast. I don't think I ever drove faster, but the others were there before us. The cab and the landau with their steaming horses were in front of the door when I arrived. I paid the man and hurried into the church. There was not a soul there save the two whom I had followed and a surpliced clergyman, who seemed to be expostulating with them. They were all three standing in a knot in front of the altar. I lounged up the side aisle like any other idler who has dropped into a church. Suddenly, to my surprise, the three at the altar faced round to me, and Godfrey Norton came running as hard as he could towards me.

"'Thank God,' he cried. 'You'll do. Come! Come!'

"'What then?' I asked.

"'Come, man, come, only three minutes, or it won't be legal.'

"I was half-dragged up to the altar, and before I knew where I was I found myself mumbling responses which were whispered in my ear, and vouching for things of which I knew nothing, and generally assisting in the secure tying up of Irene Adler, spinster, to Godfrey Norton, bachelor. It was all done in an instant, and there was the gentleman thanking me on the one side and the lady on the other, while the clergyman beamed on me in front. It was the most preposterous position in which I ever found myself in my life, and it was the thought of it that started me laughing just now. It seems that there had been some informality about their license, that the clergyman absolutely refused to marry them without a witness of some sort, and that my lucky appearance saved the bridegroom from having to sally out into the streets in search of a best man. The bride gave me a sovereign, and I mean to wear it on my watch chain in memory of the occasion." "This is a very unexpected turn of affairs," said I; "and what then?"

"Well, I found my plans very seriously menaced. It looked as if the pair might take an immediate departure, and so necessitate very prompt and energetic measures on my part. At the church door, however, they separated, he driving back to the Temple, and she to her own house. 'I shall drive out in the park at five as usual,' she said as she left him. I heard no more. They drove away in different directions, and I went off to make my own arrangements." "Which are?"

"Some cold beef and a glass of beer," he answered, ringing the bell. "I have been too busy to think of food, and I am likely to be busier still this evening. By the way, Doctor, I shall want your co-operation." "I shall be delighted."

"You don't mind breaking the law?"

"Not in the least."

"Nor running a chance of arrest?"

"Not in a good cause."

"Oh, the cause is excellent!"

"Then I am your man."

"I was sure that I might rely on you."

"But what is it you wish?"

"When Mrs. Turner has brought in the tray I will make it clear to you. Now," he said as he turned hungrily on the simple fare that our landlady had provided, "I must discuss it while I eat, for I have not much time. It is nearly five now. In two hours we must be on the scene of action. Miss Irene, or Madame, rather, returns from her drive at seven. We must be at Briony Lodge to meet her." "And what then?"

"You must leave that to me. I have already arranged what is to occur. There is only one point on which I must insist. You must not interfere, come what may. You understand?" "I am to be neutral?"

"To do nothing whatever. There will probably be some small unpleasantness. Do not join in it. It will end in my being conveyed into the house. Four or five minutes afterwards the sitting-room window will open. You are to station yourself close to that open window." "Yes."

"You are to watch me, for I will be visible to you."

"Yes."

"And when I raise my hand—so—you will throw into the room what I give you to throw, and will, at the same time, raise the cry of fire. You quite follow me?" "Entirely."

"It is nothing very formidable," he said, taking a long cigar-shaped roll from his pocket. "It is an ordinary plumber's smoke-rocket, fitted with a cap at either end to make it self-lighting. Your task is confined to that. When you raise your cry of fire, it will be taken up by quite a number of people. You may then walk to the end of the street, and I will rejoin you in ten minutes. I hope that I have made myself clear?" "I am to remain neutral, to get near the window, to watch you, and at the signal to throw in this object, then to raise the cry of fire, and to wait you at the corner of the street." "Precisely."

"Then you may entirely rely on me."

"That is excellent. I think, perhaps, it is almost time that I prepare for the new role I have to play."

He disappeared into his bedroom and returned in a few minutes in the character of an amiable and simple-minded Nonconformist clergyman. His broad black hat, his baggy trousers, his white tie, his sympathetic smile, and general look of peering and benevolent curiosity were such as Mr. John Hare alone could have equalled. It was not merely that Holmes changed his costume. His expression, his manner, his very soul seemed to vary with every fresh part that he assumed. The stage lost a fine actor, even as science lost an acute reasoner, when he became a specialist in crime.

It was a quarter past six when we left Baker Street, and it still wanted ten minutes to the hour when we found ourselves in Serpentine Avenue. It was already dusk, and the lamps were just being lighted as we paced up and down in front of Briony Lodge, waiting for the coming of its occupant. The house was just such as I had pictured it from Sherlock Holmes' succinct description, but the locality appeared to be less private than I expected. On the contrary, for a small street in a quiet neighbourhood, it was remarkably animated. There was a group of shabbily dressed men smoking and laughing in a corner, a scissors-grinder with his wheel, two guardsmen who were flirting with a nurse-girl, and several well-dressed young men who were lounging up and down with cigars in their mouths.

"You see," remarked Holmes, as we paced to and fro in front of the house, "this marriage rather simplifies matters. The photograph becomes a double-edged weapon now. The chances are that she would be as averse to its being seen by Mr. Godfrey Norton, as our client is to its coming to the eyes of his princess. Now the question is, Where are we to find the photograph?"

"Where, indeed?"

"It is most unlikely that she carries it about with her. It

is cabinet size. Too large for easy concealment about a woman's dress. She knows that the King is capable of having her waylaid and searched. Two attempts of the sort have already been made. We may take it, then, that she does not carry it about with her." "Where, then?"

"Her banker or her lawyer. There is that double possibility. But I am inclined to think neither. Women are naturally secretive, and they like to do their own secreting. Why should she hand it over to anyone else? She could trust her own guardianship, but she could not tell what indirect or political influence might be brought to bear upon a business man. Besides, remember that she had resolved to use it within a few days. It must be where she can lay her hands upon it. It must be in her own house." "But it has twice been burgled."

"Pshaw! They did not know how to look."

"But how will you look?"

"I will not look."

"What then?"

"I will get her to show me."

"But she will refuse."

"She will not be able to. But I hear the rumble of wheels. It is her carriage. Now carry out my orders to the letter."

As he spoke the gleam of the sidelights of a carriage came round the curve of the avenue. It was a smart little landau which rattled up to the door of Briony Lodge. As it pulled up, one of the loafing men at the corner dashed forward to open the door in the hope of earning a copper, but was elbowed away by another loafer, who had rushed up with the same intention. A fierce quarrel broke out, which was increased by the two guardsmen, who took sides with one of the loungers, and by the scissors-grinder, who was equally hot upon the other side. A blow was struck, and in an instant the lady, who had stepped from her carriage, was the centre of a little knot of flushed and struggling men, who struck savagely at each other with their fists and sticks. Holmes dashed into the crowd to protect the lady; but, just as he reached her, he gave a cry and dropped to the ground, with the blood running freely down his face. At his fall the guardsmen took to their heels in one direction and the loungers in the other, while a number of better dressed people, who had watched the scuffle without taking part in it, crowded in to help the lady and to attend to the injured man. Irene Adler, as I will still call her, had hurried up the steps; but she stood at the top with her superb figure outlined against the lights of the hall, looking back into the street.

"Is the poor gentleman much hurt?" she asked.

"He is dead," cried several voices.

"No, no, there's life in him!" shouted another. "But he'll be gone before you can get him to hospital."

"He's a brave fellow," said a woman. "They would have had the lady's purse and watch if it hadn't been for him. They were a gang, and a rough one, too. Ah, he's breathing now." "He can't lie in the street. May we bring him in, marm?"

"Surely. Bring him into the sitting-room. There is a comfortable sofa. This way, please!"

Slowly and solemnly he was borne into Briony Lodge and laid out in the principal room, while I still observed the proceedings from my post by the window. The lamps had been lit, but the blinds had not been drawn, so that I could see Holmes as he lay upon the couch. I do not know whether he was seized with compunction at that moment for the part he was playing, but I know that I never felt more heartily ashamed of myself in my life than when I saw the beautiful creature against whom I was conspiring, or the grace and kindliness with which she waited upon the injured man. And yet it would be the blackest treachery to Holmes to draw back now from the part which he had intrusted to me. I hardened my heart, and took the smoke-rocket from under my ulster. After all, I thought, we are not injuring her. We are but preventing her from injuring another.

Holmes had sat up upon the couch, and I saw him motion like a man who is in need of air. A maid rushed across and threw open the window. At the same instant I saw him raise his hand and at the signal I tossed my rocket into the room with a cry of "Fire!" The word was no sooner out of my mouth than the whole crowd of spectators, well dressed and ill—gentlemen, ostlers, and servant maids—joined in a general shriek of "Fire!" Thick clouds of smoke curled through the room and out at the open window. I caught a glimpse of rushing figures, and a moment later the voice of Holmes from within assuring them that it was a false alarm. Slipping through the shouting crowd I made my way to the corner of the street, and in ten minutes was rejoiced to find my friend's arm in mine, and to get away from the scene of uproar. He walked swiftly and in silence for some few minutes until we had turned down one of the quiet streets which lead towards the Edgeware Road.

"You did it very nicely, Doctor," he remarked. "Nothing could have been better. It is all right."

"You have the photograph?"

"I know where it is."

"And how did you find out?"

"She showed me, as I told you she would."

"I am still in the dark."

"I do not wish to make a mystery," said he, laughing. "The matter was perfectly simple. You, of course, saw that everyone in the street was an accomplice. They were all engaged for the evening." "I guessed as much."

"Then, when the row broke out, I had a little moist red paint in the palm of my hand. I rushed forward, fell down, clapped my hand to my face, and became a piteous spectacle. It is an old trick." "That also I could fathom."

"Then they carried me in. She was bound to have me in. What else could she do? And into her sitting-room, which was the very room which I suspected. It lay between that and her bedroom, and I was determined to see which. They laid me on a couch, I motioned for air, they were compelled to open the window, and you had your chance." "How did that help you?"

"It was all-important. When a woman thinks that her house is on fire, her instinct is at once to rush to the thing which she values most. It is a perfectly overpowering impulse, and I have more than once taken advantage of it. In the case of the Darlington Substitution Scandal it was of use to me, and also in the Arnsworth Castle business. A married woman grabs at her baby; an unmarried one reaches for her jewel-box. Now it was clear to me that our lady of to-day had nothing in the house more precious to her than what we are in quest of. She would rush to secure it. The alarm of fire was admirably done. The smoke and shouting were enough to shake nerves of steel. She responded beautifully. The photograph is in a recess behind a sliding panel just above the right bell-pull. She was there in an instant, and I caught a glimpse of it as she half drew it out. When I cried out that it was a false alarm, she replaced it, glanced at the rocket, rushed from the room, and I have not seen her since. I rose, and, making my excuses, escaped from the house. I hesitated whether to attempt to secure the photograph at once; but the coachman had come in, and as he was watching me narrowly, it seemed safer to wait. A little over-precipitance may ruin all."

"And now?" I asked.

"Our quest is practically finished. I shall call with the King to-morrow, and with you, if you care to come with us. We will be shown into the sitting-room to wait for the lady, but it is probable that when she comes she may find neither us nor the photograph. It might be a satisfaction to his Majesty to regain it with his own hands." "And when will you call?"

"At eight in the morning. She will not be up, so that we shall have a clear field. Besides, we must be prompt, for this marriage may mean a complete change in her life and habits. I must wire to the King without delay." We had reached Baker Street and had stopped at the door. He was searching his pockets for the key when someone passing said:

"Good-night, Mister Sherlock Holmes."

There were several people on the pavement at the time, but the greeting appeared to come from a slim youth in an ulster who had hurried by.

"I've heard that voice before," said Holmes, staring down the dimly lit street. "Now, I wonder who the deuce that could have been."

III.

I slept at Baker Street that night, and we were engaged upon our toast and coffee in the morning when the King of Bohemia rushed into the room.

"You have really got it!" he cried, grasping Sherlock Holmes by either shoulder and looking eagerly into his face.

"Not yet."

"But you have hopes?"

"I have hopes."

"Then, come. I am all impatience to be gone."

"We must have a cab."

"No, my brougham is waiting."

"Then that will simplify matters." We descended and started off once more for Briony Lodge.

"Irene Adler is married," remarked Holmes.

"Married! When?"

"Yesterday."

"But to whom?"

"To an English lawyer named Norton."

"But she could not love him."

"I am in hopes that she does."

"And why in hopes?"

"Because it would spare your Majesty all fear of future annoyance. If the lady loves her husband, she does not love your Majesty. If she does not love your Majesty, there is no reason why she should interfere with your Majesty's plan." "It is true. And yet—! Well! I wish she had been of my own station! What a queen she would have made!" He relapsed into a moody silence, which was not broken until we drew up in Serpentine Avenue.

The door of Briony Lodge was open, and an elderly woman stood upon the steps. She watched us with a sardonic eye as we stepped from the brougham.

"Mr. Sherlock Holmes, I believe?" said she.

"I am Mr. Holmes," answered my companion, looking at her with a questioning and rather startled gaze.

"Indeed! My mistress told me that you were likely to call. She left this morning with her husband by the 5:15 train from Charing Cross for the Continent."

"What!" Sherlock Holmes staggered back, white with chagrin and surprise. "Do you mean that she has left England?"

"Never to return."

"And the papers?" asked the King hoarsely. "All is lost."

"We shall see." He pushed past the servant and rushed into the drawing-room, followed by the King and myself.

The furniture was scattered about in every direction, with dismantled shelves and open drawers, as if the lady had hurriedly ransacked them before her flight. Holmes rushed at the bell-pull, tore back a small sliding shutter, and, plunging in his hand, pulled out a photograph and a letter. The photograph was of Irene Adler herself in evening dress, the letter was superscribed to "Sherlock Holmes, Esq. To be left till called for." My friend tore it open, and we all three read it together. It was dated at midnight of the preceding night and ran in this way:

"MY DEAR MR. SHERLOCK HOLMES,—You really did it very well. You took me in completely. Until after the alarm of fire, I had not a suspicion. But then, when I found how I had betrayed myself, I began to think. I had been warned against you months ago. I had been told that, if the King employed an agent, it would certainly be you. And your address had been given me. Yet, with all this, you made me reveal what you wanted to know. Even after I became suspicious, I found it hard to think evil of such a dear, kind old clergyman. But, you know, I have been trained as an actress myself. Male costume is nothing new to me. I often take advantage of the freedom which it gives. I sent John, the coachman, to watch you, ran upstairs, got into my walking clothes, as I call them, and came down just as you departed.

"Well, I followed you to your door, and so made sure that I was really an object of interest to the celebrated Mr. Sherlock Holmes. Then I, rather imprudently, wished you good-night, and started for the Temple to see my husband.

"We both thought the best resource was flight, when pursued by so formidable an antagonist; so you will find the nest empty when you call to-morrow. As to the photograph, your client may rest in peace. I love and am loved by a better man than he. The King may do what he will without hindrance from one whom he has cruelly wronged. I keep it only to safeguard myself, and to preserve a weapon which will always secure me from any steps which he might take in the future. I leave a photograph which he might care to possess; and I remain, dear Mr. Sherlock Holmes,

"Very truly yours,
"IRENE NORTON, née ADLER."

"What a woman—oh, what a woman!" cried the King of Bohemia, when we had all three read this epistle. "Did I not tell you how quick and resolute she was? Would she not have made an admirable queen? Is it not a pity that she was not on my level?" "From what I have seen of the lady, she seems, indeed, to be on a very different level to your Majesty," said Holmes coldly. "I am sorry that I have not been able to bring your Majesty's business to a more successful conclusion." "On the contrary, my dear sir," cried the King; "nothing could be more successful. I know that her word is inviolate. The photograph is now as safe as if it were in the fire." "I am glad to hear your Majesty say so."

"I am immensely indebted to you. Pray tell me in what way I can reward you. This ring—" He slipped an emerald snake ring from his finger and held it out upon the palm of his hand.

"Your Majesty has something which I should value even more highly," said Holmes.

"You have but to name it."

"This photograph!"

The King stared at him in amazement.

"Irene's photograph!" he cried. "Certainly, if you wish it."

"I thank your Majesty. Then there is no more to be

done in the matter. I have the honour to wish you a very good morning." He bowed, and, turning away without observing the hand which the King had stretched out to him, he set off in my company for his chambers.

And that was how a great scandal threatened to affect the kingdom of Bohemia, and how the best plans of Mr. Sherlock Holmes were beaten by a woman's wit. He used to make merry over the cleverness of women, but I have not heard him do it of late. And when he speaks of Irene Adler, or when he refers to her photograph, it is always under the honourable title of the woman.

A Correspondence and a Climax

Lucy Maud Montgomery

At sunset Sidney hurried to her room to take off the soiled and faded cotton dress she had worn while milking. She had milked eight cows and pumped water for the milk-cans afterward in the fag-end of a hot summer day. She did that every night, but tonight she had hurried more than usual because she wanted to get her letter written before the early farm bedtime. She had been thinking it out while she milked the cows in the stuffy little pen behind the barn. This monthly letter was the only pleasure and stimulant in her life. Existence would have been, so Sidney thought, a dreary, unbearable blank without it. She cast aside her milking-dress with a thrill of distaste that tingled to her rosy fingertips. As she slipped into her blue-print afternoon dress her aunt called to her from below. Sidney ran out to the dark little entry and leaned over the stair railing. Below in the kitchen there was a hubbub of laughing, crying, quarrelling children, and a reek of bad tobacco smoke drifted up to the girl's disgusted nostrils.

Aunt Jane was standing at the foot of the stairs with a lamp in one hand and a year-old baby clinging to the other. She was a big shapeless woman with a round good-natured face—cheerful and vulgar as a sunflower was Aunt Jane at all times and occasions.

"I want to run over and see how Mrs. Brixby is this evening, Siddy, and you must take care of the baby till I get back."

Sidney sighed and went downstairs for the baby. It never would have occurred to her to protest or be petulant about it. She had all her aunt's sweetness of disposition, if she resembled her in nothing else. She had not grumbled because she had to rise at four that morning, get breakfast, milk the cows, bake bread, prepare seven children for school, get dinner, preserve twenty quarts of strawberries, get tea, and milk the cows again. All her days were alike as far as hard work and dullness went, but she accepted them cheerfully and uncomplainingly. But she did resent having to look after the baby when she wanted to write her letter.

She carried the baby to her room, spread a quilt on the floor for him to sit on, and gave him a box of empty spools to play with. Fortunately he was a phlegmatic infant, fond of staying in one place, and not given to roaming about in search of adventures; but Sidney knew she would have to keep an eye on him, and it would be distracting to literary effort.

She got out her box of paper and sat down by the little table at the window with a small kerosene lamp at her elbow. The room was small—a mere box above the kitchen which Sidney shared with two small cousins. Her bed and the cot where the little girls slept filled up almost all the available space. The furniture was poor, but everything was neat—it was the only neat room in the house, indeed, for tidiness was no besetting virtue of Aunt Jane's.

Opposite Sidney was a small muslined and befrilled toilet-table, above which hung an eight-by-six-inch mirror, in which Sidney saw herself reflected as she devoutly hoped other people did not see her. Just at that particular angle one eye appeared to be as large as an orange, while the other was the size of a pea, and the mouth zigzagged from ear to ear. Sidney hated that mirror as virulently as she could hate anything. It seemed to her to typify all that was unlovely in her life. The mirror of existence into which her fresh young soul had looked for twenty years gave back to her wistful gaze just such distortions of fair hopes and ideals.

Half of the little table by which she sat was piled high with books—old books, evidently well read and well-bred books, classics of fiction and verse every one of them, and all bearing on the flyleaf the name of Sidney Richmond, thereby meaning not the girl at the table, but her college-bred young father who had died the day before she was born. Her mother had died the day after, and Sidney thereupon had come into the hands of good Aunt Jane, with those books for her dowry, since nothing else was left after the expenses of the double funeral had been paid.

One of the books had Sidney Richmond's name printed on the title-page instead of written on the flyleaf. It was a thick little volume of poems, published in his college days—musical, unsubstantial, pretty little poems, every one of which the girl Sidney loved and knew by heart.

Sidney dropped her pointed chin in her hands and looked dreamily out into the moonlit night, while she thought her letter out a little more fully before beginning to write. Her big brown eyes were full of wistfulness and romance; for Sidney was romantic, albeit a faithful and understanding acquaintance with her father's books had given to her romance refinement and reason, and the delicacy of her own nature had imparted to it a self-respecting bias.

Presently she began to write, with a flush of real excitement on her face. In the middle of things the baby choked on a small twist spool and Sidney had to catch him up by the heels and hold him head downward until the trouble was ejected. Then she had to soothe him, and finally write the rest of her letter holding him on one arm and protecting the epistle from the grabs of his sticky little fingers. It was certainly letter-writing under difficulties, but Sidney seemed to deal with them mechanically. Her soul and understanding were elsewhere.

Four years before, when Sidney was sixteen, still calling herself a schoolgirl by reason of the fact that she could be spared to attend school four months in the winter when work was slack, she had been much interested in the "Maple Leaf" department of the Montreal weekly her uncle took. It was a page given over to youthful Canadians and filled with their contributions in the way of letters, verses, and prize essays. Noms de plume were signed to these, badges were sent to those who joined the Maple Leaf Club, and a general delightful sense of mystery pervaded the department.

Often a letter concluded with a request to the club members to correspond with the writer. One such request went from Sidney under the pen-name of "Ellen Douglas." The girl was lonely in Plainfield; she had no companions or associates such as she cared for; the Maple Leaf Club represented all that her life held of outward interest, and she longed for something more.

Only one answer came to "Ellen Douglas," and that was forwarded to her by the long-suffering editor of "The Maple Leaf." It was from John Lincoln of the Bar N Ranch, Alberta. He wrote that, although his age debarred him from membership in the club (he was twenty, and the limit was eighteen), he read the letters of the department with much interest, and often had thought of answering some of the requests for correspondents. He never had done so, but "Ellen Douglas's" letter was so interesting that he had decided to write to her. Would she be kind enough to correspond with him? Life on the Bar N, ten miles from the outposts of civilization, was lonely. He was two years out from the east, and had not yet forgotten to be homesick at times.

Sidney liked the letter and answered it. Since then they had written to each other regularly. There was nothing sentimental, hinted at or implied, in the correspondence. Whatever the faults of Sidney's romantic visions were, they did not tend to precocious flirtation. The Plainfield boys, attracted by her beauty and repelled by her indifference and aloofness, could have told that. She never expected to meet John Lincoln, nor did she wish to do so. In the correspondence itself she found her pleasure.

John Lincoln wrote breezy accounts of ranch life and adventures on the far western plains, so alien and remote from snug, humdrum Plainfield life that Sidney always had the sensation of crossing a gulf when she opened a letter from the Bar N. As for Sidney's own letter, this is the way it read as she wrote it:

"The Evergreens," Plainfield.

Dear Mr. Lincoln:

The very best letter I can write in the half-hour before the carriage will be at the door to take me to Mrs. Braddon's dance shall be yours tonight. I am sitting here in the library arrayed in my smartest, newest, whitest, silkiest gown, with a string of pearls which Uncle James gave me today about my throat—the dear, glistening, sheeny things! And I am looking forward to the "dances and delight" of the evening with keen anticipation.

You asked me in your last letter if I did not sometimes grow weary of my endless round of dances and dinners and social functions. No, no, never! I enjoy every one of them, every minute of them. I love life and its bloom and brilliancy; I love meeting new people; I love the ripple of music, the hum of laughter and conversation. Every morning when I awaken the new day seems to me to be a good fairy who will bring me some beautiful gift of joy.

The gift she gave me today was my sunset gallop on my grey mare Lady. The thrill of it is in my veins yet. I distanced the others who rode with me and led the homeward canter alone, rocking along a dark, gleaming road, shadowy with tall firs and pines, whose balsam made all the air resinous around me. Before me was a long valley filled with purple dusk, and beyond it meadows of sunset and great lakes of saffron and rose where a soul might lose itself in colour. On my right was the harbour, silvered over with a rising moon. Oh, it was all glorious—the clear air with its salt-sea tang, the aroma of the pines, the laughter of my friends behind me, the spring and rhythm of Lady's grey satin body beneath me! I wanted to ride on so forever, straight into the heart of the sunset.

Then home and to dinner. We have a houseful of guests at present—one of them an old statesman with a massive silver head, and eyes that have looked into people's thoughts so long that you have an uncanny feeling that they can see right through your soul and read motives you dare not avow even to yourself. I was terribly in awe of him at first, but when I got acquainted with him I found him charming. He is not above talking delightful nonsense even to a girl. I sat by him at dinner, and he talked to me—not nonsense, either, this time. He told me of his political contests and diplomatic battles; he was wise and witty and whimsical. I felt as if I were drinking some rare, stimulating mental wine. What a privilege it is to meet such men and take a peep through their wise eyes at the fascinating game of empire-building!

I met another clever man a few evenings ago. A lot of us went for a sail on the harbour. Mrs. Braddon's house party came too. We had three big white boats that skimmed down the moonlit channel like great white sea birds. There was another boat far across the harbour, and the people in it were singing. The music drifted over the water to us, so sad and sweet and beguiling that I could have cried for very pleasure. One of Mrs. Braddon's guests said to me: "That is the soul of music with all its sense and earthliness refined away."

I hadn't thought about him before—I hadn't even caught his name in the general introduction. He was a tall, slight man, with a worn, sensitive face and iron-grey hair—a quiet man who hadn't laughed or talked. But he began to talk to me then, and I forgot all about the others. I never had listened to anybody in the least like him. He talked of books and music, of art and travel. He had been all over the world, and had seen everything everybody else had seen and everything they hadn't too, I think. I seemed to be looking into an enchanted mirror where all my own dreams and ideals were reflected back to me, but made, oh, so much more beautiful!

On my way home after the Braddon people had left us somebody asked me how I liked Paul Moore! The man I had been talking with was Paul Moore, the great novelist! I was almost glad I hadn't known it while he was talking to me—I should have been too awed and reverential to have really enjoyed his conversation. As it was, I had contradicted him twice, and he had laughed and liked it. But his books will always have a new meaning to me henceforth, through the insight he himself has given me.

It is such meetings as these that give life its sparkle for me. But much of its abiding sweetness comes from my friendship with Margaret Raleigh. You will be weary of my rhapsodies over her. But she is such a rare and wonderful woman; much older then I am, but so young in heart and soul and freshness of feeling! She is to me mother and sister and wise, clear-sighted friend. To her I go with all my perplexities and hopes and triumphs. She has sympathy and understanding for my every mood. I love life so much for giving me such a friendship!

This morning I wakened at dawn and stole away to the shore before anyone else was up. I had a delightful run-away. The long, low-lying meadows between "The Evergreens" and the shore were dewy and fresh in that first light, that was as fine and purely tinted as the heart of one of my white roses. On the beach the water was purring in little blue ripples, and, oh, the sunrise out there beyond the harbour! All the eastern Heaven was abloom with it. And there was a wind that came dancing and whistling up the channel to replace the beautiful silence with a music more beautiful still.

The rest of the folks were just coming downstairs when I got back to breakfast. They were all yawny, and some were grumpy, but I had washed my being in the sunrise and felt as blithesome as the day. Oh, life is so good to live!

Tomorrow Uncle James's new vessel, the White Lady, is to be launched. We are going to make a festive occasion of it, and I am to christen her with a bottle of cobwebby old wine.

But I hear the carriage, and Aunt Jane is calling me. I had a great deal more to say—about your letter, your big "round-up" and your tribulations with your Chinese cook —but I've only time now to say goodbye. You wish me a lovely time at the dance and a full programme, don't you?

Yours sincerely,
Sidney Richmond.

Aunt Jane came home presently and carried away her sleeping baby. Sidney said her prayers, went to bed, and slept soundly and serenely.

She mailed her letter the next day, and a month later an answer came. Sidney read it as soon as she left the post office, and walked the rest of the way home as in a nightmare, staring straight ahead of her with wide-open, unseeing brown eyes.

John Lincoln's letter was short, but the pertinent paragraph of it burned itself into Sidney's brain. He wrote:

I am going east for a visit. It is six years since I was home, and it seems like three times six. I shall go by the C.P.R., which passes through Plainfield, and I mean to stop off for a day. You will let me call and see you, won't you? I shall have to take your permission for granted, as I shall be gone before a letter from you can reach the Bar N. I leave for the east in five days, and shall look forward to our meeting with all possible interest and pleasure.

Sidney did not sleep that night, but tossed restlessly about or cried in her pillow. She was so pallid and hollow-eyed the next morning that Aunt Jane noticed it, and asked her what the matter was.

"Nothing," said Sidney sharply. Sidney had never spoken sharply to her aunt before. The good woman shook her head. She was afraid the child was "taking something."

"Don't do much today, Siddy," she said kindly. "Just lie around and take it easy till you get rested up. I'll fix you a dose of quinine."

Sidney refused to lie around and take it easy. She swallowed the quinine meekly enough, but she worked fiercely all day, hunting out superfluous tasks to do. That night she slept the sleep of exhaustion, but her dreams were unenviable and the awakening was terrible.

Any day, any hour, might bring John Lincoln to Plainfield. What should she do? Hide from him? Refuse to see him? But he would find out the truth just the same; she would lose his friendships and respect just as surely. Sidney trod the way of the transgressor, and found that its thorns pierced to bone and marrow.

Everything had come to an end—nothing was left to her! In the untried recklessness of twenty untempered years she wished she could die before John Lincoln came to Plainfield. The eyes of youth could not see how she could possibly live afterward.

Some days later a young man stepped from the C.P.R. train at Plainfield station and found his way to the one small hotel the place boasted. After getting his supper he asked the proprietor if he could direct him to "The Evergreens."

Caleb Williams looked at his guest in bewilderment. "Never heerd o' such a place," he said.

"It is the name of Mr. Conway's estate—Mr. James Conway," explained John Lincoln.

"Oh, Jim Conway's place!" said Caleb. "Didn't know that was what he called it. Sartin I kin tell you whar' to find it. You see that road out thar'? Well, just follow it straight along for a mile and a half till you come to a blacksmith's forge. Jim Conway's house is just this side of it on the right—back from the road a smart piece and no other handy. You can't mistake it."

John Lincoln did not expect to mistake it, once he found it; he knew by heart what it appeared like from Sidney's description: an old stately mansion of mellowed brick, covered with ivy and set back from the highway amid fine ancestral trees, with a pine-grove behind it, a river to the left, and a harbour beyond.

He strode along the road in the warm, ruddy sunshine of early evening. It was not a bad-looking road at all; the farmsteads sprinkled along it were for the most part snug and wholesome enough; yet somehow it was different from what he had expected it to be. And there was no harbour or glimpse of distant sea visible. Had the hotel-keeper made a mistake? Perhaps he had meant some other James Conway.

Presently he found himself before the blacksmith's forge. Beside it was a rickety, unpainted gate opening into a snake-fenced lane feathered here and there with scrubby little spruces. It ran down a bare hill, crossed a little ravine full of young white-stemmed birches, and up another bare hill to an equally bare crest where a farmhouse was perched—a farmhouse painted a stark, staring yellow and the ugliest thing in farmhouses that John Lincoln had ever seen, even among the log shacks of the west. He knew now that he had been misdirected, but as there seemed to be nobody about the forge he concluded that he had better go to the yellow house and inquire within. He passed down the lane and over the little rustic bridge that spanned the brook. Just beyond was another home-made gate of poles.

Lincoln opened it, or rather he had his hand on the hasp of twisted withes which secured it, when he was suddenly arrested by the apparition of a girl, who flashed around the curve of young birch beyond and stood before him with panting breath and quivering lips.

"I beg your pardon," said John Lincoln courteously, dropping the gate and lifting his hat. "I am looking for the house of Mr. James Conway—'The Evergreens.' Can you direct me to it?"

"That is Mr. James Conway's house," said the girl, with the tragic air and tone of one driven to desperation and an impatient gesture of her hand toward the yellow nightmare above them.

"I don't think he can be the one I mean," said Lincoln perplexedly. "The man I am thinking of has a niece, Miss Richmond."

"There is no other James Conway in Plainfield," said the girl. "This is his place—nobody calls it 'The Evergreens' but myself. I am Sidney Richmond."

For a moment they looked at each other across the

gate, sheer amazement and bewilderment holding John Lincoln mute. Sidney, burning with shame, saw that this stranger was exceedingly good to look upon—tall, clean-limbed, broad-shouldered, with clear-cut bronzed features and a chin and eyes that would have done honour to any man. John Lincoln, among all his confused sensations, was aware that this slim, agitated young creature before him was the loveliest thing he ever had seen, so lithe was her figure, so glossy and dark and silken her bare, wind-ruffled hair, so big and brown and appealing her eyes, so delicately oval her flushed cheeks. He felt that she was frightened and in trouble, and he wanted to comfort and reassure her. But how could she be Sidney Richmond?

"I don't understand," he said perplexedly.

"Oh!" Sidney threw out her hands in a burst of passionate protest. "No, and you never will understand—I can't make you understand."

"I don't understand," said John Lincoln again. "Can you be Sidney Richmond—the Sidney Richmond who has written to me for four years?"

"I am."

"Then, those letters—"

"Were all lies," said Sidney bluntly and desperately. "There was nothing true in them—nothing at all. This is my home. We are poor. Everything I told you about it and my life was just imagination."

"Then why did you write them?" he asked blankly. "Why did you deceive me?"

"Oh, I didn't mean to deceive you! I never thought of such a thing. When you asked me to write to you I wanted to, but I didn't know what to write about to a stranger. I just couldn't write you about my life here, not because it was hard, but it was so ugly and empty. So I wrote instead of the life I wanted to live—the life I did live in imagination. And when once I had begun, I had to keep it up. I found it so fascinating, too! Those letters made that other life seem real to me. I never expected to meet you. These last four days since your letter came have been dreadful to me. Oh, please go away and forgive me if you can! I know I can never make you understand how it came about."

Sidney turned away and hid her burning face against the cool white bark of the birch tree behind her. It was worse than she had even thought it would be. He was so handsome, so manly, so earnest-eyed! Oh, what a friend to lose!

John Lincoln opened the gate and went up to her. There was a great tenderness in his face, mingled with a little kindly, friendly amusement.

"Please don't distress yourself so, Sidney," he said, unconsciously using her Christian name. "I think I do understand. I'm not such a dull fellow as you take me for. After all, those letters were true—or, rather, there was truth in them. You revealed yourself more faithfully in them than if you had written truly about your narrow outward life."

Sidney turned her flushed face and wet eyes slowly toward him, a little smile struggling out amid the clouds of woe. This young man was certainly good at understanding. "You—you'll forgive me then?" she stammered.

"Yes, if there is anything to forgive. And for my own part, I am glad you are not what I have always thought you were. If I had come here and found you what I expected, living in such a home as I expected, I never could have told you or even thought of telling you what you have come to mean to me in these lonely years during which your letters have been the things most eagerly looked forward to. I should have come this evening and spent an hour or so with you, and then have gone away on the train tomorrow morning, and that would have been all.

"But I find instead just a dreamy romantic little girl, much like my sisters at home, except that she is a great deal cleverer. And as a result I mean to stay a week at Plainfield and come to see you every day, if you will let me. And on my way back to the Bar N I mean to stop off at Plainfield again for another week, and then I shall tell you something more—something it would be a little too bold to say now, perhaps, although I could say it just as well and truly. All this if I may. May I, Sidney?"

He bent forward and looked earnestly into her face. Sidney felt a new, curious, inexplicable thrill at her heart. "Oh, yes.—I suppose so," she said shyly.

"Now, take me up to the house and introduce me to your Aunt Jane," said John Lincoln in satisfied tone.

The Birthmark

Nathaniel Hawthorne

In the latter part of the last century there lived a man of science, an eminent proficient in every branch of natural philosophy, who not long before our story opens had made experience of a spiritual affinity more attractive than any chemical one. He had left his laboratory to the care of an assistant, cleared his fine countenance from the furnace smoke, washed the stain of acids from his fingers, and persuaded a beautiful woman to become his wife. In those days when the comparatively recent discovery of electricity and other kindred mysteries of Nature seemed to open paths into the region of miracle, it was not unusual for the love of science to rival the love of woman in its depth and absorbing energy. The higher intellect, the imagination, the spirit, and even the heart might all find their congenial aliment in pursuits which, as some of their ardent votaries believed, would ascend from one step of powerful intelligence to another, until the philosopher should lay his hand on the secret of creative force and perhaps make new worlds for himself. We know not whether Aylmer possessed this degree of faith in man's ultimate control over Nature. He had devoted himself, however, too unreservedly to scientific studies ever to be weaned from them by any second passion. His love for his young wife might prove the stronger of the two; but it could only be by intertwining itself with his love of science, and uniting the strength of the latter to his own.

Such a union accordingly took place, and was attended with truly remarkable consequences and a deeply impressive moral. One day, very soon after their marriage, Aylmer sat gazing at his wife with a trouble in his countenance that grew stronger until he spoke.

"Georgiana," said he, "has it never occurred to you that the mark upon your cheek might be removed?"

"No, indeed," said she, smiling; but perceiving the seriousness of his manner, she blushed deeply. "To tell you the truth it has been so often called a charm that I was simple enough to imagine it might be so."

"Ah, upon another face perhaps it might," replied her husband; "but never on yours. No, dearest Georgiana, you came so nearly perfect from the hand of Nature that this slightest possible defect, which we hesitate whether to term a defect or a beauty, shocks me, as being the visible mark of earthly imperfection."

"Shocks you, my husband!" cried Georgiana, deeply hurt; at first reddening with momentary anger, but then bursting into tears. "Then why did you take me from my mother's side? You cannot love what shocks you!"

To explain this conversation it must be mentioned that in the centre of Georgiana's left cheek there was a singular mark, deeply interwoven, as it were, with the texture and substance of her face. In the usual state of her complexion—a healthy though delicate bloom—the mark wore a tint of deeper crimson, which imperfectly defined its shape amid the surrounding rosiness. When she blushed it gradually became more indistinct, and finally vanished amid the triumphant rush of blood that bathed the whole cheek with its brilliant glow. But if any shifting motion caused her to turn pale there was the mark again, a crimson stain upon the snow, in what Aylmer sometimes deemed an almost fearful distinctness. Its shape bore not a little similarity to the human hand, though of the smallest pygmy size. Georgiana's lovers were wont to say that some fairy at her birth hour had laid her tiny hand upon the infant's cheek, and left this impress there in token of the magic endowments that were to give her such sway over all hearts. Many a desperate swain would have risked life for the privilege of pressing his lips to the mysterious hand. It must not be concealed, however, that the impression wrought by this fairy sign manual varied exceedingly, according to the difference of temperament in the beholders. Some fastidious persons—but they were exclusively of her own sex—affirmed that the bloody hand, as they chose to call it, quite destroyed the effect of Georgiana's beauty, and rendered her countenance even hideous. But it would be as reasonable to say that one of those small blue stains which sometimes occur in the purest statuary marble would convert the Eve of Powers to a monster. Masculine observers, if the birthmark did not heighten their admiration, contented themselves with wishing it away, that the world might possess one living specimen of ideal loveliness without the semblance of a flaw. After his marriage,—for he thought little or nothing of the matter before,—Aylmer discovered that this was the case with himself.

Had she been less beautiful,—if Envy's self could have found aught else to sneer at,—he might have felt his affection heightened by the prettiness of this mimic hand, now vaguely portrayed, now lost, now stealing forth again and glimmering to and fro with every pulse of emotion that throbbed within her heart; but seeing her otherwise so perfect, he found this one defect grow more and more intolerable with every moment of their united lives. It was the fatal flaw of humanity which Nature, in one shape or another, stamps ineffaceably on all her productions, either to imply that they are temporary and finite, or that their perfection must be wrought by toil and pain. The crimson hand expressed the ineludible gripe in which mortality clutches the highest and purest of earthly mould, degrading them into kindred with the lowest, and even with the very brutes, like whom their visible frames return to dust. In this manner, selecting it as the symbol of his wife's liability to sin, sorrow, decay, and death, Aylmer's sombre imagination was not long in rendering the birthmark a frightful object, causing him more trouble and horror than ever Georgiana's beauty, whether of soul or sense, had given him delight.

At all the seasons which should have been their happiest, he invariably and without intending it, nay, in spite of a purpose to the contrary, reverted to this one disastrous topic. Trifling as it at first appeared, it so connected itself with innumerable trains of thought and modes of feeling that it became the central point of all. With the morning twilight Aylmer opened his eyes upon his wife's face and recognized the symbol of imperfection; and when they sat together at the evening hearth his eyes wandered stealthily to her cheek, and beheld, flickering with the blaze of the wood fire, the spectral hand that wrote mortality where he would fain have worshipped. Georgiana soon learned to shudder at his gaze. It needed but a glance with the peculiar expression that his face often wore to change the roses of her cheek into a deathlike paleness, amid which the crimson hand was brought strongly out, like a bass-relief of ruby on the whitest marble.

Late one night when the lights were growing dim, so as hardly to betray the stain on the poor wife's cheek, she herself, for the first time, voluntarily took up the subject.

"Do you remember, my dear Aylmer," said she, with a feeble attempt at a smile, "have you any recollection of a dream last night about this odious hand?"

"None! none whatever!" replied Aylmer, starting; but then he added, in a dry, cold tone, affected for the sake of concealing the real depth of his emotion, "I might well dream of it; for before I fell asleep it had taken a pretty firm hold of my fancy."

"And you did dream of it?" continued Georgiana, hastily; for she dreaded lest a gush of tears should interrupt what she had to say. "A terrible dream! I wonder that you can forget it. Is it possible to forget this one expression?—'It is in her heart now; we must have it out!' Reflect, my husband; for by all means I would have you recall that dream."

The mind is in a sad state when Sleep, the all-involving, cannot confine her spectres within the dim region of her sway, but suffers them to break forth, affrighting this actual life with secrets that perchance belong to a deeper one. Aylmer now remembered his dream. He had fancied himself with his servant Aminadab, attempting an operation for the removal of the birthmark; but the deeper went the knife, the deeper sank the hand, until at length its tiny grasp appeared to have caught hold of Georgiana's heart; whence, however, her husband was inexorably resolved to cut or wrench it away.

When the dream had shaped itself perfectly in his memory, Aylmer sat in his wife's presence with a guilty feeling. Truth often finds its way to the mind close muffled in robes of sleep, and then speaks with uncompromising directness of matters in regard to which we practise an unconscious self-deception during our waking moments. Until now he had not been aware of the tyrannizing influence acquired by one idea over his mind, and of the lengths which he might find in his heart to go for the sake of giving himself peace.

"Aylmer," resumed Georgiana, solemnly, "I know not what may be the cost to both of us to rid me of this fatal birthmark. Perhaps its removal may cause cureless deformity; or it may be the stain goes as deep as life itself. Again: do we know that there is a possibility, on any terms, of unclasping the firm gripe of this little hand which was laid upon me before I came into the world?"

"Dearest Georgiana, I have spent much thought upon the subject," hastily interrupted Aylmer. "I am convinced of the perfect practicability of its removal."

"If there be the remotest possibility of it," continued Georgiana, "let the attempt be made at whatever risk. Danger is nothing to me; for life, while this hateful mark makes me the object of your horror and disgust,—life is a burden which I would fling down with joy. Either remove this dreadful hand, or take my wretched life! You have deep science. All the world bears witness of it. You have achieved great wonders. Cannot you remove this little, little mark, which I cover with the tips of two small fingers? Is this beyond your power, for the sake of your own peace, and to save your poor wife from madness?"

"Noblest, dearest, tenderest wife," cried Aylmer, rapturously, "doubt not my power. I have already given this matter the deepest thought—thought which might almost have enlightened me to create a being less perfect than yourself. Georgiana, you have led me deeper than ever into the heart of science. I feel myself fully competent to render this dear cheek as faultless as its fellow; and then, most beloved, what will be my triumph when I shall have corrected what Nature left imperfect in her fairest work! Even Pygmalion, when his sculptured woman assumed life, felt not greater ecstasy than mine will be."

"It is resolved, then," said Georgiana, faintly smiling. "And, Aylmer, spare me not, though you should find the birthmark take refuge in my heart at last."

Her husband tenderly kissed her cheek—her right cheek—not that which bore the impress of the crimson hand.

The next day Aylmer apprised his wife of a plan that he

had formed whereby he might have opportunity for the intense thought and constant watchfulness which the proposed operation would require; while Georgiana, likewise, would enjoy the perfect repose essential to its success. They were to seclude themselves in the extensive apartments occupied by Aylmer as a laboratory, and where, during his toilsome youth, he had made discoveries in the elemental powers of Nature that had roused the admiration of all the learned societies in Europe. Seated calmly in this laboratory, the pale philosopher had investigated the secrets of the highest cloud region and of the profoundest mines; he had satisfied himself of the causes that kindled and kept alive the fires of the volcano; and had explained the mystery of fountains, and how it is that they gush forth, some so bright and pure, and others with such rich medicinal virtues, from the dark bosom of the earth. Here, too, at an earlier period, he had studied the wonders of the human frame, and attempted to fathom the very process by which Nature assimilates all her precious influences from earth and air, and from the spiritual world, to create and foster man, her masterpiece. The latter pursuit, however, Aylmer had long laid aside in unwilling recognition of the truth—against which all seekers sooner or later stumble—that our great creative Mother, while she amuses us with apparently working in the broadest sunshine, is yet severely careful to keep her own secrets, and, in spite of her pretended openness, shows us nothing but results. She permits us, indeed, to mar, but seldom to mend, and, like a jealous patentee, on no account to make. Now, however, Aylmer resumed these half-forgotten investigations; not, of course, with such hopes or wishes as first suggested them; but because they involved much physiological truth and lay in the path of his proposed scheme for the treatment of Georgiana.

As he led her over the threshold of the laboratory, Georgiana was cold and tremulous. Aylmer looked cheerfully into her face, with intent to reassure her, but was so startled with the intense glow of the birthmark upon the whiteness of her cheek that he could not restrain a strong convulsive shudder. His wife fainted.

"Aminadab! Aminadab!" shouted Aylmer, stamping violently on the floor.

Forthwith there issued from an inner apartment a man of low stature, but bulky frame, with shaggy hair hanging about his visage, which was grimed with the vapors of the furnace. This personage had been Aylmer's underworker during his whole scientific career, and was admirably fitted for that office by his great mechanical readiness, and the skill with which, while incapable of comprehending a single principle, he executed all the details of his master's experiments. With his vast strength, his shaggy hair, his smoky aspect, and the indescribable earthiness that incrusted him, he seemed to represent man's physical nature; while Aylmer's slender figure, and pale, intellectual face, were no less apt a type of the spiritual element.

"Throw open the door of the boudoir, Aminadab," said Aylmer, "and burn a pastil."

"Yes, master," answered Aminadab, looking intently at the lifeless form of Georgiana; and then he muttered to himself, "If she were my wife, I'd never part with that birthmark."

When Georgiana recovered consciousness she found herself breathing an atmosphere of penetrating fragrance, the gentle potency of which had recalled her from her deathlike faintness. The scene around her looked like enchantment. Aylmer had converted those smoky, dingy, sombre rooms, where he had spent his brightest years in recondite pursuits, into a series of beautiful apartments not unfit to be the secluded abode of a lovely woman. The walls were hung with gorgeous curtains, which imparted the combination of grandeur and grace that no other species of adornment can achieve; and as they fell from the ceiling to the floor, their rich and ponderous folds, concealing all angles and straight lines, appeared to shut in the scene from infinite space. For aught Georgiana knew, it might be a pavilion among the clouds. And Aylmer, excluding the sunshine, which would have interfered with his chemical processes, had supplied its place with perfumed lamps, emitting flames of various hue, but all uniting in a soft, impurpled radiance. He now knelt by his wife's side, watching her earnestly, but without alarm; for he was confident in his science, and felt that he could draw a magic circle round her within which no evil might intrude.

"Where am I? Ah, I remember," said Georgiana, faintly; and she placed her hand over her cheek to hide the terrible mark from her husband's eyes.

"Fear not, dearest!" exclaimed he. "Do not shrink from me! Believe me, Georgiana, I even rejoice in this single imperfection, since it will be such a rapture to remove it."

"Oh, spare me!" sadly replied his wife. "Pray do not look at it again. I never can forget that convulsive shudder."

In order to soothe Georgiana, and, as it were, to release her mind from the burden of actual things, Aylmer now put in practice some of the light and playful secrets which science had taught him among its profounder lore. Airy figures, absolutely bodiless ideas, and forms of unsubstantial beauty came and danced before her, imprinting their momentary footsteps on beams of light. Though she had some indistinct idea of the method of these optical phenomena, still the illusion was almost perfect enough to warrant the belief that her husband possessed sway over the spiritual world. Then again, when she felt a wish to look forth from her seclusion, immediately, as if her thoughts were answered, the procession of external existence flitted across a screen. The scenery and the figures of actual life were perfectly represented, but with that bewitching, yet indescribable difference which always makes a picture, an image, or a shadow so much more attractive than the original. When wearied of this, Aylmer bade her cast her eyes upon a vessel containing a quantity of earth. She did so, with little interest at first; but was soon startled to perceive the germ of a plant shooting upward from the soil. Then came the slender stalk; the leaves gradually unfolded themselves; and amid them was a perfect and lovely flower.

"It is magical!" cried Georgiana. "I dare not touch it."

"Nay, pluck it," answered Aylmer,—"pluck it, and inhale its brief perfume while you may. The flower will wither in a few moments and leave nothing save its brown seed vessels; but thence may be perpetuated a race as ephemeral as itself."

But Georgiana had no sooner touched the flower than the whole plant suffered a blight, its leaves turning coal-black as if by the agency of fire.

"There was too powerful a stimulus," said Aylmer, thoughtfully.

To make up for this abortive experiment, he proposed to take her portrait by a scientific process of his own invention. It was to be effected by rays of light striking upon a polished plate of metal. Georgiana assented; but, on looking at the result, was affrighted to find the features of the portrait blurred and indefinable; while the minute figure of a hand appeared where the cheek should have been. Aylmer snatched the metallic plate and threw it into a jar of corrosive acid.

Soon, however, he forgot these mortifying failures. In the intervals of study and chemical experiment he came to her flushed and exhausted, but seemed invigorated by her presence, and spoke in glowing language of the resources of his art. He gave a history of the long dynasty of the alchemists, who spent so many ages in quest of the universal solvent by which the golden principle might be elicited from all things vile and base. Aylmer appeared to believe that, by the plainest scientific logic, it was altogether within the limits of possibility to discover this long-sought medium; "but," he added, "a philosopher who should go deep enough to acquire the power would attain too lofty a wisdom to stoop to the exercise of it." Not less singular were his opinions in regard to the elixir vitae. He more than intimated that it was at his option to concoct a liquid that should prolong life for years, perhaps interminably; but that it would produce a discord in Nature which all the world, and chiefly the quaffer of the immortal nostrum, would find cause to curse.

"Aylmer, are you in earnest?" asked Georgiana, looking at him with amazement and fear. "It is terrible to possess such power, or even to dream of possessing it."

"Oh, do not tremble, my love," said her husband. "I would not wrong either you or myself by working such inharmonious effects upon our lives; but I would have you consider how trifling, in comparison, is the skill requisite to remove this little hand."

At the mention of the birthmark, Georgiana, as usual, shrank as if a redhot iron had touched her cheek.

Again Aylmer applied himself to his labors. She could hear his voice in the distant furnace room giving directions to Aminadab, whose harsh, uncouth, misshapen tones were audible in response, more like the grunt or growl of a brute than human speech. After hours of absence, Aylmer reappeared and proposed that she should now examine his cabinet of chemical products and natural treasures of the earth. Among the former he showed her a small vial, in which, he remarked, was contained a gentle yet most powerful fragrance, capable of impregnating all the breezes that blow across a kingdom. They were of inestimable value, the contents of that little vial; and, as he said so, he threw some of the perfume into the air and filled the room with piercing and invigorating delight.

"And what is this?" asked Georgiana, pointing to a small crystal globe containing a gold-colored liquid. "It is so beautiful to the eye that I could imagine it the elixir of life."

"In one sense it is," replied Aylmer; "or, rather, the elixir of immortality. It is the most precious poison that ever was concocted in this world. By its aid I could apportion the lifetime of any mortal at whom you might point your finger. The strength of the dose would determine whether he were to linger out years, or drop dead in the midst of a breath. No king on his guarded throne could keep his life if I, in my private station, should deem that the welfare of millions justified me in depriving him of it."

"Why do you keep such a terrific drug?" inquired Georgiana in horror.

"Do not mistrust me, dearest," said her husband, smiling; "its virtuous potency is yet greater than its harmful one. But see! here is a powerful cosmetic. With a few drops of this in a vase of water, freckles may be washed away as easily as the hands are cleansed. A stronger infusion would take the blood out of the cheek, and leave the rosiest beauty a pale ghost."

"Is it with this lotion that you intend to bathe my cheek?" asked Georgiana, anxiously.

"Oh, no," hastily replied her husband; "this is merely

superficial. Your case demands a remedy that shall go deeper."

In his interviews with Georgiana, Aylmer generally made minute inquiries as to her sensations and whether the confinement of the rooms and the temperature of the atmosphere agreed with her. These questions had such a particular drift that Georgiana began to conjecture that she was already subjected to certain physical influences, either breathed in with the fragrant air or taken with her food. She fancied likewise, but it might be altogether fancy, that there was a stirring up of her system—a strange, indefinite sensation creeping through her veins, and tingling, half painfully, half pleasurably, at her heart. Still, whenever she dared to look into the mirror, there she beheld herself pale as a white rose and with the crimson birthmark stamped upon her cheek. Not even Aylmer now hated it so much as she.

To dispel the tedium of the hours which her husband found it necessary to devote to the processes of combination and analysis, Georgiana turned over the volumes of his scientific library. In many dark old tomes she met with chapters full of romance and poetry. They were the works of philosophers of the middle ages, such as Albertus Magnus, Cornelius Agrippa, Paracelsus, and the famous friar who created the prophetic Brazen Head. All these antique naturalists stood in advance of their centuries, yet were imbued with some of their credulity, and therefore were believed, and perhaps imagined themselves to have acquired from the investigation of Nature a power above Nature, and from physics a sway over the spiritual world. Hardly less curious and imaginative were the early volumes of the Transactions of the Royal Society, in which the members, knowing little of the limits of natural possibility, were continually recording wonders or proposing methods whereby wonders might be wrought.

But to Georgiana the most engrossing volume was a large folio from her husband's own hand, in which he had recorded every experiment of his scientific career, its original aim, the methods adopted for its development, and its final success or failure, with the circumstances to which either event was attributable. The book, in truth, was both the history and emblem of his ardent, ambitious, imaginative, yet practical and laborious life. He handled physical details as if there were nothing beyond them; yet spiritualized them all, and redeemed himself from materialism by his strong and eager aspiration towards the infinite. In his grasp the veriest clod of earth assumed a soul. Georgiana, as she read, reverenced Aylmer and loved him more profoundly than ever, but with a less entire dependence on his judgment than heretofore. Much as he had accomplished, she could not but observe that his most splendid successes were almost invariably failures, if compared with the ideal at which he aimed. His brightest diamonds were the merest pebbles, and felt to be so by himself, in comparison with the inestimable gems which lay hidden beyond his reach. The volume, rich with achievements that had won renown for its author, was yet as melancholy a record as ever mortal hand had penned. It was the sad confession and continual exemplification of the shortcomings of the composite man, the spirit burdened with clay and working in matter, and of the despair that assails the higher nature at finding itself so miserably thwarted by the earthly part. Perhaps every man of genius in whatever sphere might recognize the image of his own experience in Aylmer's journal.

So deeply did these reflections affect Georgiana that she laid her face upon the open volume and burst into tears. In this situation she was found by her husband.

"It is dangerous to read in a sorcerer's books," said he with a smile, though his countenance was uneasy and displeased. "Georgiana, there are pages in that volume which I can scarcely glance over and keep my senses. Take heed lest it prove as detrimental to you."

"It has made me worship you more than ever," said she.

"Ah, wait for this one success," rejoined he, "then worship me if you will. I shall deem myself hardly unworthy of it. But come, I have sought you for the luxury of your voice. Sing to me, dearest."

So she poured out the liquid music of her voice to quench the thirst of his spirit. He then took his leave with a boyish exuberance of gayety, assuring her that her seclusion would endure but a little longer, and that the result was already certain. Scarcely had he departed when Georgiana felt irresistibly impelled to follow him. She had forgotten to inform Aylmer of a symptom which for two or three hours past had begun to excite her attention. It was a sensation in the fatal birthmark, not painful, but which induced a restlessness throughout her system. Hastening after her husband, she intruded for the first time into the laboratory.

The first thing that struck her eye was the furnace, that hot and feverish worker, with the intense glow of its fire, which by the quantities of soot clustered above it seemed to have been burning for ages. There was a distilling apparatus in full operation. Around the room were retorts, tubes, cylinders, crucibles, and other apparatus of chemical research. An electrical machine stood ready for immediate use. The atmosphere felt oppressively close, and was tainted with gaseous odors which had been tormented forth by the processes of science. The severe and homely simplicity of the apartment, with its naked walls and brick pavement, looked strange, accustomed as Georgiana had become to the fantastic elegance of her boudoir. But what chiefly, indeed almost solely, drew her attention, was the aspect of Aylmer himself.

He was pale as death, anxious and absorbed, and hung over the furnace as if it depended upon his utmost watchfulness whether the liquid which it was distilling should be the draught of immortal happiness or misery. How different from the sanguine and joyous mien that he had assumed for Georgiana's encouragement!

"Carefully now, Aminadab; carefully, thou human machine; carefully, thou man of clay!" muttered Aylmer, more to himself than his assistant. "Now, if there be a thought too much or too little, it is all over."

"Ho! ho!" mumbled Aminadab. "Look, master! look!"

Aylmer raised his eyes hastily, and at first reddened, then grew paler than ever, on beholding Georgiana. He rushed towards her and seized her arm with a gripe that left the print of his fingers upon it.

"Why do you come hither? Have you no trust in your husband?" cried he, impetuously. "Would you throw the blight of that fatal birthmark over my labors? It is not well done. Go, prying woman, go!"

"Nay, Aylmer," said Georgiana with the firmness of which she possessed no stinted endowment, "it is not you that have a right to complain. You mistrust your wife; you have concealed the anxiety with which you watch the development of this experiment. Think not so unworthily of me, my husband. Tell me all the risk we run, and fear not that I shall shrink; for my share in it is far less than your own."

"No, no, Georgiana!" said Aylmer, impatiently; "it must not be."

"I submit," replied she calmly. "And, Aylmer, I shall quaff whatever draught you bring me; but it will be on the same principle that would induce me to take a dose of poison if offered by your hand."

"My noble wife," said Aylmer, deeply moved, "I knew not the height and depth of your nature until now. Nothing shall be concealed. Know, then, that this crimson hand, superficial as it seems, has clutched its grasp into your being with a strength of which I had no previous conception. I have already administered agents powerful enough to do aught except to change your entire physical system. Only one thing remains to be tried. If that fail us we are ruined."

"Why did you hesitate to tell me this?" asked she.

"Because, Georgiana," said Aylmer, in a low voice, "there is danger."

"Danger? There is but one danger—that this horrible stigma shall be left upon my cheek!" cried Georgiana. "Remove it, remove it, whatever be the cost, or we shall both go mad!"

"Heaven knows your words are too true," said Aylmer, sadly. "And now, dearest, return to your boudoir. In a little while all will be tested."

He conducted her back and took leave of her with a solemn tenderness which spoke far more than his words how much was now at stake. After his departure Georgiana became rapt in musings. She considered the character of Aylmer, and did it completer justice than at any previous moment. Her heart exulted, while it trembled, at his honorable love—so pure and lofty that it would accept nothing less than perfection nor miserably make itself contented with an earthlier nature than he had dreamed of. She felt how much more precious was such a sentiment than that meaner kind which would have borne with the imperfection for her sake, and have been guilty of treason to holy love by degrading its perfect idea to the level of the actual; and with her whole spirit she prayed that, for a single moment, she might satisfy his highest and deepest conception. Longer than one moment she well knew it could not be; for his spirit was ever on the march, ever ascending, and each instant required something that was beyond the scope of the instant before.

The sound of her husband's footsteps aroused her. He bore a crystal goblet containing a liquor colorless as water, but bright enough to be the draught of immortality. Aylmer was pale; but it seemed rather the consequence of a highly-wrought state of mind and tension of spirit than of fear or doubt.

"The concoction of the draught has been perfect," said he, in answer to Georgiana's look. "Unless all my science have deceived me, it cannot fail."

"Save on your account, my dearest Aylmer," observed his wife, "I might wish to put off this birthmark of mortality by relinquishing mortality itself in preference to any other mode. Life is but a sad possession to those who have attained precisely the degree of moral advancement at which I stand. Were I weaker and blinder it might be happiness. Were I stronger, it might be endured hopefully. But, being what I find myself, methinks I am of all mortals the most fit to die."

"You are fit for heaven without tasting death!" replied her husband "But why do we speak of dying? The draught cannot fail. Behold its effect upon this plant."

On the window seat there stood a geranium diseased with yellow blotches, which had overspread all its leaves. Aylmer poured a small quantity of the liquid upon the soil in which it grew. In a little time, when the roots of the plant had taken up the moisture, the unsightly blotches began to be extinguished in a living verdure.

"There needed no proof," said Georgiana, quietly. "Give me the goblet I joyfully stake all upon your word."

"Drink, then, thou lofty creature!" exclaimed Aylmer, with fervid admiration. "There is no taint of imperfection on thy spirit. Thy sensible frame, too, shall soon be all perfect."

She quaffed the liquid and returned the goblet to his hand.

"It is grateful," said she with a placid smile. "Methinks it is like water from a heavenly fountain; for it contains I know not what of unobtrusive fragrance and deliciousness. It allays a feverish thirst that had parched me for many days. Now, dearest, let me sleep. My earthly senses are closing over my spirit like the leaves around the heart of a rose at sunset."

She spoke the last words with a gentle reluctance, as if it required almost more energy than she could command to pronounce the faint and lingering syllables. Scarcely had they loitered through her lips ere she was lost in slumber. Aylmer sat by her side, watching her aspect with the emotions proper to a man the whole value of whose existence was involved in the process now to be tested. Mingled with this mood, however, was the philosophic investigation characteristic of the man of science. Not the minutest symptom escaped him. A heightened flush of the cheek, a slight irregularity of breath, a quiver of the eyelid, a hardly perceptible tremor through the frame,—such were the details which, as the moments passed, he wrote down in his folio volume. Intense thought had set its stamp upon every previous page of that volume, but the thoughts of years were all concentrated upon the last.

While thus employed, he failed not to gaze often at the fatal hand, and not without a shudder. Yet once, by a strange and unaccountable impulse he pressed it with his lips. His spirit recoiled, however, in the very act, and Georgiana, out of the midst of her deep sleep, moved uneasily and murmured as if in remonstrance. Again Aylmer resumed his watch. Nor was it without avail. The crimson hand, which at first had been strongly visible upon the marble paleness of Georgiana's cheek, now grew more faintly outlined. She remained not less pale than ever; but the birthmark with every breath that came and went, lost somewhat of its former distinctness. Its presence had been awful; its departure was more awful still. Watch the stain of the rainbow fading out the sky, and you will know how that mysterious symbol passed away.

"By Heaven! it is well-nigh gone!" said Aylmer to himself, in almost irrepressible ecstasy. "I can scarcely trace it now. Success! success! And now it is like the faintest rose color. The lightest flush of blood across her cheek would overcome it. But she is so pale!"

He drew aside the window curtain and suffered the light of natural day to fall into the room and rest upon her cheek. At the same time he heard a gross, hoarse chuckle, which he had long known as his servant Aminadab's expression of delight.

"Ah, clod! ah, earthly mass!" cried Aylmer, laughing in a sort of frenzy, "you have served me well! Matter and spirit—earth and heaven—have both done their part in this! Laugh, thing of the senses! You have earned the right to laugh."

These exclamations broke Georgiana's sleep. She slowly unclosed her eyes and gazed into the mirror which her husband had arranged for that purpose. A faint smile flitted over her lips when she recognized how barely perceptible was now that crimson hand which had once blazed forth with such disastrous brilliancy as to scare away all their happiness. But then her eyes sought Aylmer's face with a trouble and anxiety that he could by no means account for.

"My poor Aylmer!" murmured she.

"Poor? Nay, richest, happiest, most favored!" exclaimed

he. "My peerless bride, it is successful! You are perfect!"

"My poor Aylmer," she repeated, with a more than human tenderness, "you have aimed loftily; you have done nobly. Do not repent that with so high and pure a feeling, you have rejected the best the earth could offer. Aylmer, dearest Aylmer, I am dying!"

Alas! it was too true! The fatal hand had grappled with the mystery of life, and was the bond by which an angelic spirit kept itself in union with a mortal frame. As the last crimson tint of the birthmark—that sole token of human imperfection—faded from her cheek, the parting breath of the now perfect woman passed into the atmosphere, and her soul, lingering a moment near her husband, took its heavenward flight. Then a hoarse, chuckling laugh was heard again! Thus ever does the gross fatality of earth exult in its invariable triumph over the immortal essence which, in this dim sphere of half development, demands the completeness of a higher state. Yet, had Alymer reached a profounder wisdom, he need not thus have flung away the happiness which would have woven his mortal life of the selfsame texture with the celestial. The momentary circumstance was too strong for him; he failed to look beyond the shadowy scope of time, and, living once for all in eternity, to find the perfect future in the present.

At the Bay

Katherine Mansfield

I

Very early morning. The sun was not yet risen, and the whole of Crescent Bay was hidden under a white sea-mist. The big bush-covered hills at the back were smothered. You could not see where they ended and the paddocks and bungalows began. The sandy road was gone and the paddocks and bungalows the other side of it; there were no white dunes covered with reddish grass beyond them; there was nothing to mark which was beach and where was the sea. A heavy dew had fallen. The grass was blue. Big drops hung on the bushes and just did not fall; the silvery, fluffy toi-toi was limp on its long stalks, and all the marigolds and the pinks in the bungalow gardens were bowed to the earth with wetness. Drenched were the cold fuchsias, round pearls of dew lay on the flat nasturtium leaves. It looked as though the sea had beaten up softly in the darkness, as though one immense wave had come rippling, rippling—how far? Perhaps if you had waked up in the middle of the night you might have seen a big fish flicking in at the window and gone again....

Ah-Aah! sounded the sleepy sea. And from the bush there came the sound of little streams flowing, quickly, lightly, slipping between the smooth stones, gushing into ferny basins and out again; and there was the splashing of big drops on large leaves, and something else—what was it?—a faint stirring and shaking, the snapping of a twig and then such silence that it seemed some one was listening.

Round the corner of Crescent Bay, between the piled-up

masses of broken rock, a flock of sheep came pattering. They were huddled together, a small, tossing, woolly mass, and their thin, stick-like legs trotted along quickly as if the cold and the quiet had frightened them. Behind them an old sheep-dog, his soaking paws covered with sand, ran along with his nose to the ground, but carelessly, as if thinking of something else. And then in the rocky gateway the shepherd himself appeared. He was a lean, upright old man, in a frieze coat that was covered with a web of tiny drops, velvet trousers tied under the knee, and a wide-awake with a folded blue handkerchief round the brim. One hand was crammed into his belt, the other grasped a beautifully smooth yellow stick. And as he walked, taking his time, he kept up a very soft light whistling, an airy, far-away fluting that sounded mournful and tender. The old dog cut an ancient caper or two and then drew up sharp, ashamed of his levity, and walked a few dignified paces by his master's side. The sheep ran forward in little pattering rushes; they began to bleat, and ghostly flocks and herds answered them from under the sea. "Baa! Baaa!" For a time they seemed to be always on the same piece of ground. There ahead was stretched the sandy road with shallow puddles; the same soaking bushes showed on either side and the same shadowy palings. Then something immense came into view; an enormous shock-haired giant with his arms stretched out. It was the big gum-tree outside Mrs. Stubbs' shop, and as they passed by there was a strong whiff of eucalyptus. And now big spots of light gleamed in the mist. The shepherd stopped whistling; he rubbed his red nose and wet beard on his wet sleeve and, screwing up his eyes, glanced in the direction of the sea. The sun was rising. It was marvellous how quickly the mist thinned, sped away, dissolved from the shallow plain, rolled up from the bush and was gone as if in a hurry to escape; big twists and curls jostled and shouldered each other as the silvery beams broadened. The far-away sky—a bright, pure blue—was reflected in the puddles, and the drops, swimming along the telegraph poles, flashed into points of light. Now the leaping, glittering sea was so bright it made one's eyes ache to look at it. The shepherd drew a pipe, the bowl as small as an acorn, out of his breast pocket, fumbled for a chunk of speckled tobacco, pared off a few shavings and stuffed the bowl. He was a grave, fine-looking old man. As he lit up and the blue smoke wreathed his head, the dog, watching, looked proud of him.

"Baa! Baaa!" The sheep spread out into a fan. They were just clear of the summer colony before the first sleeper turned over and lifted a drowsy head; their cry sounded in the dreams of little children... who lifted their arms to drag down, to cuddle the darling little woolly lambs of sleep. Then the first inhabitant appeared; it was the Burnells' cat Florrie, sitting on the gatepost, far too early as usual, looking for their milk-girl. When she saw the old sheep-dog she sprang up quickly, arched her back, drew in her tabby head, and seemed to give a little fastidious shiver. "Ugh! What a coarse, revolting creature!" said Florrie. But the old sheep-dog, not looking up, waggled past, flinging out his legs from side to side. Only one of his ears twitched to prove that he saw, and thought her a silly young female.

The breeze of morning lifted in the bush and the smell of leaves and wet black earth mingled with the sharp smell of the sea. Myriads of birds were singing. A goldfinch flew over the shepherd's head and, perching on the tiptop of a spray, it turned to the sun, ruffling its small breast feathers. And now they had passed the fisherman's hut, passed the charred-looking little whare where Leila the milk-girl lived with her old Gran. The sheep strayed over a yellow swamp and Wag, the sheep-dog, padded after, rounded them up and headed them for the steeper, narrower rocky pass that led out of Crescent Bay and towards Daylight Cove. "Baa! Baa!" Faint the cry came as they rocked along the fast-drying road. The shepherd put away his pipe, dropping it into his breast-pocket so that the little bowl hung over. And straightway the soft airy whistling began again. Wag ran out along a ledge of rock after something that smelled, and ran back again disgusted. Then pushing, nudging, hurrying, the sheep rounded the bend and the shepherd followed after out of sight.

II

A few moments later the back door of one of the bungalows opened, and a figure in a broad-striped bathing suit flung down the paddock, cleared the stile, rushed through the tussock grass into the hollow, staggered up the sandy hillock, and raced for dear life over the big porous stones, over the cold, wet pebbles, on to the hard sand that gleamed like oil. Splish-Splosh! Splish-Splosh! The water bubbled round his legs as Stanley Burnell waded out exulting. First man in as usual! He'd beaten them all again. And he swooped down to souse his head and neck.

"Hail, brother! All hail, Thou Mighty One!" A velvety bass voice came booming over the water.

Great Scott! Damnation take it! Stanley lifted up to see a dark head bobbing far out and an arm lifted. It was Jonathan Trout—there before him! "Glorious morning!" sang the voice.

"Yes, very fine!" said Stanley briefly. Why the dickens didn't the fellow stick to his part of the sea? Why should he come barging over to this exact spot? Stanley gave a kick, a lunge and struck out, swimming overarm. But Jonathan was a match for him. Up he came, his black hair sleek on his forehead, his short beard sleek.

"I had an extraordinary dream last night!" he shouted.

What was the matter with the man? This mania for conversation irritated Stanley beyond words. And it was always the same—always some piffle about a dream he'd had, or some cranky idea he'd got hold of, or some rot he'd been reading. Stanley turned over on his back and kicked with his legs till he was a living waterspout. But even then.... "I dreamed I was hanging over a terrifically high cliff, shouting to some one below." You would be! thought Stanley. He could stick no more of it. He stopped splashing. "Look here, Trout," he said, "I'm in rather a hurry this morning." "You're WHAT?" Jonathan was so surprised—or pretended to be—that he sank under the water, then reappeared again blowing.

"All I mean is," said Stanley, "I've no time to—to—to fool about. I want to get this over. I'm in a hurry. I've work to do this morning—see?"

Jonathan was gone before Stanley had finished. "Pass, friend!" said the bass voice gently, and he slid away through the water with scarcely a ripple.... But curse the fellow! He'd ruined Stanley's bathe. What an unpractical idiot the man was! Stanley struck out to sea again, and then as quickly swam in again, and away he rushed up the beach. He felt cheated.

Jonathan stayed a little longer in the water. He floated, gently moving his hands like fins, and letting the sea rock his long, skinny body. It was curious, but in spite of everything he was fond of Stanley Burnell. True, he had a fiendish desire to tease him sometimes, to poke fun at him, but at bottom he was sorry for the fellow. There was something pathetic in his determination to make a job of everything. You couldn't help feeling he'd be caught out one day, and then what an almighty cropper he'd come! At that moment an immense wave lifted Jonathan, rode past him, and broke along the beach with a joyful sound. What a beauty! And now there came another. That was the way to live—carelessly, recklessly, spending oneself. He got on to his feet and began to wade towards the shore, pressing his toes into the firm, wrinkled sand. To take things easy, not to fight against the ebb and flow of life, but to give way to it—that was what was needed. It was this tension that was all wrong. To live—to live! And the perfect morning, so fresh and fair, basking in the light, as though laughing at its own beauty, seemed to whisper, "Why not?" But now he was out of the water Jonathan turned blue with cold. He ached all over; it was as though some one was wringing the blood out of him. And stalking up the beach, shivering, all his muscles tight, he too felt his bathe was spoilt. He'd stayed in too long.

III

Beryl was alone in the living-room when Stanley appeared, wearing a blue serge suit, a stiff collar and a spotted tie. He looked almost uncannily clean and brushed; he was going to town for the day. Dropping into his chair, he pulled out his watch and put it beside his plate.

"I've just got twenty-five minutes," he said. "You might go and see if the porridge is ready, Beryl?"

"Mother's just gone for it," said Beryl. She sat down at the table and poured out his tea.

"Thanks!" Stanley took a sip. "Hallo!" he said in an astonished voice, "you've forgotten the sugar."

"Oh, sorry!" But even then Beryl didn't help him; she pushed the basin across. What did this mean? As Stanley helped himself his blue eyes widened; they seemed to quiver. He shot a quick glance at his sister-in-law and leaned back.

"Nothing wrong, is there?" he asked carelessly, fingering his collar.

Beryl's head was bent; she turned her plate in her fingers.

"Nothing," said her light voice. Then she too looked up, and smiled at Stanley. "Why should there be?"

"O-oh! No reason at all as far as I know. I thought you seemed rather—"

At that moment the door opened and the three little girls appeared, each carrying a porridge plate. They were dressed alike in blue jerseys and knickers; their brown legs were bare, and each had her hair plaited and pinned up in what was called a horse's tail. Behind them came Mrs. Fairfield with the tray.

"Carefully, children," she warned. But they were taking the very greatest care. They loved being allowed to carry things. "Have you said good morning to your father?"

"Yes, grandma." They settled themselves on the bench opposite Stanley and Beryl.

"Good morning, Stanley!" Old Mrs. Fairfield gave him his plate.

"Morning, mother! How's the boy?"

"Splendid! He only woke up once last night. What a perfect morning!" The old woman paused, her hand on the loaf of bread, to gaze out of the open door into the garden. The sea sounded. Through the wide-open window streamed the sun on to the yellow varnished walls and bare floor. Everything on the table flashed and glittered. In the middle there was an old salad bowl filled with yellow and red nasturtiums. She smiled, and a look of deep content shone in her eyes.

"You might cut me a slice of that bread, mother," said Stanley. "I've only twelve and a half minutes before the coach passes. Has anyone given my shoes to the servant girl?"

"Yes, they're ready for you." Mrs. Fairfield was quite unruffled.

"Oh, Kezia! Why are you such a messy child!" cried Beryl despairingly.

"Me, Aunt Beryl?" Kezia stared at her. What had she done now? She had only dug a river down the middle of her porridge, filled it, and was eating the banks away. But she did that every single morning, and no one had said a word up till now.

"Why can't you eat your food properly like Isabel and Lottie?" How unfair grown-ups are!

"But Lottie always makes a floating island, don't you, Lottie?"

"I don't," said Isabel smartly. "I just sprinkle mine with sugar and put on the milk and finish it. Only babies play with their food."

Stanley pushed back his chair and got up.

"Would you get me those shoes, mother? And, Beryl, if you've finished, I wish you'd cut down to the gate and stop the coach. Run in to your mother, Isabel, and ask her where my bowler hat's been put. Wait a minute—have you children been playing with my stick?" "No, father!"

"But I put it here." Stanley began to bluster. "I remember distinctly putting it in this corner. Now, who's had it? There's no time to lose. Look sharp! The stick's got to be found." Even Alice, the servant-girl, was drawn into the chase. "You haven't been using it to poke the kitchen fire with by any chance?"

Stanley dashed into the bedroom where Linda was lying. "Most extraordinary thing. I can't keep a single possession to myself. They've made away with my stick, now!"

"Stick, dear? What stick?" Linda's vagueness on these occasions could not be real, Stanley decided. Would nobody sympathize with him?

"Coach! Coach, Stanley!" Beryl's voice cried from the gate.

Stanley waved his arm to Linda. "No time to say good-bye!" he cried. And he meant that as a punishment to her.

He snatched his bowler hat, dashed out of the house, and swung down the garden path. Yes, the coach was there waiting, and Beryl, leaning over the open gate, was laughing up at somebody or other just as if nothing had happened. The heartlessness of women! The way they took it for granted it was your job to slave away for them while they didn't even take the trouble to see that your walking-stick wasn't lost. Kelly trailed his whip across the horses.

"Good-bye, Stanley," called Beryl, sweetly and gaily. It was easy enough to say good-bye! And there she stood, idle, shading her eyes with her hand. The worst of it was Stanley had to shout good-bye too, for the sake of appearances. Then he saw her turn, give a little skip and run back to the house. She was glad to be rid of him!

Yes, she was thankful. Into the living-room she ran and called "He's gone!" Linda cried from her room: "Beryl! Has Stanley gone?" Old Mrs. Fairfield appeared, carrying the boy in his little flannel coatee.

"Gone?"

"Gone!"

Oh, the relief, the difference it made to have the man out of the house. Their very voices were changed as they called to one another; they sounded warm and loving and as if they shared a secret. Beryl went over to the table. "Have another cup of tea, mother. It's still hot." She wanted, somehow, to celebrate the fact that they could do what they liked now. There was no man to disturb them; the whole perfect day was theirs.

"No, thank you, child," said old Mrs. Fairfield, but the way at that moment she tossed the boy up and said "a-goos-a-goos-a-ga!" to him meant that she felt the same. The little girls ran into the paddock like chickens let out of a coop.

Even Alice, the servant-girl, washing up the dishes in the kitchen, caught the infection and used the precious tank water in a perfectly reckless fashion.

"Oh, these men!" said she, and she plunged the teapot into the bowl and held it under the water even after it had stopped bubbling, as if it too was a man and drowning was too good for them.

IV

"Wait for me, Isa-bel! Kezia, wait for me!"

There was poor little Lottie, left behind again, because she found it so fearfully hard to get over the stile by herself. When she stood on the first step her knees began to wobble; she grasped the post. Then you had to put one leg over. But which leg? She never could decide. And when she did finally put one leg over with a sort of stamp of despair—then the feeling was awful. She was half in the paddock still and half in the tussock grass. She clutched the post desperately and lifted up her voice. "Wait for me!" "No, don't you wait for her, Kezia!" said Isabel. "She's such a little silly. She's always making a fuss. Come on!" And she tugged Kezia's jersey. "You can use my bucket if you come with me," she said kindly. "It's bigger than yours." But Kezia couldn't leave Lottie all by herself. She ran back to her. By this time Lottie was very red in the face and breathing heavily.

"Here, put your other foot over," said Kezia.

"Where?"

Lottie looked down at Kezia as if from a mountain height.

"Here where my hand is." Kezia patted the place.

"Oh, there do you mean!" Lottie gave a deep sigh and put the second foot over.

"Now—sort of turn round and sit down and slide," said Kezia.

"But there's nothing to sit down on, Kezia," said Lottie.

She managed it at last, and once it was over she shook herself and began to beam.

"I'm getting better at climbing over stiles, aren't I, Kezia?"

Lottie's was a very hopeful nature.

The pink and the blue sunbonnet followed Isabel's bright red sunbonnet up that sliding, slipping hill. At the top they paused to decide where to go and to have a good stare at who was there already. Seen from behind, standing against the skyline, gesticulating largely with their spades, they looked like minute puzzled explorers.

The whole family of Samuel Josephs was there already with their lady-help, who sat on a camp-stool and kept order with a whistle that she wore tied round her neck, and a small cane with which she directed operations. The Samuel Josephs never played by themselves or managed their own game. If they did, it ended in the boys pouring water down the girls' necks or the girls trying to put little black crabs into the boys' pockets. So Mrs. S. J. and the poor lady-help drew up what she called a "brogramme" every morning to keep them "abused and out of bischief." It was all competitions or races or round games. Everything began with a piercing blast of the lady-help's whistle and ended with another. There were even prizes—large, rather dirty paper parcels which the lady-help with a sour little smile drew out of a bulging string kit. The Samuel Josephs fought fearfully for the prizes and cheated and pinched one another's arms—they were all expert pinchers. The only time the Burnell children ever played with them Kezia had got a prize, and when she undid three bits of paper she found a very small rusty button-hook. She couldn't understand why they made such a fuss....

But they never played with the Samuel Josephs now or even went to their parties. The Samuel Josephs were always giving children's parties at the Bay and there was always the same food. A big washhand basin of very brown fruit-salad, buns cut into four and a washhand jug full of something the lady-help called "Limmonadear." And you went away in the evening with half the frill torn off your frock or something spilled all down the front of your open-work pinafore, leaving the Samuel Josephs leaping like savages on their lawn. No! They were too awful.

On the other side of the beach, close down to the water, two little boys, their knickers rolled up, twinkled like spiders. One was digging, the other pattered in and out of the water, filling a small bucket. They were the Trout boys, Pip and Rags. But Pip was so busy digging and Rags was so busy helping that they didn't see their little cousins until they were quite close.

"Look!" said Pip. "Look what I've discovered." And he showed them an old wet, squashed-looking boot. The three little girls stared.

"Whatever are you going to do with it?" asked Kezia.

"Keep it, of course!" Pip was very scornful. "It's a find—see?"

Yes, Kezia saw that. All the same....

"There's lots of things buried in the sand," explained Pip. "They get chucked up from wrecks. Treasure. Why—you might find—"

"But why does Rags have to keep on pouring water in?"

asked Lottie.

"Oh, that's to moisten it," said Pip, "to make the work a bit easier. Keep it up, Rags."

And good little Rags ran up and down, pouring in the water that turned brown like cocoa.

"Here, shall I show you what I found yesterday?" said Pip mysteriously, and he stuck his spade into the sand. "Promise not to tell."

They promised.

"Say, cross my heart straight dinkum."

The little girls said it.

Pip took something out of his pocket, rubbed it a long time on the front of his jersey, then breathed on it and rubbed it again.

"Now turn round!" he ordered.

They turned round.

"All look the same way! Keep still! Now!"

And his hand opened; he held up to the light something that flashed, that winked, that was a most lovely green.

"It's a nemeral," said Pip solemnly.

"Is it really, Pip?" Even Isabel was impressed.

The lovely green thing seemed to dance in Pip's fingers. Aunt Beryl had a nemeral in a ring, but it was a very small one. This one was as big as a star and far more beautiful.

V

As the morning lengthened whole parties appeared over the sand-hills and came down on the beach to bathe. It was understood that at eleven o'clock the women and children of the summer colony had the sea to themselves. First the women undressed, pulled on their bathing dresses and covered their heads in hideous caps like sponge bags; then the children were unbuttoned. The beach was strewn with little heaps of clothes and shoes;

the big summer hats, with stones on them to keep them from blowing away, looked like immense shells. It was strange that even the sea seemed to sound differently when all those leaping, laughing figures ran into the waves. Old Mrs. Fairfield, in a lilac cotton dress and a black hat tied under the chin, gathered her little brood and got them ready. The little Trout boys whipped their shirts over their heads, and away the five sped, while their grandma sat with one hand in her knitting-bag ready to draw out the ball of wool when she was satisfied they were safely in.

The firm compact little girls were not half so brave as the tender, delicate-looking little boys. Pip and Rags, shivering, crouching down, slapping the water, never hesitated. But Isabel, who could swim twelve strokes, and Kezia, who could nearly swim eight, only followed on the strict understanding they were not to be splashed. As for Lottie, she didn't follow at all. She liked to be left to go in her own way, please. And that way was to sit down at the edge of the water, her legs straight, her knees pressed together, and to make vague motions with her arms as if she expected to be wafted out to sea. But when a bigger wave than usual, an old whiskery one, came lolloping along in her direction, she scrambled to her feet with a face of horror and flew up the beach again.

"Here, mother, keep those for me, will you?"

Two rings and a thin gold chain were dropped into Mrs Fairfield's lap.

"Yes, dear. But aren't you going to bathe here?"

"No-o," Beryl drawled. She sounded vague. "I'm undressing farther along. I'm going to bathe with Mrs. Harry Kember."

"Very well." But Mrs. Fairfield's lips set. She disapproved of Mrs Harry Kember. Beryl knew it.

Poor old mother, she smiled, as she skimmed over the stones. Poor old mother! Old! Oh, what joy, what bliss it was to be young....

"You look very pleased," said Mrs. Harry Kember. She sat hunched up on the stones, her arms round her knees, smoking.

"It's such a lovely day," said Beryl, smiling down at her.

"Oh my dear!" Mrs. Harry Kember's voice sounded as though she knew better than that. But then her voice always sounded as though she knew something better about you than you did yourself. She was a long, strange-looking woman with narrow hands and feet. Her face, too, was long and narrow and exhausted-looking; even her fair curled fringe looked burnt out and withered. She was the only woman at the Bay who smoked, and she smoked incessantly, keeping the cigarette between her lips while she talked, and only taking it out when the ash was so long you could not understand why it did not fall. When she was not playing bridge—she played bridge every day of her life—she spent her time lying in the full glare of the sun. She could stand any amount of it; she never had enough. All the same, it did not seem to warm her. Parched, withered, cold, she lay stretched on the stones like a piece of tossed-up driftwood. The women at the Bay thought she was very, very fast. Her lack of vanity, her slang, the way she treated men as though she was one of them, and the fact that she didn't care twopence about her house and called the servant Gladys "Glad-eyes," was disgraceful. Standing on the veranda steps Mrs. Kember would call in her indifferent, tired voice, "I say, Glad-eyes, you might heave me a handkerchief if I've got one, will you?" And Glad-eyes, a red bow in her hair instead of a cap, and white shoes, came running with an impudent smile. It was an absolute scandal! True, she had no children, and her husband.... Here the voices were always raised; they became fervent. How can he have married her? How can he, how can he? It must have been money, of course, but even then!

Mrs. Kember's husband was at least ten years younger than she was, and so incredibly handsome that he looked like a mask or a most perfect illustration in an American novel rather than a man. Black hair, dark blue eyes, red lips, a slow sleepy smile, a fine tennis player, a perfect dancer, and with it all a mystery. Harry Kember was like a man walking in his sleep. Men couldn't stand him, they couldn't get a word out of the chap; he ignored his wife just as she ignored him. How did he live? Of course there were stories, but such stories! They simply couldn't be told. The women he'd been seen with, the places he'd been seen in... but nothing was ever certain, nothing definite. Some of the women at the Bay privately thought he'd commit a murder one day. Yes, even while they talked to Mrs. Kember and took in the awful concoction she was wearing, they saw her, stretched as she lay on the beach; but cold, bloody, and still with a cigarette stuck in the corner of her mouth.

Mrs. Kember rose, yawned, unsnapped her belt buckle, and tugged at the tape of her blouse. And Beryl stepped out of her skirt and shed her jersey, and stood up in her short white petticoat, and her camisole with ribbon bows on the shoulders.

"Mercy on us," said Mrs. Harry Kember, "what a little beauty you are!"

"Don't!" said Beryl softly; but, drawing off one stocking and then the other, she felt a little beauty.

"My dear—why not?" said Mrs. Harry Kember, stamping on her own petticoat. Really—her underclothes! A pair of blue cotton knickers and a linen bodice that reminded one somehow of a pillow-case.... "And you don't wear stays, do you?" She touched Beryl's waist, and Beryl sprang away with a small affected cry. Then "Never!" she said firmly.

"Lucky little creature," sighed Mrs. Kember, unfastening her own.

Beryl turned her back and began the complicated movements of some one who is trying to take off her clothes and to pull on her bathing-dress all at one and the same time.

"Oh, my dear—don't mind me," said Mrs. Harry Kember. "Why be shy? I shan't eat you. I shan't be shocked like those other ninnies." And she gave her strange neighing laugh and grimaced at the other women.

But Beryl was shy. She never undressed in front of anybody. Was that silly? Mrs. Harry Kember made her feel it was silly, even something to be ashamed of. Why be shy indeed! She glanced quickly at her friend standing so boldly in her torn chemise and lighting a fresh cigarette; and a quick, bold, evil feeling started up in her breast. Laughing recklessly, she drew on the limp, sandy-feeling bathing-dress that was not quite dry and fastened the twisted buttons.

"That's better," said Mrs. Harry Kember. They began to go down the beach together. "Really, it's a sin for you to wear clothes, my dear. Somebody's got to tell you some day." The water was quite warm. It was that marvellous transparent blue, flecked with silver, but the sand at the bottom looked gold; when you kicked with your toes there rose a little puff of gold-dust. Now the waves just reached her breast. Beryl stood, her arms outstretched, gazing out, and as each wave came she gave the slightest little jump, so that it seemed it was the wave which lifted her so gently.

"I believe in pretty girls having a good time," said Mrs. Harry Kember. "Why not? Don't you make a mistake, my dear. Enjoy yourself." And suddenly she turned turtle, disappeared, and swam away quickly, quickly, like a rat. Then she flicked round and began swimming back. She was going to say something else. Beryl felt that she was being poisoned by this cold woman, but she longed to hear. But oh, how strange, how horrible! As Mrs. Harry Kember came up close she looked, in her black waterproof bathing-cap, with her sleepy face lifted above the water, just her chin touching, like a horrible caricature of her husband.

VI

In a steamer chair, under a manuka tree that grew in the middle of the front grass patch, Linda Burnell dreamed the morning away. She did nothing. She looked up at the dark, close, dry leaves of the manuka, at the chinks of blue between, and now and again a tiny yellowish flower dropped on her. Pretty—yes, if you held one of those flowers on the palm of your hand and looked at it closely, it was an exquisite small thing. Each pale yellow petal shone as if each was the careful work of a loving hand. The tiny tongue in the centre gave it the shape of a bell. And when you turned it over the outside was a deep bronze colour. But as soon as they flowered, they fell and were scattered. You brushed them off your frock as you talked; the horrid little things got caught in one's hair. Why, then, flower at all? Who takes the trouble—or the joy—to make all these things that are wasted, wasted.... It was uncanny.

On the grass beside her, lying between two pillows, was the boy. Sound asleep he lay, his head turned away from his mother. His fine dark hair looked more like a shadow than like real hair, but his ear was a bright, deep coral. Linda clasped her hands above her head and crossed her feet. It was very pleasant to know that all these bungalows were empty, that everybody was down on the beach, out of sight, out of hearing. She had the garden to herself; she was alone.

Dazzling white the picotees shone; the golden-eyed marigold glittered; the nasturtiums wreathed the veranda poles in green and gold flame. If only one had time to look at these flowers long enough, time to get over the sense of novelty and strangeness, time to know them! But as soon as one paused to part the petals, to discover the under-side of the leaf, along came Life and one was swept away. And, lying in her cane chair, Linda felt so light; she felt like a leaf. Along came Life like a wind and she was seized and shaken; she had to go. Oh dear, would it always be so? Was there no escape?

... Now she sat on the veranda of their Tasmanian home, leaning against her father's knee. And he promised, "As soon as you and I are old enough, Linny, we'll cut off somewhere, we'll escape. Two boys together. I have a fancy I'd like to sail up a river in China." Linda saw that river, very wide, covered with little rafts and boats. She saw the yellow hats of the boatmen and she heard their high, thin voices as they called....

"Yes, papa."

But just then a very broad young man with bright ginger hair walked slowly past their house, and slowly, solemnly even, uncovered. Linda's father pulled her ear teasingly, in the way he had.

"Linny's beau," he whispered.

"Oh, papa, fancy being married to Stanley Burnell!"

Well, she was married to him. And what was more she loved him. Not the Stanley whom every one saw, not the everyday one; but a timid, sensitive, innocent Stanley who knelt down every night to say his prayers, and who longed to be good. Stanley was simple. If he believed in people—as he believed in her, for instance—it was with his whole heart. He could not be disloyal; he could not tell a lie. And how terribly he suffered if he thought anyone—she—was not being dead straight, dead sincere with him! "This is too subtle for me!" He flung out the words, but his open, quivering, distraught look was like the look of a trapped beast.

But the trouble was—here Linda felt almost inclined to laugh, though Heaven knows it was no laughing matter—she saw her Stanley so seldom. There were glimpses, moments, breathing spaces of calm, but all the rest of the time it was like living in a house that couldn't be cured of the habit of catching on fire, on a ship that got wrecked every day. And it was always Stanley who was in the thick of the danger. Her whole time was spent in rescuing him, and restoring him, and calming him down, and listening to his story. And what was left of her time was spent in the dread of having children.

Linda frowned; she sat up quickly in her steamer chair and clasped her ankles. Yes, that was her real grudge against life; that was what she could not understand. That was the question she asked and asked, and listened in vain for the answer. It was all very well to say it was the common lot of women to bear children. It wasn't true. She, for one, could prove that wrong. She was broken, made weak, her courage was gone, through child-bearing. And what made it doubly hard to bear was, she did not love her children. It was useless pretending. Even if she had had the strength she never would have nursed and played with the little girls. No, it was as though a cold breath had chilled her through and through on each of those awful journeys; she had no warmth left to give them. As to the boy—well, thank Heaven, mother had taken him; he was mother's, or Beryl's, or anybody's who wanted him. She had hardly held him in her arms. She was so indifferent about him that as he lay there... Linda glanced down.

The boy had turned over. He lay facing her, and he was no longer asleep. His dark-blue, baby eyes were open; he looked as though he was peeping at his mother. And suddenly his face dimpled; it broke into a wide, toothless smile, a perfect beam, no less.

"I'm here!" that happy smile seemed to say. "Why don't you like me?"

There was something so quaint, so unexpected about that smile that Linda smiled herself. But she checked herself and said to the boy coldly, "I don't like babies."

"Don't like babies?" The boy couldn't believe her. "Don't like me?" He waved his arms foolishly at his mother.

Linda dropped off her chair on to the grass.

"Why do you keep on smiling?" she said severely. "If you knew what I was thinking about, you wouldn't."

But he only squeezed up his eyes, slyly, and rolled his head on the pillow. He didn't believe a word she said.

"We know all about that!" smiled the boy.

Linda was so astonished at the confidence of this little creature.... Ah no, be sincere. That was not what she felt; it was something far different, it was something so new, so.... The tears danced in her eyes; she breathed in a small whisper to the boy, "Hallo, my funny!" But by now the boy had forgotten his mother. He was serious again. Something pink, something soft waved in front of him. He made a grab at it and it immediately disappeared. But when he lay back, another, like the first, appeared. This time he determined to catch it. He made a tremendous effort and rolled right over.

VII

The tide was out; the beach was deserted; lazily flopped the warm sea. The sun beat down, beat down hot and fiery on the fine sand, baking the grey and blue and black and white-veined pebbles. It sucked up the little drop of water that lay in the hollow of the curved shells; it bleached the pink convolvulus that threaded through and through the sand-hills. Nothing seemed to move but the small sand-hoppers. Pit-pit-pit! They were never still.

Over there on the weed-hung rocks that looked at low tide like shaggy beasts come down to the water to drink, the sunlight seemed to spin like a silver coin dropped into each of the small rock pools. They danced, they quivered, and minute ripples laved the porous shores. Looking down, bending over, each pool was like a lake with pink and blue houses clustered on the shores; and oh! the vast mountainous country behind those houses—the ravines, the passes, the dangerous creeks and fearful tracks that led to the water's edge. Underneath waved the sea-forest—pink thread-like trees, velvet anemones, and orange berry-spotted weeds. Now a stone on the bottom moved, rocked, and there was a glimpse of a black feeler; now a thread-like creature wavered by and was lost. Something was happening to the pink, waving trees; they were changing to a cold moonlight blue. And now there sounded the faintest "plop." Who made that sound? What was going on down there? And how strong, how damp the seaweed smelt in the hot sun....

The green blinds were drawn in the bungalows of the summer colony. Over the verandas, prone on the paddock, flung over the fences, there were exhausted-looking bathing-dresses and rough striped towels. Each back window seemed to have a pair of sand-shoes on the sill and some lumps of rock or a bucket or a collection of pawa shells. The bush quivered in a haze of heat; the sandy road was empty except for the Trouts' dog Snooker, who lay stretched in the very middle of it. His blue eye was turned up, his legs stuck out stiffly, and he gave an occasional desperate-sounding puff, as much as to say he had decided to make an end of it and was only waiting for some kind cart to come along.

"What are you looking at, my grandma? Why do you keep stopping and sort of staring at the wall?"

Kezia and her grandmother were taking their siesta together. The little girl, wearing only her short drawers and her under-bodice, her arms and legs bare, lay on one of the puffed-up pillows of her grandma's bed, and the old woman, in a white ruffled dressing-gown, sat in a rocker at the window, with a long piece of pink knitting in her lap. This room that they shared, like the other rooms of the bungalow, was of light varnished wood and the floor was bare. The furniture was of the shabbiest, the simplest. The dressing-table, for instance, was a packing-case in a sprigged muslin petticoat, and the mirror above was very strange; it was as though a little piece of forked lightning was imprisoned in it. On the table there stood a jar of sea-pinks, pressed so tightly together they looked more like a velvet pincushion, and a special shell which Kezia had given her grandma for a pin-tray, and another even more special which she had thought would make a very nice place for a watch to curl up in.

"Tell me, grandma," said Kezia.

The old woman sighed, whipped the wool twice round her thumb, and drew the bone needle through. She was casting on.

"I was thinking of your Uncle William, darling," she said quietly.

"My Australian Uncle William?" said Kezia. She had another.

"Yes, of course."

"The one I never saw?"

"That was the one."

"Well, what happened to him?" Kezia knew perfectly well, but she wanted to be told again.

"He went to the mines, and he got a sunstroke there and died," said old Mrs. Fairfield.

Kezia blinked and considered the picture again.... A little man fallen over like a tin soldier by the side of a big black hole.

"Does it make you sad to think about him, grandma?" She hated her grandma to be sad.

It was the old woman's turn to consider. Did it make her sad? To look back, back. To stare down the years, as Kezia had seen her doing. To look after them as a woman does, long after they were out of sight. Did it make her sad? No, life was like that.

"No, Kezia."

"But why?" asked Kezia. She lifted one bare arm and began to draw things in the air. "Why did Uncle William have to die? He wasn't old."

Mrs. Fairfield began counting the stitches in threes. "It just happened," she said in an absorbed voice.

"Does everybody have to die?" asked Kezia.

"Everybody!"

"Me?" Kezia sounded fearfully incredulous.

"Some day, my darling."

"But, grandma." Kezia waved her left leg and waggled the toes. They felt sandy. "What if I just won't?"

The old woman sighed again and drew a long thread from the ball.

"We're not asked, Kezia," she said sadly. "It happens to all of us sooner or later."

Kezia lay still thinking this over. She didn't want to die. It meant she would have to leave here, leave everywhere, for ever, leave—leave her grandma. She rolled over quickly.

"Grandma," she said in a startled voice.

"What, my pet!"

"You're not to die." Kezia was very decided.

"Ah, Kezia"—her grandma looked up and smiled and shook her head—"don't let's talk about it."

"But you're not to. You couldn't leave me. You couldn't not be there." This was awful. "Promise me you won't ever do it, grandma," pleaded Kezia.

The old woman went on knitting.

"Promise me! Say never!"

But still her grandma was silent.

Kezia rolled off her bed; she couldn't bear it any longer, and lightly she leapt on to her grandma's knees, clasped her hands round the old woman's throat and began kissing her, under the chin, behind the ear, and blowing down her neck.

"Say never... say never... say never—" She gasped between the kisses. And then she began, very softly and lightly, to tickle her grandma.

"Kezia!" The old woman dropped her knitting. She swung back in the rocker. She began to tickle Kezia. "Say never, say never, say never," gurgled Kezia, while they lay there laughing in each other's arms. "Come, that's enough, my squirrel! That's enough, my wild pony!" said old Mrs. Fairfield, setting her cap straight. "Pick up my knitting." Both of them had forgotten what the "never" was about.

VIII

The sun was still full on the garden when the back door of the Burnells' shut with a bang, and a very gay figure walked down the path to the gate. It was Alice, the servant-girl, dressed for her afternoon out. She wore a white cotton dress with such large red spots on it and so many that they made you shudder, white shoes and a leghorn turned up under the brim with poppies. Of course she wore gloves, white ones, stained at the fastenings with iron-mould, and in one hand she carried a very dashed-looking sunshade which she referred to as her "perishall." Beryl, sitting in the window, fanning her freshly-washed hair, thought she had never seen such a guy. If Alice had only blacked her face with a piece of cork before she started out, the picture would have been complete. And where did a girl like that go to in a place like this? The heart-shaped Fijian fan beat scornfully at that lovely bright mane. She supposed Alice had picked up some horrible common larrikin and they'd go off into the bush together. Pity to have made herself so conspicuous; they'd have hard work to hide with Alice in that rig-out.

But no, Beryl was unfair. Alice was going to tea with Mrs Stubbs, who'd sent her an "invite" by the little boy who called for orders. She had taken ever such a liking to Mrs. Stubbs ever since the first time she went to the shop to get something for her mosquitoes.

"Dear heart!" Mrs. Stubbs had clapped her hand to her side. "I never seen anyone so eaten. You might have been attacked by canningbals."

Alice did wish there'd been a bit of life on the road though. Made her feel so queer, having nobody behind her. Made her feel all weak in the spine. She couldn't believe that some one wasn't watching her. And yet it was silly to turn round; it gave you away. She pulled up her gloves, hummed to herself and said to the distant gum-tree, "Shan't be long now." But that was hardly company.

Mrs. Stubbs's shop was perched on a little hillock just off the road. It had two big windows for eyes, a broad veranda for a hat, and the sign on the roof, scrawled MRS. STUBBS'S, was like a little card stuck rakishly in the hat crown.

On the veranda there hung a long string of bathing-dresses, clinging together as though they'd just been rescued from the sea rather than waiting to go in, and beside them there hung a cluster of sandshoes so extraordinarily mixed that to get at one pair you had to tear apart and forcibly separate at least fifty. Even then it was the rarest thing to find the left that belonged to the right. So many people had lost patience and gone off with one shoe that fitted and one that was a little too big.... Mrs. Stubbs prided herself on keeping something of everything. The two windows, arranged in the form of precarious pyramids, were crammed so tight, piled so high, that it seemed only a conjurer could prevent them from toppling over. In the left-hand corner of one window, glued to the pane by four gelatine lozenges, there was—and there had been from time immemorial—a notice.

LOST! HANSOME GOLE BROOCH
SOLID GOLD
ON OR NEAR BEACH
REWARD OFFERED

Alice pressed open the door. The bell jangled, the red serge curtains parted, and Mrs. Stubbs appeared. With her broad smile and the long bacon knife in her hand, she looked like a friendly brigand. Alice was welcomed so warmly that she found it quite difficult to keep up her "manners." They consisted of persistent little coughs and hems, pulls at her gloves, tweaks at her skirt, and a curious difficulty in seeing what was set before her or understanding what was said.

Tea was laid on the parlour table—ham, sardines, a whole pound of butter, and such a large johnny cake that it looked like an advertisement for somebody's baking-powder. But the Primus stove roared so loudly that it was useless to try to talk above it. Alice sat down on the edge of a basket-chair while Mrs. Stubbs pumped the stove still higher. Suddenly Mrs. Stubbs whipped the cushion off a chair and disclosed a large brown-paper parcel.

"I've just had some new photers taken, my dear," she shouted cheerfully to Alice. "Tell me what you think of them."

In a very dainty, refined way Alice wet her finger and put the tissue back from the first one. Life! How many there were! There were three dozzing at least. And she held it up to the light.

Mrs. Stubbs sat in an arm-chair, leaning very much to one side. There was a look of mild astonishment on her large face, and well there might be. For though the arm-chair stood on a carpet, to the left of it, miraculously skirting the carpet-border, there was a dashing water-fall. On her right stood a Grecian pillar with a giant fern-tree on either side of it, and in the background towered a gaunt mountain, pale with snow.

"It is a nice style, isn't it?" shouted Mrs. Stubbs; and Alice had just screamed "Sweetly" when the roaring of the Primus stove died down, fizzled out, ceased, and she said "Pretty" in a silence that was frightening.

"Draw up your chair, my dear," said Mrs. Stubbs, beginning to pour out. "Yes," she said thoughtfully, as she handed the tea, "but I don't care about the size. I'm having an enlargemint. All very well for Christmas cards, but I never was the one for small photers myself. You get no comfort out of them. To say the truth, I find them dis'eartening." Alice quite saw what she meant.

"Size," said Mrs. Stubbs. "Give me size. That was what my poor dear husband was always saying. He couldn't stand anything small. Gave him the creeps. And, strange as it may seem, my dear"—here Mrs. Stubbs creaked and seemed to expand herself at the memory—"it was dropsy that carried him off at the larst. Many's the time they drawn one and a half pints from 'im at the 'ospital... It seemed like a judgmint." Alice burned to know exactly what it was that was drawn from him. She ventured, "I suppose it was water."

But Mrs. Stubbs fixed Alice with her eyes and replied meaningly, "It was liquid, my dear."

Liquid! Alice jumped away from the word like a cat and came back to it, nosing and wary.

"That's 'im!" said Mrs. Stubbs, and she pointed dramatically to the life-size head and shoulders of a burly man with a dead white rose in the buttonhole of his coat that made you think of a curl of cold mutting fat. Just below, in silver letters on a red cardboard ground, were the words, "Be not afraid, it is I." "It's ever such a fine face," said Alice faintly.

The pale-blue bow on the top of Mrs. Stubbs's fair frizzy hair quivered. She arched her plump neck. What a neck she had! It was bright pink where it began and then it changed to warm apricot, and that faded to the colour of a brown egg and then to a deep creamy.

"All the same, my dear," she said surprisingly, "freedom's best!" Her soft, fat chuckle sounded like a purr. "Freedom's best," said Mrs. Stubbs again.

Freedom! Alice gave a loud, silly little titter. She felt awkward. Her mind flew back to her own kitching. Ever so queer! She wanted to be back in it again.

IX

A strange company assembled in the Burnells' washhouse after tea. Round the table there sat a bull, a rooster, a donkey that kept forgetting it was a donkey, a sheep and a bee. The washhouse was the perfect place for such a meeting because they could make as much noise as they liked, and nobody ever interrupted. It was a small tin shed standing apart from the bungalow. Against the wall there was a deep trough and in the corner a copper with a basket of clothes-pegs on top of it. The little window, spun over with cobwebs, had a piece of candle and a mouse-trap on the dusty sill. There were clotheslines criss-crossed overhead and, hanging from a peg on the wall, a very big, a huge, rusty horseshoe. The table was in the middle with a form at either side.

"You can't be a bee, Kezia. A bee's not an animal. It's a ninseck."

"Oh, but I do want to be a bee frightfully," wailed Kezia.... A tiny bee, all yellow-furry, with striped legs. She drew her legs up under her and leaned over the table. She felt she was a bee.

"A ninseck must be an animal," she said stoutly. "It makes a noise. It's not like a fish."

"I'm a bull, I'm a bull!" cried Pip. And he gave such a tremendous bellow—how did he make that noise?—that Lottie looked quite alarmed.

"I'll be a sheep," said little Rags. "A whole lot of sheep went past this morning."

"How do you know?"

"Dad heard them. Baa!" He sounded like the little lamb that trots behind and seems to wait to be carried.

"Cock-a-doodle-do!" shrilled Isabel. With her red cheeks and bright eyes she looked like a rooster.

"What'll I be?" Lottie asked everybody, and she sat there smiling, waiting for them to decide for her. It had to be an easy one.

"Be a donkey, Lottie." It was Kezia's suggestion. "Hee-haw! You can't forget that."

"Hee-haw!" said Lottie solemnly. "When do I have to say it?"

"I'll explain, I'll explain," said the bull. It was he who

had the cards. He waved them round his head. "All be quiet! All listen!" And he waited for them. "Look here, Lottie." He turned up a card. "It's got two spots on it—see? Now, if you put that card in the middle and somebody else has one with two spots as well, you say 'Hee-haw,' and the card's yours." "Mine?" Lottie was round-eyed. "To keep?"

"No, silly. Just for the game, see? Just while we're playing." The bull was very cross with her.

"Oh, Lottie, you are a little silly," said the proud rooster.

Lottie looked at both of them. Then she hung her head; her lip quivered. "I don't want to play," she whispered. The others glanced at one another like conspirators. All of them knew what that meant. She would go away and be discovered somewhere standing with her pinny thrown over her head, in a corner, or against a wall, or even behind a chair.

"Yes, you do, Lottie. It's quite easy," said Kezia.

And Isabel, repentant, said exactly like a grown-up, "Watch me, Lottie, and you'll soon learn."

"Cheer up, Lot," said Pip. "There, I know what I'll do. I'll give you the first one. It's mine, really, but I'll give it to you. Here you are." And he slammed the card down in front of Lottie.

Lottie revived at that. But now she was in another difficulty. "I haven't got a hanky," she said; "I want one badly, too."

"Here, Lottie, you can use mine." Rags dipped into his sailor blouse and brought up a very wet-looking one, knotted together. "Be very careful," he warned her. "Only use that corner. Don't undo it. I've got a little starfish inside I'm going to try and tame." "Oh, come on, you girls," said the bull. "And mind—you're not to look at your cards. You've got to keep your hands under the table till I say 'Go.'"

Smack went the cards round the table. They tried with all their might to see, but Pip was too quick for them. It was very exciting, sitting there in the washhouse; it was all they could do not to burst into a little chorus of animals before Pip had finished dealing.

"Now, Lottie, you begin."

Timidly Lottie stretched out a hand, took the top card off her pack, had a good look at it—it was plain she was counting the spots—and put it down.

"No, Lottie, you can't do that. You mustn't look first. You must turn it the other way over."

"But then everybody will see it the same time as me," said Lottie.

The game proceeded. Mooe-ooo-er! The bull was terrible. He charged over the table and seemed to eat the cards up.

Bss-ss! said the bee.

Cock-a-doodle-do! Isabel stood up in her excitement and moved her elbows like wings.

Baa! Little Rags put down the King of Diamonds and Lottie put down the one they called the King of Spain. She had hardly any cards left.

"Why don't you call out, Lottie?"

"I've forgotten what I am," said the donkey woefully.

"Well, change! Be a dog instead! Bow-wow!"

"Oh yes. That's much easier." Lottie smiled again. But when she and Kezia both had a one Kezia waited on purpose. The others made signs to Lottie and pointed. Lottie turned very red; she looked bewildered, and at last she said, "Hee-haw! Ke-zia." "Ss! Wait a minute!" They were in the very thick of it when the bull stopped them, holding up his hand. "What's that? What's that noise?"

"What noise? What do you mean?" asked the rooster.

"Ss! Shut up! Listen!" They were mouse-still. "I thought I

heard a—a sort of knocking," said the bull.

"What was it like?" asked the sheep faintly.

No answer.

The bee gave a shudder. "Whatever did we shut the door for?" she said softly. Oh, why, why had they shut the door?

While they were playing, the day had faded; the gorgeous sunset had blazed and died. And now the quick dark came racing over the sea, over the sand-hills, up the paddock. You were frightened to look in the corners of the washhouse, and yet you had to look with all your might. And somewhere, far away, grandma was lighting a lamp. The blinds were being pulled down; the kitchen fire leapt in the tins on the mantelpiece.

"It would be awful now," said the bull, "if a spider was to fall from the ceiling on to the table, wouldn't it?"

"Spiders don't fall from ceilings."

"Yes, they do. Our Min told us she'd seen a spider as big as a saucer, with long hairs on it like a gooseberry."

Quickly all the little heads were jerked up; all the little bodies drew together, pressed together.

"Why doesn't somebody come and call us?" cried the rooster.

Oh, those grown-ups, laughing and snug, sitting in the lamp-light, drinking out of cups! They'd forgotten about them. No, not really forgotten. That was what their smile meant. They had decided to leave them there all by themselves.

Suddenly Lottie gave such a piercing scream that all of them jumped off the forms, all of them screamed too. "A face—a face looking!" shrieked Lottie.

It was true, it was real. Pressed against the window was a pale face, black eyes, a black beard.

"Grandma! Mother! Somebody!"

But they had not got to the door, tumbling over one

another, before it opened for Uncle Jonathan. He had come to take the little boys home.

X

He had meant to be there before, but in the front garden he had come upon Linda walking up and down the grass, stopping to pick off a dead pink or give a top-heavy carnation something to lean against, or to take a deep breath of something, and then walking on again, with her little air of remoteness. Over her white frock she wore a yellow, pink-fringed shawl from the Chinaman's shop.

"Hallo, Jonathan!" called Linda. And Jonathan whipped off his shabby panama, pressed it against his breast, dropped on one knee, and kissed Linda's hand.

"Greeting, my Fair One! Greeting, my Celestial Peach Blossom!" boomed the bass voice gently. "Where are the other noble dames?"

"Beryl's out playing bridge and mother's giving the boy his bath.... Have you come to borrow something?"

The Trouts were for ever running out of things and sending across to the Burnells' at the last moment.

But Jonathan only answered, "A little love, a little kindness;" and he walked by his sister-in-law's side.

Linda dropped into Beryl's hammock under the manuka-tree, and Jonathan stretched himself on the grass beside her, pulled a long stalk and began chewing it. They knew each other well. The voices of children cried from the other gardens. A fisherman's light cart shook along the sandy road, and from far away they heard a dog barking; it was muffled as though the dog had its head in a sack. If you listened you could just hear the soft swish of the sea at full tide sweeping the pebbles. The sun was sinking.

"And so you go back to the office on Monday, do you,

Jonathan?" asked Linda.

"On Monday the cage door opens and clangs to upon the victim for another eleven months and a week," answered Jonathan.

Linda swung a little. "It must be awful," she said slowly.

"Would ye have me laugh, my fair sister? Would ye have me weep?"

Linda was so accustomed to Jonathan's way of talking that she paid no attention to it.

"I suppose," she said vaguely, "one gets used to it. One gets used to anything."

"Does one? Hum!" The "Hum" was so deep it seemed to boom from underneath the ground. "I wonder how it's done," brooded Jonathan; "I've never managed it."

Looking at him as he lay there, Linda thought again how attractive he was. It was strange to think that he was only an ordinary clerk, that Stanley earned twice as much money as he. What was the matter with Jonathan? He had no ambition; she supposed that was it. And yet one felt he was gifted, exceptional. He was passionately fond of music; every spare penny he had went on books. He was always full of new ideas, schemes, plans. But nothing came of it all. The new fire blazed in Jonathan; you almost heard it roaring softly as he explained, described and dilated on the new thing; but a moment later it had fallen in and there was nothing but ashes, and Jonathan went about with a look like hunger in his black eyes. At these times he exaggerated his absurd manner of speaking, and he sang in church—he was the leader of the choir—with such fearful dramatic intensity that the meanest hymn put on an unholy splendour.

"It seems to me just as imbecile, just as infernal, to have to go to the office on Monday," said Jonathan, "as it always has done and always will do. To spend all the best years of one's life sitting on a stool from nine to five, scratching in somebody's ledger! It's a queer use to make of one's... one and only life, isn't it? Or do I fondly dream?" He rolled over on the grass and looked up at Linda. "Tell me, what is the difference between my life and that of an ordinary prisoner. The only difference I can see is that I put myself in jail and nobody's ever going to let me out. That's a more intolerable situation than the other. For if I'd been—pushed in, against my will—kicking, even—once the door was locked, or at any rate in five years or so, I might have accepted the fact and begun to take an interest in the flight of flies or counting the warder's steps along the passage with particular attention to variations of tread and so on. But as it is, I'm like an insect that's flown into a room of its own accord. I dash against the walls, dash against the windows, flop against the ceiling, do everything on God's earth, in fact, except fly out again. And all the while I'm thinking, like that moth, or that butterfly, or whatever it is, 'The shortness of life! The shortness of life!' I've only one night or one day, and there's this vast dangerous garden, waiting out there, undiscovered, unexplored."

"But, if you feel like that, why—" began Linda quickly.

"Ah!" cried Jonathan. And that "ah!" was somehow almost exultant. "There you have me. Why? Why indeed? There's the maddening, mysterious question. Why don't I fly out again? There's the window or the door or whatever it was I came in by. It's not hopelessly shut—is it? Why don't I find it and be off? Answer me that, little sister." But he gave her no time to answer.

"I'm exactly like that insect again. For some reason"—Jonathan paused between the words—"it's not allowed, it's forbidden, it's against the insect law, to stop banging and flopping and crawling up the pane even for an instant. Why don't I leave the office? Why don't I seriously consider, this moment, for instance, what it is that prevents me leaving? It's not as though I'm tremendously tied. I've two boys to provide for, but, after all, they're boys. I could cut off to sea, or get a job up-country, or —" Suddenly he smiled at Linda and said in a changed voice, as if he were confiding a secret, "Weak... weak. No stamina. No anchor. No guiding principle, let us call it." But then the dark velvety voice rolled out: Would ye hear the story

How it unfolds itself. . .

and they were silent.

The sun had set. In the western sky there were great masses of crushed-up rose-coloured clouds. Broad beams of light shone through the clouds and beyond them as if they would cover the whole sky. Overhead the blue faded; it turned a pale gold, and the bush outlined against it gleamed dark and brilliant like metal. Sometimes when those beams of light show in the sky they are very awful. They remind you that up there sits Jehovah, the jealous God, the Almighty, Whose eye is upon you, ever watchful, never weary. You remember that at His coming the whole earth will shake into one ruined graveyard; the cold, bright angels will drive you this way and that, and there will be no time to explain what could be explained so simply.... But to-night it seemed to Linda there was something infinitely joyful and loving in those silver beams. And now no sound came from the sea. It breathed softly as if it would draw that tender, joyful beauty into its own bosom.

"It's all wrong, it's all wrong," came the shadowy voice of Jonathan. "It's not the scene, it's not the setting for... three stools, three desks, three inkpots and a wire blind." Linda knew that he would never change, but she said, "Is it too late, even now?"

"I'm old—I'm old," intoned Jonathan. He bent towards her, he passed his hand over his head. "Look!" His black hair was speckled all over with silver, like the breast plumage of a black fowl.

Linda was surprised. She had no idea that he was grey. And yet, as he stood up beside her and sighed and stretched, she saw him, for the first time, not resolute, not gallant, not careless, but touched already with age. He looked very tall on the darkening grass, and the thought crossed her mind, "He is like a weed." Jonathan stooped again and kissed her fingers.

"Heaven reward thy sweet patience, lady mine," he murmured. "I must go seek those heirs to my fame and fortune...." He was gone.

XI

Light shone in the windows of the bungalow. Two square patches of gold fell upon the pinks and the peaked marigolds. Florrie, the cat, came out on to the veranda, and sat on the top step, her white paws close together, her tail curled round. She looked content, as though she had been waiting for this moment all day.

"Thank goodness, it's getting late," said Florrie. "Thank goodness, the long day is over." Her greengage eyes opened.

Presently there sounded the rumble of the coach, the crack of Kelly's whip. It came near enough for one to hear the voices of the men from town, talking loudly together. It stopped at the Burnells' gate.

Stanley was half-way up the path before he saw Linda. "Is that you, darling?"

"Yes, Stanley."

He leapt across the flower-bed and seized her in his arms. She was enfolded in that familiar, eager, strong embrace.

"Forgive me, darling, forgive me," stammered Stanley, and he put his hand under her chin and lifted her face to him.

"Forgive you?" smiled Linda. "But whatever for?"

"Good God! You can't have forgotten," cried Stanley Burnell. "I've thought of nothing else all day. I've had the hell of a day. I made up my mind to dash out and telegraph, and then I thought the wire mightn't reach you before I did. I've been in tortures, Linda." "But, Stanley," said Linda, "what must I forgive you for?"

"Linda!"—Stanley was very hurt—"didn't you realize—you must have realized—I went away without saying good-bye to you this morning? I can't imagine how I can have done such a thing. My confounded temper, of course. But—well"—and he sighed and took her in his arms again—"I've suffered for it enough to-day." "What's that you've got in your hand?" asked Linda. "New gloves? Let me see."

"Oh, just a cheap pair of wash-leather ones," said Stanley humbly. "I noticed Bell was wearing some in the coach this morning, so, as I was passing the shop, I dashed in and got myself a pair. What are you smiling at? You don't think it was wrong of me, do you?" "On the con-trary, darling," said Linda, "I think it was most sensible."

She pulled one of the large, pale gloves on her own fingers and looked at her hand, turning it this way and that. She was still smiling.

Stanley wanted to say, "I was thinking of you the whole time I bought them." It was true, but for some reason he couldn't say it. "Let's go in," said he.

XII

Why does one feel so different at night? Why is it so exciting to be awake when everybody else is asleep? Late—it is very late! And yet every moment you feel more and more wakeful, as though you were slowly, almost with every breath, waking up into a new, wonderful, far more thrilling and exciting world than the daylight one. And what is this queer sensation that you're a conspirator? Lightly, stealthily you move about your room. You take something off the dressing-table and put it down again without a sound. And everything, even the bed-post, knows you, responds, shares your secret....

You're not very fond of your room by day. You never think about it. You're in and out, the door opens and slams, the cupboard creaks. You sit down on the side of your bed, change your shoes and dash out again. A dive down to the glass, two pins in your hair, powder your nose and off again. But now—it's suddenly dear to you. It's a darling little funny room. It's yours. Oh, what a joy it is to own things! Mine—my own!

"My very own for ever?"

"Yes." Their lips met.

No, of course, that had nothing to do with it. That was all nonsense and rubbish. But, in spite of herself, Beryl saw so plainly two people standing in the middle of her room. Her arms were round his neck; he held her. And now he whispered, "My beauty, my little beauty!" She jumped off her bed, ran over to the window and kneeled on the window-seat, with her elbows on the sill. But the beautiful night, the garden, every bush, every leaf, even the white palings, even the stars, were conspirators too. So bright was the moon that the flowers were bright as by day; the shadow of the nasturtiums, exquisite lily-like leaves and wide-open flowers, lay across the silvery veranda. The manuka-tree, bent by the southerly winds, was like a bird on one leg stretching out a wing.

But when Beryl looked at the bush, it seemed to her the bush was sad.

"We are dumb trees, reaching up in the night, imploring we know not what," said the sorrowful bush.

It is true when you are by yourself and you think about life, it is always sad. All that excitement and so on has a way of suddenly leaving you, and it's as though, in the silence, somebody called your name, and you heard your name for the first time. "Beryl!" "Yes, I'm here. I'm Beryl. Who wants me?"

"Beryl!"

"Let me come."

It is lonely living by oneself. Of course, there are relations, friends, heaps of them; but that's not what she means. She wants some one who will find the Beryl they none of them know, who will expect her to be that Beryl always. She wants a lover.

"Take me away from all these other people, my love. Let us go far away. Let us live our life, all new, all ours, from the very beginning. Let us make our fire. Let us sit down to eat together. Let us have long talks at night." And the thought was almost, "Save me, my love. Save me!"

... "Oh, go on! Don't be a prude, my dear. You enjoy yourself while you're young. That's my advice." And a high rush of silly laughter joined Mrs. Harry Kember's loud, indifferent neigh.

You see, it's so frightfully difficult when you've nobody. You're so at the mercy of things. You can't just be rude. And you've always this horror of seeming inexperienced and stuffy like the other ninnies at the Bay. And—and it's fascinating to know you've power over people. Yes, that is fascinating....

Oh why, oh why doesn't "he" come soon?

If I go on living here, thought Beryl, anything may happen to me.

"But how do you know he is coming at all?" mocked a small voice within her.

But Beryl dismissed it. She couldn't be left. Other

people, perhaps, but not she. It wasn't possible to think that Beryl Fairfield never married, that lovely fascinating girl.

"Do you remember Beryl Fairfield?"

"Remember her! As if I could forget her! It was one summer at the Bay that I saw her. She was standing on the beach in a blue"—no, pink—"muslin frock, holding on a big cream"—no, black—"straw hat. But it's years ago now." "She's as lovely as ever, more so if anything."

Beryl smiled, bit her lip, and gazed over the garden. As she gazed, she saw somebody, a man, leave the road, step along the paddock beside their palings as if he was coming straight towards her. Her heart beat. Who was it? Who could it be? It couldn't be a burglar, certainly not a burglar, for he was smoking and he strolled lightly. Beryl's heart leapt; it seemed to turn right over, and then to stop. She recognized him.

"Good evening, Miss Beryl," said the voice softly.

"Good evening."

"Won't you come for a little walk?" it drawled.

Come for a walk—at that time of night! "I couldn't. Everybody's in bed. Everybody's asleep."

"Oh," said the voice lightly, and a whiff of sweet smoke reached her. "What does everybody matter? Do come! It's such a fine night. There's not a soul about."

Beryl shook her head. But already something stirred in her, something reared its head.

The voice said, "Frightened?" It mocked, "Poor little girl!"

"Not in the least," said she. As she spoke that weak thing within her seemed to uncoil, to grow suddenly tremendously strong; she longed to go!

And just as if this was quite understood by the other, the voice said, gently and softly, but finally, "Come along!"

Beryl stepped over her low window, crossed the veranda, ran down the grass to the gate. He was there before her.

"That's right," breathed the voice, and it teased, "You're not frightened, are you? You're not frightened?"

She was; now she was here she was terrified, and it seemed to her everything was different. The moonlight stared and glittered; the shadows were like bars of iron. Her hand was taken.

"Not in the least," she said lightly. "Why should I be?"

Her hand was pulled gently, tugged. She held back.

"No, I'm not coming any farther," said Beryl.

"Oh, rot!" Harry Kember didn't believe her. "Come along! We'll just go as far as that fuchsia bush. Come along!"

The fuchsia bush was tall. It fell over the fence in a shower. There was a little pit of darkness beneath.

"No, really, I don't want to," said Beryl.

For a moment Harry Kember didn't answer. Then he came close to her, turned to her, smiled and said quickly, "Don't be silly! Don't be silly!"

His smile was something she'd never seen before. Was he drunk? That bright, blind, terrifying smile froze her with horror. What was she doing? How had she got here? the stern garden asked her as the gate pushed open, and quick as a cat Harry Kember came through and snatched her to him.

"Cold little devil! Cold little devil!" said the hateful voice.

But Beryl was strong. She slipped, ducked, wrenched free.

"You are vile, vile," said she.

"Then why in God's name did you come?" stammered Harry Kember.

Nobody answered him.

A cloud, small, serene, floated across the moon. In that

moment of darkness the sea sounded deep, troubled. Then the cloud sailed away, and the sound of the sea was a vague murmur, as though it waked out of a dark dream. All was still.

The Door in the Wall

H. G. Wells

I

One confidential evening, not three months ago, Lionel Wallace told me this story of the Door in the Wall. And at the time I thought that so far as he was concerned it was a true story.

He told it me with such a direct simplicity of conviction that I could not do otherwise than believe in him. But in the morning, in my own flat, I woke to a different atmosphere, and as I lay in bed and recalled the things he had told me, stripped of the glamour of his earnest slow voice, denuded of the focussed shaded table light, the shadowy atmosphere that wrapped about him and the pleasant bright things, the dessert and glasses and napery of the dinner we had shared, making them for the time a bright little world quite cut off from every-day realities, I saw it all as frankly incredible. "He was mystifying!" I said, and then: "How well he did it!. . . . . It isn't quite the thing I should have expected him, of all people, to do well." Afterwards, as I sat up in bed and sipped my morning tea, I found myself trying to account for the flavour of reality that perplexed me in his impossible reminiscences, by supposing they did in some way suggest, present, convey—I hardly know which word to use—experiences it was otherwise impossible to tell.

Well, I don't resort to that explanation now. I have got over my intervening doubts. I believe now, as I believed at the moment of telling, that Wallace did to the very best of his ability strip the truth of his secret for me. But whether he himself saw, or only thought he saw, whether he himself was the possessor of an inestimable privilege, or the victim of a fantastic dream, I cannot pretend to guess. Even the facts of his death, which ended my doubts forever, throw no light on that. That much the reader must judge for himself.

I forget now what chance comment or criticism of mine moved so reticent a man to confide in me. He was, I think, defending himself against an imputation of slackness and unreliability I had made in relation to a great public movement in which he had disappointed me. But he plunged suddenly. "I have" he said, "a preoccupation—" "I know," he went on, after a pause that he devoted to the study of his cigar ash, "I have been negligent. The fact is—it isn't a case of ghosts or apparitions—but—it's an odd thing to tell of, Redmond—I am haunted. I am haunted by something—that rather takes the light out of things, that fills me with longings . . . . ." He paused, checked by that English shyness that so often overcomes us when we would speak of moving or grave or beautiful things. "You were at Saint Athelstan's all through," he said, and for a moment that seemed to me quite irrelevant. "Well"—and he paused. Then very haltingly at first, but afterwards more easily, he began to tell of the thing that was hidden in his life, the haunting memory of a beauty and a happiness that filled his heart with insatiable longings that made all the interests and spectacle of worldly life seem dull and tedious and vain to him.

Now that I have the clue to it, the thing seems written visibly in his face. I have a photograph in which that look of detachment has been caught and intensified. It reminds me of what a woman once said of him—a woman who had loved him greatly. "Suddenly," she said, "the interest goes out of him. He forgets you. He doesn't care a rap for you—under his very nose . . . . ." Yet the interest was not always out of him, and when he was holding his attention to a thing Wallace could contrive to be an extremely successful man. His career, indeed, is set with successes. He left me behind him long ago; he soared up over my head, and cut a figure in the world that I couldn't cut—anyhow. He was still a year short of forty, and they say now that he would have been in office and very probably in the new Cabinet if he had lived. At school he always beat me without effort—as it were by nature. We were at school together at Saint Athelstan's College in West Kensington for almost all our school time. He came into the school as my co-equal, but he left far above me, in a blaze of scholarships and brilliant performance. Yet I think I made a fair average running. And it was at school I heard first of the Door in the Wall—that I was to hear of a second time only a month before his death.

To him at least the Door in the Wall was a real door leading through a real wall to immortal realities. Of that I am now quite assured.

And it came into his life early, when he was a little fellow between five and six. I remember how, as he sat making his confession to me with a slow gravity, he reasoned and reckoned the date of it. "There was," he said, "a crimson Virginia creeper in it—all one bright uniform crimson in a clear amber sunshine against a white wall. That came into the impression somehow, though I don't clearly remember how, and there were horse-chestnut leaves upon the clean pavement outside the green door. They were blotched yellow and green, you know, not brown nor dirty, so that they must have been new fallen. I take it that means October. I look out for horse-chestnut leaves every year, and I ought to know.

"If I'm right in that, I was about five years and four months old."

He was, he said, rather a precocious little boy—he learned to talk at an abnormally early age, and he was so sane and "old-fashioned," as people say, that he was permitted an amount of initiative that most children scarcely attain by seven or eight. His mother died when he was born, and he was under the less vigilant and authoritative care of a nursery governess. His father was a stern, preoccupied lawyer, who gave him little attention, and expected great things of him. For all his brightness he found life a little grey and dull I think. And one day he wandered.

He could not recall the particular neglect that enabled him to get away, nor the course he took among the West Kensington roads. All that had faded among the incurable blurs of memory. But the white wall and the green door stood out quite distinctly.

As his memory of that remote childish experience ran, he did at the very first sight of that door experience a peculiar emotion, an attraction, a desire to get to the door and open it and walk in. And at the same time he had the clearest conviction that either it was unwise or it was wrong of him—he could not tell which—to yield to this attraction. He insisted upon it as a curious thing that he knew from the very beginning—unless memory has played him the queerest trick—that the door was unfastened, and that he could go in as he chose.

I seem to see the figure of that little boy, drawn and repelled. And it was very clear in his mind, too, though why it should be so was never explained, that his father would be very angry if he went through that door.

Wallace described all these moments of hesitation to me with the utmost particularity. He went right past the door, and then, with his hands in his pockets, and making an infantile attempt to whistle, strolled right along beyond the end of the wall. There he recalls a number of mean, dirty shops, and particularly that of a plumber and decorator, with a dusty disorder of earthenware pipes, sheet lead ball taps, pattern books of wall paper, and tins of enamel. He stood pretending to examine these things, and coveting, passionately desiring the green door.

Then, he said, he had a gust of emotion. He made a run for it, lest hesitation should grip him again, he went plump with outstretched hand through the green door and let it slam behind him. And so, in a trice, he came into the garden that has haunted all his life.

It was very difficult for Wallace to give me his full sense of that garden into which he came.

There was something in the very air of it that exhilarated, that gave one a sense of lightness and good happening and well being; there was something in the sight of it that made all its colour clean and perfect and subtly luminous. In the instant of coming into it one was exquisitely glad—as only in rare moments and when one is young and joyful one can be glad in this world. And everything was beautiful there . . . . . Wallace mused before he went on telling me. "You see," he said, with the doubtful inflection of a man who pauses at incredible things, "there were two great panthers there . . . Yes, spotted panthers. And I was not afraid. There was a long wide path with marble-edged flower borders on either side, and these two huge velvety beasts were playing there with a ball. One looked up and came towards me, a little curious as it seemed. It came right up to me, rubbed its soft round ear very gently against the small hand I held out and purred. It was, I tell you, an enchanted garden. I know. And the size? Oh! it stretched far and wide, this way and that. I believe there were hills far away. Heaven knows where West Kensington had suddenly got to. And somehow it was just like coming home.

"You know, in the very moment the door swung to behind me, I forgot the road with its fallen chestnut leaves, its cabs and tradesmen's carts, I forgot the sort of gravitational pull back to the discipline and obedience of home, I forgot all hesitations and fear, forgot discretion, forgot all the intimate realities of this life. I became in a moment a very glad and wonder-happy little boy—in another world. It was a world with a different quality, a warmer, more penetrating and mellower light, with a faint clear gladness in its air, and wisps of sun-touched cloud in the blueness of its sky. And before me ran this long wide path, invitingly, with weedless beds on either side, rich with untended flowers, and these two great panthers. I put my little hands fearlessly on their soft fur, and caressed their round ears and the sensitive corners under their ears, and played with them, and it was as though they welcomed me home. There was a keen sense of home-coming in my mind, and when presently a tall, fair girl appeared in the pathway and came to meet me, smiling, and said Well?' to me, and lifted me, and kissed me, and put me down, and led me by the hand, there was no amazement, but only an impression of delightful rightness, of being reminded of happy things that had in some strange way been overlooked. There were broad steps, I remember, that came into view between spikes of delphinium, and up these we went to a great avenue between very old and shady dark trees. All down this avenue, you know, between the red chapped stems, were marble seats of honour and statuary, and very tame and friendly white doves . . . . . "And along this avenue my girl-friend led me, looking down—I recall the pleasant lines, the finely-modelled chin of her sweet kind face—asking me questions in a soft, agreeable voice, and telling me things, pleasant things I know, though what they were I was never able to recall . . . And presently a little Capuchin monkey, very clean, with a fur of ruddy brown and kindly hazel eyes, came down a tree to us and ran beside me, looking up at me and grinning, and presently leapt to my shoulder. So we went on our way in great happiness . . . ." He paused.

"Go on," I said.

"I remember little things. We passed an old man musing among laurels, I remember, and a place gay with paroquets, and came through a broad shaded colonnade to a spacious cool palace, full of pleasant fountains, full of beautiful things, full of the quality and promise of heart's desire. And there were many things and many people, some that still seem to stand out clearly and some that are a little vague, but all these people were beautiful and kind. In some way—I don't know how—it was conveyed to me that they all were kind to me, glad to have me there, and filling me with gladness by their gestures, by the touch of their hands, by the welcome and love in their eyes. Yes—" He mused for awhile. "Playmates I found there. That was very much to me, because I was a lonely little boy. They played delightful games in a grass-covered court where there was a sun-dial set about with flowers. And as one played one loved . . . .

"But—it's odd—there's a gap in my memory. I don't remember the games we played. I never remembered. Afterwards, as a child, I spent long hours trying, even with tears, to recall the form of that happiness. I wanted to play it all over again—in my nursery—by myself. No! All I remember is the happiness and two dear playfellows who were most with me . . . . Then presently came a sombre dark woman, with a grave, pale face and dreamy eyes, a sombre woman wearing a soft long robe of pale purple, who carried a book and beckoned and took me aside with her into a gallery above a hall—though my playmates were loth to have me go, and ceased their game and stood watching as I was carried away. 'Come back to us!' they cried. 'Come back to us soon!' I looked up at her face, but she heeded them not at all. Her face was very gentle and grave. She took me to a seat in the gallery, and I stood beside her, ready to look at her book as she opened it upon her knee. The pages fell open. She pointed, and I looked, marvelling, for in the living pages of that book I saw myself; it was a story about myself, and in it were all the things that had happened to me since ever I was born . . . . "It was wonderful to me, because the pages of that book were not pictures, you understand, but realities."

Wallace paused gravely—looked at me doubtfully.

"Go on," I said. "I understand."

"They were realities—yes, they must have been; people moved and things came and went in them; my dear mother, whom I had near forgotten; then my father, stern and upright, the servants, the nursery, all the familiar things of home. Then the front door and the busy streets, with traffic to and fro: I looked and marvelled, and looked half doubtfully again into the woman's face and turned the pages over, skipping this and that, to see more of this book, and more, and so at last I came to myself hovering and hesitating outside the green door in the long white wall, and felt again the conflict and the fear.

"'And next?' I cried, and would have turned on, but the cool hand of the grave woman delayed me.

"'Next?' I insisted, and struggled gently with her hand, pulling up her fingers with all my childish strength, and as she yielded and the page came over she bent down upon me like a shadow and kissed my brow.

"But the page did not show the enchanted garden, nor

the panthers, nor the girl who had led me by the hand, nor the playfellows who had been so loth to let me go. It showed a long grey street in West Kensington, on that chill hour of afternoon before the lamps are lit, and I was there, a wretched little figure, weeping aloud, for all that I could do to restrain myself, and I was weeping because I could not return to my dear play-fellows who had called after me, 'Come back to us! Come back to us soon!' I was there. This was no page in a book, but harsh reality; that enchanted place and the restraining hand of the grave mother at whose knee I stood had gone—whither have they gone?" He halted again, and remained for a time, staring into the fire.

"Oh! the wretchedness of that return!" he murmured.

"Well?" I said after a minute or so.

"Poor little wretch I was—brought back to this grey world again! As I realised the fulness of what had happened to me, I gave way to quite ungovernable grief. And the shame and humiliation of that public weeping and my disgraceful homecoming remain with me still. I see again the benevolent-looking old gentleman in gold spectacles who stopped and spoke to me—prodding me first with his umbrella. 'Poor little chap,' said he; 'and are you lost then?'—and me a London boy of five and more! And he must needs bring in a kindly young policeman and make a crowd of me, and so march me home. Sobbing, conspicuous and frightened, I came from the enchanted garden to the steps of my father's house.

"That is as well as I can remember my vision of that garden—the garden that haunts me still. Of course, I can convey nothing of that indescribable quality of translucent unreality, that difference from the common things of experience that hung about it all; but that—that is what happened. If it was a dream, I am sure it was a day-time and altogether extraordinary dream . . . . . . H'm!—naturally there followed a terrible questioning, by my aunt, my father, the nurse, the governess—everyone . . . . . . "I tried to tell them, and my father gave me my first thrashing for telling lies. When afterwards I tried to tell my aunt, she punished me again for my wicked persistence. Then, as I said, everyone was forbidden to listen to me, to hear a word about it. Even my fairy tale books were taken away from me for a time—because I was 'too imaginative.' Eh? Yes, they did that! My father belonged to the old school . . . . . And my story was driven back upon myself. I whispered it to my pillow—my pillow that was often damp and salt to my whispering lips with childish tears. And I added always to my official and less fervent prayers this one heartfelt request: 'Please God I may dream of the garden. Oh! take me back to my garden! Take me back to my garden!' "I dreamt often of the garden. I may have added to it, I may have changed it; I do not know . . . . . All this you understand is an attempt to reconstruct from fragmentary memories a very early experience. Between that and the other consecutive memories of my boyhood there is a gulf. A time came when it seemed impossible I should ever speak of that wonder glimpse again." I asked an obvious question.

"No," he said. "I don't remember that I ever attempted to find my way back to the garden in those early years. This seems odd to me now, but I think that very probably a closer watch was kept on my movements after this misadventure to prevent my going astray. No, it wasn't until you knew me that I tried for the garden again. And I believe there was a period—incredible as it seems now—when I forgot the garden altogether—when I was about eight or nine it may have been. Do you remember me as a kid at Saint Athelstan's?" "Rather!"

"I didn't show any signs did I in those days of having a secret dream?"

II

He looked up with a sudden smile.

"Did you ever play North-West Passage with me? . . . . . No, of course you didn't come my way!"

"It was the sort of game," he went on, "that every imaginative child plays all day. The idea was the discovery of a North-West Passage to school. The way to school was plain enough; the game consisted in finding some way that wasn't plain, starting off ten minutes early in some almost hopeless direction, and working one's way round through unaccustomed streets to my goal. And one day I got entangled among some rather low-class streets on the other side of Campden Hill, and I began to think that for once the game would be against me and that I should get to school late. I tried rather desperately a street that seemed a cul de sac, and found a passage at the end. I hurried through that with renewed hope. 'I shall do it yet,' I said, and passed a row of frowsy little shops that were inexplicably familiar to me, and behold! there was my long white wall and the green door that led to the enchanted garden!

"The thing whacked upon me suddenly. Then, after all, that garden, that wonderful garden, wasn't a dream!" . . . He paused.

"I suppose my second experience with the green door marks the world of difference there is between the busy life of a schoolboy and the infinite leisure of a child. Anyhow, this second time I didn't for a moment think of going in straight away. You see . . . For one thing my mind was full of the idea of getting to school in time—set on not breaking my record for punctuality. I must surely have felt some little desire at least to try the door—yes, I must have felt that . . . . . But I seem to remember the attraction of the door mainly as another obstacle to my overmastering determination to get to school. I was immediately interested by this discovery I had made, of course—I went on with my mind full of it—but I went on. It didn't check me. I ran past tugging out my watch, found I had ten minutes still to spare, and then I was going downhill into familiar surroundings. I got to school, breathless, it is true, and wet with perspiration, but in time. I can remember hanging up my coat and hat . . . Went right by it and left it behind me. Odd, eh?" He looked at me thoughtfully. "Of course, I didn't know then that it wouldn't always be there. School boys have limited imaginations. I suppose I thought it was an awfully jolly thing to have it there, to know my way back to it, but there was the school tugging at me. I expect I was a good deal distraught and inattentive that morning, recalling what I could of the beautiful strange people I should presently see again. Oddly enough I had no doubt in my mind that they would be glad to see me . . . Yes, I must have thought of the garden that morning just as a jolly sort of place to which one might resort in the interludes of a strenuous scholastic career.

"I didn't go that day at all. The next day was a half holiday, and that may have weighed with me. Perhaps, too, my state of inattention brought down impositions upon me and docked the margin of time necessary for the detour. I don't know. What I do know is that in the meantime the enchanted garden was so much upon my mind that I could not keep it to myself.

"I told—What was his name?—a ferrety-looking youngster

we used to call Squiff."

"Young Hopkins," said I.

"Hopkins it was. I did not like telling him, I had a feeling that in some way it was against the rules to tell him, but I did. He was walking part of the way home with me; he was talkative, and if we had not talked about the enchanted garden we should have talked of something else, and it was intolerable to me to think about any other subject. So I blabbed.

"Well, he told my secret. The next day in the play interval I found myself surrounded by half a dozen bigger boys, half teasing and wholly curious to hear more of the enchanted garden. There was that big Fawcett—you remember him?—and Carnaby and Morley Reynolds. You weren't there by any chance? No, I think I should have remembered if you were . . . . . "A boy is a creature of odd feelings. I was, I really believe, in spite of my secret self-disgust, a little flattered to have the attention of these big fellows. I remember particularly a moment of pleasure caused by the praise of Crawshaw—you remember Crawshaw major, the son of Crawshaw the composer?—who said it was the best lie he had ever heard. But at the same time there was a really painful undertow of shame at telling what I felt was indeed a sacred secret. That beast Fawcett made a joke about the girl in green—." Wallace's voice sank with the keen memory of that shame. "I pretended not to hear," he said. "Well, then Carnaby suddenly called me a young liar and disputed with me when I said the thing was true. I said I knew where to find the green door, could lead them all there in ten minutes. Carnaby became outrageously virtuous, and said I'd have to—and bear out my words or suffer. Did you ever have Carnaby twist your arm? Then perhaps you'll understand how it went with me. I swore my story was true. There was nobody in the school then to save a chap from Carnaby though Crawshaw put in a word or so. Carnaby had got his game. I grew excited and red-eared, and a little frightened, I behaved altogether like a silly little chap, and the outcome of it all was that instead of starting alone for my enchanted garden, I led the way presently—cheeks flushed, ears hot, eyes smarting, and my soul one burning misery and shame—for a party of six mocking, curious and threatening school-fellows.

"We never found the white wall and the green door .. ."

"You mean?—"

"I mean I couldn't find it. I would have found it if I could.

"And afterwards when I could go alone I couldn't find it. I never found it. I seem now to have been always looking for it through my school-boy days, but I've never come upon it again."

"Did the fellows—make it disagreeable?"

"Beastly . . . . . Carnaby held a council over me for wanton lying. I remember how I sneaked home and upstairs to hide the marks of my blubbering. But when I cried myself to sleep at last it wasn't for Carnaby, but for the garden, for the beautiful afternoon I had hoped for, for the sweet friendly women and the waiting playfellows and the game I had hoped to learn again, that beautiful forgotten game . . . . . "I believed firmly that if I had not told— . . . . . I had bad times after that —crying at night and wool-gathering by day. For two terms I slackened and had bad reports. Do you remember? Of course you would! It was you—your beating me in mathematics that brought me back to the grind again."

III

For a time my friend stared silently into the red heart

of the fire. Then he said: "I never saw it again until I was seventeen.

"It leapt upon me for the third time—as I was driving to Paddington on my way to Oxford and a scholarship. I had just one momentary glimpse. I was leaning over the apron of my hansom smoking a cigarette, and no doubt thinking myself no end of a man of the world, and suddenly there was the door, the wall, the dear sense of unforgettable and still attainable things.

"We clattered by—I too taken by surprise to stop my cab until we were well past and round a corner. Then I had a queer moment, a double and divergent movement of my will: I tapped the little door in the roof of the cab, and brought my arm down to pull out my watch. 'Yes, sir!' said the cabman, smartly. 'Er—well—it's nothing,' I cried. 'My mistake! We haven't much time! Go on!' and he went on . . . "I got my scholarship. And the night after I was told of that I sat over my fire in my little upper room, my study, in my father's house, with his praise—his rare praise—and his sound counsels ringing in my ears, and I smoked my favourite pipe—the formidable bulldog of adolescence—and thought of that door in the long white wall. 'If I had stopped,' I thought, 'I should have missed my scholarship, I should have missed Oxford—muddled all the fine career before me! I begin to see things better!' I fell musing deeply, but I did not doubt then this career of mine was a thing that merited sacrifice.

"Those dear friends and that clear atmosphere seemed very sweet to me, very fine, but remote. My grip was fixing now upon the world. I saw another door opening—the door of my career."

He stared again into the fire. Its red lights picked out a stubborn strength in his face for just one flickering moment, and then it vanished again.

"Well", he said and sighed, "I have served that career. I have done—much work, much hard work. But I have dreamt of the enchanted garden a thousand dreams, and seen its door, or at least glimpsed its door, four times since then. Yes—four times. For a while this world was so bright and interesting, seemed so full of meaning and opportunity that the half-effaced charm of the garden was by comparison gentle and remote. Who wants to pat panthers on the way to dinner with pretty women and distinguished men? I came down to London from Oxford, a man of bold promise that I have done something to redeem. Something—and yet there have been disappointments . . . . . "Twice I have been in love—I will not dwell on that—but once, as I went to someone who, I know, doubted whether I dared to come, I took a short cut at a venture through an unfrequented road near Earl's Court, and so happened on a white wall and a familiar green door. 'Odd!' said I to myself, 'but I thought this place was on Campden Hill. It's the place I never could find somehow—like counting Stonehenge—the place of that queer day dream of mine.' And I went by it intent upon my purpose. It had no appeal to me that afternoon.

"I had just a moment's impulse to try the door, three steps aside were needed at the most—though I was sure enough in my heart that it would open to me—and then I thought that doing so might delay me on the way to that appointment in which I thought my honour was involved. Afterwards I was sorry for my punctuality—I might at least have peeped in I thought, and waved a hand to those panthers, but I knew enough by this time not to seek again belatedly that which is not found by seeking. Yes, that time made me very sorry . . . . . "Years of hard work after that and never a sight of the door. It's only recently it has come back to me. With it there has come a sense as though some thin tarnish had spread itself over my world. I began to think of it as a sorrowful and bitter thing that I should never see that door again. Perhaps I was suffering a little from overwork—perhaps it was what I've heard spoken of as the feeling of forty. I don't know. But certainly the keen brightness that makes effort easy has gone out of things recently, and that just at a time with all these new political developments—when I ought to be working. Odd, isn't it? But I do begin to find life toilsome, its rewards, as I come near them, cheap. I began a little while ago to want the garden quite badly. Yes—and I've seen it three times." "The garden?"

"No—the door! And I haven't gone in!"

He leaned over the table to me, with an enormous sorrow in his voice as he spoke. "Thrice I have had my chance—thrice! If ever that door offers itself to me again, I swore, I will go in out of this dust and heat, out of this dry glitter of vanity, out of these toilsome futilities. I will go and never return. This time I will stay . . . . . I swore it and when the time came—I didn't go.

"Three times in one year have I passed that door and failed to enter. Three times in the last year.

"The first time was on the night of the snatch division on the Tenants' Redemption Bill, on which the Government was saved by a majority of three. You remember? No one on our side—perhaps very few on the opposite side—expected the end that night. Then the debate collapsed like eggshells. I and Hotchkiss were dining with his cousin at Brentford, we were both unpaired, and we were called up by telephone, and set off at once in his cousin's motor. We got in barely in time, and on the way we passed my wall and door—livid in the moonlight, blotched with hot yellow as the glare of our lamps lit it, but unmistakable. 'My God!' cried I.

'What?' said Hotchkiss. 'Nothing!' I answered, and the moment passed.

"'I've made a great sacrifice,' I told the whip as I got in. They all have,' he said, and hurried by.

"I do not see how I could have done otherwise then. And the next occasion was as I rushed to my father's bedside to bid that stern old man farewell. Then, too, the claims of life were imperative. But the third time was different; it happened a week ago. It fills me with hot remorse to recall it. I was with Gurker and Ralphs—it's no secret now you know that I've had my talk with Gurker. We had been dining at Frobisher's, and the talk had become intimate between us. The question of my place in the reconstructed ministry lay always just over the boundary of the discussion. Yes—yes. That's all settled. It needn't be talked about yet, but there's no reason to keep a secret from you . . . . . Yes—thanks! thanks! But let me tell you my story.

"Then, on that night things were very much in the air. My position was a very delicate one. I was keenly anxious to get some definite word from Gurker, but was hampered by Ralphs' presence. I was using the best power of my brain to keep that light and careless talk not too obviously directed to the point that concerns me. I had to. Ralphs' behaviour since has more than justified my caution . . . . . Ralphs, I knew, would leave us beyond the Kensington High Street, and then I could surprise Gurker by a sudden frankness. One has sometimes to resort to these little devices. . . . . And then it was that in the margin of my field of vision I became aware once more of the white wall, the green door before us down the road.

"We passed it talking. I passed it. I can still see the shadow of Gurker's marked profile, his opera hat tilted forward over his prominent nose, the many folds of his neck wrap going before my shadow and Ralphs' as we sauntered past.

"I passed within twenty inches of the door. 'If I say good-night to them, and go in,' I asked myself, 'what will happen?' And I was all a-tingle for that word with Gurker.

"I could not answer that question in the tangle of my other problems. 'They will think me mad,' I thought. 'And suppose I vanish now!—Amazing disappearance of a prominent politician!' That weighed with me. A thousand inconceivably petty worldlinesses weighed with me in that crisis."

Then he turned on me with a sorrowful smile, and, speaking slowly; "Here I am!" he said.

"Here I am!" he repeated, "and my chance has gone from me. Three times in one year the door has been offered me—the door that goes into peace, into delight, into a beauty beyond dreaming, a kindness no man on earth can know. And I have rejected it, Redmond, and it has gone—"

"How do you know?"

"I know. I know. I am left now to work it out, to stick to the tasks that held me so strongly when my moments came. You say, I have success—this vulgar, tawdry, irksome, envied thing. I have it." He had a walnut in his big hand. "If that was my success," he said, and crushed it, and held it out for me to see.

"Let me tell you something, Redmond. This loss is destroying me. For two months, for ten weeks nearly now, I have done no work at all, except the most necessary and urgent duties. My soul is full of inappeasable regrets. At nights—when it is less likely I shall be recognised—I go out. I wander. Yes. I wonder what people would think of that if they knew. A Cabinet Minister, the responsible head of that most vital of all departments, wandering alone—grieving—sometimes near audibly lamenting—for a door, for a garden!" IV

I can see now his rather pallid face, and the unfamiliar sombre fire that had come into his eyes. I see him very vividly to-night. I sit recalling his words, his tones, and last evening's Westminster Gazette still lies on my sofa, containing the notice of his death. At lunch to-day the club was busy with him and the strange riddle of his fate.

They found his body very early yesterday morning in a deep excavation near East Kensington Station. It is one of two shafts that have been made in connection with an extension of the railway southward. It is protected from the intrusion of the public by a hoarding upon the high road, in which a small doorway has been cut for the convenience of some of the workmen who live in that direction. The doorway was left unfastened through a misunderstanding between two gangers, and through it he made his way . . . . . My mind is darkened with questions and riddles.

It would seem he walked all the way from the House that night—he has frequently walked home during the past Session—and so it is I figure his dark form coming along the late and empty streets, wrapped up, intent. And then did the pale electric lights near the station cheat the rough planking into a semblance of white? Did that fatal unfastened door awaken some memory?

Was there, after all, ever any green door in the wall at all?

I do not know. I have told his story as he told it to me. There are times when I believe that Wallace was no more than the victim of the coincidence between a rare but not unprecedented type of hallucination and a careless trap, but that indeed is not my profoundest belief. You may think me superstitious if you will, and foolish; but, indeed, I am more than half convinced that he had in truth, an abnormal gift, and a sense, something—I know not what—that in the guise of wall and door offered him an outlet, a secret and peculiar passage of escape into another and altogether more beautiful world. At any rate, you will say, it betrayed him in the end. But did it betray him? There you touch the inmost mystery of these dreamers, these men of vision and the imagination. We see our world fair and common, the hoarding and the pit. By our daylight standard he walked out of security into darkness, danger and death. But did he see like that?

An Honest Thief

Fyodor Dostoevsky

One morning, just as I was about to set off to my office, Agrafena, my cook, washerwoman and housekeeper, came in to me and, to my surprise, entered into conversation.

She had always been such a silent, simple creature that, except her daily inquiry about dinner, she had not uttered a word for the last six years. I, at least, had heard nothing else from her.

"Here I have come in to have a word with you, sir," she began abruptly; "you really ought to let the little room."

"Which little room?"

"Why, the one next the kitchen, to be sure."

"What for?"

"What for? Why because folks do take in lodgers, to be sure."

"But who would take it?"

"Who would take it? Why, a lodger would take it, to be sure."

"But, my good woman, one could not put a bedstead in it; there wouldn't be room to move! Who could live in it?"

"Who wants to live there! As long as he has a place to sleep in. Why, he would live in the window."

"In what window?"

"In what window! As though you didn't know! The one in the passage, to be sure. He would sit there, sewing or doing anything else. Maybe he would sit on a chair, too. He's got a chair; and he has a table, too; he's got everything."

"Who is 'he' then?"

"Oh, a good man, a man of experience. I will cook for him. And I'll ask him three roubles a month for his board and lodging."

After prolonged efforts I succeeded at last in learning from Agrafena that an elderly man had somehow managed to persuade her to admit him into the kitchen as a lodger and boarder. Any notion Agrafena took into her head had to be carried out; if not, I knew she would give me no peace. When anything was not to her liking, she at once began to brood, and sank into a deep dejection that would last for a fortnight or three weeks. During that period my dinners were spoiled, my linen was mislaid, my floors went unscrubbed; in short, I had a great deal to put up with. I had observed long ago that this inarticulate woman was incapable of conceiving a project, of originating an idea of her own. But if anything like a notion or a project was by some means put into her feeble brain, to prevent its being carried out meant, for a time, her moral assassination. And so, as I cared more for my peace of mind than for anything else, I consented forthwith.

"Has he a passport anyway, or something of the sort?"

"To be sure, he has. He is a good man, a man of experience; three roubles he's promised to pay."

The very next day the new lodger made his appearance in my modest bachelor quarters; but I was not put out by this, indeed I was inwardly pleased. I lead as a rule a very lonely hermit's existence. I have scarcely any friends; I hardly ever go anywhere. As I had spent ten years never coming out of my shell, I had, of course, grown used to solitude. But another ten or fifteen years or more of the same solitary existence, with the same Agrafena, in the same bachelor quarters, was in truth a somewhat cheerless prospect. And therefore a new inmate, if well-behaved, was a heaven-sent blessing.

Agrafena had spoken truly: my lodger was certainly a man of experience.

From his passport it appeared that he was an old soldier, a fact which I should have known indeed from his face. An old soldier is easily recognised. Astafy Ivanovitch was a favourable specimen of his class. We got on very well together. What was best of all, Astafy Ivanovitch would sometimes tell a story, describing some incident in his own life. In the perpetual boredom of my existence such a story-teller was a veritable treasure. One day he told me one of these stories. It made an impression on me. The following event was what led to it.

I was left alone in the flat; both Astafy and Agrafena were out on business of their own. All of a sudden I heard from the inner room somebody--I fancied a stranger--come in; I went out; there actually was a stranger in the passage, a short fellow wearing no overcoat in spite of the cold autumn weather.

"What do you want?"

"Does a clerk called Alexandrov live here?"

"Nobody of that name here, brother. Good-bye."

"Why, the dvornik told me it was here," said my visitor, cautiously retiring towards the door.

"Be off, be off, brother, get along."

Next day after dinner, while Astafy Ivanovitch was fitting on a coat which he was altering for me, again some one came into the passage. I half opened the door.

Before my very eyes my yesterday's visitor, with perfect composure, took my wadded greatcoat from the peg and, stuffing it under his arm, darted out of the flat. Agrafena stood all the time staring at him, agape with astonishment and doing nothing for the protection of my property. Astafy Ivanovitch flew in pursuit of the thief and ten minutes later came back out of breath and empty-handed. He had vanished completely.

"Well, there's a piece of luck, Astafy Ivanovitch!"

"It's a good job your cloak is left! Or he would have put you in a plight, the thief!"

But the whole incident had so impressed Astafy Ivanovitch that I forgot the theft as I looked at him. He could not get over it. Every minute or two he would drop the work upon which he was engaged, and would describe over again how it had all happened, how he had been standing, how the greatcoat had been taken down before his very eyes, not a yard away, and how it had come to pass that he could not catch the thief. Then he would sit down to his work again, then leave it once more, and at last I saw him go down to the dvornik to tell him all about it, and to upbraid him for letting such a thing happen in his domain. Then he came back and began scolding Agrafena.

Then he sat down to his work again, and long afterwards he was still muttering to himself how it had all happened, how he stood there and I was here, how before our eyes, not a yard away, the thief took the coat off the peg, and so on. In short, though Astafy Ivanovitch understood his business, he was a terrible slow-coach and busy-body.

"He's made fools of us, Astafy Ivanovitch," I said to him in the evening, as I gave him a glass of tea. I wanted to while away the time by recalling the story of the lost greatcoat, the frequent repetition of which, together with the great earnestness of the speaker, was beginning to become very amusing.

"Fools, indeed, sir! Even though it is no business of mine, I am put out.

It makes me angry though it is not my coat that was lost. To my thinking there is no vermin in the world worse than a thief. Another takes what you can spare, but a thief steals the work of your hands, the sweat of your brow, your time ... Ugh, it's nasty! One can't speak of it! it's too vexing. How is it you don't feel the loss of your property, sir?"

"Yes, you are right, Astafy Ivanovitch, better if the thing had been burnt; it's annoying to let the thief have it, it's disagreeable."

"Disagreeable! I should think so! Yet, to be sure, there are thieves and thieves. And I have happened, sir, to come across an honest thief."

"An honest thief? But how can a thief be honest, Astafy Ivanovitch?"

"There you are right indeed, sir. How can a thief be honest? There are none such. I only meant to say that he was an honest man, sure enough, and yet he stole. I was simply sorry for him."

"Why, how was that, Astafy Ivanovitch?"

"It was about two years ago, sir. I had been nearly a year out of a place, and just before I lost my place I made the acquaintance of a poor lost creature. We got acquainted in a public-house. He was a drunkard, a vagrant, a beggar, he had been in a situation of some sort, but from his drinking habits he had lost his work. Such a ne'er-do-weel! God only knows what he had on! Often you wouldn't be sure if he'd a shirt under his coat; everything he could lay his hands upon he would drink away. But he was not one to quarrel; he was a quiet fellow. A soft, good-natured chap. And he'd never ask, he was ashamed; but you could see for yourself the poor fellow wanted a drink, and you would stand it him. And so we got friendly, that's to say, he stuck to me.... It was all one to me. And what a man he was, to be sure! Like a little dog he would follow me; wherever I went there he would be; and all that after our first meeting, and he as thin as a thread-paper! At first it was 'let me stay the night'; well, I let him stay.

"I looked at his passport, too; the man was all right.

"Well, the next day it was the same story, and then the third day he came again and sat all day in the window and stayed the night. Well, thinks I, he is sticking to me; give him food and drink and shelter at night, too--here am I, a poor man, and a hanger-on to keep as well! And before he came to me, he used to go in the same way to a government clerk's; he attached himself to him; they were always drinking together; but he, through trouble of some sort, drank himself into the grave. My man was called Emelyan Ilyitch. I pondered and pondered what I was to do with him.

To drive him away I was ashamed. I was sorry for him; such a pitiful, God-forsaken creature I never did set eyes on. And not a word said either; he does not ask, but just sits there and looks into your eyes like a dog.

To think what drinking will bring a man down to!

"I keep asking myself how am I to say to him: 'You must be moving, Emelyanoushka, there's nothing for you here, you've come to the wrong place; I shall soon not have a bite for myself, how am I to keep you too?'

"I sat and wondered what he'd do when I said that to him. And I seemed to see how he'd stare at me, if he were to hear me say that, how long he would sit and not understand a word of it. And when it did get home to him at last, how he would get up from the window, would take up his bundle--I can see it now, the red-check handkerchief full of holes, with God knows what wrapped up in it, which he had always with him, and then how he would set his shabby old coat to rights, so that it would look decent and keep him warm, so that no holes would be seen--he was a man of delicate feelings!

And how he'd open the door and go out with tears in

his eyes. Well, there's no letting a man go to ruin like that.... One's sorry for him.

"And then again, I think, how am I off myself? Wait a bit, Emelyanoushka, says I to myself, you've not long to feast with me: I shall soon be going away and then you will not find me.

"Well, sir, our family made a move; and Alexandr Filimonovitch, my master (now deceased, God rest his soul), said, 'I am thoroughly satisfied with you, Astafy Ivanovitch; when we come back from the country we will take you on again.' I had been butler with them; a nice gentleman he was, but he died that same year. Well, after seeing him off, I took my belongings, what little money I had, and I thought I'd have a rest for a time, so I went to an old woman I knew, and I took a corner in her room. There was only one corner free in it. She had been a nurse, so now she had a pension and a room of her own. Well, now good-bye, Emelyanoushka, thinks I, you won't find me now, my boy.

"And what do you think, sir? I had gone out to see a man I knew, and when I came back in the evening, the first thing I saw was Emelyanoushka! There he was, sitting on my box and his check bundle beside him; he was sitting in his ragged old coat, waiting for me. And to while away the time he had borrowed a church book from the old lady, and was holding it wrong side upwards. He'd scented me out! My heart sank. Well, thinks I, there's no help for it--why didn't I turn him out at first? So I asked him straight off: Have you brought your passport, Emelyanoushka?'

"I sat down on the spot, sir, and began to ponder: will a vagabond like that be very much trouble to me? And on thinking it over it seemed he would not be much trouble. He must be fed, I thought. Well, a bit of bread in the morning, and to make it go down better I'll buy him an onion. At midday I should have to give him another bit of bread and an onion; and in the evening, onion again with kvass, with some more bread if he wanted it. And if some cabbage soup were to come our way, then we should both have had our fill. I am no great eater myself, and a drinking man, as we all know, never eats; all he wants is herb-brandy or green vodka. He'll ruin me with his drinking, I thought, but then another idea came into my head, sir, and took great hold on me. So much so that if Emelyanoushka had gone away I should have felt that I had nothing to live for, I do believe.... I determined on the spot to be a father and guardian to him. I'll keep him from ruin, I thought, I'll wean him from the glass! You wait a bit, thought I; very well, Emelyanoushka, you may stay, only you must behave yourself; you must obey orders.

"Well, thinks I to myself, I'll begin by training him to work of some sort, but not all at once; let him enjoy himself a little first, and I'll look round and find something you are fit for, Emelyanoushka. For every sort of work a man needs a special ability, you know, sir. And I began to watch him on the quiet; I soon saw Emelyanoushka was a desperate character. I began, sir, with a word of advice: I said this and that to him. 'Emelyanoushka,'

said I, 'you ought to take a thought and mend your ways. Have done with drinking! Just look what rags you go about in: that old coat of yours, if I may make bold to say so, is fit for nothing but a sieve. A pretty state of things! It's time to draw the line, sure enough.' Emelyanoushka sat and listened to me with his head hanging down. Would you believe it, sir? It had come to such a pass with him, he'd lost his tongue through drink and could not speak a word of sense. Talk to him of cucumbers and he'd answer back about beans! He would listen and listen to me and then heave such a sigh. 'What are you sighing for, Emelyan Ilyitch?' I asked him.

"'Oh, nothing; don't you mind me, Astafy Ivanovitch. Do you know there were two women fighting in the street to-day, Astafy Ivanovitch? One upset the other woman's basket of cranberries by accident.'

"'Well, what of that?'

"'And the second one upset the other's cranberries on purpose and trampled them under foot, too.'

"'Well, and what of it, Emelyan Ilyitch?'

"'Why, nothing, Astafy Ivanovitch, I just mentioned it.'

"'"Nothing, I just mentioned it!" Emelyanoushka, my boy, I thought, you've squandered and drunk away your brains!'

"'And do you know, a gentleman dropped a money-note on the pavement in Gorohovy Street, no, it was Sadovy Street. And a peasant saw it and said, "That's my luck"; and at the same time another man saw it and said, "No, it's my bit of luck. I saw it before you did."'

"'Well, Emelyan Ilyitch?'

"'And the fellows had a fight over it, Astafy Ivanovitch. But a policeman came up, took away the note, gave it back to the gentleman and threatened to take up both the men.'

"'Well, but what of that? What is there edifying about it, Emelyanoushka?'

"'Why, nothing, to be sure. Folks laughed, Astafy Ivanovitch.'

"'Ach, Emelyanoushka! What do the folks matter? You've sold your soul for a brass farthing! But do you know what I have to tell you, Emelyan Ilyitch?'

"'What, Astafy Ivanovitch?'

"'Take a job of some sort, that's what you must do. For the hundredth time I say to you, set to work, have some mercy on yourself!'

"'What could I set to, Astafy Ivanovitch? I don't know what job I could set to, and there is no one who will take me on, Astafy Ivanovitch.'

"'That's how you came to be turned off, Emelyanoushka, you drinking man!'

"'And do you know Vlass, the waiter, was sent for to the office to-day, Astafy Ivanovitch?'

"'Why did they send for him, Emelyanoushka?' I asked.

"'I could not say why, Astafy Ivanovitch. I suppose they wanted him there, and that's why they sent for him.'

"A-ach, thought I, we are in a bad way, poor Emelyanoushka! The Lord is chastising us for our sins. Well, sir, what is one to do with such a man?

"But a cunning fellow he was, and no mistake. He'd listen and listen to me, but at last I suppose he got sick of it. As soon as he sees I am beginning to get angry, he'd pick up his old coat and out he'd slip and leave no trace. He'd wander about all day and come back at night drunk. Where he got the money from, the Lord only knows; I had no hand in that.

"'No,' said I, 'Emelyan Ilyitch, you'll come to a bad end. Give over drinking, mind what I say now, give it up! Next time you come home in liquor, you can spend the night on the stairs. I won't let you in!'

"After hearing that threat, Emelyanoushka sat at home that day and the next; but on the third he slipped off again. I waited and waited; he didn't come back. Well, at least I don't mind owning, I was in a fright, and I felt for the man too. What have I done to him? I thought. I've scared him away. Where's the poor fellow gone to now? He'll get lost maybe. Lord have mercy upon us!

"Night came on, he did not come. In the morning I went out into the porch; I looked, and if he hadn't gone to sleep in the porch! There he was with his head on the step, and chilled to the marrow of his bones.

"'What next, Emelyanoushka, God have mercy on you! Where will you get to next!'

"'Why, you were--sort of--angry with me, Astafy Ivanovitch, the other day, you were vexed and promised to put me to sleep in the porch, so I didn't--sort of--venture to come in, Astafy Ivanovitch, and so I lay down here....'

"I did feel angry and sorry too.

"'Surely you might undertake some other duty, Emelyanoushka, instead of lying here guarding the steps,' I said.

"'Why, what other duty, Astafy Ivanovitch?'

"'You lost soul'--I was in such a rage, I called him that--'if you could but learn tailoring work! Look at your old rag of a coat! It's not enough to have it in tatters, here you are sweeping the steps with it! You might take a needle and boggle up your rags, as decency demands. Ah, you drunken man!'

"What do you think, sir? He actually did take a needle. Of course I said it in jest, but he was so scared he set to work. He took off his coat and began threading the needle. I watched him; as you may well guess, his eyes were all red and bleary, and his hands were all of a shake. He kept shoving and shoving the thread and could not get it through the eye of the needle; he kept screwing his eyes up and wetting the thread and twisting it in his fingers--it was no good! He gave it up and looked at me.

"'Well,' said I, 'this is a nice way to treat me! If there had been folks by to see, I don't know what I should have done! Why, you simple fellow, I said it you in joke, as a reproach. Give over your nonsense, God bless you!

Sit quiet and don't put me to shame, don't sleep on my stairs and make a laughing-stock of me.'

"'Why, what am I to do, Astafy Ivanovitch? I know very

well I am a drunkard and good for nothing! I can do nothing but vex you, my bene--bene--factor....'

"And at that his blue lips began all of a sudden to quiver, and a tear ran down his white cheek and trembled on his stubbly chin, and then poor Emelyanoushka burst into a regular flood of tears. Mercy on us! I felt as though a knife were thrust into my heart! The sensitive creature! I'd never have expected it. Who could have guessed it? No, Emelyanoushka, thought I, I shall give you up altogether. You can go your way like the rubbish you are.

"Well, sir, why make a long story of it? And the whole affair is so trifling; it's not worth wasting words upon. Why, you, for instance, sir, would not have given a thought to it, but I would have given a great deal--if I had a great deal to give--that it never should have happened at all.

"I had a pair of riding breeches by me, sir, deuce take them, fine, first-rate riding breeches they were too, blue with a check on it. They'd been ordered by a gentleman from the country, but he would not have them after all; said they were not full enough, so they were left on my hands.

It struck me they were worth something. At the second-hand dealer's I ought to get five silver roubles for them, or if not I could turn them into two pairs of trousers for Petersburg gentlemen and have a piece over for a waistcoat for myself. Of course for poor people like us everything comes in. And it happened just then that Emelyanoushka was having a sad time of it. There he sat day after day: he did not drink, not a drop passed his lips, but he sat and moped like an owl. It was sad to see him--he just sat and brooded. Well, thought I, either you've not got a copper to spend, my lad, or else you're turning over a new leaf of yourself, you've given it up, you've listened to reason. Well, sir, that's how it was with us; and just then came a holiday. I went to vespers; when I came home I found Emelyanoushka sitting in the window, drunk and rocking to and fro.

"Ah! so that's what you've been up to, my lad! And I went to get something out of my chest. And when I looked in, the breeches were not there.... I rummaged here and there; they'd vanished. When I'd ransacked everywhere and saw they were not there, something seemed to stab me to the heart. I ran first to the old dame and began accusing her; of Emelyanoushka I'd not the faintest suspicion, though there was cause for it in his sitting there drunk.

"'No,' said the old body, 'God be with you, my fine gentleman, what good are riding breeches to me? Am I going to wear such things? Why, a skirt I had I lost the other day through a fellow of your sort ... I know nothing; I can tell you nothing about it,' she said.

"'Who has been here, who has been in?' I asked.

"'Why, nobody has been, my good sir,' says she; 'I've been here all the while; Emelyan Ilyitch went out and came back again; there he sits, ask him.'

"'Emelyanoushka,' said I, 'have you taken those new riding breeches for anything; you remember the pair I made for that gentleman from the country?'

"'No, Astafy Ivanovitch,' said he; 'I've not--sort of--touched them.'

"I was in a state! I hunted high and low for them--they were nowhere to be found. And Emelyanoushka sits there rocking himself to and fro. I was squatting on my heels facing him and bending over the chest, and all at once I stole a glance at him.... Alack, I thought; my heart suddenly grew hot within me and I felt myself flushing up too. And suddenly Emelyanoushka looked at me.

"'No, Astafy Ivanovitch,' said he, 'those riding breeches

of yours, maybe, you are thinking, maybe, I took them, but I never touched them.'

"'But what can have become of them, Emelyan Ilyitch?'

"'No, Astafy Ivanovitch,' said he, 'I've never seen them.'

"'Why, Emelyan Ilyitch, I suppose they've run off of themselves, eh?'

"'Maybe they have, Astafy Ivanovitch.'

"When I heard him say that, I got up at once, went up to him, lighted the lamp and sat down to work to my sewing. I was altering a waistcoat for a clerk who lived below us. And wasn't there a burning pain and ache in my breast! I shouldn't have minded so much if I had put all the clothes I had in the fire. Emelyanoushka seemed to have an inkling of what a rage I was in. When a man is guilty, you know, sir, he scents trouble far off, like the birds of the air before a storm.

"'Do you know what, Astafy Ivanovitch,' Emelyanoushka began, and his poor old voice was shaking as he said the words, 'Antip Prohoritch, the apothecary, married the coachman's wife this morning, who died the other day—'

"I did give him a look, sir, a nasty look it was; Emelyanoushka understood it too. I saw him get up, go to the bed, and begin to rummage there for something. I waited--he was busy there a long time and kept muttering all the while, 'No, not there, where can the blessed things have got to!' I waited to see what he'd do; I saw him creep under the bed on all fours. I couldn't bear it any longer. 'What are you crawling about under the bed for, Emelyan Ilyitch?' said I.

"'Looking for the breeches, Astafy Ivanovitch. Maybe they've dropped down there somewhere.'

"'Why should you try to help a poor simple man like me,' said I, 'crawling on your knees for nothing, sir?'--I called him that in my vexation.

"'Oh, never mind, Astafy Ivanovitch, I'll just look. They'll turn up, maybe, somewhere.'

"'H'm,' said I, 'look here, Emelyan Ilyitch!'

"'What is it, Astafy Ivanovitch?' said he.

"'Haven't you simply stolen them from me like a thief and a robber, in return for the bread and salt you've eaten here?' said I.

"I felt so angry, sir, at seeing him fooling about on his knees before me.

"'No, Astafy Ivanovitch.'

"And he stayed lying as he was on his face under the bed. A long time he lay there and then at last crept out. I looked at him and the man was as white as a sheet. He stood up, and sat down near me in the window and sat so for some ten minutes.

"'No, Astafy Ivanovitch,' he said, and all at once he stood up and came towards me, and I can see him now; he looked dreadful. 'No, Astafy Ivanovitch,' said he, 'I never--sort of--touched your breeches.'

"He was all of a shake, poking himself in the chest with a trembling finger, and his poor old voice shook so that I was frightened, sir, and sat as though I was rooted to the window-seat.

"'Well, Emelyan Ilyitch,' said I, 'as you will, forgive me if I, in my foolishness, have accused you unjustly. As for the breeches, let them go hang; we can live without them. We've still our hands, thank God; we need not go thieving or begging from some other poor man; we'll earn our bread.'

"Emelyanoushka heard me out and went on standing there before me. I looked up, and he had sat down. And there he sat all the evening without stirring.

At last I lay down to sleep. Emelyanoushka went on sitting in the same place. When I looked out in the morning, he was lying curled up in his old coat on the bare floor; he felt too crushed even to come to bed.

Well, sir, I felt no more liking for the fellow from that day, in fact for the first few days I hated him. I felt as one may say as though my own son had robbed me, and done me a deadly hurt. Ach, thought I, Emelyanoushka, Emelyanoushka! And Emelyanoushka, sir, went on drinking for a whole fortnight without stopping. He was drunk all the time, and regularly besotted. He went out in the morning and came back late at night, and for a whole fortnight I didn't get a word out of him. It was as though grief was gnawing at his heart, or as though he wanted to do for himself completely.

At last he stopped; he must have come to the end of all he'd got, and then he sat in the window again. I remember he sat there without speaking for three days and three nights; all of a sudden I saw that he was crying. He was just sitting there, sir, and crying like anything; a perfect stream, as though he didn't know how his tears were flowing. And it's a sad thing, sir, to see a grown-up man and an old man, too, crying from woe and grief.

"'What's the matter, Emelyanoushka?' said I.

"He began to tremble so that he shook all over. I spoke to him for the first time since that evening.

"'Nothing, Astafy Ivanovitch.'

"'God be with you, Emelyanoushka, what's lost is lost. Why are you moping about like this?' I felt sorry for him.

"'Oh, nothing, Astafy Ivanovitch, it's no matter. I want to find some work to do, Astafy Ivanovitch.'

"'And what sort of work, pray, Emelyanoushka?'

"'Why, any sort; perhaps I could find a situation such as I used to have.

I've been already to ask Fedosay Ivanitch. I don't like to be a burden on you, Astafy Ivanovitch. If I can find a situation, Astafy Ivanovitch, then I'll pay it you all back, and make you a return for all your hospitality.'

"'Enough, Emelyanoushka, enough; let bygones be bygones--and no more to be said about it. Let us go on as we used to do before.'

"'No, Astafy Ivanovitch, you, maybe, think--but I never touched your riding breeches.'

"'Well, have it your own way; God be with you, Emelyanoushka.'

"'No, Astafy Ivanovitch, I can't go on living with you, that's clear. You must excuse me, Astafy Ivanovitch.'

"'Why, God bless you, Emelyan Ilyitch, who's offending you and driving you out of the place--am I doing it?'

"'No, it's not the proper thing for me to live with you like this, Astafy Ivanovitch. I'd better be going.'

"He was so hurt, it seemed, he stuck to his point. I looked at him, and sure enough, up he got and pulled his old coat over his shoulders.

"'But where are you going, Emelyan Ilyitch? Listen to reason: what are you about? Where are you off to?'

"'No, good-bye, Astafy Ivanovitch, don't keep me now'--and he was blubbering again--'I'd better be going. You're not the same now.'

"'Not the same as what? I am the same. But you'll be lost by yourself like a poor helpless babe, Emelyan Ilyitch.'

"'No, Astafy Ivanovitch, when you go out now, you lock up your chest and it makes me cry to see it, Astafy Ivanovitch. You'd better let me go, Astafy Ivanovitch, and forgive me all the trouble I've given you while I've been living with you.'

"Well, sir, the man went away. I waited for a day; I expected he'd be back in the evening--no. Next day no sign of him, nor the third day either. I began to get frightened; I was so worried, I couldn't drink, I couldn't eat, I couldn't sleep. The fellow had quite disarmed me.

On the fourth day I went out to look for him; I peeped into all the taverns, to inquire for him--but no, Emelyanoushka was lost. 'Have you managed to keep yourself alive, Emelyanoushka?' I wondered. 'Perhaps he is lying dead under some hedge, poor drunkard, like a sodden log.' I went home more dead than alive.

Next day I went out to look for him again. And I kept cursing myself that I'd been such a fool as to let the man go off by himself. On the fifth day it was a holiday--in the early morning I heard the door creak. I looked up and there was my Emelyanoushka coming in. His face was blue and his hair was covered with dirt as though he'd been sleeping in the street; he was as thin as a match. He took off his old coat, sat down on the chest and looked at me. I was delighted to see him, but I felt more upset about him than ever. For you see, sir, if I'd been overtaken in some sin, as true as I am here, sir, I'd have died like a dog before I'd have come back. But Emelyanoushka did come back. And a sad thing it was, sure enough, to see a man sunk so low. I began to look after him, to talk kindly to him, to comfort him.

"'Well, Emelyanoushka,' said I, 'I am glad you've come back. Had you been away much longer I should have gone to look for you in the taverns again to-day. Are you hungry?'

"'No, Astafy Ivanovitch.'

"'Come, now, aren't you really? Here, brother, is some cabbage soup left over from yesterday; there was meat in it; it is good stuff. And here is some bread and onion. Come, eat it, it'll do you no harm.'

"I made him eat it, and I saw at once that the man had not tasted food for maybe three days--he was as hungry as a wolf. So it was hunger that had driven him to me. My heart was melted looking at the poor dear. 'Let me run to the tavern,' thought I, 'I'll get something to ease his heart, and then we'll make an end of it. I've no more anger in my heart against you, Emelyanoushka!' I brought him some vodka. 'Here, Emelyan Ilyitch, let us have a drink for the holiday. Like a drink? And it will do you good.' He held out his hand, held it out greedily; he was just taking it, and then he stopped himself. But a minute after I saw him take it, and lift it to his mouth, spilling it on his sleeve. But though he got it to his lips he set it down on the table again.

"'What is it, Emelyanoushka?'

"'Nothing, Astafy Ivanovitch, I--sort of—'

"'Won't you drink it?'

"'Well, Astafy Ivanovitch, I'm not--sort of--going to drink any more, Astafy Ivanovitch.'

"'Do you mean you've given it up altogether, Emelyanoushka, or are you only not going to drink to-day?'

"He did not answer. A minute later I saw him rest his head on his hand.

"'What's the matter, Emelyanoushka, are you ill?'

"'Why, yes, Astafy Ivanovitch, I don't feel well.'

"I took him and laid him down on the bed. I saw that he really was ill: his head was burning hot and he was shivering with fever. I sat by him all day; towards night he was worse. I mixed him some oil and onion and kvass and bread broken up.

"'Come, eat some of this,' said I, 'and perhaps you'll be better.' He shook his head. 'No,' said he, 'I won't have any dinner to-day, Astafy Ivanovitch.'

"I made some tea for him, I quite flustered our old woman--he was no better. Well, thinks I, it's a bad look-out! The third morning I went for a medical gentleman. There was one I knew living close by, Kostopravov by name. I'd made his acquaintance when I was in service with the Bosomyagins; he'd attended me.

The doctor come and looked at him. 'He's in a bad way,' said he, 'it was no use sending for me. But if you like I can give him a powder.' Well, I didn't give him a powder, I thought that's just the doctor's little game; and then the fifth day came.

"He lay, sir, dying before my eyes. I sat in the window with my work in my hands. The old woman was heating the stove. We were all silent. My heart was simply breaking over him, the good-for-nothing fellow; I felt as if it were a son of my own I was losing. I knew that Emelyanoushka was looking at me. I'd seen the man all the day long making up his mind to say something and not daring to.

"At last I looked up at him; I saw such misery in the poor fellow's eyes.

He had kept them fixed on me, but when he saw that I was looking at him, he looked down at once.

"'Astafy Ivanovitch.'

"'What is it, Emelyanoushka?'

"'If you were to take my old coat to a second-hand dealer's, how much do you think they'd give you for it, Astafy Ivanovitch?'

"'There's no knowing how much they'd give. Maybe they would give me a rouble for it, Emelyan Ilyitch.'

"But if I had taken it they wouldn't have given a farthing for it, but would have laughed in my face for bringing such a trumpery thing. I simply said that to comfort the poor fellow, knowing the simpleton he was.

"'But I was thinking, Astafy Ivanovitch, they might give you three roubles for it; it's made of cloth, Astafy Ivanovitch. How could they only give one rouble for a cloth coat?'

"'I don't know, Emelyan Ilyitch,' said I, 'if you are thinking of taking it you should certainly ask three roubles to begin with.'

"Emelyanoushka was silent for a time, and then he addressed me again"'Astafy Ivanovitch.'

"'What is it, Emelyanoushka?' I asked.

"'Sell my coat when I die, and don't bury me in it. I can lie as well without it; and it's a thing of some value--it might come in useful.'

"I can't tell you how it made my heart ache to hear him. I saw that the death agony was coming on him. We were silent again for a bit. So an hour passed by. I looked at him again: he was still staring at me, and when he met my eyes he looked down again.

"'Do you want some water to drink, Emelyan Ilyitch?' I asked.

"'Give me some, God bless you, Astafy Ivanovitch.'

"I gave him a drink.

"'Thank you, Astafy Ivanovitch,' said he.

"'Is there anything else you would like, Emelyanoushka?'

"'No, Astafy Ivanovitch, there's nothing I want, but I--sort of—'

"'What?'

"'I only—'

"'What is it, Emelyanoushka?'

"'Those riding breeches—it was—sort of—I who took them—Astafy Ivanovitch.'

"'Well, God forgive you, Emelyanoushka,' said I, 'you poor, sorrowful creature. Depart in peace.'

"And I was choking myself, sir, and the tears were in my eyes. I turned aside for a moment.

"'Astafy Ivanovitch—'

"I saw Emelyanoushka wanted to tell me something; he was trying to sit up, trying to speak, and mumbling something. He flushed red all over suddenly, looked at me ... then I saw him turn white again, whiter and whiter, and he seemed to sink away all in a minute. His head fell back, he drew one breath and gave up his soul to God."

The Box of Robbers

Lyman Frank Baum

No one intended to leave Martha alone that afternoon, but it happened that everyone was called away, for one reason or another. Mrs. McFarland was attending the weekly card party held by the Women's Anti-Gambling League. Sister Nell's young man had called quite unexpectedly to take her for a long drive. Papa was at the office, as usual. It was Mary Ann's day out. As for Emeline, she certainly should have stayed in the house and looked after the little girl; but Emeline had a restless nature.

"Would you mind, miss, if I just crossed the alley to speak a word to Mrs. Carleton's girl?" she asked Martha.

"'Course not," replied the child. "You'd better lock the back door, though, and take the key, for I shall be upstairs."

"Oh, I'll do that, of course, miss," said the delighted maid, and ran away to spend the afternoon with her friend, leaving Martha quite alone in the big house, and locked in, into the bargain.

The little girl read a few pages in her new book, sewed a few stitches in her embroidery and started to "play visiting" with her four favorite dolls. Then she remembered that in the attic was a doll's playhouse that hadn't been used for months, so she decided she would dust it and put it in order.

Filled with this idea, the girl climbed the winding stairs to the big room under the roof. It was well lighted by three dormer windows and was warm and pleasant. Around the walls were rows of boxes and trunks, piles of old carpeting, pieces of damaged furniture, bundles of discarded clothing and other odds and ends of more or less value. Every well-regulated house has an attic of this sort, so I need not describe it.

The doll's house had been moved, but after a search Martha found it away over in a corner near the big chimney.

She drew it out and noticed that behind it was a black wooden chest which Uncle Walter had sent over from Italy years and years ago—before Martha was born, in fact. Mamma had told her about it one day; how there was no key to it, because Uncle Walter wished it to remain unopened until he returned home; and how this wandering uncle, who was a mighty hunter, had gone into Africa to hunt elephants and had never been heard from afterwards.

The little girl looked at the chest curiously, now that it had by accident attracted her attention.

It was quite big—bigger even than mamma's traveling trunk—and was studded all over with tarnished brassheaded nails. It was heavy, too, for when Martha tried to lift one end of it she found she could not stir it a bit. But there was a place in the side of the cover for a key. She stooped to examine the lock, and saw that it would take a rather big key to open it.

Then, as you may suspect, the little girl longed to open Uncle Walter's big box and see what was in it. For we are all curious, and little girls are just as curious as the rest of us.

"I don't b'lieve Uncle Walter'll ever come back," she thought. "Papa said once that some elephant must have killed him. If I only had a key—" She stopped and clapped her little hands together gayly as she remembered a big basket of keys on the shelf in the linen closet. They were of all sorts and sizes; perhaps one of them would unlock the mysterious chest!

She flew down the stairs, found the basket and returned with it to the attic. Then she sat down before the brass-studded box and began trying one key after another in the curious old lock. Some were too large, but most were too small. One would go into the lock but would not turn; another stuck so fast that she feared for a time that she would never get it out again. But at last, when the basket was almost empty, an oddly-shaped, ancient brass key slipped easily into the lock. With a cry of joy Martha turned the key with both hands; then she heard a sharp "click," and the next moment the heavy lid flew up of its own accord!

The little girl leaned over the edge of the chest an instant, and the sight that met her eyes caused her to start back in amazement.

Slowly and carefully a man unpacked himself from the chest, stepped out upon the floor, stretched his limbs and then took off his hat and bowed politely to the astonished child.

He was tall and thin and his face seemed badly tanned or sunburnt.

Then another man emerged from the chest, yawning and rubbing his eyes like a sleepy schoolboy. He was of middle size and his skin seemed as badly tanned as that of the first.

While Martha stared open-mouthed at the remarkable sight a third man crawled from the chest. He had the same complexion as his fellows, but was short and fat.

All three were dressed in a curious manner. They wore short jackets of red velvet braided with gold, and knee breeches of sky-blue satin with silver buttons. Over their stockings were laced wide ribbons of red and yellow and blue, while their hats had broad brims with high, peaked crowns, from which fluttered yards of bright-colored ribbons.

They had big gold rings in their ears and rows of knives and pistols in their belts. Their eyes were black and glittering and they wore long, fierce mustaches, curling at the ends like a pig's tail.

"My! but you were heavy," exclaimed the fat one, when he had pulled down his velvet jacket and brushed the dust from his sky-blue breeches. "And you squeezed me all out of shape."

"It was unavoidable, Luigi," responded the thin man, lightly; "the lid of the chest pressed me down upon you. Yet I tender you my regrets."

"As for me," said the middle-sized man, carelessly rolling a cigarette and lighting it, "you must acknowledge I have been your nearest friend for years; so do not be disagreeable."

"You mustn't smoke in the attic," said Martha, recovering herself at sight of the cigarette. "You might set the house on fire."

The middle-sized man, who had not noticed her before, at this speech turned to the girl and bowed.

"Since a lady requests it," said he, "I shall abandon my cigarette," and he threw it on the floor and extinguished it with his foot.

"Who are you?" asked Martha, who until now had been too astonished to be frightened.

"Permit us to introduce ourselves," said the thin man, flourishing his hat gracefully. "This is Lugui," the fat man nodded; "and this is Beni," the middle-sized man bowed; "and I am Victor. We are three bandits—Italian bandits."

"Bandits!" cried Martha, with a look of horror.

"Exactly. Perhaps in all the world there are not three other bandits so terrible and fierce as ourselves," said Victor, proudly.

"'Tis so," said the fat man, nodding gravely.

"But it's wicked!" exclaimed Martha.

"Yes, indeed," replied Victor. "We are extremely and tremendously wicked. Perhaps in all the world you could not find three men more wicked than those who now stand before you."

"'Tis so," said the fat man, approvingly.

"But you shouldn't be so wicked," said the girl; "it's—it's—naughty!"

Victor cast down his eyes and blushed.

"Naughty!" gasped Beni, with a horrified look.

"'Tis a hard word," said Luigi, sadly, and buried his face in his hands.

"I little thought," murmured Victor, in a voice broken by emotion, "ever to be so reviled—and by a lady! Yet, perhaps you spoke thoughtlessly. You must consider, miss, that our wickedness has an excuse. For how are we to be bandits, let me ask, unless we are wicked?"

Martha was puzzled and shook her head, thoughtfully. Then she remembered something.

"You can't remain bandits any longer," said she, "because you are now in America."

"America!" cried the three, together.

"Certainly. You are on Prairie avenue, in Chicago. Uncle Walter sent you here from Italy in this chest."

The bandits seemed greatly bewildered by this announcement. Lugui sat down on an old chair with a broken rocker and wiped his forehead with a yellow silk handkerchief. Beni and Victor fell back upon the chest and looked at her with pale faces and staring eyes.

When he had somewhat recovered himself Victor spoke.

"Your Uncle Walter has greatly wronged us," he said, reproachfully. "He has taken us from our beloved Italy, where bandits are highly respected, and brought us to a strange country where we shall not know whom to rob or how much to ask for a ransom."

"'Tis so!" said the fat man, slapping his leg sharply.

"And we had won such fine reputations in Italy!" said Beni, regretfully.

"Perhaps Uncle Walter wanted to reform you," suggested Martha.

"Are there, then, no bandits in Chicago?" asked Victor.

"Well," replied the girl, blushing in her turn, "we do not call them bandits."

"Then what shall we do for a living?" inquired Beni, despairingly.

"A great deal can be done in a big American city," said the child. "My father is a lawyer" (the bandits shuddered), "and my mother's cousin is a police inspector."

"Ah," said Victor, "that is a good employment. The police need to be inspected, especially in Italy."

"Everywhere!" added Beni.

"Then you could do other things," continued Martha, encouragingly. "You could be motor men on trolley cars, or clerks in a department store. Some people even become aldermen to earn a living."

The bandits shook their heads sadly.

"We are not fitted for such work," said Victor. "Our business is to rob."

Martha tried to think.

"It is rather hard to get positions in the gas office," she said, "but you might become politicians."

"No!" cried Beni, with sudden fierceness; "we must not abandon our high calling. Bandits we have always been, and bandits we must remain!"

"'Tis so!" agreed the fat man.

"Even in Chicago there must be people to rob," remarked Victor, with cheerfulness.

Martha was distressed.

"I think they have all been robbed," she objected.

"Then we can rob the robbers, for we have experience and talent beyond the ordinary," said Beni.

"Oh, dear; oh, dear!" moaned the girl; "why did Uncle Walter ever send you here in this chest?"

The bandits became interested.

"That is what we should like to know," declared Victor, eagerly.

"But no one will ever know, for Uncle Walter was lost while hunting elephants in Africa," she continued, with conviction.

"Then we must accept our fate and rob to the best of our ability," said Victor. "So long as we are faithful to our beloved profession we need not be ashamed."

"'Tis so!" cried the fat man.

"Brothers! we will begin now. Let us rob the house we are in."

"Good!" shouted the others and sprang to their feet.

Beni turned threateningly upon the child.

"Remain here!" he commanded. "If you stir one step your blood will be on your own head!" Then he added, in a gentler voice: "Don't be afraid; that's the way all bandits talk to their captives. But of course we wouldn't hurt a young lady under any circumstances."

"Of course not," said Victor.

The fat man drew a big knife from his belt and flourished it about his head.

"S'blood!" he ejaculated, fiercely.

"S'bananas!" cried Beni, in a terrible voice.

"Confusion to our foes!" hissed Victor.

And then the three bent themselves nearly double and crept stealthily down the stairway with cocked pistols in their hands and glittering knives between their teeth, leaving Martha trembling with fear and too horrified to even cry for help.

How long she remained alone in the attic she never knew, but finally she heard the catlike tread of the returning bandits and saw them coming up the stairs in single file.

All bore heavy loads of plunder in their arms, and Lugui was balancing a mince pie on the top of a pile of her mother's best evening dresses. Victor came next with an armful of bric-a-brac, a brass candelabra and the parlor clock. Beni had the family Bible, the basket of silverware from the sideboard, a copper kettle and papa's fur overcoat.

"Oh, joy!" said Victor, putting down his load; "it is pleasant to rob once more."

"Oh, ecstacy!" said Beni; but he let the kettle drop on his toe and immediately began dancing around in anguish, while he muttered queer words in the Italian language.

"We have much wealth," continued Victor, holding the mince pie while Lugui added his spoils to the heap; "and all from one house! This America must be a rich place."

With a dagger he then cut himself a piece of the pie and handed the remainder to his comrades. Whereupon all three sat upon the floor and consumed the pie while Martha looked on sadly.

"We should have a cave," remarked Beni; "for we must store our plunder in a safe place. Can you tell us of a secret cave?" he asked Martha.

"There's a Mammoth cave," she answered, "but it's in Kentucky. You would be obliged to ride on the cars a long time to get there."

The three bandits looked thoughtful and munched their pie silently, but the next moment they were startled by the ringing of the electric doorbell, which was heard plainly even in the remote attic.

"What's that?" demanded Victor, in a hoarse voice, as the three scrambled to their feet with drawn daggers.

Martha ran to the window and saw it was only the postman, who had dropped a letter in the box and gone away again. But the incident gave her an idea of how to get rid of her troublesome bandits, so she began wringing her hands as if in great distress and cried out: "It's the police!"

The robbers looked at one another with genuine alarm, and Lugui asked, tremblingly:

"Are there many of them?"

"A hundred and twelve!" exclaimed Martha, after pretending to count them.

"Then we are lost!" declared Beni; "for we could never fight so many and live."

"Are they armed?" inquired Victor, who was shivering as if cold.

"Oh, yes," said she. "They have guns and swords and pistols and axes and—and—"

"And what?" demanded Lugui.

"And cannons!"

The three wicked ones groaned aloud and Beni said, in a hollow voice:

"I hope they will kill us quickly and not put us to the torture. I have been told these Americans are painted Indians, who are bloodthirsty and terrible."

"'Tis so!" gasped the fat man, with a shudder.

Suddenly Martha turned from the window.

"You are my friends, are you not?" she asked.

"We are devoted!" answered Victor.

"We adore you!" cried Beni.

"We would die for you!" added Lugui, thinking he was about to die anyway.

"Then I will save you," said the girl.

"How?" asked the three, with one voice.

"Get back into the chest," she said. "I will then close the lid, so they will be unable to find you."

They looked around the room in a dazed and irresolute way, but she exclaimed:

"You must be quick! They will soon be here to arrest you."

Then Lugui sprang into the chest and lay fat upon the bottom. Beni tumbled in next and packed himself in the back side. Victor followed after pausing to kiss her hand to the girl in a graceful manner.

Then Martha ran up to press down the lid, but could not make it catch.

"You must squeeze down," she said to them.

Lugui groaned.

"I am doing my best, miss," said Victor, who was nearest the top; "but although we fitted in very nicely before, the chest now seems rather small for us."

"'Tis so!" came the muffled voice of the fat man from the bottom.

"I know what takes up the room," said Beni.

"What?" inquired Victor, anxiously.

"The pie," returned Beni.

"'Tis so!" came from the bottom, in faint accents.

Then Martha sat upon the lid and pressed it down with all her weight. To her great delight the lock caught, and, springing down, she exerted all her strength and turned the key.

This story should teach us not to interfere in matters that do not concern us. For had Martha refrained from opening Uncle Walter's mysterious chest she would not have been obliged to carry downstairs all the plunder the robbers had brought into the attic.

Beyond the Bayou

Kate Chopin

The bayou curved like a crescent around the point of land on which La Folle's cabin stood. Between the stream and the hut lay a big abandoned field, where cattle were pastured when the bayou supplied them with water enough. Through the woods that spread back into unknown regions the woman had drawn an imaginary line, and past this circle she never stepped. This was the form of her only mania.

She was now a large, gaunt black woman, past thirty-five. Her real name was Jacqueline, but every one on the plantation called her La Folle, because in childhood she had been frightened literally "out of her senses," and had never wholly regained them.

It was when there had been skirmishing and sharpshooting all day in the woods. Evening was near when P'tit Maître, black with powder and crimson with blood, had staggered into the cabin of Jacqueline's mother, his pursuers close at his heels. The sight had stunned her childish reason.

She dwelt alone in her solitary cabin, for the rest of the quarters had long since been removed beyond her sight and knowledge. She had more physical strength than most men, and made her patch of cotton and corn and tobacco like the best of them. But of the world beyond the bayou she had long known nothing, save what her morbid fancy conceived.

People at Bellissime had grown used to her and her way, and they thought nothing of it. Even when "Old Mis'" died, they did not wonder that La Folle had not crossed the bayou, but had stood upon her side of it, wailing and lamenting.

P'tit Maître was now the owner of Bellissime. He was a middle-aged man, with a family of beautiful daughters about him, and a little son whom La Folle loved as if he had been her own. She called him Chéri, and so did every one else because she did.

None of the girls had ever been to her what Chéri was. They had each and all loved to be with her, and to listen to her wondrous stories of things that always happened "yonda, beyon' de bayou." But none of them had stroked her black hand quite as Chéri did, nor rested their heads against her knee so confidingly, nor fallen asleep in her arms as he used to do. For Chéri hardly did such things now, since he had become the proud possessor of a gun, and had had his black curls cut off.

That summer—the summer Chéri gave La Folle two black curls tied with a knot of red ribbon—the water ran so low in the bayou that even the little children at Bellissime were able to cross it on foot, and the cattle were sent to pasture down by the river. La Folle was sorry when they were gone, for she loved these dumb companions well, and liked to feel that they were there, and to hear them browsing by night up to her own enclosure.

It was Saturday afternoon, when the fields were deserted. The men had flocked to a neighboring village to do their week's trading, and the women were occupied with household affairs,—La Folle as well as the others. It was then she mended and washed her handful of clothes, scoured her house, and did her baking.

In this last employment she never forgot Chéri. To-day she had fashioned croquignoles of the most fantastic and alluring shapes for him. So when she saw the boy come trudging across the old field with his gleaming little new rifle on his shoulder, she called out gayly to him, "Chéri! Chéri!" But Chéri did not need the summons, for he was coming straight to her. His pockets all bulged out with almonds and raisins and an orange that he had secured for her from the very fine dinner which had been given that day up at his father's house.

He was a sunny-faced youngster of ten. When he had emptied his pockets, La Folle patted his round red cheek, wiped his soiled hands on her apron, and smoothed his hair. Then she watched him as, with his cakes in his hand, he crossed her strip of cotton back of the cabin, and disappeared into the wood.

He had boasted of the things he was going to do with his gun out there.

"You think they got plenty deer in the wood, La Folle?" he had inquired, with the calculating air of an experienced hunter.

"Non, non!" the woman laughed. "Don't you look fo' no deer, Chéri. Dat's too big. But you bring La Folle one good fat squirrel fo' her dinner to-morrow, an' she goin' be satisfi'." "One squirrel ain't a bite. I'll bring you mo' 'an one, La Folle," he had boasted pompously as he went away.

When the woman, an hour later, heard the report of the boy's rifle close to the wood's edge, she would have thought nothing of it if a sharp cry of distress had not followed the sound.

She withdrew her arms from the tub of suds in which they had been plunged, dried them upon her apron, and as quickly as her trembling limbs would bear her, hurried to the spot whence the ominous report had come.

It was as she feared. There she found Chéri stretched upon the ground, with his rifle beside him. He moaned piteously:—

"I'm dead, La Folle! I'm dead! I'm gone!"

"Non, non!" she exclaimed resolutely, as she knelt beside him. "Put you' arm 'roun' La Folle's nake, Chéri. Dat's nuttin'; dat goin' be nuttin'." She lifted him in her powerful arms.

Chéri had carried his gun muzzle-downward. He had stumbled,—he did not know how. He only knew that he had a ball lodged somewhere in his leg, and he thought that his end was at hand. Now, with his head upon the woman's shoulder, he moaned and wept with pain and fright.

"Oh, La Folle! La Folle! it hurt so bad! I can' stan' it, La Folle!"

"Don't cry, mon bébé, mon bébé, mon Chéri!" the woman spoke soothingly as she covered the ground with long strides. "La Folle goin' mine you; Doctor Bonfils goin' come make mon Chéri well agin." She had reached the abandoned field. As she crossed it with her precious burden, she looked constantly and restlessly from side to side. A terrible fear was upon her,—the fear of the world beyond the bayou, the morbid and insane dread she had been under since childhood.

When she was at the bayou's edge she stood there, and shouted for help as if a life depended upon it:—

"Oh, P'tit Maître! P'tit Maître! Venez donc! Au secours! Au secours!"

No voice responded. Chéri's hot tears were scalding her neck. She called for each and every one upon the place, and still no answer came.

She shouted, she wailed; but whether her voice remained unheard or unheeded, no reply came to her frenzied cries. And all the while Chéri moaned and wept and entreated to be taken home to his mother.

La Folle gave a last despairing look around her. Extreme terror was upon her. She clasped the child close against her breast, where he could feel her heart beat like a muffled hammer. Then shutting her eyes, she ran suddenly down the shallow bank of the bayou, and never stopped till she had climbed the opposite shore.

She stood there quivering an instant as she opened her eyes. Then she plunged into the footpath through the trees.

She spoke no more to Chéri, but muttered constantly, "Bon Dieu, ayez pitié La Folle! Bon Dieu, ayez pitié moi!"

Instinct seemed to guide her. When the pathway spread clear and smooth enough before her, she again closed her eyes tightly against the sight of that unknown and terrifying world.

A child, playing in some weeds, caught sight of her as she neared the quarters. The little one uttered a cry of dismay.

"La Folle!" she screamed, in her piercing treble. "La Folle done cross de bayer!"

Quickly the cry passed down the line of cabins.

"Yonda, La Folle done cross de bayou!"

Children, old men, old women, young ones with infants in their arms, flocked to doors and windows to see this awe-inspiring spectacle. Most of them shuddered with superstitious dread of what it might portend. "She totin' Chéri!" some of them shouted.

Some of the more daring gathered about her, and followed at her heels, only to fall back with new terror when she turned her distorted face upon them. Her eyes were bloodshot and the saliva had gathered in a white foam on her black lips.

Some one had run ahead of her to where P'tit Maître sat with his family and guests upon the gallery.

"P'tit Maître! La Folle done cross de bayou! Look her! Look her yonda totin' Chéri!" This startling intimation was the first which they had of the woman's approach.

She was now near at hand. She walked with long

strides. Her eyes were fixed desperately before her, and she breathed heavily, as a tired ox.

At the foot of the stairway, which she could not have mounted, she laid the boy in his father's arms. Then the world that had looked red to La Folle suddenly turned black,—like that day she had seen powder and blood.

She reeled for an instant. Before a sustaining arm could reach her, she fell heavily to the ground.

When La Folle regained consciousness, she was at home again, in her own cabin and upon her own bed. The moon rays, streaming in through the open door and windows, gave what light was needed to the old black mammy who stood at the table concocting a tisane of fragrant herbs. It was very late.

Others who had come, and found that the stupor clung to her, had gone again. P'tit Maître had been there, and with him Doctor Bonfils, who said that La Folle might die.

But death had passed her by. The voice was very clear and steady with which she spoke to Tante Lizette, brewing her tisane there in a corner.

"Ef you will give me one good drink tisane, Tante Lizette, I b'lieve I'm goin' sleep, me."

And she did sleep; so soundly, so healthfully, that old Lizette without compunction stole softly away, to creep back through the moonlit fields to her own cabin in the new quarters.

The first touch of the cool gray morning awoke La Folle. She arose, calmly, as if no tempest had shaken and threatened her existence but yesterday.

She donned her new blue cottonade and white apron, for she remembered that this was Sunday. When she had made for herself a cup of strong black coffee, and drunk it with relish, she quitted the cabin and walked across the old familiar field to the bayou's edge again.

She did not stop there as she had always done before, but crossed with a long, steady stride as if she had done this all her life.

When she had made her way through the brush and scrub cottonwood-trees that lined the opposite bank, she found herself upon the border of a field where the white, bursting cotton, with the dew upon it, gleamed for acres and acres like frosted silver in the early dawn.

La Folle drew a long, deep breath as she gazed across the country. She walked slowly and uncertainly, like one who hardly knows how, looking about her as she went.

The cabins, that yesterday had sent a clamor of voices to pursue her, were quiet now. No one was yet astir at Bellissime. Only the birds that darted here and there from hedges were awake, and singing their matins.

When La Folle came to the broad stretch of velvety lawn that surrounded the house, she moved slowly and with delight over the springy turf, that was delicious beneath her tread.

She stopped to find whence came those perfumes that were assailing her senses with memories from a time far gone.

There they were, stealing up to her from the thousand blue violets that peeped out from green, luxuriant beds. There they were, showering down from the big waxen bells of the magnolias far above her head, and from the jessamine clumps around her.

There were roses, too, without number. To right and left palms spread in broad and graceful curves. It all looked like enchantment beneath the sparkling sheen of dew.

When La Folle had slowly and cautiously mounted the many steps that led up to the veranda, she turned to look back at the perilous ascent she had made. Then she caught sight of the river, bending like a silver bow at the foot of Bellissime. Exultation possessed her soul.

La Folle rapped softly upon a door near at hand. Chéri's mother soon cautiously opened it. Quickly and cleverly she dissembled the astonishment she felt at seeing La Folle.

"Ah, La Folle! Is it you, so early?"

"Oui, madame. I come ax how my po' li'le Chéri do, 's mo'nin'."

"He is feeling easier, thank you, La Folle. Dr. Bonfils says it will be nothing serious. He's sleeping now. Will you come back when he awakes?"

"Non, madame. I'm goin' wait yair tell Chéri wake up." La Folle seated herself upon the topmost step of the veranda.

A look of wonder and deep content crept into her face as she watched for the first time the sun rise upon the new, the beautiful world beyond the bayou.

The Mantle

Nicholas Gogol

In a certain Russian ministerial department——

But it is perhaps better that I do not mention which department it was. There are in the whole of Russia no persons more sensitive than Government officials. Each of them believes if he is annoyed in any way, that the whole official class is insulted in his person.

Recently an Isprawnik (country magistrate)—I do not know of which town—is said to have drawn up a report with the object of showing that, ignoring Government orders, people were speaking of Isprawniks in terms of contempt. In order to prove his assertions, he forwarded with his report a bulky work of fiction, in which on about every tenth page an Isprawnik appeared generally in a drunken condition.

In order therefore to avoid any unpleasantness, I will not definitely indicate the department in which the scene of my story is laid, and will rather say "in a certain chancellery."

Well, in a certain chancellery there was a certain man who, as I cannot deny, was not of an attractive appearance. He was short, had a face marked with smallpox, was rather bald in front, and his forehead and cheeks were deeply lined with furrows—to say nothing of other physical imperfections. Such was the outer aspect of our hero, as produced by the St Petersburg climate.

As regards his official rank—for with us Russians the official rank must always be given—he was what is usually known as a permanent titular councillor, one of those unfortunate beings who, as is well known, are made a butt of by various authors who have the bad habit of attacking people who cannot defend themselves.

Our hero's family name was Bashmatchkin; his baptismal name Akaki Akakievitch. Perhaps the reader may think this name somewhat strange and far-fetched, but he can be assured that it is not so, and that circumstances so arranged it that it was quite impossible to give him any other name.

This happened in the following way. Akaki Akakievitch was born, if I am not mistaken, on the night of the 23rd of March. His deceased mother, the wife of an official and a very good woman, immediately made proper arrangements for his baptism. When the time came, she was lying on the bed before the door. At her right hand stood the godfather, Ivan Ivanovitch Jeroshkin, a very important person, who was registrar of the senate; at her left, the godmother Anna Semenovna Byelobrushkova, the wife of a police inspector, a woman of rare virtues.

Three names were suggested to the mother from which to choose one for the child—Mokuja, Sossuja, or Khozdazat.

"No," she said, "I don't like such names."

In order to meet her wishes, the church calendar was opened in another place, and the names Triphiliy, Dula, and Varakhasiy were found.

"This is a punishment from heaven," said the mother. "What sort of names are these! I never heard the like! If it had been Varadat or Varukh, but Triphiliy and Varakhasiy!"

They looked again in the calendar and found Pavsikakhiy and Vakhtisiy.

"Now I see," said the mother, "this is plainly fate. If there is no help for it, then he had better take his father's name, which was Akaki."

So the child was called Akaki Akakievitch. It was baptised, although it wept and cried and made all kinds of grimaces, as though it had a presentiment that it would one day be a titular councillor.

We have related all this so conscientiously that the reader himself might be convinced that it was impossible for the little Akaki to receive any other name. When and how he entered the chancellery and who appointed him, no one could remember. However many of his superiors might come and go, he was always seen in the same spot, in the same attitude, busy with the same work, and bearing the same title; so that people began to believe he had come into the world just as he was, with his bald forehead and official uniform.

In the chancellery where he worked, no kind of notice was taken of him. Even the office attendants did not rise from their seats when he entered, nor look at him; they took no more notice than if a fly had flown through the room. His superiors treated him in a coldly despotic manner. The assistant of the head of the department, when he pushed a pile of papers under his nose, did not even say "Please copy those," or "There is something interesting for you," or make any other polite remark such as well-educated officials are in the habit of doing. But Akaki took the documents, without worrying himself whether they had the right to hand them over to him or not, and straightway set to work to copy them.

His young colleagues made him the butt of their ridicule and their elegant wit, so far as officials can be said to possess any wit. They did not scruple to relate in his presence various tales of their own invention regarding his manner of life and his landlady, who was seventy years old. They declared that she beat him, and inquired of him when he would lead her to the marriage altar. Sometimes they let a shower of scraps of paper fall on his head, and told him they were snowflakes.

But Akaki Akakievitch made no answer to all these

attacks; he seemed oblivious of their presence. His work was not affected in the slightest degree; during all these interruptions he did not make a single error in copying. Only when the horse-play grew intolerable, when he was held by the arm and prevented writing, he would say "Do leave me alone! Why do you always want to disturb me at work?" There was something peculiarly pathetic in these words and the way in which he uttered them.

One day it happened that when a young clerk, who had been recently appointed to the chancellery, prompted by the example of the others, was playing him some trick, he suddenly seemed arrested by something in the tone of Akaki's voice, and from that moment regarded the old official with quite different eyes. He felt as though some supernatural power drew him away from the colleagues whose acquaintance he had made here, and whom he had hitherto regarded as well-educated, respectable men, and alienated him from them. Long afterwards, when surrounded by gay companions, he would see the figure of the poor little councillor and hear the words "Do leave me alone! Why will you always disturb me at work?" Along with these words, he also heard others: "Am I not your brother?" On such occasions the young man would hide his face in his hands, and think how little humane feeling after all was to be found in men's hearts; how much coarseness and cruelty was to be found even in the educated and those who were everywhere regarded as good and honourable men.

Never was there an official who did his work so zealously as Akaki Akakievitch. "Zealously," do I say? He worked with a passionate love of his task. While he copied official documents, a world of varied beauty rose before his eyes. His delight in copying was legible in his face. To form certain letters afforded him special satisfaction, and when he came to them he was quite another man; he began to smile, his eyes sparkled, and he pursed up his lips, so that those who knew him could see by his face which letters he was working at.

Had he been rewarded according to his zeal, he would perhaps—to his own astonishment—have been raised to the rank of civic councillor. However, he was not destined, as his colleagues expressed it, to wear a cross at his buttonhole, but only to get hæmorrhoids by leading a too sedentary life.

For the rest, I must mention that on one occasion he attracted a certain amount of attention. A director, who was a kindly man and wished to reward him for his long service, ordered that he should be entrusted with a task more important than the documents which he usually had to copy. This consisted in preparing a report for a court, altering the headings of various documents, and here and there changing the first personal pronoun into the third.

Akaki undertook the work; but it confused and exhausted him to such a degree that the sweat ran from his forehead and he at last exclaimed: "No! Please give me again something to copy." From that time he was allowed to continue copying to his life's end.

Outside this copying nothing appeared to exist for him. He did not even think of his clothes. His uniform, which was originally green, had acquired a reddish tint. The collar was so narrow and so tight that his neck, although of average length, stretched far out of it, and appeared extraordinarily long, just like those of the cats with movable heads, which are carried about on trays and sold to the peasants in Russian villages.

Something was always sticking to his clothes—a piece of thread, a fragment of straw which had been flying about, etc. Moreover he seemed to have a special predilection for passing under windows just when something not very clean was being thrown out of them, and therefore he constantly carried about on his hat pieces of orange-peel and such refuse. He never took any notice of what was going on in the streets, in contrast to his colleagues who were always watching people closely and whom nothing delighted more than to see someone walking along on the opposite pavement with a rent in his trousers.

But Akaki Akakievitch saw nothing but the clean, regular lines of his copies before him; and only when he collided suddenly with a horse's nose, which blew its breath noisily in his face, did the good man observe that he was not sitting at his writing-table among his neat duplicates, but walking in the middle of the street.

When he arrived home, he sat down at once to supper, ate his cabbage-soup hurriedly, and then, without taking any notice how it tasted, a slice of beef with garlic, together with the flies and any other trifles which happened to be lying on it. As soon as his hunger was satisfied, he set himself to write, and began to copy the documents which he had brought home with him. If he happened to have no official documents to copy, he copied for his own satisfaction political letters, not for their more or less grand style but because they were directed to some high personage.

When the grey St Petersburg sky is darkened by the veil of night, and the whole of officialdom has finished its dinner according to its gastronomical inclinations or the depth of its purse—when all recover themselves from the perpetual scratching of bureaucratic pens, and all the cares and business with which men so often needlessly burden themselves, they devote the evening to recreation. One goes to the theatre; another roams about the streets, inspecting toilettes; another whispers flattering words to some young girl who has risen like a star in his modest official circle. Here and there one visits a colleague in his third or fourth story flat, consisting of two rooms with an entrance-hall and kitchen, fitted with some pretentious articles of furniture purchased by many abstinences.

In short, at this time every official betakes himself to some form of recreation—playing whist, drinking tea, and eating cheap pastry or smoking tobacco in long pipes. Some relate scandals about great people, for in whatever situation of life the Russian may be, he always likes to hear about the aristocracy; others recount well-worn but popular anecdotes, as for example that of the commandant to whom it was reported that a rogue had cut off the horse's tail on the monument of Peter the Great.

But even at this time of rest and recreation, Akaki Akakievitch remained faithful to his habits. No one could say that he had ever seen him in any evening social circle. After he had written as much as he wanted, he went to bed, and thought of the joys of the coming day, and the fine copies which God would give him to do.

So flowed on the peaceful existence of a man who was quite content with his post and his income of four hundred roubles a year. He might perhaps have reached an extreme old age if one of those unfortunate events had not befallen him, which not only happen to titular but to actual privy, court, and other councillors, and also to persons who never give advice nor receive it.

In St Petersburg all those who draw a salary of four hundred roubles or thereabouts have a terrible enemy in our northern cold, although some assert that it is very good for the health. About nine o'clock in the morning, when the clerks of the various departments betake themselves to their offices, the cold nips their noses so vigorously that most of them are quite bewildered. If at this time even high officials so suffer from the severity of the cold in their own persons that the tears come into their eyes, what must be the sufferings of the titular councillors, whose means do not allow of their protecting themselves against the rigour of winter? When they have put on their light cloaks, they must hurry through five or six streets as rapidly as possible, and then in the porter's lodge warm themselves and wait till their frozen official faculties have thawed.

For some time Akaki had been feeling on his back and shoulders very sharp twinges of pain, although he ran as fast as possible from his dwelling to the office. After well considering the matter, he came to the conclusion that these were due to the imperfections of his cloak. In his room he examined it carefully, and discovered that in two or three places it had become so thin as to be quite transparent, and that the lining was much torn.

This cloak had been for a long time the standing object of jests on the part of Akaki's merciless colleagues. They had even robbed it of the noble name of "cloak," and called it a cowl. It certainly presented a remarkable appearance. Every year the collar had grown smaller, for every year the poor titular councillor had taken a piece of it away in order to repair some other part of the cloak; and these repairs did not look as if they had been done by the skilled hand of a tailor. They had been executed in a very clumsy way and looked remarkably ugly.

After Akaki Akakievitch had ended his melancholy examination, he said to himself that he must certainly take his cloak to Petrovitch the tailor, who lived high up in a dark den on the fourth floor.

With his squinting eyes and pock-marked face, Petrovitch certainly did not look as if he had the honour to make frock-coats and trousers for high officials—that is to say, when he was sober, and not absorbed in more pleasant diversions.

I might dispense here with dwelling on this tailor; but since it is the custom to portray the physiognomy of every separate personage in a tale, I must give a better or worse description of Petrovitch. Formerly when he was a simple serf in his master's house, he was merely called Gregor. When he became free, he thought he ought to adorn himself with a new name, and dubbed himself Petrovitch; at the same time he began to drink lustily, not only on the high festivals but on all those which are marked with a cross in the calendar. By thus solemnly celebrating the days consecrated by the Church, he considered that he was remaining faithful to the traditions of his childhood; and when he quarrelled with his wife, he shouted that she was an earthly minded creature and a German. Of this lady we have nothing more to relate than that she was the wife of Petrovitch, and that she did not wear a kerchief but a cap on her head. For the rest, she was not pretty; only the soldiers looked at her as they passed, then they twirled their moustaches and walked on, laughing.

Akaki Akakievitch accordingly betook himself to the tailor's attic. He reached it by a dark, dirty, damp staircase, from which, as in all the inhabited houses of the poorer class in St Petersburg, exhaled an effluvia of spirits vexatious to nose and eyes alike. As the titular councillor climbed these slippery stairs, he calculated what sum Petrovitch could reasonably ask for repairing his cloak, and determined only to give him a rouble.

The door of the tailor's flat stood open in order to provide an outlet for the clouds of smoke which rolled from the kitchen, where Petrovitch's wife was just then cooking fish. Akaki, his eyes smarting, passed through the kitchen without her seeing him, and entered the room where the tailor sat on a large, roughly made, wooden table, his legs crossed like those of a Turkish pasha, and, as is the custom of tailors, with bare feet. What first arrested attention, when one approached him, was his thumb nail, which was a little misshapen but as hard and strong as the shell of a tortoise. Round his neck were hung several skeins of thread, and on his knees lay a tattered coat. For some minutes he had been trying in vain to thread his needle. He was first of all angry with the gathering darkness, then with the thread.

"Why the deuce won't you go in, you worthless scoundrel!" he exclaimed.

Akaki saw at once that he had come at an inopportune moment. He wished he had found Petrovitch at a more favourable time, when he was enjoying himself—when, as his wife expressed it, he was having a substantial ration of brandy. At such times the tailor was extraordinarily ready to meet his customer's proposals with bows and gratitude to boot. Sometimes indeed his wife interfered in the transaction, and declared that he was drunk and promised to do the work at much too low a price; but if the customer paid a trifle more, the matter was settled.

Unfortunately for the titular councillor, Petrovitch had just now not yet touched the brandy flask. At such moments he was hard, obstinate, and ready to demand an exorbitant price.

Akaki foresaw this danger, and would gladly have turned back again, but it was already too late. The tailor's single eye—for he was one-eyed—had already noticed him, and Akaki Akakievitch murmured involuntarily "Good day, Petrovitch."

"Welcome, sir," answered the tailor, and fastened his glance on the titular councillor's hand to see what he had in it.

"I come just—merely—in order—I want—"

We must here remark that the modest titular councillor

was in the habit of expressing his thoughts only by prepositions, adverbs, or particles, which never yielded a distinct meaning. If the matter of which he spoke was a difficult one, he could never finish the sentence he had begun. So that when transacting business, he generally entangled himself in the formula "Yes—it is indeed true that——" Then he would remain standing and forget what he wished to say, or believe that he had said it.

"What do you want, sir?" asked Petrovitch, scrutinising him from top to toe with a searching look, and contemplating his collar, sleeves, coat, buttons—in short his whole uniform, although he knew them all very well, having made them himself. That is the way of tailors whenever they meet an acquaintance.

Then Akaki answered, stammering as usual, "I want—Petrovitch—this cloak—you see—it is still quite good, only a little dusty—and therefore it looks a little old. It is, however, still quite new, only that it is worn a little—there in the back and here in the shoulder—and there are three quite little splits. You see it is hardly worth talking about; it can be thoroughly repaired in a few minutes." Petrovitch took the unfortunate cloak, spread it on the table, contemplated it in silence, and shook his head. Then he stretched his hand towards the window-sill for his snuff-box, a round one with the portrait of a general on the lid. I do not know whose portrait it was, for it had been accidentally injured, and the ingenious tailor had gummed a piece of paper over it.

After Petrovitch had taken a pinch of snuff, he examined the cloak again, held it to the light, and once more shook his head. Then he examined the lining, took a second pinch of snuff, and at last exclaimed, "No! that is a wretched rag! It is beyond repair!"

At these words Akaki's courage fell.

"What!" he cried in the querulous tone of a child. "Can

this hole really not be repaired? Look! Petrovitch; there are only two rents, and you have enough pieces of cloth to mend them with."

"Yes, I have enough pieces of cloth; but how should I sew them on? The stuff is quite worn out; it won't bear another stitch."

"Well, can't you strengthen it with another piece of cloth?"

"No, it won't bear anything more; cloth after all is only cloth, and in its present condition a gust of wind might blow the wretched mantle into tatters."

"But if you could only make it last a little longer, do you see—really——"

"No!" answered Petrovitch decidedly. "There is nothing more to be done with it; it is completely worn out. It would be better if you made yourself foot bandages out of it for the winter; they are warmer than stockings. It was the Germans who invented stockings for their own profit." Petrovitch never lost an opportunity of having a hit at the Germans. "You must certainly buy a new cloak," he added.

"A new cloak?" exclaimed Akaki Akakievitch, and it grew dark before his eyes. The tailor's work-room seemed to go round with him, and the only object he could clearly distinguish was the paper-patched general's portrait on the tailor's snuff-box. "A new cloak!" he murmured, as though half asleep. "But I have no money." "Yes, a new cloak," repeated Petrovitch with cruel calmness.

"Well, even if I did decide on it—how much——"

"You mean how much would it cost?"

"Yes."

"About a hundred and fifty roubles," answered the tailor, pursing his lips. This diabolical tailor took a special pleasure in embarrassing his customers and watching the expression of their faces with his squinting single eye.

"A hundred and fifty roubles for a cloak!" exclaimed Akaki Akakievitch in a tone which sounded like an outcry —possibly the first he had uttered since his birth.

"Yes," replied Petrovitch. "And then the marten-fur collar and silk lining for the hood would make it up to two hundred roubles."

"Petrovitch, I adjure you!" said Akaki Akakievitch in an imploring tone, no longer hearing nor wishing to hear the tailor's words, "try to make this cloak last me a little longer."

"No, it would be a useless waste of time and work."

After this answer, Akaki departed, feeling quite crushed; while Petrovitch, with his lips firmly pursed up, feeling pleased with himself for his firmness and brave defence of the art of tailoring, remained sitting on the table.

Meanwhile Akaki wandered about the streets like a somnambulist, at random and without an object. "What a terrible business!" he said to himself. "Really, I could never have believed that it would come to that. No," he continued after a short pause, "I could not have guessed that it would come to that. Now I find myself in a completely unexpected situation—in a difficulty that——" As he thus continued his monologue, instead of approaching his dwelling, he went, without noticing it, in quite a wrong direction. A chimney-sweep brushed against him and blackened his back as he passed by. From a house where building was going on, a bucket of plaster of Paris was emptied on his head. But he saw and heard nothing. Only when he collided with a sentry, who, after he had planted his halberd beside him, was shaking out some snuff from his snuff-box with a bony hand, was he startled out of his reverie.

"What do you want?" the rough guardian of civic order exclaimed. "Can't you walk on the pavement properly?"

This sudden address at last completely roused Akaki

from his torpid condition. He collected his thoughts, considered his situation clearly, and began to take counsel with himself seriously and frankly, as with a friend to whom one entrusts the most intimate secrets.

"No!" he said at last. "To-day I will get nothing from Petrovitch—to-day he is in a bad humour—perhaps his wife has beaten him—I will look him up again next Sunday. On Saturday evenings he gets intoxicated; then the next day he wants a pick-me-up—his wife gives him no money—I squeeze a ten-kopeck piece into his hand; then he will be more reasonable and we can discuss the cloak further." Encouraged by these reflections, Akaki waited patiently till Sunday. On that day, having seen Petrovitch's wife leave the house, he betook himself to the tailor's and found him, as he had expected, in a very depressed state as the result of his Saturday's dissipation. But hardly had Akaki let a word fall about the mantle than the diabolical tailor awoke from his torpor and exclaimed, "No, nothing can be done; you must certainly buy a new cloak." The titular councillor pressed a ten-kopeck piece into his hand.

"Thanks, my dear friend," said Petrovitch; "that will get me a pick-me-up, and I will drink your health with it. But as for your old mantle, what is the use of talking about it? It isn't worth a farthing. Let me only get to work; I will make you a splendid one, I promise!"

But poor Akaki Akakievitch still importuned the tailor to repair his old one.

"No, and again no," answered Petrovitch. "It is quite impossible. Trust me; I won't take you in. I will even put silver hooks and eyes on the collar, as is now the fashion."

This time Akaki saw that he must follow the tailor's advice, and again all his courage sank. He must have a new mantle made. But how should he pay for it? He certainly expected a Christmas bonus at the office; but that money had been allotted beforehand. He must buy a pair of trousers, and pay his shoemaker for repairing two pairs of boots, and buy some fresh linen. Even if, by an unexpected stroke of good luck, the director raised the usual bonus from forty to fifty roubles, what was such a small amount in comparison with the immense sum which Petrovitch demanded? A mere drop of water in the sea.

At any rate, he might expect that Petrovitch, if he were in a good humour, would lower the price of the cloak to eighty roubles; but where were these eighty roubles to be found? Perhaps he might succeed if he left no stone unturned, in raising half the sum; but he saw no means of procuring the other half. As regards the first half, he had been in the habit, as often as he received a rouble, of placing a kopeck in a money-box. At the end of each half-year he changed these copper coins for silver. He had been doing this for some time, and his savings just now amounted to forty roubles. Thus he already had half the required sum. But the other half!

Akaki made long calculations, and at last determined that he must, at least for a whole year, reduce some of his daily expenses. He would have to give up his tea in the evening, and copy his documents in his landlady's room, in order to economise the fuel in his own. He also resolved to avoid rough pavements as much as possible, in order to spare his shoes; and finally to give out less washing to the laundress.

At first he found these deprivations rather trying; but gradually he got accustomed to them, and at last took to going to bed without any supper at all. Although his body suffered from this abstinence, his spirit derived all the richer nutriment from perpetually thinking about his new cloak. From that time it seemed as though his nature had completed itself; as though he had married and possessed a companion on his life journey. This companion was the thought of his new cloak, properly wadded and lined.

From that time he became more lively, and his character grew stronger, like that of a man who has set a goal before himself which he will reach at all costs. All that was indecisive and vague in his gait and gestures had disappeared. A new fire began to gleam in his eyes, and in his bold dreams he sometimes even proposed to himself the question whether he should not have a marten-fur collar made for his coat.

These and similar thoughts sometimes caused him to be absent-minded. As he was copying his documents one day he suddenly noticed that he had made a slip. "Ugh!" he exclaimed, and crossed himself.

At least once a month he went to Petrovitch to discuss the precious cloak with him, and to settle many important questions, e.g. where and at what price he should buy the cloth, and what colour he should choose.

Each of these visits gave rise to new discussions, but he always returned home in a happier mood, feeling that at last the day must come when all the materials would have been bought and the cloak would be lying ready to put on.

This great event happened sooner than he had hoped. The director gave him a bonus, not of forty or fifty, but of five-and-sixty roubles. Had the worthy official noticed that Akaki needed a new mantle, or was the exceptional amount of the gift only due to chance?

However that might be, Akaki was now richer by twenty roubles. Such an access of wealth necessarily hastened his important undertaking. After two or three more months of enduring hunger, he had collected his eighty roubles. His heart, generally so quiet, began to beat violently; he hastened to Petrovitch, who accompanied him to a draper's shop. There, without hesitating, they bought a very fine piece of cloth. For more than half a year they had discussed the matter incessantly, and gone round the shops inquiring prices. Petrovitch examined the cloth, and said they would not find anything better. For the lining they chose a piece of such firm and thickly woven linen that the tailor declared it was better than silk; it also had a splendid gloss on it. They did not buy marten fur, for it was too dear, but chose the best catskin in the shop, which was a very good imitation of the former.

It took Petrovitch quite fourteen days to make the mantle, for he put an extra number of stitches into it. He charged twelve roubles for his work, and said he could not ask less; it was all sewn with silk, and the tailor smoothed the sutures with his teeth.

At last the day came—I cannot name it certainly, but it assuredly was the most solemn in Akaki's life—when the tailor brought the cloak. He brought it early in the morning, before the titular councillor started for his office. He could not have come at a more suitable moment, for the cold had again begun to be very severe.

Petrovitch entered the room with the dignified mien of an important tailor. His face wore a peculiarly serious expression, such as Akaki had never seen on it. He was fully conscious of his dignity, and of the gulf which separates the tailor who only repairs old clothes from the artist who makes new ones.

The cloak had been brought wrapped up in a large, new, freshly washed handkerchief, which the tailor carefully opened, folded, and placed in his pocket. Then he proudly took the cloak in both hands and laid it on Akaki Akakievitch's shoulders. He pulled it straight behind to see how it hung majestically in its whole length. Finally he wished to see the effect it made when unbuttoned. Akaki, however, wished to try the sleeves, which fitted wonderfully well. In brief, the cloak was irreproachable, and its fit and cut left nothing to be desired.

While the tailor was contemplating his work, he did not forget to say that the only reason he had charged so little for making it, was that he had only a low rent to pay and had known Akaki Akakievitch for a long time; he declared that any tailor who lived on the Nevski Prospect would have charged at least five-and-sixty roubles for making up such a cloak.

The titular councillor did not let himself be involved in a discussion on the subject. He thanked him, paid him, and then sallied forth on his way to the office.

Petrovitch went out with him, and remained standing in the street to watch Akaki as long as possible wearing the mantle; then he hurried through a cross-alley and came into the main street again to catch another glimpse of him.

Akaki went on his way in high spirits. Every moment he was acutely conscious of having a new cloak on, and smiled with sheer self-complacency. His head was filled with only two ideas: first that the cloak was warm, and secondly that it was beautiful. Without noticing anything on the road, he marched straight to the chancellery, took off his treasure in the hall, and solemnly entrusted it to the porter's care.

I do not know how the report spread in the office that Akaki's old cloak had ceased to exist. All his colleagues hastened to see his splendid new one, and then began to congratulate him so warmly that he at first had to smile with self-satisfaction, but finally began to feel embarrassed.

But how great was his surprise when his cruel

colleagues remarked that he should formally "handsel" his cloak by giving them a feast! Poor Akaki was so disconcerted and taken aback, that he did not know what to answer nor how to excuse himself. He stammered out, blushing, that the cloak was not so new as it appeared; it was really second-hand.

One of his superiors, who probably wished to show that he was not too proud of his rank and title, and did not disdain social intercourse with his subordinates, broke in and said, "Gentlemen! Instead of Akaki Akakievitch, I will invite you to a little meal. Come to tea with me this evening. To-day happens to be my birthday." All the others thanked him for his kind proposal, and joyfully accepted his invitation. Akaki at first wished to decline, but was told that to do so would be grossly impolite and unpardonable, so he reconciled himself to the inevitable. Moreover, he felt a certain satisfaction at the thought that the occasion would give him a new opportunity of displaying his cloak in the streets. This whole day for him was like a festival day. In the cheerfullest possible mood he returned home, took off his cloak, and hung it up on the wall after once more examining the cloth and the lining. Then he took out his old one in order to compare it with Petrovitch's masterpiece. His looks passed from one to the other, and he thought to himself, smiling, "What a difference!" He ate his supper cheerfully, and after he had finished, did not sit down as usual to copy documents. No; he lay down, like a Sybarite, on the sofa and waited. When the time came, he made his toilette, took his cloak, and went out.

I cannot say where was the house of the superior official who so graciously invited his subordinates to tea. My memory begins to grow weak, and the innumerable streets and houses of St Petersburg go round so confusedly in my head that I have difficulty in finding my way about them. So much, however, is certain: that the honourable official lived in a very fine quarter of the city, and therefore very far from Akaki Akakievitch's dwelling.

At first the titular councillor traversed several badly lit streets which seemed quite empty; but the nearer he approached his superior's house, the more brilliant and lively the streets became. He met many people, among whom were elegantly dressed ladies, and men with beaverskin collars. The peasants' sledges, with their wooden seats and brass studs, became rarer; while now every moment appeared skilled coachmen with velvet caps, driving lacquered sleighs covered with bearskins, and fine carriages.

At last he reached the house whither he had been invited. His host lived in a first-rate style; a lamp hung before his door, and he occupied the whole of the second story. As Akaki entered the vestibule, he saw a long row of galoshes; on a table a samovar was smoking and hissing; many cloaks, some of them adorned with velvet and fur collars, hung on the wall. In the adjoining room he heard a confused noise, which assumed a more decided character when a servant opened the door and came out bearing a tray full of empty cups, a milk-jug, and a basket of biscuits. Evidently the guests had been there some time and had already drunk their first cup of tea.

After hanging his cloak on a peg, Akaki approached the room in which his colleagues, smoking long pipes, were sitting round the card-table and making a good deal of noise. He entered the room, but remained standing by the door, not knowing what to do; but his colleagues greeted him with loud applause, and all hastened into the vestibule to take another look at his cloak. This excitement quite robbed the good titular councillor of his composure; but in his simplicity of heart he rejoiced at the praises which were lavished on his precious cloak. Soon afterwards his colleagues left him to himself and resumed their whist parties.

Akaki felt much embarrassed, and did not know what to do with his feet and hands. Finally he sat down by the players; looked now at their faces and now at the cards; then he yawned and remembered that it was long past his usual bedtime. He made an attempt to go, but they held him back and told him that he could not do so without drinking a glass of champagne on what was for him such a memorable day.

Soon supper was brought. It consisted of cold veal, cakes, and pastry of various kinds, accompanied by several bottles of champagne. Akaki was obliged to drink two glasses of it, and found everything round him take on a more cheerful aspect. But he could not forget that it was already midnight and that he ought to have been in bed long ago. From fear of being kept back again, he slipped furtively into the vestibule, where he was pained to find his cloak lying on the ground. He carefully shook it, brushed it, put it on, and went out.

The street-lamps were still alight. Some of the small ale-houses frequented by servants and the lower classes were still open, and some had just been shut; but by the beams of light which shone through the chinks of the doors, it was easy to see that there were still people inside, probably male and female domestics, who were quite indifferent to their employers' interests.

Akaki Akakievitch turned homewards in a cheerful mood. Suddenly he found himself in a long street where it was very quiet by day and still more so at night. The surroundings were very dismal. Only here and there hung a lamp which threatened to go out for want of oil; there were long rows of wooden houses with wooden fences, but no sign of a living soul. Only the snow in the street glimmered faintly in the dim light of the half-extinguished lanterns, and the little houses looked melancholy in the darkness.

Akaki went on till the street opened into an enormous square, on the other side of which the houses were scarcely visible, and which looked like a terrible desert. At a great distance—God knows where!—glimmered the light in a sentry-box, which seemed to stand at the end of the world. At the same moment Akaki's cheerful mood vanished. He went in the direction of the light with a vague sense of depression, as though some mischief threatened him. On the way he kept looking round him with alarm. The huge, melancholy expanse looked to him like a sea. "No," he thought to himself, "I had better not look at it"; and he continued his way with his eyes fixed on the ground. When he raised them again he suddenly saw just in front of him several men with long moustaches, whose faces he could not distinguish. Everything grew dark before his eyes, and his heart seemed to be constricted.

"That is my cloak!" shouted one of the men, and seized him by the collar. Akaki tried to call for help. Another man pressed a great bony fist on his mouth, and said to him, "Just try to scream again!" At the same moment the unhappy titular councillor felt the cloak snatched away from him, and simultaneously received a kick which stretched him senseless in the snow. A few minutes later he came to himself and stood up; but there was no longer anyone in sight. Robbed of his cloak, and feeling frozen to the marrow, he began to shout with all his might; but his voice did not reach the end of the huge square. Continuing to shout, he ran with the rage of despair to the sentinel in the sentry-box, who, leaning on his halberd, asked him why the deuce he was making such a hellish noise and running so violently.

When Akaki reached the sentinel, he accused him of being drunk because he did not see that passers-by were robbed a short distance from his sentry-box.

"I saw you quite well," answered the sentinel, "in the middle of the square with two men; I thought you were friends. It is no good getting so excited. Go to-morrow to the police inspector; he will take up the matter, have the thieves searched for, and make an examination."

Akaki saw there was nothing to be done but to go home. He reached his dwelling in a state of dreadful disorder, his hair hanging wildly over his forehead, and his clothes covered with snow. When his old landlady heard him knocking violently at the door, she sprang up and hastened thither, only half-dressed; but at the sight of Akaki started back in alarm. When he told her what had happened, she clasped her hands together and said, "You should not go to the police inspector, but to the municipal Superintendent of the district. The inspector will put you off with fine words, and do nothing; but I have known the Superintendent for a long time. My former cook, Anna, is now in his service, and I often see him pass by under our windows. He goes to church on all the festival-days, and one sees at once by his looks that he is an honest man." After hearing this eloquent recommendation, Akaki retired sadly to his room. Those who can picture to themselves such a situation will understand what sort of a night he passed. As early as possible the next morning he went to the Superintendent's house. The servants told him that he was still asleep. At ten o'clock he returned, only to receive the same reply. At twelve o'clock the Superintendent had gone out.

About dinner-time the titular councillor called again, but the clerks asked him in a severe tone what was his business with their superior. Then for the first time in his life Akaki displayed an energetic character. He declared that it was absolutely necessary for him to speak with the Superintendent on an official matter, and that anyone who ventured to put difficulties in his way would have to pay dearly for it.

This left them without reply. One of the clerks departed, in order to deliver his message. When Akaki was admitted to the Superintendent's presence, the latter's way of receiving his story was somewhat singular. Instead of confining himself to the principal matter—the theft, he asked the titular councillor how he came to be out so late, and whether he had not been in suspicious company.

Taken aback by such a question, Akaki did not know what to answer, and went away without knowing whether any steps would be taken in the matter or not.

The whole day he had not been in his office—a perfectly new event in his life. The next day he appeared there again with a pale face and restless aspect, in his old cloak, which looked more wretched than ever. When his colleagues heard of his misfortune, some were cruel enough to laugh; most of them, however, felt a sincere sympathy with him, and started a subscription for his benefit; but this praiseworthy undertaking had only a very insignificant result, because these same officials had been lately called upon to contribute to two other subscriptions—in the first case to purchase a portrait of their director, and in the second to buy a work which a friend of his had published.

One of them, who felt sincerely sorry for Akaki, gave him some good advice for want of something better. He told him it was a waste of time to go again to the Superintendent, because even in case that this official succeeded in recovering the cloak, the police would keep it till the titular councillor had indisputably proved that he was the real owner of it. Akaki's friend suggested to him to go to a certain important personage, who because of his connection with the authorities could expedite the matter.

In his bewilderment, Akaki resolved to follow this advice. It was not known what position this personage occupied, nor how high it really was; the only facts known were that he had only recently been placed in it, and that there must be still higher personages than himself, as he was leaving no stone unturned in order to get promotion. When he entered his private room, he made his subordinates wait for him on the stairs below, and no one had direct access to him. If anyone called with a request to see him, the secretary of the board informed the Government secretary, who in his turn passed it on to a higher official, and the latter informed the important personage himself.

That is the way business is carried on in our Holy Russia. In the endeavour to resemble the higher officials, everyone imitates the manners of his superiors. Not long ago a titular councillor, who was appointed to the headship of a little office, immediately placed over the door of one of his two tiny rooms the inscription "Council-chamber." Outside it were placed servants with red collars and lace-work on their coats, in order to announce petitioners, and to conduct them into the chamber which was hardly large enough to contain a chair.

But let us return to the important personage in question. His way of carrying things on was dignified and imposing, but a trifle complicated. His system might be summed up in a single word—"severity." This word he would repeat in a sonorous tone three times in succession, and the last time turn a piercing look on the person with whom he happened to be speaking. He might have spared himself the trouble of displaying so much disciplinary energy; the ten officials who were under his command feared him quite sufficiently without it. As soon as they were aware of his approach, they would lay down their pens, and hasten to station themselves in a respectful attitude as he passed by. In converse with his subordinates, he preserved a stiff, unbending attitude, and generally confined himself to such expressions as "What do you want? Do you know with whom you are speaking? Do you consider who is in front of you?" For the rest, he was a good-natured man, friendly and amiable with his acquaintances. But the title of "District-Superintendent" had turned his head. Since the time when it had been bestowed upon him, he lived for a great part of the day in a kind of dizzy self-intoxication. Among his equals, however, he recovered his equilibrium, and then showed his real amiability in more than one direction; but as soon as he found himself in the society of anyone of less rank than himself, he entrenched himself in a severe taciturnity. This situation was all the more painful for him as he was quite aware that he might have passed his time more agreeably.

All who watched him at such moments perceived clearly that he longed to take part in an interesting conversation, but that the fear of displaying some unguarded courtesy, of appearing too confidential, and thereby doing a deadly injury to his dignity, held him back. In order to avoid such a risk, he maintained an unnatural reserve, and only spoke from time to time in monosyllables. He had driven this habit to such a pitch that people called him "The Tedious," and the title was well deserved.

Such was the person to whose aid Akaki wished to

appeal. The moment at which he came seemed expressly calculated to flatter the Superintendent's vanity, and accordingly to help forward the titular councillor's cause.

The high personage was seated in his office, talking cheerfully with an old friend whom he had not seen for several years, when he was told that a gentleman named Akakievitch begged for the honour of an interview.

"Who is the man?" asked the Superintendent in a contemptuous tone.

"An official," answered the servant.

"He must wait. I have no time to receive him now."

The high personage lied; there was nothing in the way of his granting the desired audience. His friend and himself had already quite exhausted various topics of conversation. Many long, embarrassing pauses had occurred, during which they had lightly tapped each other on the shoulder, saying, "So it was, you see."

"Yes, Stepan."

But the Superintendent refused to receive the petitioner, in order to show his friend, who had quitted the public service and lived in the country, his own importance, and how officials must wait in the vestibule till he chose to receive them.

At last, after they had discussed various other subjects with other intervals of silence, during which the two friends leaned back in their chairs and blew cigarette smoke in the air, the Superintendent seemed suddenly to remember that someone had sought an interview with him. He called the secretary, who stood with a roll of papers in his hand at the door, and told him to admit the petitioner.

When he saw Akaki approaching with his humble expression, wearing his shabby old uniform, he turned round suddenly towards him and said "What do you want?" in a severe voice, accompanied by a vibrating intonation which at the time of receiving his promotion he had practised before the looking-glass for eight days.

The modest Akaki was quite taken aback by his harsh manner; however, he made an effort to recover his composure, and to relate how his cloak had been stolen, but did not do so without encumbering his narrative with a mass of superfluous detail. He added that he had applied to His Excellence in the hope that through his making a representation to the police inspector, or some other high personage, the cloak might be traced.

The Superintendent found Akaki's method of procedure somewhat unofficial. "Ah, sir," he said, "don't you know what steps you ought to take in such a case? Don't you know the proper procedure? You should have handed in your petition at the chancellery. This in due course would have passed through the hands of the chief clerk and director of the bureau. It would then have been brought before my secretary, who would have made a communication to you." "Allow me," replied Akaki, making a strenuous effort to preserve the remnants of his presence of mind, for he felt that the perspiration stood on his forehead, "allow me to remark to Your Excellence that I ventured to trouble you personally in this matter because secretaries—secretaries are a hopeless kind of people." "What! How! Is it possible?" exclaimed the Superintendent. "How could you say such a thing? Where have you got your ideas from? It is disgraceful to see young people so rebellious towards their superiors." In his official zeal the Superintendent overlooked the fact that the titular councillor was well on in the fifties, and that the word "young" could only apply to him conditionally, i.e. in comparison with a man of seventy. "Do you also know," he continued, "with whom you are speaking? Do you consider before whom you are standing? Do you consider, I ask you, do you consider?"

As he spoke, he stamped his foot, and his voice grew deeper.

Akaki was quite upset—nay, thoroughly frightened; he trembled and shook and could hardly remain standing upright. Unless one of the office servants had hurried to help him, he would have fallen to the ground. As it was, he was dragged out almost unconscious.

But the Superintendent was quite delighted at the effect he had produced. It exceeded all his expectations, and filled with satisfaction at the fact that his words made such an impression on a middle-aged man that he lost consciousness, he cast a side-glance at his friend to see what effect the scene had produced on him. His self-satisfaction was further increased when he observed that his friend also was moved, and looked at him half-timidly.

Akaki had no idea how he got down the stairs and crossed the street, for he felt more dead than alive. In his whole life he had never been so scolded by a superior official, let alone one whom he had never seen before.

He wandered in the storm which raged without taking the least care of himself, nor sheltering himself on the side-walk against its fury. The wind, which blew from all sides and out of all the narrow streets, caused him to contract inflammation of the throat. When he reached home he was unable to speak a word, and went straight to bed.

Such was the result of the Superintendent's lecture.

The next day Akaki had a violent fever. Thanks to the St Petersburg climate, his illness developed with terrible rapidity. When the doctor came, he saw that the case was already hopeless; he felt his pulse and ordered him some poultices, merely in order that he should not die without some medical help, and declared at once that he had only two days to live. After giving this opinion, he said to Akaki's landlady, "There is no time to be lost; order a pine coffin, for an oak one would be too expensive for this poor man." Whether the titular councillor heard these words, whether they excited him and made him lament his tragic lot, no one ever knew, for he was delirious all the time. Strange pictures passed incessantly through his weakened brain. At one time he saw Petrovitch the tailor and asked him to make a cloak with nooses attached for the thieves who persecuted him in bed, and begged his old landlady to chase away the robbers who were hidden under his coverlet. At another time he seemed to be listening to the Superintendent's severe reprimand, and asking his forgiveness. Then he uttered such strange and confused remarks that the old woman crossed herself in alarm. She had never heard anything of the kind in her life, and these ravings astonished her all the more because the expression "Your Excellency" constantly occurred in them. Later on he murmured wild disconnected words, from which it could only be gathered that his thoughts were continually revolving round a cloak.

At last Akaki breathed his last. Neither his room nor his cupboard were officially sealed up, for the simple reason that he had no heir and left nothing behind him but a bundle of goose-quills, a notebook of white paper, three pairs of socks, some trouser buttons, and his old coat.

Into whose possession did these relics pass? Heaven only knows! The writer of this narrative has never inquired.

Akaki was wrapped in his shroud, and laid to rest in the churchyard. The great city of St Petersburg continued its life as though he had never existed. Thus disappeared a human creature who had never possessed a patron or friend, who had never elicited real hearty sympathy from anyone, nor even aroused the curiosity of the naturalists, though they are most eager to subject a rare insect to microscopic examination.

Without a complaint he had borne the scorn and contempt of his colleagues; he had proceeded on his quiet way to the grave without anything extraordinary happening to him—only towards the end of his life he had been joyfully excited by the possession of a new cloak, and had then been overthrown by misfortune.

Some days after his conversation with the Superintendent, his superior in the chancellery, where no one knew what had become of him, sent an official to his house to demand his presence. The official returned with the news that no one would see the titular councillor any more.

"Why?" asked all the clerks.

"Because he was buried four days ago."

In such a manner did Akaki's colleagues hear of his death.

The next day his place was occupied by an official of robuster fibre, a man who did not trouble to make so many fair transcripts of state documents.

. . . . . .

It seems as though Akaki's story ended here, and that there was nothing more to be said of him; but the modest titular councillor was destined to attract more notice after his death than during his life, and our tale now assumes a somewhat ghostly complexion.

One day there spread in St Petersburg the report that near the Katinka Bridge there appeared every night a spectre in a uniform like that of the chancellery officials; that he was searching for a stolen cloak, and stripped all passers-by of their cloaks without any regard for rank or title. It mattered not whether they were lined with wadding, mink, cat, otter, bear, or beaverskin; he took all he could get hold of. One of the titular councillor's former colleagues had seen the ghost, and quite clearly recognised Akaki. He ran as hard as he could and managed to escape, but had seen him shaking his fist in the distance. Everywhere it was reported that councillors, and not only titular councillors but also state-councillors, had caught serious colds in their honourable backs on account of these raids.

The police adopted all possible measures in order to get this ghost dead or alive into their power, and to inflict an exemplary punishment on him; but all their attempts were vain.

One evening, however, a sentinel succeeded in getting hold of the malefactor just as he was trying to rob a musician of his cloak. The sentinel summoned with all the force of his lungs two of his comrades, to whom he entrusted the prisoner while he sought for his snuff-box in order to bring some life again into his half-frozen nose. Probably his snuff was so strong that even a ghost could not stand it. Scarcely had the sentinel thrust a grain or two up his nostrils than the prisoner began to sneeze so violently that a kind of mist rose before the eyes of the sentinels. While the three were rubbing their eyes, the prisoner disappeared. Since that day, all the sentries were so afraid of the ghost that they did not even venture to arrest the living but shouted to them from afar "Go on! Go on!" Meanwhile the ghost extended his depredations to the other side of the Katinka Bridge, and spread dismay and alarm in the whole of the quarter.

But now we must return to the Superintendent, who is the real origin of our fantastic yet so veracious story. First of all we must do him the justice to state that after Akaki's departure he felt a certain sympathy for him. He was by no means without a sense of justice—no, he possessed various good qualities, but his infatuation about his title hindered him from showing his good side. When his friend left him, his thoughts began to occupy themselves with the unfortunate titular councillor, and from that moment onwards he saw him constantly in his mind's eye, crushed by the severe reproof which had been administered to him. This image so haunted him that at last one day he ordered one of his officials to find out what had become of Akaki, and whether anything could be done for him.

When the messenger returned with the news that the poor man had died soon after that interview, the Superintendent felt a pang in his conscience, and remained the whole day absorbed in melancholy brooding.

In order to banish his unpleasant sensations, he went in the evening to a friend's house, where he hoped to find pleasant society and what was the chief thing, some other officials of his own rank, so that he would not be obliged to feel bored. And in fact he did succeed in throwing off his melancholy thoughts there; he unbent and became lively, took an active part in the conversation, and passed a very pleasant evening. At supper he drank two glasses of champagne, which, as everyone knows, is an effective means of heightening one's cheerfulness.

As he sat in his sledge, wrapped in his mantle, on his way home, his mind was full of pleasant reveries. He thought of the society in which he had passed such a cheerful evening, and of all the excellent jokes with which he had made them laugh. He repeated some of them to himself half-aloud, and laughed at them again.

From time to time, however, he was disturbed in this cheerful mood by violent gusts of wind, which from some corner or other blew a quantity of snowflakes into his face, lifted the folds of his cloak, and made it belly like a sail, so that he had to exert all his strength to hold it firmly on his shoulders. Suddenly he felt a powerful hand seize him by the collar. He turned round, perceived a short man in an old, shabby uniform, and recognised with terror Akaki's face, which wore a deathly pallor and emaciation.

The titular councillor opened his mouth, from which issued a kind of corpse-like odour, and with inexpressible fright the Superintendent heard him say, "At last I have you—by the collar! I need your cloak. You did not trouble about me when I was in distress; you thought it necessary to reprimand me. Now give me your cloak." The high dignitary nearly choked. In his office, and especially in the presence of his subordinates, he was a man of imposing manners. He only needed to fix his eye on one of them and they all seemed impressed by his pompous bearing. But, as is the case with many such officials, all this was only outward show; at this moment he felt so upset that he seriously feared for his health. Taking off his cloak with a feverish, trembling hand, he handed it to Akaki, and called to his coachman, "Drive home quickly." When the coachman heard this voice, which did not sound as it usually did, and had often been accompanied by blows of a whip, he bent his head cautiously and drove on apace.

Soon afterwards the Superintendent found himself at home. Cloakless, he retired to his room with a pale face and wild looks, and had such a bad night that on the following morning his daughter exclaimed "Father, are you ill?" But he said nothing of what he had seen, though a very deep impression had been made on him. From that day onwards he no longer addressed to his subordinates in a violent tone the words, "Do you know with whom you are speaking? Do you know who is standing before you?" Or if it ever did happen that he spoke to them in a domineering tone, it was not till he had first listened to what they had to say.

Strangely enough, from that time the spectre never appeared again. Probably it was the Superintendent's cloak which he had been seeking so earnestly; now he had it and did not want anything more. Various persons, however, asserted that this formidable ghost was still to be seen in other parts of the city. A sentinel went so far as to say that he had seen him with his own eyes glide like a furtive shadow behind a house. But this sentinel was of such a nervous disposition that he had been chaffed about his timidity more than once. Since he did not venture to seize the flitting shadow, he stole after it in the darkness; but the shadow turned round and shouted at him "What do you want?" shaking an enormous fist, such as no man had ever possessed.

"I want nothing," answered the sentry, quickly retiring.

This shadow, however, was taller than the ghost of the titular councillor, and had an enormous moustache. He went with great strides towards the Obuchoff Bridge, and disappeared in the darkness.

Up In Michigan

Ernest Miller Hemingway

Jim Gilmore came to Hortons Bay from Canada. He bought the blacksmith shop from old man Horton. Jim was short and dark with big mustaches and big hands. He was a good horseshoer and did not look much like a blacksmith even with his leather apron on. He lived upstairs above the blacksmith shop and took his meals at A. J. Smith's.

Liz Coates worked for Smith's. Mrs. Smith, who was a very large clean woman, said Liz Coates was the neatest girl she'd ever seen. Liz had good legs and always wore clean gingham aprons and Jim noticed that her hair was always neat behind. He liked her face because it was so jolly but he never thought about her.

Liz liked Jim very much. She liked it the way he walked over from the shop and often went to the kitchen door to watch for him to start down the road. She liked it about his mustache. She liked it about how white his teeth were when he smiled. She liked it very much that he didn't look like a blacksmith. She liked it how much A. J. Smith and Mrs. Smith liked Jim. One day she found that she liked it the way the hair was black on his arms and how white they were above the tanned line when he washed up in the washbasin outside the house. Liking that made her feel funny.

Hortons Bay, the town, was only five houses on the main road between Boyne City and Charlevoix. There was the general store and postoffice with a high false front and maybe a wagon hitched out in front, Smith's house, Stroud's house, Fox's house, Horton's house and Van Hoosen's house. The houses were in a big grove of elm trees and the road was very sandy. There was farming country and timber each way up the road. Up the road a ways was the Methodist church and down the road the other direction was the township school. The blacksmith shop was painted red and faced the school.

A steep sandy road ran down the hill to the bay through the timber. From Smith's back door you could look out across the woods that ran down to the lake and across the bay. It was very beautiful in the spring and summer, the bay blue and bright and usually whitecaps on the lake out beyond the point from the breeze blowing from Charlevoix and Lake Michigan. From Smith's back door Liz could see ore barges way out in the lake going toward Boyne City. When she looked at them they didn't seem to be moving at all but if she went in and dried some more dishes and then came out again they would be out of sight beyond the point.

All the time now Liz was thinking about Jim Gilmore. He didn't seem to notice her much. He talked about the shop to A. J. Smith and about the Republican Party and about James G. Blaine. In the evenings he read the Toledo Blade and the Grand Rapids paper by the lamp in the front room or went out spearing fish in the bay with a jacklight with A. J. Smith. In the fall he and Smith and Charley Wyman took a wagon and tent, grub, axes, their rifles and two dogs and went on a trip to the pine plains beyond Vanderbilt deer hunting. Liz and Mrs. Smith were cooking for four days for them before they started. Liz wanted to make something special for Jim to take but she didn't finally because she was afraid to ask Mrs. Smith for the eggs and flour and afraid if she bought them Mrs. Smith would catch her cooking. It would have been all right with Mrs. Smith but Liz was afraid.

All the time Jim was gone on the deer hunting trip Liz thought about him. It was awful while he was gone. She couldn't sleep well from thinking about him but she discovered it was fun to think about him too. If she let herself go it was better. The night before they were to come back she didn't sleep at all, that is she didn't think she slept because it was all mixed up in a dream about not sleeping and really not sleeping. When she saw the wagon coming down the road she felt weak and sick sort of inside. She couldn't wait till she saw Jim and it seemed as though everything would be all right when he came. The wagon stopped outside under the big elm and Mrs. Smith and Liz went out. All the men had beards and there were three deer in the back of the wagon, their thin legs sticking stiff over the edge of the wagon box. Mrs. Smith kissed Alonzo and he hugged her. Jim said "Hello Liz." and grinned. Liz hadn't known just what would happen when Jim got back but she was sure it would be something. Nothing had happened. The men were just home that was all. Jim pulled the burlap sacks off the deer and Liz looked at them. One was a big buck. It was stiff and hard to lift out of the wagon.

"Did you shoot it Jim?" Liz asked.

"Yeah. Aint it a beauty?" Jim got it onto his back to carry to the smokehouse.

That night Charley Wyman stayed to supper at Smith's. It was too late to get back to Charlevoix. The men washed up and waited in the front room for supper.

"Aint there something left in that crock Jimmy?" A. J. Smith asked and Jim went out to the wagon in the barn and fetched in the jug of whiskey the men had taken hunting with them. It was a four gallon jug and there was quite a little slopped back and forth in the bottom. Jim took a long pull on his way back to the house. It was hard to lift such a big jug up to drink out of it. Some of the whiskey ran down on his shirt front. The two men smiled when Jim came in with the jug. A. J.

Smith sent for glasses and Liz brought them. A. J. poured out three big shots.

"Well here's looking at you A. J." said Charley Wyman.

"That damn big buck Jimmy." said A. J.

"Here's all the ones we missed A. J." said Jim and downed his liquor.

"Tastes good to a man."

"Nothing like it this time of year for what ails you."

"How about another boys?"

"Here's how A. J."

"Down the creek boys."

"Here's to next year."

Jim began to feel great. He loved the taste and the feel of whisky. He was glad to be back to a comfortable bed and warm food and the shop. He had another drink. The men came in to supper feeling hilarious but acting very respectable. Liz sat at the table after she put on the food and ate with the family. It was a good dinner. The men ate seriously. After supper they went into the front room again and Liz cleaned off with Mrs. Smith. Then Mrs. Smith went up stairs and pretty soon Smith came out and went up stairs too. Jim and Charley were still in the front room. Liz was sitting in the kitchen next to the stove pretending to read a book and thinking about Jim. She didn't want to go to bed yet because she knew Jim would be coming out and she wanted to see him as he went out so she could take the way he looked up to bed with her.

She was thinking about him hard and then Jim came out. His eyes were shining and his hair was a little rumpled. Liz looked down at her book. Jim came over back of her chair and stood there and she could feel him breathing and then he put his arms around her. Her breasts felt plump and firm and the nipples were erect under his hands. Liz was terribly frightened, no one had ever touched her, but she thought, "He's come to me finally. He's really come." She held herself stiff because she was so frightened and did not know anything else to do and then Jim held her tight against the chair and kissed her. It was such a sharp, aching, hurting feeling that she thought she couldn't stand it. She felt Jim right through the back of the chair and she couldn't stand it and then something clicked inside of her and the feeling was warmer and softer. Jim held her tight hard against the chair and she wanted it now and Jim whispered, "Come on for a walk." Liz took her coat off the peg on the kitchen wall and they went out the door. Jim had his arm around her and every little way they stopped and pressed against each other and Jim kissed her. There was no moon and they walked ankle deep in the sandy road through the trees down to the dock and the warehouse on the bay. The water was lapping in the piles and the point was dark across the bay. It was cold but Liz was hot all over from being with Jim. They sat down in the shelter of the warehouse and Jim pulled Liz close to him. She was frightened. One of Jim's hands went inside her dress and stroked over her breast and the other hand was in her lap. She was very frightened and didn't know how he was going to go about things but she snuggled close to him. Then the hand that felt so big in her lap went away and was on her leg and started to move up it.

"Don't Jim". Liz said. Jim slid the hand further up.

"You musn't Jim. You musn't". Neither Jim nor Jim's big hand paid any attention to her.

The boards were hard. Jim had her dress up and was trying to do something to her. She was frightened but she wanted it. She had to have it but it frightened her.

"You musn't do it Jim. You musn't."

"I got to. I'm going to. You know we got to."

"No we haven't Jim. We aint got to. Oh it isn't right.

Oh it's so big and it hurts so. You can't. Oh Jim. Jim. Oh."

The hemlock planks of the dock were hard and splintery and cold and Jim was heavy on her and he had hurt her. Liz pushed him, she was so uncomfortable and cramped. Jim was asleep. He wouldn't move. She worked out from under him and sat up and straightened her skirt and coat and tried to do something with her hair. Jim was sleeping with his mouth a little open. Liz leaned over and kissed him on the cheek. He was still asleep. She lifted his head a little and shook it. He rolled his head over and swallowed. Liz started to cry. She walked over to the edge of the dock and looked down to the water. There was a mist coming up from the bay. She was cold and miserable and everything felt gone. She walked back to where Jim was lying and shook him once more to make sure. She was crying.

"Jim" she said, "Jim. Please Jim".

Jim stirred and curled a little tighter. Liz took off her coat and leaned over and covered him with it. She tucked it around him neatly and carefully. Then she walked across the dock and up the steep sandy road to go to bed. A cold mist was coming up through the woods from the bay.

How the Whale Got His Throat

Joseph Rudyard Kipling

IN the sea, once upon a time, O my Best Beloved, there was a Whale, and he ate fishes. He ate the starfish and the garfish, and the crab and the dab, and the plaice and the dace, and the skate and his mate, and the mackereel and the pickereel, and the really truly twirly-whirly eel. All the fishes he could find in all the sea he ate with his mouth—so! Till at last there was only one small fish left in all the sea, and he was a small 'Stute Fish, and he swam a little behind the Whale's right ear, so as to be out of harm's way. Then the Whale stood up on his tail and said, 'I'm hungry.' And the small 'Stute Fish said in a small 'stute voice, 'Noble and generous Cetacean, have you ever tasted Man?' 'No,' said the Whale. 'What is it like?'

'Nice,' said the small 'Stute Fish. 'Nice but nubbly.'

'Then fetch me some,' said the Whale, and he made the sea froth up with his tail.

'One at a time is enough,' said the 'Stute Fish. 'If you swim to latitude Fifty North, longitude Forty West (that is magic), you will find, sitting on a raft, in the middle of the sea, with nothing on but a pair of blue canvas breeches, a pair of suspenders (you must not forget the suspenders, Best Beloved), and a jack-knife, one ship-wrecked Mariner, who, it is only fair to tell you, is a man of infinite-resource-and-sagacity.' So the Whale swam and swam to latitude Fifty North, longitude Forty West, as fast as he could swim, and on a raft, in the middle of the sea, with nothing to wear except a pair of blue canvas breeches, a pair of suspenders (you must particularly remember the suspenders, Best

Beloved), and a jack-knife, he found one single, solitary shipwrecked Mariner, trailing his toes in the water. (He had his mummy's leave to paddle, or else he would never have done it, because he was a man of infinite-resource-and-sagacity.) Then the Whale opened his mouth back and back and back till it nearly touched his tail, and he swallowed the shipwrecked Mariner, and the raft he was sitting on, and his blue canvas breeches, and the suspenders (which you must not forget), and the jack-knife—He swallowed them all down into his warm, dark, inside cup-boards, and then he smacked his lips—so, and turned round three times on his tail.

But as soon as the Mariner, who was a man of infinite-resource-and-sagacity, found himself truly inside the Whale's warm, dark, inside cup-boards, he stumped and he jumped and he thumped and he bumped, and he pranced and he danced, and he banged and he clanged, and he hit and he bit, and he leaped and he creeped, and he prowled and he howled, and he hopped and he dropped, and he cried and he sighed, and he crawled and he bawled, and he stepped and he lepped, and he danced hornpipes where he shouldn't, and the Whale felt most unhappy indeed. (Have you forgotten the suspenders?) So he said to the 'Stute Fish, 'This man is very nubbly, and besides he is making me hiccough. What shall I do?'

'Tell him to come out,' said the 'Stute Fish.

So the Whale called down his own throat to the shipwrecked Mariner, 'Come out and behave yourself. I've got the hiccoughs.'

'Nay, nay!' said the Mariner. 'Not so, but far otherwise. Take me to my natal-shore and the white-cliffs-of-Albion, and I'll think about it.' And he began to dance more than ever.

'You had better take him home,' said the 'Stute Fish to the Whale.

'I ought to have warned you that he is a man of infinite-resource-and-sagacity.'

So the Whale swam and swam and swam, with both flippers and his tail, as hard as he could for the hiccoughs; and at last he saw the Mariner's natal-shore and the white-cliffs-of-Albion, and he rushed half-way up the beach, and opened his mouth wide and wide and wide, and said, 'Change here for Winchester, Ashuelot, Nashua, Keene, and stations on the Fitchburg Road;' and just as he said 'Fitch' the Mariner walked out of his mouth. But while the Whale had been swimming, the Mariner, who was indeed a person of infinite-resource-and-sagacity, had taken his jack-knife and cut up the raft into a little square grating all running criss-cross, and he had tied it firm with his suspenders (now, you know why you were not to forget the suspenders!), and he dragged that grating good and tight into the Whale's throat, and there it stuck! Then he recited the following Sloka, which, as you have not heard it, I will now proceed to relate— By means of a grating

I have stopped your ating.

For the Mariner he was also an Hi-ber-ni-an. And he stepped out on the shingle, and went home to his mother, who had given him leave to trail his toes in the water; and he married and lived happily ever afterward. So did the Whale. But from that day on, the grating in his throat, which he could neither cough up nor swallow down, prevented him eating anything except very, very small fish; and that is the reason why whales nowadays never eat men or boys or little girls.

The small 'Stute Fish went and hid himself in the mud under the Door-sills of the Equator. He was afraid that the Whale might be angry with him.

The Sailor took the jack-knife home. He was wearing the blue canvas breeches when he walked out on the shingle. The suspenders were left behind, you see, to tie the grating with; and that is the end of that tale.

WHEN the cabin port-holes are dark and green
Because of the seas outside;
When the ship goes wop (with a wiggle between)
And the steward falls into the soup-tureen,
And the trunks begin to slide;
When Nursey lies on the floor in a heap,
And Mummy tells you to let her sleep,
And you aren't waked or washed or dressed,
Why, then you will know (if you haven't guessed)
You're 'Fifty North and Forty West!'